FLIGHT OF THE SEAHAWKS

BOOK TWO: THE SEABIRDS TRILOGY

JESSICA GLASNER

Printed in the United States of America

First Printing: 978-1-7337629-4-6

Hope House Press

www.hopehousepress.co

www.glasnerhouse.co

To the 110,000 Jewish Immigrants who participated in Aliyah Bet,
and to my equally brave parents, who, likewise, sold all they had to buy the
pearl of great price.

A HISTORICAL NOTE

*I*n 1939, a match igniting World War II struck the red phosphorous exterior strip of its box and burst into flames. Within two short years, the small fire explodes into an uncontainable conflagration sweeping across Europe, burning through Africa, the Middle East, and China.

Piper and Peter escape Europe alive and unscathed, not unlike Piper's cousins, the Adleman sisters, who find themselves *en route* to the Holy Land. They are among the lucky ones. 1941 marked the beginning of *Endlösung der Judenfrage,* Hitler's Final Solution to systematically rid Germany and Europe of Jews, Poles, Gypsies, and others the Nazi Party deemed undesirable, through forced labor, ghettos, and systemized murder in death camps.

It looks like all hope is lost to save free Europe. Italy, Poland, Yugoslavia, Greece, Hungary, Romania, Slovakia, Austria, Czecho-slovakia, Denmark, the Netherlands, and parts of France—including Paris—have fallen to Nazi Germany.

Hitler betrays his Soviet ally and attacks the USSR. In response, the Soviets regroup and form an alliance with the British.

Now, only Great Britain, Free-France, and a weakened USSR

stand against the encroaching evil Axis Powers. While the United States supplies food and arms to the British, it clings to its isolationist policies and refuses to involve itself in battle.

The fighting is intense. There is massive bloodshed on both sides.

The flames of war burn hotter. European Jews, along with countless other displaced refugees, are trapped without a home. The United States denies refugee status to most who escape Germany and Nazi-occupied territories. Hundreds of thousands must return to Germany to perish in death camps.

But not all suffer this tragic fate. In God's mercy, a remnant escapes to the British Mandate of Palestine, a region promised to the Jewish people by Lord Balfour.

Unfortunately, Balfour's promise is not one the British are keen to keep. And the Jews are not the only group promised a homeland in Palestine. The Arabs demand the region for themselves. And because the British need Arab oil to fight the Nazis, they allow only a handful of Jews to immigrate into Palestine a year to appease the Arab population, putting the lives of millions of displaced Jewish refugees in harm's way.

THE SEAHAWKS IS INSPIRED by the freedom fighters who, against incredible odds, battled against Nazis, British blockades, and Arab opposition, to establish a homeland for Jewish refugees of the Holocaust.

Several characters are real: Hannah Senesh, Albert Einstein, Orde Wingate, Henrietta Szold, Bertha Spafford, among others. All conversations and scenarios involving these characters are fictional unless otherwise noted. However, I have done my best to adhere to the spirit of the times and the historicity of the real persons. I've also taken some creative license with some locations, dates, and events, such as Einstein's presence in Palestine in 1940.

While the Adleman sisters are fictional, their struggles and journeys of faith are based on the lives of personal friends and family.

Ultimately, the men and women whose stories of hope and perseverance through extraordinary stress and trauma inspired this book. I hope they inspire you as they do me. They teach us that even when it seems the world is going up in flames, *"The path of the righteous is like the morning sun, shining ever brighter till the full light of day."* (Proverbs 4:18)

"From where is this quiet in your hearts? From where have you learned strength?"[1]

— *HANNAH SENESH*

THE BEGINNING OF THE MIDDLE

The winding road to the lighthouse was slick with black ice. I gripped the steering wheel until my knuckles turned white and eased on and off the accelerator as Peter and I inched forward.

"It looks alright from here," he said.

"How can you tell? It's almost dark." Peering out the windshield, I could just barely make out the outline of the old house and the tower. A light was glowing through the window in my aunt's study. Mr. Henderson must have already arrived. I hoped he had the fire going by now.

The old Ford pickup Peter had bought the day before slid forward several inches, and I slammed on the brakes.

"I can't do this!" I glanced at Peter. "You could make it from here, couldn't you? It's just a short walk."

Peter looked down at his leg. "Seriously?"

I groaned heavily. "Next time, you drive."

"I can't move my ankle yet enough to hit the gas." Comfortingly, he put his hand on my shoulder and said, "One inch at a time. You can do it."

"I hate this."

"Just think of once we make it inside. Our own house, just the two of us." He winked and added, "And Mr. Henderson."

Swallowing, I shifted the gear back to drive and prayed under my breath that we would not go right over the edge and plunge into the swirling dark waters below. "To get to our home is like a trial by fire! Why didn't Edie tell us about the ice?"

"It's October. Usually, there isn't any ice in October." Peter looked straight ahead nervously as I rounded the corner and, thankfully, hit gravel once more. "We'll put chains on the tires tomorrow. Edie probably has some in the shed."

"She didn't own a car so I doubt she has chains." I pulled up to the front walk next to Mr. Henderson's old Model T and took the keys out of the ignition.

"We'll buy some in town then."

"Let me work up the courage to get behind the wheel again." A strong, frigid wind threatened to keep the door shut, and I threw myself against it, bracing myself against the cold. My hair and scarf whipped around my face as I made my way to Peter's side and opened the door. "Here," I helped him out, "lean on me."

Carefully, one step at a time, we made our way up the winding pathway to the front door. The sound of the waves and wind roared, and the sun disappeared behind the western horizon.

We were finally home.

Peter pushed the front door open. "I'm sorry I can't carry you over the threshold."

"Shall I carry you?"

"No, we tried that last time. It didn't work out so well."

"Your leg was in a full cast, it got caught on the door."

"Let's not and say we did, how about that?"

Suddenly, a wrinkled face appeared. "So the newlyweds made it at last."

"Mr. Henderson?" I asked, extending my hand.

"The same. The very same." The old man's watery eyes glistened.

8

"Come on in before you let the heat out. I've just started the fire for you both."

"Oh good." Peter smiled and rubbed his hands together.

Old Man Henderson bustled about us like a concerned mother hen. "You know, your Aunt Edie wrote me and said she was giving the house away now that she's married to a Scottish baron or another. Said she was giving it to you, Piper, and your new war hero husband to live in for a while before he goes back to school. Imagine my surprise when she said the war hero was none other than our Peter. You've done real well for yourself." He slapped Peter heartily on the back and took his arm, helping him into the deep leather chair by the fire. "A medal and a bride!"

Carefully, Peter sat back as I took off my coat.

He turned towards me and said, "I brought you my famous walnut pie. It's on the counter in the kitchen."

"I didn't know you could cook, Mr. Henderson."

"I'm a surprising sort, Ms. Piper. And there's hot water on if you want some tea." He winked before adding, "I'll let you two honeymooners get on by yourselves now. I'm sure you're tired."

We were tired. Three weeks at sea, the train, the drive... two years in war-torn Europe. Yes. We were tired.

"Thank you," I said, slipping my low block heels off, "for everything. The pie. The fire... for taking care of the old place."

"Anything for Edie," he said, cracking a smile that revealed a missing tooth. "You should know, the faucet is dripping in the bathroom, and there is a cracked window in the bedroom. I put some cardboard over it, but it will need mending before winter hits. It's bound to be a record year. October and there's ice already. So, what else do you kids need?"

"Not a thing, Mr. Henderson."

"Then I'll be going home now." He marched to the coat rack and pulled on his thick wool seaman's coat. Before opening the door, he faced me and said quietly, "You both look older."

"We are older," I responded.

"Yes. Yes… I suppose you are." Then, dropping his creaking voice even more and tilting his head in Peter's direction, he asked. "Is he alright?"

I nodded. "He'll be alright, after some time."

"Well," he tenderly patted my cheek, "if you need anything at all, you know where I live." His eyes lit up suddenly. "Any chance you play cards?"

"Believe it or not, Mr. Henderson, I do."

"Ooh da lolly! I've been itching for a game or two. How's Thursday?"

Peter called for me, and I looked apologetically at the old man. "I'll get back to you."

He nodded understandingly and disappear into the coming darkness, the mechanical rattle of the Model T disappearing into the crash of the ocean's windy roar.

My socked feet padded into the study and stopped in front of the fire. I took the poker and prodded it, sending sparks flying up the chimney. I felt Peter staring at me, and I turned to him.

"Hi."

"Hi yourself." Peter smiled up at me. "What was he whispering about?"

"He's lonely, I think. Like this old place." I glanced around the room. It was all the same, just as Edie and I had left it. The jars of shells and feathers. A pile of canvases and my portrait leaning against the wall. The big old radio. It was all familiar, and yet, not so. Without Edie, the house felt empty and mournfully quiet.

"You ought to invite him over."

"Oh no," I said, firmly planting my hand on my hip. "I've *finally* got you all to myself."

"You've had me all to yourself for a while now." He gave me that old playful look, subconsciously rubbing the small fine hairs on his chin. He hadn't shaved in a week and had that scruffy, relaxed look I'd grown to love.

I checked the pocket watch that my parents had given me on my

16th birthday in Switzerland. It was 5:03 pm. I did a quick calculation. One month, two days, four hours, and 21 minutes. But who was counting? What was it that Mother had said? *It's so you don't lose hope, because God's timing is always perfect. You may think you are too late when you are only too early.*

I knelt down by the chair and leaned my head on his knee, the one that had not been shredded by shrapnel. The last time we'd been in that room, we'd been so different, so young.

The Peter I'd married was almost a different man than the Peter I'd fallen in love with. Oh, he was still Peter. Same beautiful blue eyes and wispy blonde hair. He still loved fishing. But he'd seen so much, been hurt so badly. Sometimes, at night, he'd cry out in pain. The doctors said there was nerve damage. And then I'd catch him staring into space, looking at nothing in particular. My father warned me it was something that happened to soldiers sometimes.

He'd come out of it, I told myself. We'd be ourselves again, one day. One day, he would laugh that deep honest laugh I remembered. Because he was alive. And because he had me. He just needed space and time, and that's exactly what he had in the lighthouse perched above the Atlantic on the coast of Maine, space and time.

The fire crackled and popped and big fat snowflakes began to fall steadily from the window. Plenty of time, I thought.

"Piper,"

"Yes?"

He didn't answer, and I lifted my head and turned to look at him. His blue eyes stared into mine.

"What is it?" I asked carefully. The memories were too near, too raw for me to press too hard. He needed me to listen to his silence. What he didn't say was sometimes louder than anything he actually said, which wasn't much these days.

"I'm happy to be back," he exhaled, not finishing his thought.

"You are?"

"I thought I was going to die out there." He held my hand, looking at my fingers. "I'm almost relieved I got hurt... I'm no hero,

Piper. I was afraid that day. I've never been so scared in my life. It makes me ashamed."

"Everyone gets scared, Peter. It's okay. We are far away from the war now. We're safe."

It was as though he didn't hear me. His thoughts were jumbled and twisted. "I don't deserve the medal. Not when all those other men died." He grasped my hand. "I... don't know what to do anymore."

"You are going to go back to school and make something of yourself, remember?"

"That's not what I mean." He struggled to say more, and then, gave up.

My heart caught in my chest, and for a moment, I wanted to hold him in my arms and take all his pain away. But I couldn't.

A shiver ran through my body, and I stood up. Early October, and it was already snowing. I wondered what sort of winter was in store for us in my aunt's old lighthouse.

It was 1941. I was 18, and Peter, 21. We were young and old at the same time. And we were hungry. I stood up and went to cut Mr. Henderson's famous walnut pie for supper.

She arrived on the first day of December, moments before the storm hit. In the interim, Peter had patched the window and fixed the leak. The ice had melted, and the sun had come out. And then, the temperature dropped, and the ice came back thicker and stronger than before. But by then, we had chains. Which meant we could drive into town once a week and see a film.

Sitting across from me in the kitchen, rubbing her fingers around a steaming mug of tea nervously, I noticed the dark circles under her eyes. She was thinner than I remembered and taller too.

"I won't stay for long. Just until I have things worked out." The wind howled outside, and the barren vines rattled against the house. My cousin looked like a scared cat.

A *wet* scared cat.

She'd walked the 7 miles from the bus stop in the snow. I'd put her in a hot bath and then in my extra set of wool pajamas and wrapped her in an old handmade quilt made of pink and blue and green calico. And now, the gale in full swing, we all sat down.

"Edie said you wouldn't mind." Her eyes darted to the study where Peter was listening to the news and then back to me.

Examining my cousin closely, I responded, "Of course not. Technically, this is still her house. We are only here for a few more weeks. Before the next term starts. Then we move to Boston."

"Boston?"

I nodded. "Peter's going back to finish his education."

Grace managed a small smile. "I really do appreciate you letting me stay. I had to get away, I had to think. I tried my hardest when I went back to Scotland, I really did, but with the twins starting to walk, and all the other children running around like mad, I couldn't focus."

"But why not go back to Palestine?"

"Oh, I just couldn't. Not now. Not… yet." She took a sip of tea.

"Where are Katrine and Lorelei? Why not stay with them?" I pressed.

"Lorelei? Tending the wounded in the North African desert?" She shook her head. "And Katrine's got her hands full enough in Jerusalem. And besides, Jerusalem is too close to—" she stopped herself before saying anything else.

I may have been younger than my cousin, but not by much. I could smell a problem a mile away. And Grace had a problem. I put my hand on the table. "The last we heard, you had escaped Hungary. What's going on. Are you in some sort of trouble?"

"No. It's nothing like that. It's personal."

"I see." I waited, but she refused to go on. "Grace, tell me what happened."

Grace clenched her fist and then stretched out her fingers. Her light brown hair was pulled back into a bun, still damp from the bath and dripping slightly. Standing suddenly, she said: "Just wait a second. Where's my bag?"

"I put it in your room. It's my old one, on the left."

She nodded and left, the sound of her footsteps going up the stairs slowly fading. Quickly, the sound carried back down, and she reappeared, a large manilla folder in her hands. She pushed it across the table to me. "It's from Edie, for you."

"For me?"

"She told me how you were the girl reporter for the Scotsman while you lived in Scotland. She said they turned you into a great editor, even if you still struggle to write. 'An eye for catching the whiff of a story.'" She paused and looked around briefly. "There are quite a few paintings of birds in this place."

I held the package lightly, shocked. "A whole book?"

Grace raised her eyebrows and nodded. "After I arrived in Scotland, after Hungary…" She paused for a moment before continuing, "She had one of her 'episodes.' You know, where she doesn't eat or drink or talk to anyone, and everyone thinks she's angry, but it is really that she's thinking very hard. Apparently, she'd started it right after we left Scotland. But my arrival gave her the gusto, and missing plot points, to finish it."

"How long did her, uh, episode last?"

"Two weeks. And then, she gave me this packet and shipped us both off to… here."

Out of the manilla envelope emerged a rather large stack of typed papers with a handwritten note pinned to the front.

Piper dear, you simply must give me your completely honest opinion! It turned out to be much more of an adventure story then I set out to write. (But life is like that, isn't it? You and I both know that more than anyone else!) And I might as well tell you now it's about your cousins. I thought I might leave that a surprise, considering that I usually write fiction. But given how desperately I need your input before sending it in to the publishers, I thought I'd put all my cards on the table. No pun intended! So do read it as quickly as you can, and let me know what you really, really think. I'm itching to discuss it with you. Keeping the whole thing secret this long has just about been my end. I don't know how I would have gotten this far along in my writing if Horatio wasn't gone every other weekend at the Naval Academy, training all those darling young cadets... I'm rambling. Read it, and then we'll talk.

Your ever-adoring aunt,

Philipa Edith Gordan-Macleay.

P.S. Don't ask me why I wrote my full name. I think I just like seeing my new last name. Macleay!

"A novel?" I asked, my jaw dropping slightly.

"Novel, memoir, fiction, history... its fiction and fact all mixed up." She paused before adding, "It's Edie. She embellishes things. But you'll get the picture."

My mind was spinning. So Edie had finally finished another novel. Her first in decades. And she wanted me to edit it!

Grace looked towards the study. "What have you and Peter been up to these days?"

"We read. I'm making a scrapbook of all the pictures I took in Europe and Scotland. I even took up knitting." I sighed.

I saw her eye the cane. "Was he hurt badly?" she asked.

"Yes." I didn't speak for a moment. "But sometimes, I think he was hurt somewhere *inside* more. Does that make any sense, Grace? He's so quiet all the time. His leg pains him terribly, and it wakes him up. Or maybe the dreams wake him up. He won't say which."

"It's the war. What he saw," she said simply. "I wish I didn't understand, but I'm afraid I do."

Grace looked at me penetratingly. "Piper, I—are you happy, with Peter?"

"He's my best friend."

"But he's so... different from when I met him before."

"I married him for better or worse. He's a little worse right now, but he'll get better."

"But if he doesn't?" Her eyebrow raised slightly. "You don't know that he'll get better."

"Grace, he will always be my best friend. I love him when he's down and when he's happy. He'll always be my Peter. He'll always be the best time I ever had."

Grace looked at me with fresh eyes, and it was then that I realized how tired she really looked. In the study, I heard the theme song to the Cisco Kid come on. "Why don't we get cozy in the study."

Tonight's show, "The Disappearing Bullet," centered on a man swindled in a card game who loses everything and is framed for murder. "I'm always on the edge of my seat with this program."

"I don't think so." Grace stood up and wrapped the quilt around her shoulders. "It's very cold here, you know?"

"I know."

Grace stared at the wall.

"Well, we don't have to listen to the show. We could read and listen to records. Edie's got a great Encyclopedia…"

She laughed out loud.

"I'm serious! It's sort of meditative."

"I just need to crawl into bed." She came around the table and wrapped her long, thin arms around me, kissed me, and wiped a tear off her cheek. Then, she turned and silently ascended the stairs to her room.

I downed the remains of my tea and exhaled. Outside, the snowflakes were descending with rapidity, and the wind, if possible, had picked up even more. A cousin on the run and a wounded husband. Yep, it was growing into quite the storm.

"She wants you to edit it?" Peter called from the study.

"I'm honestly happy for the work." I looked up. "We are trapped inside all day with the weather. Mr. Henderson comes by once a week, and we play cards and eat walnut pie. We venture into town once a week for supplies and to watch *To Be or Not to Be* for the umpteenth time…"

"You like Carole Lombard," Peter protested.

"I love Carole Lombard. That's not the point."

With the manuscript in hand, I poured another mug of tea and wandered from the kitchen towards Peter.

"Where is Grace?"

"In bed." I went to my aunt's old desk (that was now mine) and looked over the photographs I had spread out earlier in the afternoon. There was one of Rudolf Hess, one of Hitler's sidekicks, and his airplane after it crashed near Horatio's land.

It had landed on the front page of the Scotsman, and I was very proud of it.

Peter stared out the window into the black night. "Piper?"

"Ummhmm?"

"What if this is it?"

"What if *what's* it?"

"This," he spread his hands out. "We wake up. We eat oatmeal. I putter around and do nothing. You putter around and mess with your photographs and make sweaters."

"We are sort of on vacation." My eyes rested on the photograph. The corner was slightly bent.

"What if God is finished with me? You know, what if this is the end of the road?"

I looked up, horrified.

"Peter, how can you say that?"

"I can't walk. I'm not good for anything anymore." He looked down. "Sometimes I wonder why you waited for me."

I walked around the desk and nestled into his lap, kissing him squarely. "You're the best friend I ever had or ever will have. And don't talk foolishness. Just because you have a slight limp doesn't mean God isn't going to use you. It just means He just hasn't told you how yet. Be patient. The season changed."

"Winter is here." He frowned.

"Don't be so depressing." I punched him playfully. "That's not what I meant! For crying out loud, Peter, you are the one who is supposed to tell me this sort of stuff. I feel out of my league encouraging you." He looked into my eyes. "And," I added, "you can walk. Just not as fast as before. Slowing down isn't always a bad thing. Remember the tortoise and the hare."

He looked down. When he looked back up, he whispered, "I love you, Piper."

"I love you too."

For a moment, we didn't move, and the air was very still. On the radio, a commercial for denture adhesive droned on and on with three girls singing in an annoyingly high pitch, crooning the catchphrase, "Dalley's Dentures, for daily dental delight."

He exhaled. "We are a little too serious for newlyweds, don't you think?"

"Don't *I* think?"

Edie's manuscript on the desk, sitting where had I left it, caught my eye. Well, if he wanted to lighten the mood, it would serve well enough, I should think.

I went to the radio and switched it off. "We are going to read this together. You can help me make suggestions. The male perspective and all that."

"Do men buy your aunt's books?"

I shrugged. "No idea. She only ever wrote the one."

"What about the Cisco Kid?"

"Who cares?" I put another log on the fire and sat down in the other leather chair and opened up the manuscript.

"Do you want to read or do you want me to read?"

He shrugged, and I cleared my throat. "All right then, I'll read."

The Flight of the Seahawks
A Novel by Edith Gordan-Macleay

An epic drama of love and romance in a time of war, as told to the authoress by her three (for all events and purposes) adopted daughters through letters and verbal testimony. Certain names and circumstances may or may not have been altered for the sake of dramatic flow. However, the authoress has done her best to stick to the truth, i.e., the *essence of* the story.

CHAPTER 1

ON BOARD THE ATHENA

The *Athena* was a rust bucket. The kind that stunk in the summer, froze in the winter and creaked like it was about to crack in two at any given moment. Thankfully, it was winter. That meant the smell of vomit and sweat wasn't quite as unbearable as it could have been. Still, it smelled awful, offending Katrine Adleman's bourgeois sensibilities. That, and the insufferable, constant creaking kept her wide awake. She hadn't had a real solid sleep since they'd set out from Chelsea four days before.

She glanced over at her sisters. Lorelei had leaned up against the filthy iron wall, her head sunk into her chin, deep in sleep. Grace had curled her long frame up in a ball, using Lorelei's lap as a pillow, a dirty blanket on the hard floor beneath her. Katrine watched her chest rise and fall, in awe of how her sisters had the innate ability to sleep anywhere.

From her sisters, her eyes traveled to the dark forms of sleeping young bodies - all 250 of them - crammed into the hull of the salvaged fishing vessel, which was anything but the *Grey Goose*. Each one needed a bath.

Katrine tried not to breathe. She had to get some fresh air, and she had to get some right now. Stealthily, she stood up and buttoned up the thick wool sweater from Scotland. They may have been nearing the Mediterranean, but it was still December. With the agility of a dancer, she stepped over the teenagers sprawled all over and silently ascended the stairs to the deck. The cold, clean air rushed over her like a shower. Grasping the edge of the rail, she immediately felt cleansed, refreshed, and more wide awake than ever.

"Still up, eh?" A voice said.

Katrine looked behind her. The voice was Harry's. He was sitting on the ground, legs stretched out, his back against the pilot's cabin.

She looked back at the sea. "You're one to talk. I haven't seen you sleep once since we came on board."

"I don't need sleep." He smiled up at her playfully. The moon was very bright and reflected off the water.

It was so bright she could see his dark curls were askew. The length made him look extra boyish. Though Katrine knew that he was in his early forties, he could have passed for 20 years old at that moment. And for some reason, it made her feel extra-annoyed at the man who continually had the ability to unnerve her. "Sure. Just like you don't need a haircut."

"What? You don't like it?" He ran his hand back through his hair self-consciously. "I did shave my mustache."

"I noticed."

He motioned to the spot beside him. "Want to sit down?" His red-rimmed eyes were underlined with dark circles.

Katrine shook her head, but then, on second thought, eased down - though not beside him. Instead, she leaned against the rail, and faced him, pulling her knees up close to her chest. Neither spoke for a moment.

"Two hundred and fifty teenagers," she said after a minute. "A fishing boat built in the last century. . . You really surprised me, Harry. Boy, when you deliver, you deliver."

He bowed as though he were a magician who had accomplished some fabulous trick. "Baby, when Harry snaps his fingers," he snapped, "things happen." Then, with less bravado, he continued, "The Jewish Fund is stretched pretty thin these days. At least we are able to get the kids in. No one else is allowed."

Katrine grimaced. In her four days aboard the *Athena*, she'd begun to see that the reality of what Harry and the rest of the Zionists were trying to accomplish was almost, to put it lightly, impossible.

Everything about what they were doing appeared crazy.

But then, everything that had happened actually was crazy. Katrine's world had turned upside down. Her parents were dead, or as good as dead. All she'd known and loved in Germany was as good as dead too. All she had left were her sisters and the promise of a new life in Palestine.

For many Jews, the idea of returning to Eretz Israel was a dream come true. For Katrine, not so much. In truth, she hadn't really thought of Eretz Israel at all. Her whole life was in Germany. Now, her whole life was in shambles.

But still, she knew she should be grateful. The British, under pressure from the Arabs, had shut down all Jewish immigration to Palestine. Only 3,400 Jewish teenage refugees from the Kindertransport were permitted visas. She and Lorelei and Grace were a part of this group. It was a miracle that she and her sisters had papers that said they were teenagers and looks young enough to fool even the Germans.

But knowing you should be grateful and actually being grateful are two different things. At the moment, all Katrine felt was uncomfortable, slightly seasick, tired, and deep down, afraid.

"I don't understand you at all, Harry," she said after a minute. "A country built by teenagers?" She thought of the children in the hold. Of such stock, she was sure, countries were *not* made.

"By people like you, Katrine. And me." He stopped and looked intensely at her. "Katrine, when you step foot on the land, you will understand. It's different. It's... *ours*."

The way he said 'ours' caused a prick of pain to run through Katrine's heart. *Ours?* She thought. *My home is in Germany! A beautiful home. A beautiful life. . .* the thoughts trailed off.

She shook her head. "Harry, I'm on this boat because I've nowhere else to go."

She stood up abruptly and looked down at him. "What are you really doing here, Harry? You're from America. You don't need to be here. You could have everything. A normal life! I would do anything to be in America."

"You really don't get it, do you?" He shot Katrine a look. "America! Sure, there are no Nazis in power. But they are there. And there's the more subtle stuff. I'm not allowed to join the country club in my neighborhood because of my last name."

"You play golf?"

"No. Tennis is more my style." Harry exhaled. "But it's the principle of the thing."

"Okay, so no golf. But you can still do and be anything you want. You can live without fear," Katrine pushed.

"Not so. Over 50 percent of Americans think that Jews are different and should be restricted. That's not good news, Katrine. You of all people should know that better than anyone."[2]

She froze, but Harry kept going. "Last December, 2,000 protestors marched through New York demanding that Jews escaping Germany be sent back to where they came from. They got what they wanted." He paused and then added, "So in answer to your question, a Jew cannot have everything in America. And they cannot live without fear. But you know what's worse?"[3]

She shook her head.

"American Jews don't get it. They are oblivious. They think America is the new promised land. It's not."

Katrine listened intently.

"They don't want to rock the boat. They are worried and fear that supporting a Jewish State will make things uncomfortable in their little New Jersey suburbs. They are like you. They like things comfortable." He stood up and stepped towards her. "But sometimes things have got to get uncomfortable before they get comfortable."

Harry had stepped past Katrine's invisible zone of personal space, making her feel the very definition of uncomfortable. She pulled away and looked at him. He was strange, she thought. And very driven.

"Any more words of wisdom?" She put her hand on her hip cynically.

"You really should try to get some sleep. Big day tomorrow."

She turned to go but then stopped and asked quietly, "How much longer?"

Harry's shoulders shrugged, "Two hours, more or less. We should be crossing into British-"

Out of nowhere, a bright spotlight hit the deck, and a loud voice on a bullhorn cried, "*ATHENA*! CALLING *ATHENA*! YOU ARE NO LONGER ON INTERNATIONAL WATERS. PREPARE TO BE BOARDED BY HIS MAJESTY'S GOVERNMENT!"

Harry groaned and turned with Katrine so they were shoulder to shoulder, with both of their faces illuminated by the piercing light coming from a British Patrol boat. "Like I said, we should be crossing into British waters anytime now."

She could feel the tension emanating from his body. It sent a shiver down her spine. Harry was usually so... confident. This wasn't a good sign.

Domoskenos, the captain of the *Athena*, answered the destroyer, "THIS IS *ATHENA*. MESSAGE RECEIVED. WE ARE UNARMED AND AUTHORIZED TO PORT IN HAIFA."

Katrine looked at Harry. "What now?"

"They'll board. Domoskenos knows the drill."

"And?"

"And hopefully, they'll keep their side of the deal. I worked my you-know-what off for these visas. A lot of people did."

"How do you know you can trust the Greek man?" Katrine looked towards the glow coming from the pilot's cabin.

"This isn't his first rodeo. He hates the British almost as much as I do... And we've certainly paid him enough."

Unconvinced, Katrine arched her brows. "Comforting thought."

Harry gripped the side of the railing until his knuckles turned white. They could see the motorboat speeding towards them, the spray of the water glowing in the moonlight. He next spoke without looking at her. "Go wake the youngsters up. His Royal Majesty's bell-bottoms will want to check the paperwork of each and every one."

Then, before she could leave, he reached out and gave her hand a gentle squeeze and shot her a knowing smile. "I'll see you around, okay?"

Confused, Katrine's mouth turned down. "What do you mean?"

"Never you mind. Just go get the kids up, okay?"

~

"WHAT IS IT? What's the matter?" Morris whispered loudly as Katrine's feet padded down the stairs into the hold. The lanky 14-year-old sat up with a start, blinking his bright hazel eyes in the light coming through the portal from the deck. Katrine's hand sought the light switch and flipped it on.

Clapping her hands together, she spoke quickly. "Everybody up! Come on now. Esther! Ruth!" She gently shook the identical twin girls asleep near the stairs. The room began to stir.

Morris repeated his question, louder now.

"The British are boarding the boat," she answered, trying to keep her voice steady, but stern. She meant business. "Help me get everyone up on the deck!"

Morris snapped into gear. In less than six months, he'd gone from a carefree boy, the youngest of five, to a refugee. And a man. He may not have been in high school yet, but he'd gained enough maturity through the forced fires of the Warsaw Ghetto and clandestine escapes to mirror men four times his age.

"Adam! Pawal! Marcel!" Morris jumped from one

adolescent to the next, poking and prodding them awake. Within two minutes, all were wide awake. There was no need for anyone to dress; all slept with the few clothes they had on. Each one had only been allowed a small valise as they escaped wherever they had come from.

A hush of nervous German, Czech, and Polish filled the hold. Lorelei and Grace were up now, making their way up after Katrine. Shouts from the deck made them stop short. The British were boarding. The girls huddled three steps down from the top, listening carefully.

Grace snapped her fingers together and motioned for the young people to be quiet. No one moved. All eyes traveled upwards towards the deck.

Lorelei leaned towards Katrine. "I can't hear what they're saying."

Suddenly, a dark double-breasted reefer jacket and matching trousers appeared at the top of the stairs. The man in the suit was the captain of the patrol boat, evidenced by his distinctive cap and the insignia on his left shoulder—and his undeniable air of authority.

The girls stood up quite straight, staring at the intruders.

"What have we here?" The captain spoke with the well-educated accent of an Oxford man. He looked down his long thin nose and settled his watery, repulsive eyes on girls. Slowly, they traveled past their faces towards the cargo: 250 teenagers. He sneered. "School trip?"

Grace lifted her chin defiantly. "All of these

children have visas. We have every right to be here!"

"I'm sure you do." He tilted his head disarmingly to the side, continuing, "Just like all the Jews trying to get into Palestine. Like little ants, seeping through the cracks. But the law's the law. And the law says you have to go back to where you came from." The captain was very smooth, proper, charming, and, in a word, reptilian.

Just before Grace was about to respond with words she would no doubt have regretted, Captain Domoskenos pushed through.

"You!" Domoskenos pushed his fat finger at the British captain's chest. The man stared at the finger disdainfully.

"You may address me as Captain Jones."

The Greek always seemed angry, but at this moment, he was nearly bursting with rage. "All of them - all of the children - they have the papers you want so bad."

"*Badly*," Jones corrected.

Domoskenos ignored him and addressed the children. "Show the man your visas, yes?"

From pockets and purses, hidden in secret linings sewn in jackets, the children produced their papers. The papers that promised life; the papers that many had died to produce.

Captain Jones nodded to several able-bodied seamen who clambered down the hold. One by one, they checked each visa.

A stressed silence filled the cramped space. The men looked back at Captain Jones and gave the all clear. It was true, each and every one, including Katrine, Grace, and Lorelei, had the proper papers.

Captain Jones stroked his chin, his voice dripping with sarcasm. "Well then. I stand reproved. It looks like you are all indeed going to Palestine."

"Sir! Sir!" A British sailor shoved Domoskenos aside. "He's not on board. We looked everywhere, Captain. The American is not here."

"Blast it!" Jones cursed under his breath. He frowned. "You're sure, really sure?"

"American? We have no American on board!" Domoskenos interjected.

Katrine, Lorelei, and Grace shared a look. Was it possible they were looking for Harry?

The sailor looked at Domoskenos. "That's what I said."

Captain Jones shouted down to the children. "All of you, listen up. Was there an American on this ship? A man about my height, with brown hair and glasses?" Then he commanded to Katrine, "If you would translate, please. I assume none of the Yids speak English!"

She did, and the children shook their heads 'no,' intuitively understanding that, apparently, Harry must never have been on board.

Captain Jones turned his attention on the sisters. "No American? Who is in charge of this operation?"

They looked at one another. Katrine swallowed and choked out an unsteady, "I am."

"What?" Captain Jones glared at her.

"I am in charge," she repeated, gaining confidence this time around. "And I am not an American."

Captain Jones took her passport out of her hands and checked it carefully. "It says here you're British. You obviously were raised some-where... else."

"Germany," Katrine answered truthfully. "My adoptive parents are British. Well, at least my father is. I mean, he's Scottish. My adoptive mother is American." She was gaining speed. "Perhaps that is the confusion?"

Inside, she began to panic. *He must be looking for Harry!* She thought. *Wherever was he hiding? How had he disappeared so quickly!*

"No." He looked disdainfully from young face to young face. "We are not looking for a German-British-American young woman." He grimaced and muttered to himself, "We must have received faulty information."

Captain Domoskenos poked out his chest. "So there is no American on board. You get off my boat now, yes? Everything is in order, yes? You go now."

Captain Jones turned on his heel and marched down the deck, disappearing over the side. But not before throwing the Greek a mock salute.

The sisters, with Morris close behind them, stood by Domoskenos on the side of the ship. The sun had begun to rise, awakening the day with a brilliant flash followed by a spectacular show of reds and oranges and yellows. The British Patrol Boat, with its captain and crew safely aboard, chugged towards the rising orb until they could no longer look at it.

"Good riddance!" Domoskenos raised his fist in the air.

"Where is he? What happened to Harry?" Katrine asked the captain.

"I told you, there is no American onboard this boat."

Grace turned her head. "Whatever do you mean? He must be hiding somewhere!"

"Harry is gone," he answered. "Your American is no longer on this ship."

Lorelei and Katrine simultaneously protested, "But how!?"

"Our ways are much too complicated for such pretty girls as you. Don't trouble your thoughts? Yes?" He gave them a look that begged them to not ask any more questions.

"Well, is he coming back?" Katrine asked, undeterred.

"Harry comes! Harry goes! He doesn't tell old Domoskenos when! Now, we land soon. I've things to do, yes?"

Grace looked from Lorelei to Katrine. All three were thinking the same thing; they had 250 youngsters in the hold of an old fishing boat. In an hour they would be in Haifa, and their one contact was AWOL.

Katrine groaned. *"Of course* Harry would disappear at a time like this! What are we going to do?"

Morris leaned against the rails. "Who knew that Harry was a wanted man? I bet they stopped our boat just to look for him." Crossing his arms and looking very young, he continued, "Don't you worry, Miss Grace, Miss

Katrine, and you, Miss Lorelei. I'll take care of you."

"That's very gentlemanly of you, Morris," Lorelei answered. To Katrine, she said, "I'm sure the Jewish National Fund will have someone to meet us at the dock. It will all be alright."

"And if they don't? What if-"

Morris put his hand on Katrine's back, "You worry too much, Miss Katrine. It will be fine. I trust God. Look how far we've come. He's bringing us to Palestine. We are almost there!"

"You really trust God, Morris?" Lorelei asked.

"My father was a rabbi. In Warsaw. He would do anything to be on this boat."

"He raised you very well," Katrine said.

From the bullhorn, the voice of Domoskenos blared over the ship.

Grace looked at Morris. "Happen to speak Greek?"

"No, I-" He leaned over the rails and then cried out, "I can see it! It's there! Look! It's land!" Out of his back pocket, Morris pulled out a small skull cap and slipped it onto his head. Then, he whispered, "Baruch Hashem."

CHAPTER 2

ERETZ ISRAEL

*I*t was with a great tangled mess of feelings that the Adleman sisters disembarked the *Athena*. They watched as some of the more religious teenagers, Morris included, fell upon their knees and kissed the ground.

Others stood in numb silence, looking up at the glittering new city of Haifa, perched tenuously on the slopes of Mount Carmel, where Elijah, so many years before, had challenged the prophets of Baal and the fire of God consumed his sacrifice.[4] All were struck with the stark contrasts of the white stone buildings, the cliff-like mountain range, the striking blue sky, and piercingly bright sun.

The harbor was a cacophony of Arabic, Hebrew, and English. Factories near the water let out the long whistles of steam engines. Horns blared in the traffic around the Old City center near the bay. A bracing wind whipped along the coast. And a British immigration officer lifted a bullhorn to his lips, announcing that all the passengers of the *Athena* were to be processed at Building 7.

Slowly, the sisters wound their way towards a small official looking building, the size of a garden shed.

"It's very different from Kingsbarns," Grace tugged on her eldest sister's arm, "don't you think Katrine?"

In a strange sort of daze, Katrine nodded, entering the open door to the immigration office. A half-hour later, she stood outside Building 7, her immigration papers in hand, her sisters by her side.

Lorelei looked at the teenagers of the *Athena* milling about. "Oh Katrine, what are we going to do with them all?"

Just as Katrine was about to reply that she had absolutely no idea and sink down to the curb and cry, a rather grandmotherly woman waved cheerily in their direction. She was dressed in a smart suit and a stylish velvet hat, and was well-rounded in all the right places to make her look and feel sweetly comforting. Her smile was equally reassuring. "Are you the Adleman girls? You simply must be! You look just the way Harry said you would when he wrote me!"

Katrine's jaw dropped slightly.

The old woman moved towards them with supernatural vivacity and kept on talking. "I'm so sorry I'm late. I usually meet every single boat, but I got held up at a checkpoint. You'll get used to it." She grasped Grace's hand, then Lorelei's, and then, she stared right into

Katrine's soul. "My name's Henrietta Szold.[5] I'm from Baltimore, and I'm an old friend of Harry's. In fact, I'm practically his mother."

Her eyes traveled past Katrine's shoulder to the teenagers. "Well, I think it's time we get all of you home, don't you?"

Home? Had there ever been a sweeter word? Katrine's eyes welled up with tears. "Yes, I think that is a very, very good idea."

It took about an hour to divide the children up between the busses going to three different Youth Aliyah Villages throughout the region. The Adleman sisters were assigned to a new one in the Northern Galilee, Kibbutz Kinneret.

"Move over, girls," Henrietta said, squeezing between Grace and Lorelei in the back seat of the old dusty bus as the engine revved to life. "I've got business that way and thought I'd hitch a ride."

"Mrs. Szold," Grace began, curious about this old woman who had so swiftly organized and distributed the *Athena*'s children. Every child had received a bottle of fresh milk and white bread spread thick with butter to eat on the bus. Each one had also received an enormous hug from Henrietta that seemed to wash away all apprehension and fear of what might come next.

"*Ms.* Szold," Henrietta corrected. "And between us, you can call me Aunt Henrietta. Everyone else does. To my great sadness, I never married. And I've no children."

The three sisters did not speak, surprised at the old woman's forthrightness.

"I'm sure you're wondering what I'm doing here," Henrietta said, smiling knowingly.

They nodded as the bus driver switched gears and plunged down the congested streets of the Old City of Haifa.

"Over 30 years ago, I came here with my mother. You know, on one of those tours of the Holy Land. What I saw horrified me. Jews living without proper plumbing or sanitation! It was horrible! For crying out loud, it's the 20th century, and there were all these families living like medieval peasants."

Katrine's eyes were glued out the window at the passing scenery. A British motorcade went past. Then, they were forced to stop and wait for an old shepherd to pass with a herd of sheep.

Henrietta pushed her white hair firmly back under her velvet hat. "It's a long trip to the Galilee these days. The roads are awful and the British will probably stop us at least three times to check our papers." From her shiny leather purse, Henrietta produced a tin of lemon drops. After taking one, she passed it to the girls.

Their new friend then continued her story, "Well, I said to myself, 'Henrietta! You've simply got to do something about this!' So I did."

"What did you do?" Grace pressed, sucking on her candy like a 12-year-old and nearly looking like one.

"I went back to Baltimore, and I founded a group called Hadassah, made up of good strong Jewish girls like you."

Katrine squirmed uncomfortably.

"A few years later, I came back with a whole team of doctors and nurses and dentists. We built a hospital. It's in Jerusalem. But now my job is to meet every boat of Youth Aliyah, like the *Athena*." She took one more lemon drop and popped it in her mouth. "So now that I've talked myself out of a job, why don't you young ladies tell me about yourselves? Any chance one of you is a nurse? We desperately need some more nurses. And we'll need more very soon."

The girls shook their heads.

"Well," Henrietta answered kindly, "that's all right. I'm sure we'll find *something* for you to do."

∼

LORELEI POKED KATRINE. "Look! Oh Katrine, look! It's the Galilee!"

"We call it the Kinneret, in Hebrew. It means 'harp.' The lake is in the shape of a harp." Henrietta dabbed her lipstick with a hand-kerchief.

Lorelei shook her head. They had been driving

for hours and hours and had hit one roadblock after another. The British had been clamping down hard on the Jews ever since the last Arab revolt. And then there was the simple fact that the roads were old and narrow and there were a fair number of horses and donkey carts mixed in with ancient trucks and busses that consistently broke down.

Their bus had reached the crest of a hill, and now the lake stretched out before them, in all its glory. Palm trees were scattered along the shoreline. Fishermen in little boats threw nets over the side, just as their fathers, and their fathers before them, had.

"Where do the fishermen live?" Grace asked, squinting her eyes.

"Some live in Tiberias," Henrietta answered. "There are also a few small Arab villages along the coast. And just across the lake is Lebanon and Syria and Jordan."

"So close?" Katrine asked.

The bus began to wind its way down the narrow road. Henrietta nodded and patted Katrine's knee. "There now, we're almost there. Why, in fact, we are here!" She pointed down at a collection of white bungalows set in the middle of a field of palm trees. "Behold, Kibbutz Kinneret."

They could see a small crowd forming near the gate. The girls were all dressed the same as the boys, in khaki shorts and pullover sweaters. A distinguished looking man in his late 50s wearing wire-rimmed glasses waved and smiled as the bus pulled in.

"Welcome! Welcome, children!" he said over and over again, as the bus emptied. He made a beeline for Henrietta and kissed her hand.

"Enough of that, Caleb!" The old woman swatted him playfully. "I want to introduce you to the Adleman girls, Grace, Lorelei, and Katrine."

He bowed stiffly as Henrietta continued, "And this is my dear friend and colleague, Dr. Caleb Herring. You'll all be in very good hands. He was the chief surgeon at Vienna General Hospital."

Dr. Herring's smile did not fade as he said, "That was a long time ago. Before my wife and I were forced out."

"Well, for the sake of Kibbutz Kinneret, I am glad you were forced out." Henrietta inhaled and then said, "Now Caleb, these children are hungry. What have you got for dinner?"

"All in good time, Henrietta," Dr. Herring chuckled. "The sun is not yet set, yes? We've still time for a little tour, I think, and time for the newcomers to get their bearings." He turned to a young man and woman standing off to the side, both dressed in the same khaki uniform. "Dafna, you take the girls to their dorms, and Uri, you take the boys. Make sure everyone's settled, and then get them to the dining room by 7:00, yes?"

He turned back to the sisters and Henrietta. "I'll take you to your room. I thought the dormitory might be a little much. Harry told me all about you in his letter." He looked at Katrine, and she fought the blush she felt creeping up her neck and burning onto her cheek.

41

"We've an empty bungalow right now until we find a better place for all three of you. It's not perfect," Dr. Herring continued, "but it is better than anything else we can offer. The children will have a home here forever, they will grow up strong and healthy. The kibbutz has everything they could ever need."

From there, Dr. Herring pointed out the chicken house with over 200 chickens. On one side of the kibbutz was an orange grove. On the other, an olive grove. Five donkeys, two horses, and seven very good and beloved milk cows.

"We've a school and a library. We work and learn on rotation. Hebrew and Arabic classes, Tanach classes - that's Hebrew for *Bible* - and engineering classes."

"Bible classes?" Lorelei asked.

"Oh yes. We think it is very important for our children to learn the Hebrew Scriptures. How better to understand their new home, don't you agree?" Without waiting for a reply, Dr. Herring began to walk towards the dormitories. "Several of my personal students are local Arabs preparing for university in France. Three very bright boys. One's father is the head of the village - and a dear friend of mine. I offered to teach the boys so they would not have to go to the school in Jerusalem. It's rather far and would have been inconvenient." The white stucco walls glowed as though it had been freshly scrubbed. The teenagers who milled about seemed unusually mature and content. They smiled politely as Dr. Herring passed, eyeing the sisters and their fashionable dresses with a curious, if occasionally suspect, expression.

"I thought the Arabs and the Jews didn't get along," Katrine asked quietly. "We'd heard you had little to do with one another."

"Little to do?" He stopped, looking at Katrine directly. His voice was not unkind, but it was firm. "We sell them our produce, and we hire them during harvest to lend an extra hand. Our children study side by side." Pausing, he tilted his head toward the fields beyond the courtyard. "While our worlds may be different, Ms. Adleman, we get along quite well with our neighbors."

With that, he turned and continued his tour.

"As members of the kibbutz, this is all yours. We all own it collectively. We vote on everything, even the youngsters. We share in the profits, we suffer the losses - together." Dr. Herring explained as he pushed the door open to one of the dorms - the girl's one. Dafna stood off to the side, observing the newcomers unpack their few belongings. She glanced up as they stepped inside. "Shalom Abba," she said.

"My daughter, Dafna," Dr. Herring said proudly. "She was born here, on this very land. She is a Sabra."

Henrietta sunk down onto one of the beds and explained, "That means a Jew born on the soil."

"Tough on the outside, sweet on the inside." Dr. Herring kissed Dafna's cheek.

She brushed him away. "Come on, Father!"

"Don't think anything of her," Dr. Herring said, addressing the sisters. "She is indeed very sweet on the inside. It just takes some work to get there."

Henrietta laughed. "Uri certainly found out. I hear congratulations are in order."

Now it was Dafna's turn to blush. "Oh, Aunt Henrietta! Daddy told you? I… Well… I don't know what to say! He only asked me last night!"

"Then you better marry him tomorrow." Henrietta stood up. "Now," she checked her watch, "it's nearly seven. Let's not keep everyone waiting, Caleb."

Dafna seemed very young, standing there so embarrassed. Katrine leaned into Henrietta as they followed Dr. Herring back down the dirt path to the communal dining room. "How old is Dafna?"

"18, I think." Henrietta looked at Katrine.

"The children grow up here very quickly, don't they?"

"They have to. To survive." Henrietta answered.

THE DINING ROOM was a large wooden structure with windows that opened out to the lake. Long tables were set with white tablecloths and set with platters of salads, challah, and roasted chickens. The smell of lemon and garlic filled the room. Each newcomer sat between two of the 'old-timers.' They eyed the food in awe. It had been, for some, many, many months since they had seen such bounty.

Dr. Herring stood up moved to the front of the

room. He stood on a small platform, and the group quieted.

"I want to welcome each and every one of you to Kibbutz Kinneret." Dr. Herring's voice carried to the back of the room as a cool breeze from the lake swept through the open windows.

"You are now members of this kibbutz! This is your home. You will never live in fear again for being a Jew. Here, in the land of your forefathers, you are safe. I want you to be proud of who you are, do you understand?" His voice rose. "Shabbat Shalom!"

Morris had also been assigned to Kibbutz Kinneret. The boy caught Katrine's eyes and smiled widely. He looked as though he were in heaven.

The room erupted in a mass of young voices shouting out "Shabbat Shalom!"

Dr. Herring took a loaf of bread and began to pray "Blessed are You, Lord God, Ruler of the universe, who has brought forth bread from the earth. . ."

Lorelei fingered the thin gold bracelet on her wrist and fought back tears. They had celebrated Shabbat on occasion, though her family had been far from observant. The words were, nevertheless, familiar. And truly, almost too much.

THREE HOURS LATER, Katrine collapsed on her back on her bed in their bungalow. She didn't bother taking her dress off or washing her face. "I don't think I can do it."

Grace pulled one of her leather loafers off and then the other. "What do you mean?"

Lorelei dug her brush out of her valise and began to brush her long blond hair, one stroke at a time.

Katrine stared at the ceiling. "You heard that girl at dinner - that 'Dafna.'" Her voice took on a mocking tone as she continued to imitate. "We all share our clothes here. So tomorrow we'll get you some shorts. They're better for farming."

"I like the shorts," Grace answered.

But Katrine pressed on. "And can you imagine me? Milking a cow? And then all that rot about choosing a new name, a Hebrew name. I like my name just the way it is, thank you very much"

Lorelei put the brush down. "I think it's a very nice sentiment. We're Hebrews now. Why not choose new names? I was thinking of something like Tzivia. Henrietta said it means 'Doe,' like a deer."

Katrine sat up violently. "Because Mama and Papa chose our names, and they're beautiful, and they're ours."

"All right, all right." Lorelei came over to Katrine and rubbed her back. "You don't have to change your name."

"I'm turning the light off now," Grace said, switching off the lamp. Both Lorelei and Grace crawled into the same bed as Katrine, though there were two other beds in the room. "I'm telling you, Katrine, it's going to be alright. I like it here. I feel safe. And I think Dafna and Uri are two of the nicest people I've met in ages."

Katrine didn't answer. Within two minutes, both her younger sisters had fallen fast asleep.

"Oh Harry," she whispered in the darkness, "what have you gotten me into now?"

CHAPTER 3

KIBBUTZNIKS

*H*enrietta sat across from the Adleman sisters in the communal dining room. They had now been on the kibbutz for four days. In those four days, they had brushed horses, milked cows under Edna's expert supervision, and gathered eggs.

Each afternoon had been spent clearing the new east field, picking dates from the palm trees (perched high on ladders), and checking the orange trees for bugs or other pests.

The girls were outfitted in the obligatory khaki shorts and heavy leather sandals and then plunged headfirst into their first Hebrew lesson. Katrine's hair was pulled back into a low bun. Her fair skin was burned, and her nose was peeling. Even in December, the Galilee was warm, and the sun, intense. Grace's nose was covered in freckles. And Lorelei's olive skin was taking on a warm tanned glow.

Henrietta observed them closely. "You look healthy. I always say there is nothing better for people than to be working hard in the sun and fresh air." She pushed a glass of orange juice towards Katrine. "Drink this, it's full of vitamins."

"I'm really not very hungry," Katrine protested. She was never one for a large breakfast, but on the kibbutz, as on most farms, breakfast was the main meal of the day. There were hard-boiled eggs, sliced bread, giant bowls of tomatoes and cucumbers (salad for breakfast at first seemed a very novel idea!), and bowls of a thick paste of mashed beans they called 'hummus.' It was all very different from the delicate pastries and thick brown bread and butter of Berlin, and, of course, Horatio and Edie's Scottish oatmeal and cream back in Kingsbarns.

"How's your Hebrew coming along?" Henrietta asked.

Grace frowned. "It's not as easy for us as some of the others. Papa and Mama didn't think we needed to learn Hebrew as kids." Like many German-Jewish refugees, she refused to speak her mother-tongue in protest against the land of her birth, the land that had rejected her so violently.

Katrine grimaced. "Music and dancing lessons were more important. We were just like any other German family."

"Except that you were Jewish," Henrietta pointed out.

Katrine looked down and stared at her hands.

49

There were blisters on her palms from hoeing. Every muscle in her body ached. "Dafna is a very firm Hebrew teacher."

Lorelei interjected, "Ani me-da-be-ret ktsat iv-rit?"

Henrietta looked like a proud mother hen. "So you speak a little Hebrew, do you? Well done! By the time I come back, you'll be speaking like a native."

"By the time you come back?" Lorelei asked, suddenly concerned. "You're leaving?"

"I have to go back to Jerusalem. My business here is complete, and I'm needed at the hospital. We are working on opening a new neonatal wing."

Lorelei looked down, and the old woman reached across the table and took her hand. "But I'm sure you will be just fine."

At that moment, Dafna poked her head into the dining room. "Aunt Henrietta! The bus is here."

With that, Henrietta stood up and kissed each of the Adleman girls on the cheek. She stopped near Katrine's ear and whispered, "Those blisters will heal soon enough, and they'll make you stronger in the end."

WITHIN ONE MONTH Katrine's blisters had hardened into calluses. The days blended together in a constant stream of work, lessons, meals, and sleep.

The rains came and went, turning the fields into a sloggy mess. Hanukkah came and went. It had felt quite odd to the Adleman girls, who were used to Christmas trees and cold weather next to their menorahs. But there were still donuts, thanks to Mrs. Herring. The work came, but it never went. In fact, the work on the kibbutz never stopped.

Every afternoon, around 2:00 or so, Morris, would lead a small cart pulled by a donkey into the field. In the cart was a large barrel filled with water and a tray of sandwiches. The young man always brought the donkey underneath a large Acacia tree, and the weary laborers would lean up against the knotty roots and rocks in the Acacia's shade, eating slowly.

Today, Morris was accompanied by a very thin and very silent boy. The boy had dark circles under his eyes and a sad down-turned mouth. Morris motioned for the boy to start filling up the metal cups with water.

Dafna put her hands on her hips and wiped her brow. "Who's this, Morris?"

"His name is Borris. He only speaks Russian. He walked all the way from Russia. Can you believe that!"

Borris mechanically filled up one cup at a time, shooting a shy glance at the group of teenagers circling up around the cart.

Katrine took a cup. "That's impossible. You can't walk from Russia."

"Well, Borris did." Dafna looked at Katrine. "Besides, lots of people have tried it. Not many make it, but some do. I met a man who came here around the same time as my dad. He walked all the way from Russia - to escape the Tsar."

51

Morris's face took on an other-worldly look. "Fear not, for I am with you. I will bring your descendants from the east, and gather you from the west. I will say to the north, 'Give them up!' And to the south, 'do not keep them back!' Bring my sons from afar, and my daughters from the ends of the earth."[6]

"What's that?" Lorelei asked, sipping her water.

Dafna shot her a look that said, 'don't you know anything?' and then answered, "That's Scripture. The Prophet Isaiah wrote it."

Lorelei shrugged. She had never read much Scripture. Her father had been a math teacher, not a rabbi.

Morris began passing out the sandwiches. "That's us. The sons and daughters from the ends of the earth."

Katrine took her sandwich and eased onto the ground. It was tuna salad. *Again.* Her arms hurt from the last hour of attacking hard soil that refused to soften. To no one in particular, she groaned and let out, "I'm all for gender equality and all that, but I am certain a man could do a more efficient job at clearing stones than me."

Dafna, who had remained standing, replied, "Well, we don't have the luxury here of going to cafes all day and shopping or whatever it is you did back there in Germany. Here, women have to work just as hard as the men in the fields, or we would never be able to build anything at all. It is the only way."

Katrine seriously doubted it was the *only* way,

but she had a vague suspicion that now was not the time to try to convince Dafna otherwise.

"Here, we don't care about vanities like makeup and dresses," the girl preached on, self-righteously.

"What's the matter with makeup and dresses?" Grace asked.

"They're 'extra.' Completely unnecessary. Why, in Europe and America, women spend hours on permanent waves and lipstick and false eyelashes… and for what purpose?"

"To look pretty, and because it's fun," Grace answered.

"Uri likes me exactly how I am. Why, if he were to see me all dressed up like a picture in a magazine, I'd feel so unlike myself, I wouldn't know what to do!"

Katrine smiled. "Certainly, you would like Uri to take you out somewhere special, him wearing a smart tuxedo, and your beautiful auburn hair done up, swishing around on a dance floor while the band plays 'Isn't it Romantic?'"

Dafna's brow furrowed and a complex, pained expression came across her face. Then, she picked up her shovel and marched back to her row and began digging vigorously.

"What's the matter with her?" Morris said, after a moment.

"I don't know," Katrine answered, "but I'm going to find out."

∾

"WHAT ARE YOU DOING HERE?" Dafna asked, surprised to see Katrine standing on the small porch outside the women's dorm.

Katrine didn't answer. Instead, she stepped inside and glanced around. It was empty, just as she had expected. Everyone had just left for dinner. "Dafna, do you mind if we talk?"

"I was just going to dinner." She was acting even more like a prickly pear than usual.

"Well, you can wait a few more minutes. I've got ten years on you, give or take, so you can at least give me that out of respect."

"We are equals on this kibbutz." Dafna put her hand on her hip and pursed her lips together.

"Then for the sake of equality, give me the time of day." Katrine smiled and held out a paper bag. "I brought you something."

Dafna's eyes narrowed. She took the bag and opened it cautiously. Neatly folded and tied in a ribbon was Katrine's best dress, the evening gown that Horatio and Edie had bought for her at the Bijenkorf in Holland. The dress was white silk with delicate ruffles all around the neck.

Katrine saw the fingers lovingly caress the soft fabric. She knew immediately that she had found a chink in the girl's armor. Her suspicion was correct.

"I know you 'don't care about vanities like makeup and dresses,' but that doesn't mean you shouldn't have a nice dress for yourself."

"But why?" Dafna asked though she did not let go of the dress. "I don't need a dress! I'd feel silly wearing something like this!"

"Don't feel silly," Katrine answered. "Just

give yourself permission to feel like and look like the beautiful woman you are."

"You've seen what I do all day." Dafna looked at Katrine.

"I know exactly what you do every day, and that's why you need this dress. You're just about my size, and I thought it might be nice the next time Uri takes you dancing."

Dafna's eyes opened wide and filled with tears. Katrine had struck a nerve. "Oh, Katrine. Don't you see, Uri has never taken me dancing. Why we've only ever been hiking together." She looked down. "When you were talking, I realized how provincial we must seem to you and your sisters. How rough around the edges."

"Certainly you go out sometimes? To Tel Aviv or Haifa? I hear there are some very swanky places in the cities."

Dafna shrugged. "It's hard to leave the kibbutz. There is always so much to be done. And with Amos gone…"

"Amos?"

"My elder brother. He joined the RAF. He's fighting the Germans with the Royal Air Force."

"I see."

By now, Dafna had untied the ribbon and was holding the dress up to her shoulders.

"It may be a little long. But I'll have Grace fit it to you."

Dafna's eyes met Katrine's. "You really want me to have this?"

"I think you need to have it if only so when you see it hanging up you can tell yourself that one day, if you ever have the chance to go dancing, you'll be prepared. It's good for the soul. Besides, I'll never have a reason to wear it now. My nightclub days are over." Katrine gave a little shrug of her shoulders.

"You used to go to nightclubs?" Dafna asked.

Katrine sat down on the edge of the bed, "My sisters and I used to work at one of sorts, after my parents were arrested. We had a singing group at an underground jazz club. They paid us in borscht."

"In borscht? What an unusual life you must have had."

"Not so unusual, I think. But certainly different from here."

"What did you do, back in Germany?"

"I studied medieval history in college and was planning to get my master's degree until the Jews were expelled from the universities."

"And Lorelei?"

"She was going to get married. The Nazis killed him."

The young sabra's face fell. "Were *you* ever in love?"

This was met with a dry humorless laugh. "I never got as high of marks in that subject as I would have liked. I generally have terrible taste in men. Or men have terrible taste in me."

"What about Grace?" Dafna asked.

"She's young. She didn't know what she wanted to do yet. Now, her parents are dead, and she is trying with everything in her to make a life for herself on this kibbutz. She loves it."

Katrine stood up. "Well, the next time Uri wants to do something special with you, come to me. Grace will do your hair, and Lorelei, your makeup. And maybe we'll sing something to you both from behind a tree for a picnic. How does that sound? The Adleman Sisters for a private performance."

Dafna's eyes welled up. "You've been very kind to me."

~

THE NEXT NIGHT, Grace, Katrine, and Lorelei were startled awake by a rapping on their door. Grace sat up and was just about to switch on the lamp when Lorelei grabbed her hand to stop her. "Don't turn the lamp on! What if it is an Arab raid?"

Grace paused before saying, "Why would the Arabs knock on our door? Wouldn't they just start shooting?"

Katrine was now on her feet and moving towards the door. "It's not an Arab raid. You know the villages around here. We depend on them, and they depend on us! Dr. Herring is the only good doctor for miles. They are not going to shoot him!"

"Who's there?" she called loudly.

"It's me! Dafna!"

Instantly, Katrine threw open the door. There Dafna stood, along with Uri.

"Sorry for the late notice, but these things are always last minute," Uri said. He held Dafna's hand.

"What things?" Grace asked, now behind Katrine.

"Put your clothes on and find out!" Dafna laughed, a playful gleam in her eye.

Ten minutes later, the Adleman sisters were squished in the back of an old truck and headed up the steep canyon road that rose above the Galilee. The oldest children from the village, along with Uri and Dafna, made up the rest of the party. The moon illuminated the Yavne'el Valley and its thick rows of olive trees. They passed a group of Bedouins camped on the side of the road, their herd of camels peacefully watching the truck sputter past.

Morris poked Grace. "Do you know where we are going?"

Grace shook her head, her eyes bright with excitement.

By then, they were out of the valley and working their way towards an enormous hill that rose like a great mound from the valley's floor.

"I think we are in the Jezreel Valley," Morris said.

"How do you know that?" Grace asked.

"I know what direction we've been driving. I can follow the stars."

Grace smiled. "So... where does that put us?"

The truck began to climb up the hill through a small Arab village, and Dafna motioned for Grace to be quiet. "We don't want to wake up the whole of Shibli," she said.

"Shibli?" Morris whispered.

"This village."

Moments later, Uri parked the truck and helped the girls out of the back. Everyone was given a canteen and told to be quiet and follow closely.

And so began the Adleman sisters' first hike up Mount Tabor.

"I knew it!" Morris practically squealed with delight. "I just knew it was going to be Mount Tabor!"

"I think a better name for it is Mount Never Ending." Katrine paused to catch her breath, but Dafna grabbed her hand and pulled her forward, exclaiming, "Come on, Katrine! We are almost there!"

Up and up the little group went, winding up the steep switchbacks, the air growing colder and colder as the elevation increased. They passed a group of cattle roaming about.

"They belong to the monks," Uri explained. They could see the outline of a large church on the top of the hill now, glowing white against the night sky. "The monks never come down. All their food is brought to them every week on the backs of donkeys," he finished.

Lorelei stopped short. "Do you all hear that?" she asked, drawing back.

They all listened closely. It was the sound of singing. Dafna then clapped her hands together. "Oh good! They are already here!"

She was suddenly overcome with energy and began to practically run up the mountain, Uri not far behind.

Huffing and puffing, the rest of the group finally reached the top of the mountain. There, in a clearing, were nearly 100 young people. Someone had brought a guitar. There was a bonfire, and they were all singing a lovely melody in Hebrew. Many of the boys and girls were dancing in a circle, their feet moving so fast in an intricate pattern that it made Katrine's head spin.

Before the girls could catch their breath, they were swept up in the circle. Around and around they swung, arms interlaced with strangers who felt like family, until they knew not which way was up and which was down.

Katrine, desperately thirsty, pulled away and collapsed onto the ground, drinking deeply from her canteen. When she looked up, Dafna was smiling down at her. "Welcome to our nightclub!"

"Whoever are all these people?" Katrine asked, pushing herself back against the ruins of an old stone wall.

Dafna fell upon the ground and propped herself up on one elbow. "They are the leaders from all the Youth Villages. A special meeting was called. Apparently, there is news."

Just then, the music died down, and a man motioned for everyone to sit. All eyes turned to him expectantly.

His eyes suddenly caught Katrine's.

It was Harry.

CHAPTER 4

THE ADLEMAN SISTERS GET DRAFTED

*H*arry looked at Katrine for another moment, more than a bit surprised. Then, as though he remembered where he was, he stepped closer to the light of the bonfire. "I'm sure you are all wondering why you've been summoned here tonight," he began.

The young people glanced at one another expectantly. Harry began to pace, his clear voice carrying over the group.

"I've just been to see Ben Gurion and the other leaders."

"The Arab population is demanding independence from the British Mandate, and they do not want us here. Their antics shut down open-ended Jewish immigration and land purchases. Britain can't handle any more conflict with the Arabs in Palestine alongside a war with Germany. By keeping the Jews away from Palestine, they hope to win back the Arab's support."[7] He paused a moment and continued, "And now we have intel that the Grand Mufti has ties with Hitler. We've intercepted wires of the Mufti congratulating Hitler and expressing his excitement to see fascism spread through the Middle East."[8]

"No surprise there," Dafna whispered vehemently.

Katrine remained focused on Harry, who had stopped pacing. He looked very handsome in the moonlight. "Over two decades ago, the British promised that they would support a national home for the Jewish people in Palestine, in a letter from Foreign Secretary Arthur Balfour to Lord Rothschild. Now that they need Arab support, and Arab oil, for the war, they don't want to remember that promise."[9]

"The British have made a lot of promises," a young man called out, "to the Arabs, and to us. Even to France."[10]

"It doesn't matter what promises the British made," Harry said. "They'll say whatever they can to get what they want."

"And that puts us where?" the young man answered.

"Good question." Harry clasped his hands behind his back. "It puts us in a very precarious position. The Arabs are going to do everything they can so we can't stay. The British are probably not going to do much to stop them."

A young woman sitting near Harry got up on her knees, her brow furrowed in anger. "And what are we supposed to do? Hitler killed my parents! I cannot go back to Vienna!"

"I know, I know," Harry said, putting his

hands up to calm her down. "And America, the UK, and just about everywhere else has shut their borders."[11]

Harry put his hands down as the truth sunk in. The world did not want them. They had nowhere to go. No one to turn to.

"So what are we going to do?" Dafna called out.

"There is plenty of room in this land for all of us, the Arabs and the Jews. We don't want to take their land or throw them out. All the land we have is land we bought, fair and square. And there are many Arabs who agree. It's just that their leader, the Mufti, also happens to be a closet Nazi."

Katrine's head spun. The British were appeasing the Arabs, who were partial to Hitler. Yet, the British were also the only ones brave enough to stand up to Hitler. What an awful twisted mess.

Harry began to pace again. "We can't rely on the British. That's clear enough now. However, we also *must* support them." He paused before continuing, "And on that note, I'm going to introduce a great friend to the Jewish people, Captain Orde Wingate."[12]

A tall, thin man with a long, angular nose stepped into the light of the fire. He wore the uniform of a senior British army officer and had a strange glint in his eye.

"Many of you know who I am," he said, his accent richly Scottish. "I am a modern-day Gideon. I'm not Jewish, but I am a deeply religious Christian and a devoted Zionist. I'm with you, because you're God's people, and the creation of a Jewish state is a fulfillment of prophecy! That's why I'm here. That's why you are here. It doesn't matter what promises my government made or didn't make. It's God's promises that matter. And he's the one who promised this day would come!"

Katrine leaned into Dafna and whispered, "Is he all right," She tapped her head, "you know, up there?"

Captain Wingate raised his voice and continued, "Here we stand on Mount Tabor! According to the book of Judges, this is where the Israelites attacked and vanquished Sisera and the Canaanites under the great General Barak and the prophetess, Deborah. Right here! On this very ground!"

Dafna whispered, her eyes never leaving Captain Wingate's face, "Dad says he's stark raving mad. But everyone also admits he is a military genius."

"And now," Captain Orde Wingate raised his fist, the fire glowed off his face eerily, "some of you will be asked to volunteer for His Royal Majesty's forces. They need all the help they can get to defeat Hitler. The British are asking for your cooperation. They fear the Axis Powers are going to break through in North Africa. The location of Palestine is key in holding the Middle East. There is even talk about forming a Jewish Brigade."

"What good is that going to do?" someone cried out. "We help the Brits defeat Hitler, and then they are going to give away our land

and the Arabs are going to push us into the sea?"

"Ah!" Captain Wingate pointed his finger at the young man, "that is where the rest of you come in. Consider yourselves drafted. You have all been chosen to become members of the Palmach."

Lorelei and Grace inched their way to Katrine and leaned in. "Do you have any idea what this guy is talking about?" Grace whispered.

Katrine shook her head.

He took a proud, militaristic stance. "The Haganah, the Jewish military organization founded by the Zionists in Palestine to guard the settlements, has decided to form a brand-new elite strike force. *This* is the Palmach. This is to prepare for the possibility of a British withdrawal and a German invasion."[13] He looked solemnly from face to face. "You all know what that would mean."

Lorelei, Grace, and Katrine shared a knowing glance. It would mean certain death. More concentration camps. Forced labor. It would mean the end.

"I've several trusted officers under my command who will begin to train you in guerilla tactics and sabotage. They will arrive at your various kibbutzim within the month." He stopped for a moment before saying, "And meanwhile, we are going to smuggle as many of you out of the grip of the Nazis in Europe and into the country as we can." He paused, letting his news sink in.

A slight glow on the horizon announced that night was over. A moment later, the burning fire of the sun appeared, eclipsing the dying flames of the bonfire. Suddenly, the Jezreel Valley, far below their perch on the side of the mountain, was ablaze with the light of day. They were so high up, you could see clouds hanging above the plains and fields and olive groves. A great stillness enveloped the group.

And then, the clear voice, of a young boy or girl, Katrine could not tell, sang out, welcoming the dawn, "Kol 'od balevav penimah..."

Dafna whispered the translation to the haunting melody that many of the group were now singing. *"O while within a Jewish heart, yearns true a Jewish soul, and Jewish glances turning East to Zion fondly dart, O then our hope—it is not dead, our ancient hope and true, to be a nation free and forevermore Zion and Jerusalem at our core."*[14]

The eerie melody ended as night fully dissolved in the sun's rays. Dafna's eyes were glued on Captain Wingate, whose back was turned from the group towards the valley. "It is called Ha Tikvah."

"The Hope?" Grace asked, testing her Hebrew skills.

Everyone was on their feet now, speaking in small groups with a tense sort of hush.

As Katrine eased herself up, she noticed Harry making his way towards her. He had a funny look on his face.

"I thought you were on the lam," she said flatly.

"It's nice to see you too, Katrine."

Grace stifled a smile and pulled Lorelei and

Dafna away, saying, "Come on, girls, I want to see the ruins of the old church," leaving Harry and Katrine all alone.

"How'd you do it?" Katrine crossed her arms.

"What?"

"Disappear off the *Athena*?"

"I had a friend on the patrol boat. It was all planned from the beginning. Hitched a ride in one of the blow-up lifeboat boxes that just so happened not to have a lifeboat in it."

"And then?" Katrine arched one eyebrow.

"Oh, between Wingate and the Jewish Agency, I keep myself busy. You are looking at a bonafide spy."

She crossed her arms, turning her head to look at Wingate, who was deep in conversation with Uri. "How do you know you can trust him?"

"Wingate?"

She nodded.

"He's eccentric, a genius, and quotes the Bible like he was there when it was written. Sure, he might be a little crazy. But only a crazy man would want to help us, right? You can trust him."

"I'm not even sure I trust you. You left us on the *Athena*."

"It all worked out, didn't it?" Harry asked.

"Depends on how you define 'worked out.' I plow fields now. Look at my hands!" She held up a calloused palm.

He took her hand in his. "They look alright, in my expert opinion."

She pulled her hand away awkwardly.

"You sort of surprised me, Ms. Adleman."

"How's that?"

"I wasn't expecting to see you here."

She lifted her chin up. "Why ever not?"

"You don't strike me as a very secure Zionist."

"I'm not. I was invited here," she answered, leveling him with a steely gaze.

"By who?"

"Dafna and Uri."

"That means they trust you."

She stopped, unable to answer.

He suddenly became bashful and couldn't look at her face. But if he had, he would have noticed a distinct softening about her eyes. "I certainly trust you…" he said quietly.

Then, abruptly changing the subject, he began poking the remains of a wall behind her with a stick. "Old crusader ruins."

"Really?"

"They're everywhere around here. And caves and alcoves. All very mysterious. Legend has it that the caves are where the King of Salem met with Abraham."[15]

"You mean Melchizedek?"

Harry nodded. "And the chapel was built by Christians to commemorate Christ's ascension." She followed his gaze towards the beautiful stone building. She could make out Lorelei, Grace, and Dafna sitting on the steps.

Katrine sighed. "So much on one hill. Who built them? The ruins, I mean." She moved closer to the wall and knelt down. "You know, I used to study medieval history, in another life." She looked up at him. "Was Richard the Lionheart ever here?"

"I don't know… I'm more of a modern history guy. Like, the last ten years, if you get my drift."

A cow mooed from inside the courtyard of the ruins.

Just then, Uri joined Harry and leaned up against the old crusader wall. "Have you seen Dafna?" the young man asked. "I've got to talk to her. Something just came up."

"She's up there with the girls." Harry jerked his head in the direction of the chapel. He scratched his chin and said half to himself, "Can't live with em—"

"Can't live without em!" Uri finished, slapping Harry heartily on the back.

CHAPTER 5

KATHERINA

*H*arry led the charge up a steep incline where rumor had it, they would find a field of flowers.

"Well, *I* couldn't do it!" Katrine said, huffing after Harry. Lorelei, Grace, and Morris followed behind.

"Do *what*?" Lorelei asked, adjusting the funny little cloth hat, called a 'kova tembel,' on her head.

"Just get married," she snapped her fingers, "like that!"

Harry turned back to Katrine. "You don't strike me as someone who does anything 'like that.'"

Marching on, she answered, "I don't. I'm very thoughtful. The craziest thing I ever did was get on the *Athena*. And I still thought about that for a whole week before doing it! Uri proposed to Dafna two months ago! He decides to volunteer for the RAF yesterday. And now, we're hiking to who knows where to pick wildflowers for the wedding. It seems rather foolhardy. You, however," she said, referring to Harry, "are not like that."

"Are you saying I'm foolhardy?" Harry asked. "Or not?"

"You know exactly what I mean!"

"I'm only here because I've got a week of vacation, and I'm the only one who knows where the wildflowers are. I couldn't send all you newbies up here on your own, now could I? That wouldn't be responsible." Harry stepped up the pace. "Besides, they didn't need my help in the kitchen or building the huppa."

"I think it's romantic," Grace answered.

"And that's another question!" Katrine was breathing heavily. "Why in the world would you know where wildflowers are? You're a man!"

Harry shouted back to Morris, "What do you think, Morris?"

"About what? Getting married or doing crazy things? Or knowing where flowers are?"

"Your pick!"

Morris stopped. "Even fools are thought wise if they keep silent, and discerning if they hold their tongues."[16]

"What is that supposed to mean?" Grace asked the young man.

"Oh the wise, wise words of Solomon," Harry chuckled.

"I think I was just put down, but I don't know exactly how," Katrine shot Morris a sideways glance, "and by a kid."

They kept marching, the sun rising higher and hotter by the minute.

Before Morris could explain himself, the trail evened out, opening onto a magnificent plain of flowers. The Jezreel Valley was a sea of color. Spring had nipped at winter's heels. A surprise burst of heat had forced the flowers to bloom earlier than usual. All thoughts of fools disappeared into the oblivion of flora and fauna.

"All right," Harry said. "Lorelei, Grace, Morris—you take those flowers over there to the east. Katrine, you and I will tackle the west. Operation Wedding commence!"

KATRINE AND HARRY worked in silence, picking one bloom at a time. Mrs. Herring had loaned them a large quilt that they'd spread on the ground. Slowly, a pile of bright pink, orange, and red flowers formed. They could then carefully carry the mound of flowers back without damaging the blooms.

Harry worked quickly, deftly picking one bloom after another in a steady rhythm. "You know, I really do love flowers," he said.

It was hot. Very hot. Katrine took a long sip from her canteen. "Harry Stenetsky, the brave spy and lover of flowers."

"There are a lot of things you don't know about me, Katrine." He was unfazed and didn't stop picking.

"All right, what sort of flower is this?" She

picked a lacy yellow bloom and tossed it onto the quilt.

"Ferula communis. Common Giant Fennel."

"And this?" she pointed to a delicate flower that looked rather like an iris, more than a little surprised.

"Iris Haynei. They also call it a Gilboa Iris." He bent down and plucked a bright pink flower. "This one is a linum pubescens, known as a Hairy Pink Flax."

Looking carefully, he suddenly spotted what he was looking for and gleefully exclaimed, "There it is, this one's rare! It's an Ophrys Umbilicata."

"A what?" Katrine stepped closer and bent down to examine the flower, feeling rather irked.

"A Carmel Bee-Orchid." He looked at Katrine's face. "They are pretty unique."

"How do you know all this? The names and everything."

"My father was into horticulture." He picked the flower and stood up alongside her. "See," he said, "doesn't the flower look like a bee?"

He was standing too close again. It made her nervous. "I suppose so," she stammered and stepped backward.

At that point, Grace and Lorelei swept up, holding large bunches in their hands. They looked from Katrine to Harry and then to the flower.

"What's going on?" Grace asked.

"We've just about finished..." Katrine mumbled.

Then, looking at the flower, Lorelei

exclaimed, "Oh my, Katrine! Have you ever seen a flower like that?"

"It's an Ophrys Umbilicata," Harry said confidently.

"Yes, yes," Katrine said. "We know. A Toffee Bee Orchid."

"Carmel Bee-Orchid," Harry corrected. "'*Carmel*'—not like the candy, like the mountain."

Katrine rolled her eyes.

Lorelei took the flower in her hand as Grace said (as only a sister can say), "Don't mind her. Katrine always gets upset when someone knows something she doesn't know. It makes her feel insecure."

"That's not true!" Katrine retorted.

"That wasn't kind, Grace!" Lorelei, the habitual peacekeeper between bossy Katrine and outspoken Grace, shot Grace a disapproving look.

Grace shrugged. "We all know that's why you and that professor what's-his-name—"

"Grace!" Lorelei said firmly, growing embarrassed for both of her sisters and trying to salvage the moment before it got worse. "That's enough." Lorelei gave the flower back to Harry.

It was too late. Katrine's face had turned beet red, and she was stammering, "This is not the time or the place to bring up Jonathan! I ought to—" Her brain stopped then. She had no idea what she ought to do.

Harry, oblivious, held up the flower as a peace offering. Then, impulsively, he reached out and pushed the bee-like orchid into

Katrine's hand. "I think I'm going to start calling you 'Kate.'"

Grace smirked. "You know, she played Kate in *The Taming of the Shrew* in high school!"

"You're kidding! I played Petruchio in college! 'Come, come, you wasp. I'faith you are too angry,'[17] he laughed, quoting the play. Impishly he added, "Who's Jonathan?"

Katrine glared at him and then at Grace and Lorelei. She refused the flower, quoting ruefully, "'If I be waspish, best beware my sting.'"[18]

"Talk about perfect casting! You're really good!" He continued, enjoying the drama, "'Nay, come, Kate, come. You must not look so sour.'"[19]

Her face froze, pain written all over it.

Realizing how distressed she was, he instantly retreated. "I'm sorry. I was just playing around."

"I know. I—" she swallowed, wanting to cry for some unknown reason. "I've forgotten how to play, that's all."

"Understandable… And don't worry. I've got bee immunity. It will come back, like riding a bike."

He smiled, and she managed a small smile back. Who knows? She thought. Maybe he was right. Maybe she would remember how to play one day.

Morris suddenly shouted from across the field, "Harry! Harry. Come here! I found something!"

"Excuse me, fair Kate!" He bowed and jogged towards Morris, who was hunched over and looking at something on the ground intensely.

Katrine turned to Lorelei and Grace.

"That was rude." Her shoulders sagged, and a deep hurt registered in her eyes.

Grace realized she had gone too far and instantly felt awful. "Oh Katrine, I'm sorry. I didn't mean anything by it."

"I know," Katrine sighed. "That doesn't mean it didn't hurt."

"You'll forgive me?"

Katrine looked at her younger sister, and as usual, couldn't stay mad. Softening, she reached out and squeezed Grace's hand, assuring her that all was forgotten.

The heaviness lifted, and Grace ran towards Morris and Harry, leaving Katrine and Lorelei behind.

As Katrine was about to move forward, she felt Lorelei hold her back. Her face was very serious.

"What Grace said may not have been very nice, but that doesn't mean it isn't true."

"What do you mean?" Katrine's lips parted in a question.

"I mean, there is only one person here not being very nice, and that's you. He's sort of wonderful, and you are the only person who doesn't see it. You are normally the most composed, polite, thoughtful woman I've ever been around. But when you are with Harry, it's like you become a different human being. You freeze up." Exhaling, she added, "If you ask me, I think he likes you."

"He's a lot older…" Katrine trailed off. She wanted to argue with Lorelei, but she couldn't. She knew her sister spoke the truth.

"You and I both know that doesn't matter. You are older than him inside by a million years. When you are both as far past 21 as you are, well, all's fair in love and war."

Katrine looked towards Harry. He turned around and stared at her briefly before turning his attention back to what Morris was showing him.

Lorelei put her hand on her sister's arm softly. "He's undertaken to woo the curst Katharina. Yea, and to marry her, if her dowry please."[20]

Katrine stared after him. "He'll woo a thousand, point the day of marriage, make feasts, invite friends, and proclaim the banns, yet never means to wed where he hath woo'd. Now must the world point at poor Katharina, and say, 'Lo, there is mad Petruchio's wife, if it would please him to come and marry her!'"[21]

"Oh Lorelei, face it!" she continued, "He'll be just like the others. He'll make me fall madly in love with him, and then he'll leave me. If I can convince him, and myself, that I don't like him, we'll all be saved months of pain."

"That's a terrible plan."

"I never was great at relationships, but it's the best I can come up with. Trust me, he's no Petruchio."

"You don't know that." Lorelei drew Katrine in, leaning her head on her shoulder. "He's not like the others. He's not Jonathan. For one thing, he's a grown man. Not a 15-year-old in a man's body. You should try again."

"I will if you will." Katrine stared at

Lorelei's wrist and the gold chain that hung about it.

Lorelei was unprepared for that sort of response and stammered uncomfortably, "This is about you, not me."

With that, Morris shouted across the field, "Hey you two! Get over here!"

LATER THAT EVENING, once the dining room had cleared out, Katrine, Lorelei, Grace, Harry, Dafna, Uri, and Mr. Herring all sat at one of the long tables, leaning over a small stone object.

Katrine picked it up and examined it closely. "My best guess is that it's a signet cylinder. But it's not medieval, I know enough to know that. It's much, much older."

"What's a signet cylinder?" Grace took the object from her sister's hand.

Katrine leaned back. "It's a stamp or an engraving. They are usually set in stone—like this one. Or metal. Or even crystal."

Mrs. Herring arrived from the kitchen carrying a plate of rugelach, a thin pastry filled with date paste and cinnamon, still warm from the oven. She set the plate down and pulled up a chair. Mr. Herring pecked her on the cheek and said, "Look what we have here, Mama! A real ancient treasure. Morris found it when he was picking flowers."

The portly woman took the stone object and

lifted it very close to her glasses. "What is it?"

Katrine inhaled before answering, "A seal. See those markings that look like writing?"

Mrs. Herring nodded.

"Someone important would have used it to seal a document, proving its authenticity. I don't know what language it is. Maybe ancient Hebrew, or Aramaic, or even Babylonian. So many people have lived around here…"

"It's ancient Hebrew!" Morris said triumphantly, entering the dining room, a large book in his hands. He set the book down and opened to the page he'd found. "See! I found this book on ancient languages in the library. The script matches the ancient Hebrew cursive."

They all looked. It was true.

Dr. Herring looked at the group gravely. "Well, if that's the case, this could be quite an important find."

Katrine's eyes glowed with excitement. "We'll have to get it authenticated!" In answer to the questioning stares, she explained, "You know, we need to find an expert who can tell us if it is the real deal. It could be worth a lot of money."

"It could be worth a lot of money?" Harry spoke half to himself, half to no one in particular.

Taking the seal out of his wife's hands, Dr. Herring replied, "We'll keep it in the safe until we decide what is best to be done with it."

THE NEXT MORNING, Grace put her artist's eye to good use in directing Lorelei and Katrine as they arranged the flowers on the huppa. "A few more red ones to the right!" she commanded. "Some of the wheat, yes, that's good. Perfect! We're done!"

Four wooden poles were planted in the earth, stretched out over the top was a beautiful prayer shawl fringed in blue. The wedding ceremony would take place underneath.

Katrine helped Lorelei off the stepstool, and the three girls stepped back to examine their handiwork. "Definitely worthy of a wedding," Lorelei said, quite proud.

"It's not red roses, but it will have to do," Katrine sighed. "At least Dafna will have a lovely dress."

The courtyard between the library and the dining room was lined with chairs in preparation for the coming festivities. Everyone was coming. Of course, the kibbutz. But then there were two other kibbutzim nearby and the neighboring Arab village. Apparently, in this corner of the world, 'close friends and family' meant everyone you'd ever met.

"I thought we were enemies with the Arabs," Lorelei said, glancing towards the dining room. A smell of something delicious roasting wafted towards them. "I can't understand why the Herrings insisted on inviting them."

Grace brushed the hair away from her face. "The Herrings are very close with several of the local Arab families. Their children grew up side by side. Some of the older children even attend high school classes at the school here on the kibbutz, remember?"

"It's all so confusing," Lorelei said. She had forgotten momentarily that three Arab teenagers were enrolled in the kibbutz school's classes for higher mathematics. The three boys were adamant about trying to learn all they could so they could study in France. Dr. Herring was the only one qualified to teach such advanced studies for miles around.

"They don't want violence any more than we do, I suppose," Katrine sighed.

"Some do, some don't. Dr. Herring told me all about it." Grace reached their bungalow and opened the door. "Just like some of us. Have you heard about the Irgun?"

"What's that?" Lorelei asked.

"It's a group here in Palestine. They don't think it's enough to just defend ourselves, which is the whole point of the Haganah. 'Only armed force will ensure the Jewish state,' and all that sort of talk. Some people say they're terrorists,"[22] Grace answered, stepping inside. "In that bombing last week at the Rex Cinema in Jerusalem, five Arabs were killed. And they say the Irgun was behind it."

"How awful!" Lorelei splashed water on her face from the small washstand. "Those poor people, just going to see a movie! What sort of person would do such a thing? It's so senseless!"

Grace's lips were tight. "They are angry. They

think that terrorism is the only way to get what they want."

"And what do they want?"

"A place to call home," Grace had changed out of her dress and was now carefully buttoning up a pink flimsy shift. She started brushing her hair, "just like us."

Twisting up her long blonde hair in front of the old mirror, Lorelei frowned. "But that's not the way to do it! By hurting innocent people!"

Grace stood behind Lorelei, staring at their reflections in the mirror. "To quote our young rabbi Morris, 'we are all capable of more evil than we could ever imagine.'"

Katrine's face appeared, significantly shorter in the mirror than her two sisters. She managed a funny little grin. "That boy needs to get out more," she said.

Glancing at the clock her face froze. They only had two hours to prepare for the wedding. "Now, we better hurry. Dafna will be here any minute! I better get the curling iron heating up."

CHAPTER 6

TROUBLE AT SUNSET

*D*afna's wedding was the first wedding to ever be held at Kibbutz Kinneret, so it took on a feeling of unprecedented importance. Amos, her elder brother serving with His Royal Majesty's Air Force, was unable to attend the wedding. He was not married and appeared to be so well adjusted to bachelor life that few believed he would ever settle down. Meanwhile, Dafna was the lake region's darling. She recklessly rode her ginger horse all over the hills. It was almost the same color as her hair.

Loved by all, fawned over, petted over, generally given whatever she wanted when she wanted it, Dafna had somehow still turned out impressively well (if occasionally self-centered, but who can blame a child with such an upbringing!). Her character matched her physical strength, which was more than most women her age could boast. Uri had fallen in love with her instantly, the day he'd arrived on one of Henrietta Stolz's busses. She'd been there, right next to her father, waving the bus in, her hair reflecting the sunlight.

And now, they were to be married.

Mrs. Herring knocked on the door of the bungalow and shouted merrily, "Girls, it's nearly time! All the guests are here."

Grace opened the door, and instantly, Mrs. Herring burst into tears. She had never seen Dafna look so beautiful. Katrine's dress was a dream on her daughter.

"Oh, Mama!" Dafna protested, "You mustn't cry!"

Mrs. Herring wiped her eyes with a handkerchief. She wore her best Shabbat frock, a simple, well-made black suit. "Dafna, what a dress!" she said, fingering the thin fabric. It fit her perfectly. "And your hair! It's perfect. You are a perfect bride, and it will be a perfect wedding!" Turning to Katrine, Lorelei, and Grace, she added, "She's never looked prettier. Thank you, girls!"

"Yes, thank you," Dafna agreed, taking one last look in the mirror.

Grace reached out and tamed a loose curl. "There, *now* it's perfect."

Sighing, Dafna turned back around. "Almost perfect. Amos isn't here."

Her mother reached out and squeezed her hand tenderly. "There wasn't enough time to arrange his leave."

"My mother used to say that missing those who are not with us helps us appreciate who we have

with us that much more," Katrine said, holding
the door open.

"No sweet without the bitter, yes?" Dafna
said.

"Rather, sometimes the bitter makes the sweet
sweeter." Katrine kissed her cheek. "So, my
dear, how about we go to a wedding?"

As far as weddings go, Dafna and Uri's was very
sweet and nearly perfect. It was spring. They
were young and in love. The flowers were plen-
tiful and bright. The seven blessings were given
with grace and poise. Uri broke the glass with a
voracious stomp.

And then, after the rings were exchanged,
everyone exploded in shouts of 'mazel tov!' and
'good luck!'

After that, everyone sat down to an abundant,
if bland, dinner of schnitzel, crispy potato
pancakes, pickled herring, and plates of cooked
cabbage. If there had been no bowls of fresh
dates and pulpy orange juice from the kibbutz on
the table, you would have sworn you were in
Poland or Hungary.

It was after the wedding, at the reception in
the courtyard, that 'it' happened. They'd
already cut the cake and were just getting
started on the dancing.

Just as the Adleman sisters sang the last
notes of "Erev Shel Shoshanim" (and what Jewish
wedding would be complete without that song!)
and the guests swayed in somber recognition of

the seriousness of the ceremony, a few brave and strong guests hoisted Dafna and Uri up on chairs above the crowd as everyone began to sing the much rowdier "Hava Nagila." The song is rather infectious, with the words 'everyone rejoice' repeating over and over. The circle of dancing merrymakers grew faster and faster as the song grew louder and louder. Dafna and Uri tried not to look down or fall off the chairs, poised precariously above the heads of their friends and family.

Somehow, Harry and Katrine wound up next to each other in the circle. They were whirling around, very very fast, with Harry's strong arm pulling Katrine along. It took every ounce of her brain-power to concentrate on the steps and not land flat on her face. Every once in a while, he would look back at her, breathless and happy.

It was then that the shot rang out.

While the shot was loud enough to stop the dancing, it was the blood-curdling scream that followed that sent the reception scrambling for cover. "It's a gun! A sniper!" someone shouted.

Dafna and Uri were practically dropped to the ground, the groom dragging his bride behind a tree.

Harry threw himself over Katrine before pulling her under the table where the remains of the cake sat. She was protesting loudly, calling for Lorelei and Grace. But Harry was stronger. "The girls can take care of them-selves!" he shouted. And he was right—Katrine's sisters were already nearly back to the bungalow. From under the table cloth, Katrine saw them escape inside. She breathed a sigh of relief.

Nearly everyone had found some sort of cover or another. Everyone except one man who lay still on the center of the dance floor. He had a bright red stain on his white dress shirt. Katrine whispered loudly, "Oh Harry! Who is it?"

Harry squinted and whispered, "I can't tell. Don't move, okay."

She jerked her head 'yes.'

Harry's whisper became even quieter. "The guards on duty will sweep the property line. Odds are, the sniper got what he came for. They'll give the all clear signal."

"What if they're dead?"

"Who?"

"The guards, what if the sniper killed the guards?"

Harry swallowed. "I don't know. We'll run for the dining room. I know where the extra gun is hidden."

"We have one gun? There are over 200 people on this kibbutz! How can we possibly defend ourselves?"

"You ask that to the British. They're the ones who confiscated all our guns."

Katrine felt sick. The whole kibbutz seemed deathly still. For five minutes, no one dared stir from their hiding places.

Finally, from over a loudspeaker on the roof of the dining room, a young man's voice said, "Kibbutz Kinneret, this is the all clear. The parameters have been secured. There is no sniper on the grounds. It is safe to come out. Repeat. It is safe to come out."

Harry wiped nervous sweat off his face. Immediately, he ran to the dance floor. As everyone emerged from behind the dormitories and rocks and trees, Harry knelt down by the man who had been shot.

"He's still breathing!" he announced, as Dr. and Mrs. Herring pushed through the guests. Lorelei, Katrine, and Grace hung together, looking down on the man. Dafna clung to Uri's arm, looking whiter than Katrine's dress.

"Oh no," she said, her voice trembling.

"Who is it?" Harry asked.

Dr. Herring was on the ground now, taking the man's vitals. Inching closer, Katrine could see he was a little older, perhaps in his mid 60s. He was dark and rather handsome. Even though he was unconscious, the man's kindness was evident.

"It is Mahmoud Kanaan." Dr. Herring shot a look at Lorelei and his wife, who stood closest to him. "In my office, get my black bag. I'll also need boiling water and clean sheets. You know the drill."

"I don't know the drill!" his wife protested. "No one's ever been shot here before."

Dr. Herring glared at her.

"Where do you want them?" Lorelei asked, her lips tense. She was serious and in control. Faced with a crisis, Lorelei always seemed to hunker down and simply know what to do and how to do it. This was one of those times.

"The dining room. We'll use one of the tables." Dr. Herring turned back to the patient.

Lorelei pulled Mrs. Herring along. "I need you to show me where everything is."

By now, the three Arab teenagers who attended the kibbutz school pushed through. One choked back a sob, crying out in Arabic, "Ab-be!" or 'my father!' He looked around wildly. "It cannot be, not my father! He is not dead, is he?"

Dr. Herring frowned. "Calm yourself, Amir. Your father is alive."

The boy, still shaking, exhaled. "Thanks be to Allah."

Looking at Uri, Harry, and Amir, Dr. Herring commanded they carefully carry the wounded gentleman into the dining room. He was concerned the bullet was under a rib. But thankfully, it had missed his heart. If they removed the bullet quickly, he had a fair chance of living. The man's breathing was uneven and shallow.

It took a solid ten minutes for the boys to move Mahmoud to the dining room. When they arrived, Lorelei and Mrs. Herring had set up something that almost looked like a surgery.

With that, Dr. Herring barred the door to the dining room from the wedding guests. He shut it, locked it, and set to work on removing the bullet. Lorelei would have left, but Dr. Herring asked her to stay. He needed two sets of hands, and hers, he thought, seemed steady enough.

And so, the remainder of the reception was spent waiting nervously outside the dining room, wondering whether Mahmoud the kind, Mahmoud the wise, Mahmoud the widower, Mahmoud the forward-thinking leader of the little village who had sacrificed much so his only son could go to engineering school and bring back the right way to build buildings and have modern plumbing, whether Mahmoud the friend, would live or die.

~

SIX HOURS LATER, Lorelei emerged looking haggard and worn but peaceful. The surgery was over, she announced, and Dr. Herring had miraculously removed the bullet. Amir looked up expectantly. "I can see my father now?"

Lorelei nodded. "He's awake."

As Amir practically ran inside the dining room, Lorelei scanned the courtyard. Most of the wedding guests had thinned out. The neighboring Kibbutzniks had returned to their Kibbutzim. Most of the younger Kibbutz Kinneret members were back in their dorms. Dafna was asleep on the steps, her head resting on Uri's shoulder. Grace, Katrine, and Harry all leaned against the porch beams. The moon was very bright, and the courtyard was flooded with light.

Dafna's eyes fluttered awake, "What happened?"

All eyes settled on Lorelei.

"Dr. Herring is an expert. There is no doubt that Mahmoud will be alright, by and by. If no infection sets in." She frowned and added, "He said he knew something like this would happen."

"What do you mean?" Harry pressed. "It was random, the sniper could have hit anyone."

She shook her head. "No. Mahmoud received a warning. He said, once he came to, that he'd been targeted because of his friendship with Dr. Herring. There's been pressure from the Arab

League to cut off all ties to the kibbutz and to us… No 'fraternizing with the enemy.'"

"But we are not Mahmoud's enemy!" Dafna cried. "Why, his wife used to watch me as a baby! When she passed away, my parents helped raise Amir. We are almost like family."

No one spoke.

Lorelei swallowed. "I'm no expert, certainly, but from what I can gather, there are those in the Arab League, those who are aligned with the Mufti in Jerusalem, who will do anything to keep there from being peace between the Arabs and the Jews."

"But to shoot Mahmoud?" Katrine looked toward the door of the dining room.

"He is the leader of the village. It sends a strong message." Harry rubbed his hand back through his hair. Katrine realized that this familiar action was what he always did when he was stressed. "He can't come back here you know. They'll kill him for sure."

"And what of the boys?" Dafna asked. "They've worked so hard! What of their education?"

"Their lives are more important," Lorelei answered. "It's better for everyone if they keep their distance. But still," she sighed, "it is very sad." She looked at Katrine and Grace. "Both Dr. Herring and Mahmoud cried. They are close. I had no idea how close. Like brothers."

"Two philosophers, trying to create a better world for their children," Harry said sadly.

~

At DAWN, Dafna and Uri caught the early bus to Haifa, where they were to spend their honeymoon. It was not the most auspicious start to a marriage, but, in the words of Harry, it could have been a lot worse. At its best, it was a wedding no one would forget for a very long time.

"You know," Morris's voice reached a high falsetto, "Uri and Dafna's wedding? The one where no one died? You were there, weren't you, darling?"

"But someone could have died," Dr. Herring said gravely. "And that's the whole point. We need more nurses and doctors."

It was the next morning, and Dr. and Mrs. Herring, Katrine, Lorelei, Grace, and Harry were slowly recovering over coffee and leftover wedding cake. No one had much of an appetite.

"What we really need are more guards," Grace said, scalding the roof of her mouth with the steaming liquid. "If we'd had more guards, the sniper never would have made it onto the property!"

"Who's to say the sniper sneaked onto the kibbutz?" Katrine picked at the corner of the cake, the caramel filling slightly hardened. "For all we know, it could have been one of the invited guests. It all happened so quickly. He could have slipped away during the hora, shot Mahmoud, and then scattered with the rest of us. We never did search the guests to see if anyone had a gun. Or, he could have hidden it"

Harry's shoulders slumped. "We should have

searched the guests! It is the only plausible explanation for the way it all happened!"

Mrs. Herring was indignant. "That would have been terribly rude! Search our daughter's wedding guests! Besides, we know each and every one of those people like family." She set her fork down firmly.

"Obviously, whoever it was does not feel the same way about you or Mahmoud." The smile on Harry's face was grim.

"And if you ask me," Grace threw in, "the really rude thing was to shoot someone at a wedding. It does not get more inconsiderate than that!"

Dr. Herring rapped his fork on his coffee cup. "You are right, Grace. Yes. We do need more guards. But we also need more medical personnel." He looked at Lorelei. "Henrietta Stolz has a new nursing school in Jerusalem. I want you to enroll. I saw great talent in you last night. You have the makings of a natural nurse, even a doctor, should you choose."

Lorelei looked at him blankly. "Me? A nurse? I… I've only done secretarial work."

"I know," Dr. Herring said. "But this is a kibbutz, and you are a member of the kibbutz now. We decide as a group what is best for you and the group. I believe what's best for all is if you go to Jerusalem for your training and return."

Lorelei said nothing. It was impossible to read her thoughts.

"We'll put it to a vote then?" Dr. Herring

said. "Who agrees that Lorelei ought to become a nurse?"

Harry, Dr. Herring, Mrs. Herring, and Grace all lifted their hands up.

Katrine stared at Lorelei, shocked that such a thing could be decided without Lorelei's consent! "You don't have to go if you don't want to, Lorelei!" She cried.

"Oh," Lorelei answered, her eyes widening, "it's not that I don't want to. I just… I just don't know what I want!"

"Then it's settled." Dr. Herring put a fatherly hand on her shoulder. "It's for the best, trust me. For you and for the kibbutz. You are a smart, good girl. You'll do well."

She managed a slight laugh. "I honestly did not love climbing date trees. But I will miss the horses." Her eyes met Dr. Herring's. "When do I leave?"

"I want you to go tomorrow morning. You're expected."

Katrine felt claustrophobic. She cried out, "So soon!"

She couldn't lose her sister! Not after all they'd gone through! Not when their lives were just starting to calm down.

"I've some business in Jerusalem and was planning on heading out tomorrow. I'll make sure she arrives safely," Harry said. He caught a look in Dr. Herring's eye. "What is it? There's something else, isn't there?"

"Yes," Dr. Herring answered, "there is. With all the violence, I don't feel safe with the antiquity Morris found hanging about in my office safe. I want you and Katrine to take it to a friend of mine at the Hebrew University of Jerusalem. He'll know the best use for it."

"Me?" Katrine asked. "Why me?"

"If the seal is real, and we decide to do with it what I assume we will do with it, you will be as much needed as Harry."

"Are you talking about Operation Smith?" Harry asked, frowning.

Dr. Herring nodded.

"So, who votes Katrine goes with Harry?"

Everyone, except for Harry, raised their hands.

Dr. Herring smiled. "See? It's all settled."

"And what of Grace?" Katrine looked at her youngest sister, feeling extremely protective.

"She'll be fine right here." Mrs. Herring lovingly patted Grace's cheek.

"All settled," Katrine repeated, marching back to the bungalow with her sisters. "Everything's all settled! Except, it's absolutely not settled!"

Grace, suddenly the oldest in spirit, drew Katrine into a hug, "It's for the best Katrine, just as Dr. Herring said. We all have different jobs to do."

Lorelei put her arms around both her sisters, "And we'll be back together again before we know it!"

THE NEXT MORNING

~

Grace came down the stairs fully dressed the next morning. She wore an olive-green plaid wool dress and fur-lined winter booties. Her hair was in a low ponytail she'd tied with a small red velvet ribbon. "My, the view of the sea!" She exhaled and sat down heavily at the table.

"How do you want your eggs?" I asked, standing by the stove.

"Scrambled." She poured herself coffee from the urn. "It's so different from any other sea I've ever seen. The colors are magnificent…"

Peter watched her as she took a sip. She was talkative this morning, almost cheerful. She held up her fork and declared, "God, may there be no end, to sea, to sand, water's splash, lightning's flash, the prayer of man."[23]

"My, that's rather deep for 8:00 in the morning. Did you write that?" Peter asked.

She shook her head. "No. I wish I did. A friend of mine wrote it."

"Who?"

"Hannah." She stopped short, withdrawing into herself and stirring an absurd amount of sugar into her coffee.

"Are you feeling alright?" Peter asked.

"Just fine," she said, adding yet another teaspoon to her cup. Feeling his gaze, she looked up and asked, "What?"

"Oh, nothing." He shrugged and took a bite of his own eggs—poached on toast.

We were all silent for a moment, and then, as though remembering a question he'd been waiting to ask, Peter said, "I'm curious, what's this about the glass stomping at the wedding?"

"So you made it to the wedding?" She looked towards me as I nodded and brought over her plate of scrambled eggs.

Grace pushed the eggs on her plate back and forth. "It is supposed to remind the Jews of the destruction of the Temple in Jerusalem by the Romans. Before the groom stomps down on the glass, he says, 'If I forget thee, O Jerusalem, let my right hand forget her cunning. If I do not remember thee, let my tongue cleave to the roof of my mouth. If I prefer not Jerusalem above my chief joy...'"

"How... celebratory," I answered, back at the stove and cracking my own eggs into the browning butter. Celebratory? Seriously, I checked myself. Was that really the best word I could have used? Well, it was early in the morning. No one can be that creative so early, right?

"It's from Psalm 137."

Peter shifted in his seat, and, against his will, let out a groan that betrayed the pain he usually tried to hide.

Grace stared at him and, her voice decidedly lower, asked, "Can I ask what happened to you, to your leg?"

I could tell Peter was deciding whether or not to answer. "It was off the coast of North Africa. A few months after Algeria... I got caught in some crossfire."

"Got caught in some crossfire?" I turned from my eggs, sizzling over the stove. "He's being humble. He, and I quote, 'at the risk of his life went above and beyond the call of duty.'"

"Really, Piper," Peter tried to stop me.

"They were off trying to capture an enemy German submarine off the coast. Peter actually boarded the sub, knowing at any moment that the U-boat might sink or blow up by exploding demolition charges," I continued, flipping the eggs and breaking the yoke. "Ugh. I hate when I do that." I grimaced.

"Piper," Peter hated talking about what had happened, "please."

"Let me finish. She should know what you did!" I looked at Grace. "He braved the danger of enemy gunfire and plunged through the tower hatch and managed, with the rest of his men, to capture the submarine."

"We didn't manage to keep the thing afloat for long though. It sunk after we towed it a couple hundred miles." Peter sighed. "It had been too badly damaged in the battle."

"Did many people die?"

He looked down. "Yes."

"Do you think about them often?"

I looked from Peter to Grace and then back to Peter.

Abruptly, she stood up. "I think I'll take a walk today."

I looked outside. The sky was grey and heavy. It had snowed all night, covering the rocks around the lighthouse with piles of icy, white, billowy puffs. The sea reflected the grey sky and churned with abnormal ferocity. "It looks like another rough day. Are you sure you want to go out? I was going to start working on Edie's book again. I'll read it to you if you like."

"Oh no. I lived it already, remember? Besides, I can't seem to stay still these days. I've got to stretch my legs. I even have the shoes for it!" She daintily lifted up her fur-lined booties and gave a little cheerful click with her heels.

Peter's mouth twitched, and Grace immediately said, "Oh Peter, I'm sorry. That was thoughtless of me."

"Don't worry about it, Grace." He looked up. "Take my coat. It's hanging up. And wear gloves."

"Don't be gone too long!" I called after her. "I'm making lobster pie for lunch!" She answered with the slam of a door.

Peter's frown deepened as he looked out the window. There was Grace, wandering aimlessly over the rocks. She sat down on one overlooking the ocean. "She does look like a hawk out there, doesn't she? All alone, sort of fierce."

"Yeah, a fierce fur-lined bootied hawk wearing a coat that's too big. Very, very fierce." I stood up and scraped Grace's uneaten eggs into the garbage. "Maybe I should go talk to her."

"She'll talk when she's good and ready. Let her be." Peter stood up and leaned on his cane. "I'll be upstairs. I need to lie down."

"You're going back to bed?"

"There's nothing else to do. I can't stretch my leg no matter how hard I want to."

"Peter!"

"I'm sorry. I know I'm acting like a grump… I'm just a little tired, that's all." He came over and kissed my cheek. "It's all this vacationing. It's exhausting."

"Well, if you need something to do…" I looked up at him, willing him with my eyes to tell me what was the matter. But he was clammed up so tight, I needed some sort of wrench to open him up. I wrapped my arms around him and pressed my face against his chest. I could hear his heart beating.

"What is it this time? Polishing the banister or reorganizing the junk drawer?"

"Nothing like that. I was thinking you could read out loud to me."

"Oh." Peter was surprised. "Really?"

"Why not? You have to be tired of the sound of my voice by now. And I want to work on the new scarf I started, and I can't read and knit at the same time."

"Your wish," he bowed, "is my command!"

CHAPTER 7

JERUSALEM OF GOLD

*H*arry rubbed his hands together vigorously. "Obviously, those are pickles and raw onions. And this is the oxtail soup. Majadra —that's rice and lentils with a sprinkling of browned onions, and of course, the kubbeh soup. Two of them actually. The red one is a little more sour than the green one."

"Kubbe?" Katrine poked at the dumpling-like object floating in the bright-red fragrant broth. Everything on the table was unfamiliar and smelled strongly of chillies, onions, and cinnamon.

"They are famous for them. The family who owns the restaurant is up at three in the morning to get everything cooking. They sell out by two in the afternoon."

Lorelei and Katrine took a tentative spoonful of the soup. "I've never shared soup with someone before." Lorelei smiled. "From the same bowl, I mean."

Harry caught the waiter, a man with a long dark beard, dark skin, and eyes so brown, they appeared black. "You've outdone yourself again, Moshe!" Harry patted him on the back. "I dream about your food whenever I am gone."

The man smiled and in a heavily accented English said, "Shokran, my dear friend. You honor my house to return so often! And this time with such lovely friends. They brighten this grey courtyard." A shout from the kitchen followed by a long worried stream of Arabic, sent the man scurrying back inside.

Harry chuckled. "Moshe has four sons running the kitchen. It gets exciting."

"You call him Moshe, a Jewish name if there ever was one, but he looks like an Arab. *And* he speaks Arabic… I don't understand." Katrine nibbled at her pickle spear.

"He would agree with you. He's what they call an Arab Jew.[24] He's originally from Turkey, and his wife is from Lebanon. Arabic was their first language. They eat Arabic-style food. Before they came to Palestine, he tells me, they lived in tents in the desert, like nomads. Now they live up on top of the restaurant in a little apartment. All the stalls in the Machane Yehuda Shuk have apartments on top. Most of the vendors live in them with their families."

Katrine looked towards the kitchen. "I had no idea!"

"A lot of people don't," Harry said. Then,

looking at her plate, he smiled, "You like your food?"

"Very much," both girls responded simultaneously.

It had taken eight hours to reach Jerusalem once they'd boarded the bus at four that morning. If the roads had been modern and clear, the drive might have lasted half that time. But as it was, the roads were in desperate need of repair, as was the bus. It lumbered up the hills surrounding the great city at the breakneck speed of 15 miles per hour. By the time they were deposited on Jaffa, outside the Machane Yehuda Shuk, all three were dirty, hungry and irritable.

Harry said, "You should see the Arab Shuk in the Old City. It's a whole different world."

"You mean, everyone doesn't shop here?" Lorelei asked. They had passed countless stalls of butchers, fishmongers, piles of dried fruit and pastries, fresh rounds of flatbread stacked a mile high, cheese shops... it seemed everything you could possibly need or imagine was at the shuk.

"Since the riots, everyone likes to keep their distance. Arab markets for the Arabs, Jewish markets for the Jews."

"And the Arab Jews?" Katrine frowned.

Harry stared at her blankly. "You don't get it, do you?"

She shrugged.

After a quick chug of his lemonade, he asked, "You've got the seal, right?"

Katrine patted her purse protectively and

nodded tersely. "So, will we go to the university right after this?"

Harry shook his head. "I thought we'd get settled in the hotel first, get cleaned up a bit. Then, this afternoon, we'll drop Lorelei off at the apartment Henrietta secured." He turned to Lorelei. "Your roommate, Rebecca Hampton, is one of the chief nurses at the hospital."

"All right." Lorelei shrugged. "My life feels very out of my hands."

"We all only think we have some sort of control," Harry laughed. "By the time you reach my age, you'll know it's all a facade."

Suddenly, two white-haired elderly men in rumpled shirts that were rolled up over their elbows sauntered into the courtyard. Both were deeply entrenched in some sort of conversation. "Oh my goodness," Harry breathed, "it's David Ben Gurion, the head of the Jewish Agency… And I think that's Albert Einstein."

"What is Dr. Einstein doing here?" Lorelei's mouth opened slightly. "My father would be," she quickly corrected herself, *"would have been* so pleased to meet him."

"Do you want to meet him?"

She really did want to, but she could tell the two men were very concerned about whatever it was they were discussing, and she did not want to interrupt. "No… no. Let them enjoy their lunch without a bunch of gaggling fans." Wistfully, she stared at the table, dabbing her mouth with her napkin.

"You take us to the most interesting places,

Harry," Katrine said. She meant it this time, no cynical smirk, no hint of sarcasm.

"I don't know what to say," Harry said. "I'm not used to you being so polite."

"Just say you're welcome." She smiled softly. "And take me to the hotel. I'm so tired I can barely stand up, Einstein or no Einstein."

"I'll take you back here some time if you want…" Harry said, helping her out of her chair.

"What about me!" Lorelei cried, half-joking.

Harry floundered. "You'll be busy in school."

THE HOTEL WAS LOCATED right on the corner of Jaffa and Ben Yehuda Street in the 'New City,' or, as Harry explained, the part of Jerusalem outside the ancient walls that circled about the 'Old City.'

Jerusalem was a city within a city, Harry explained rounding the corner and holding the door open to the hotel. The sign above the rickety door, 'The Inn of the Orient,' hung slightly askew.

"The King David was booked tonight, but I was able to secure you a room there tomorrow night,"[25] Harry looked at Katrine apologetically as her sharp eyes took in the dusty well-worn carpet on the lobby floor, the cat sleeping on the front desk, and the leftover dishes from breakfast on several of the tables of the adjoining dining room.

"This will do just fine, I'm sure," Lorelei said, lugging her suitcase through the door.

"All we need is a clean bed and a place to bathe. Isn't that right, Katrine?"

Harry was at the front desk and soon had their keys in his hand. One for the girls' room and one for his own. He passed Katrine her key, "You are on floor four. I'm directly beneath you. You need anything, just stomp, and I'll come running."

The seedy front-desk clerk eyed the sisters. Katrine was so tired, she couldn't care less. All she wanted was to lie down.

"So, you two girls get some beauty rest, and we'll meet up in an hour and a half right here, okay?" Harry asked.

The sisters nodded their heads as a young boy appeared and took their suitcases. Numbly, they followed the silent bellhop up four flights of stairs and watched as he opened the door to their room. He stepped inside, set their bags down, and took the coins Katrine offered from her little purse. He pointed down the hall and Katrine frowned. It was a *communal* bathroom.

"Harry said he booked a different hotel for you tomorrow." Lorelei put her hand on Katrine's arm and pulled her back inside the small room. It had a very creaky bed, a washbasin, and a dirty window. But the linens appeared clean enough.

Katrine didn't bother taking off her shoes. "Who's to say it will be any better?" Her eyes fluttered shut with disjointed pictures of Albert Einstein, piles of dried fruit and spices, and Harry's curly hair darting through her half-awake dreams. She barely felt Lorelei squeeze in next to her.

Within 30 seconds, both women were sound asleep, snoring loudly.

Lorelei awoke first and checked her dainty pocket watch. They had slept exactly an hour and a half. Katrine groaned heavily and turned over. Lorelei shrugged and stood up off the tiny bed, moving towards the window. It creaked open, and she noticed the cracks of dirt all along the pane. It hadn't been properly cleaned in years. Of course, Lorelei didn't know about dust storms yet. But she would soon enough.

To her left, she watched the donkey carts and old vehicles make their way up Jaffa towards the Machane Yehuda Market, kicking up plumes of dust. Directly below, a group of Yeshiva students were arguing loudly over some portion of the Torah. Her Hebrew was not yet good enough to understand the gist of the argument. One was so emphatic his face turned beet red. She laughed to herself and turned to the right. There, in the distance, rose a large stone wall glowing gold in the late afternoon sun.

"Oh Katrine!" she burst out.

Katrine sat up quickly. "What?"

"I think I see it! It's Jerusalem!"

"We are in Jerusalem," Katrine answered dryly.

"No! Not that one. I mean the old one, the real one!"

Katrine was up on her feet now. She squeezed up next to Lorelei and looked out towards the city. Something caught in her heart, an unexpected emotion that rose up and threatened to send forth tears.

"Oh my," was all she said, and then, gathering herself, she added, "I do believe you're right."

They stood there staring a moment longer. Finally, Katrine pulled herself away and snapped her suitcase open. She selected a light blue suit and a matching little hat and began to change. She glanced at Lorelei. "You are going to change, aren't you?"

Still looking out the window, she nodded. "Yes, just one more minute."

"You are going to have months and months to look at that!" Katrine had opened Lorelei's suitcase by now and threw her a fresh blouse. "You're moving here, remember?"

"Oh yes," Lorelei turned, a stunned look on her face, "I'd almost forgotten. I am going to live… *here*."

~

HARRY, freshly shaved and wearing a crisp white shirt, was sitting in the lobby reading a paper when the girls emerged. The bellboy was immediately deployed back to their room to gather Lorelei's large suitcase and smaller valise.

Harry folded up the paper and stood up. He and Katrine awkwardly eyed one another.

"Where's Lorelei's apartment?" she asked.

"On the other side of town. East Jerusalem. Not far from the University..."

"How far?"

"Two, maybe three miles." He shrugged.

"We'll need a cab." Katrine looked at Lorelei's bags as Harry thrust a wad of coins into the bellboy's outstretched hand. "They are much too cumbersome for a three-mile hike."

"I'm standing right here." Lorelei looked perturbed. They were talking like she wasn't even there.

"Already ordered one." Harry smiled and opened the door. "Ladies first!"

Outside the hotel, a cab and driver waited patiently. Harry passed him the address of Lorelei's new apartment, scribbled on a scrap of paper. He then helped the girls into the back-seat, while the driver loaded Lorelei's suit-cases onto the roof, carefully tying them down.

Wordlessly, he got into the driver's seat and started the engine. The car ambled up Jaffa, narrowly avoiding street children and a herd of donkeys. Looming in front of them rose the walls of the Old City, cast in a sad sort of reddish-orange glow.

"Jaffa Gate is down that way," Harry said as the cab veered left. "And that," he pointed towards a large opening in the wall, "is Damascus Gate. The Arab Shuk is right inside."

"There are so many people!" Lorelei exclaimed. The entrance to the gate was teeming with men in long robes and women covered from head to foot, with only small slits for their eyes. Other men wore regular suits, but tall turbans on their heads. Many sported long thin mustaches.

"Some of the women are dressed just like us," Katrine said. "Look, those girls look like they are coming from a Catholic girl's school!"

"They probably are," Harry said. "There are all types in the Old City. Catholics, Armenians, Muslims, Jews. All together."

By now, the Old City was behind them, and the cab was turning into a beautiful neighborhood of tall trees and large Arab-style mansions. A particularly lovely manor, shaded by Acacias and date palms, stood at the end of the street. "That's it." Harry checked the address.

Both girls inhaled, surprisingly pleased. "You mean, that's where I am going to live?" Lorelei broke out into an enormous grin.

"Don't get too excited." Harry got out of the cab and began to untie the suitcases with the driver's help. "It was divided up into apartments decades ago. Some of these mansions are a couple hundred years old. The neighborhood's been around a while."

Lorelei looked up at the ornate facade. It was enormously inviting and cool.

"It looks like something out of the *Arabian Nights*." Katrine came up behind her and squeezed her elbow. "Shall we go in?"

Lorelei adjusted her hat, a brown flat one that was tilted 'just so' over her large green eyes. "Yes, let's go in."

REBECCA HAMPTON WAS a petite blonde from Ireland with big blue eyes. When she was 12 years old, she'd sat in church as a missionary spoke one Sunday morning—an elderly doctor who worked with children in Africa. Rebecca hadn't known it at the time —she wouldn't have had the language for it— but she had received 'a calling,' and she took it very seriously. In fact, that morning at church had set in motion the wheels that would take little Rebecca from high school, to nursing school, and eventually, all the way to Palestine.

"She's a very good nurse," Harry said, putting down the larger suitcase and knocking on the door of Apartment 12. "Henrietta said that she's one of the best in Jerusalem. Lot's of experience."

They had climbed up five flights of stairs and were still breathing heavily. As the door swung open, Lorelei's mouth opened slightly. "Rebecca?"

"Call me Becky." The woman blushed slightly.

"You have to forgive me," Lorelei said. "I thought you were going to be a lot older! You can't be more than—"

"I'm 28 years old," Becky laughed. "I know, it surprises people." Her laugh was infectious.

"And your accent?" Lorelei couldn't quite place it.

"Irish, through and through."

Soft jazz music played from a gramophone in the small living room. The whole apartment was clean, bright. There were big arches opening onto a small balcony. "Come in." Becky led Lorelei, Katrine, and Harry inside.

"I hope you won't mind living with me," Becky said to Lorelei. Turning to Harry, she pointed to an open door off the side of the balcony. "You can take her bags in that room there."

"Why would I mind?" Lorelei looked puzzled. She thought Becky seemed lovely. In fact, she thought Becky seemed much too stylish and fun to be a nurse.

"Because I'm a Christian and you're Jewish."

Lorelei grinned. "I don't keep kosher, have no fear."

Becky laughed again. "Good. Because this is by far the easiest place you could live. We are on the slope of Mount Scopus. On the top is the new Hadassah Hospital, where you will have your classes. And the rent is cheap."

"How do you know Henrietta?" Katrine asked.

"I teach at the hospital. She heard through the grapevine that I was searching for a roommate."

Harry re-emerged from the bedroom. "I'm sorry to interrupt, but Katrine and I have an appointment at the university in half an hour. We've got to head out."

Katrine scanned the apartment. "I think this will certainly do. I'm almost jealous of you."

Becky turned to Katrine. "You are welcome of course, anytime! We have a very comfortable couch."

Katrine looked at the couch, a well-worn red velvet. "Maybe we can meet up for lunch tomorrow?"

Lorelei shook her head. "No. Classes start tomorrow. I'll be busy all day…"

Harry waited for Katrine by the door. "Professor Hildesheimer will be waiting, Katrine."

"Right, of course." Katrine swallowed the lump of fear in her throat, wondering when she would see her sister again. The two clung to one another for a brief second, and Katrine whispered, suddenly very afraid, "Lorelei, you don't have to do this."

"I know." Lorelei hugged Katrine close. "You go on. I'll be just fine."

With that, Katrine tore herself away, unable to look Lorelei in the eye. She felt a small tear streak down her face. She felt very alone and very unsure of where she was supposed to be.

A few moments later, Becky and Lorelei were standing on the balcony, watching Katrine and Harry get back in the cab.

"It's such a beautiful home." Lorelei's hands felt the rough iron of the balcony fence. The sound of children in the garden wafted upwards as a gentle warm breeze blew through the palm trees, rustling softly.

"It used to belong to a sheik, a long time ago. Now, a rabbi and his seven children live right below us, and a wealthy Muslim family has the entire upper level and a garden on the roof. You'll get to know all of them, by and by."

"Oh my," Lorelei said. "And the other homes?"

"Lots of wealthy Arab families, primarily. The neighborhood's called Sheikh Jarrah. The legend says that it was named after the personal physician to Saladin."[26]

"Who liberated Jerusalem from the Crusaders?"

Becky nodded. "I like it because I'm a nurse, and it seems ideal to live in a place named after a doctor." A moment or two later, Becky said, "Your sister seems pretty nervous. Is she all right?"

113

"I hope so." Lorelei turned back inside, frowning.

"Is it, what was his name again, Harry?"

"I think it's men in general. Only, she doesn't know that."

CHAPTER 8

WHAT 'IT' WAS AND WHAT THEY DECIDED TO DO WITH 'IT'

*H*arry leaned back in his chair. "So what do you think, Professor?"

Professor Hildesheimer was hunched over a magnifying glass. "I cannot be sure." The professor was a tall thin man in his early sixties. Strong and wiry, his once white skin had turned permanently reddish-brown from summers out at dig sites throughout the Middle East. His hair was sandy colored, with flecks of grey just at the temples, and thinning out on the top.

Katrine looked through his bookshelf. One title after another, German, French, English… books on Assyrians, Babylonians, the Hebrews. They had titles like *The Levant and her Ancient Peoples*, *An Introduction to Biblical Pottery*, and *A Simple Guide to Reading Cuneiform, the Language of Babylon*. She also noted every single issue of *Near Eastern Archeology of Ancient Mesopotamia.*

Interspersed through the volumes were bits of pots and little clay animals and people. Katrine's fingers carefully brushed the top of a stone statue of a well-rounded female form.

"You like my little Ishtar?"

Katrine twisted her head back. The professor was watching her.

"Ishtar?" she asked.

"She's nearly 3,100 years old." He smiled and added, "And one of my favorites. I've a warehouse bursting with crates of precious finds."

"You need a museum."

"You are not the first to say such a thing."

Katrine pulled her hand back and returned to her chair behind the professor's desk. Her tea was tepid, but she took another sip anyway. They'd been there for over an hour, and still, the professor had not told them anything. He took the seal in his hands and rubbed the etched letters carefully, his consternation growing. Again, he repeated, "I cannot be sure."

A moment later, he looked up at Harry. "You will let me do something, yes?"

"Sure, whatever." Harry shrugged. "You're the expert."

"Let me consult with my colleague, Professor Weinberger. He's in the research lab. It will only take me a little time."

"How much time do you need?" Harry asked.

"Thirty minutes. Why don't you take Miss Katrine to see the view, and by the time you come back, I won't be sure, but I will be more sure."

Confused, Harry answered, "Sure. You go talk to your friend," Harry stood up and opened the door, "and I'll take Katrine to go see the view. And then you will still not be sure."

"But I will be more sure."

Katrine and Harry were out of the office now, not totally sure of what to do with themselves.

"So, how about that view?"

"How about it?" Katrine laughed.

"I think it's that way." He pointed to the left.

"Lead the way!" She plunged after him. He walked quickly, and she had to skip to keep up.

The campus was beautiful. The buildings were spaced apart, built with big Jerusalem stones. In between, orderly gardens with tall cedars and pines and brilliant green lawns with winding paths connected them all. Suddenly, Harry stopped. Walking directly towards them was a man with a shock of white hair and wire-rimmed glasses. It was Dr. Einstein.

Harry stuttered. "Excuse us!"

"You are excused. Now, if you would allow me to pass." He smiled good-naturedly.

Harry didn't make way for the old man. He could feel something was up. Harry leaned in and said, "Dr. Einstein?"[27]

"You are a little old to want an autograph, aren't you?"

"I was just wondering…" Harry didn't finish his thought.

"What I'm doing here?" Dr. Einstein rubbed his

forehead. "I'm going to my office, right over there." He pointed at a particularly pleasant building. "I used to teach here, you know. I'm the chairman of the Academics Committee."

Harry's eyes narrowed. He did not teach here *anymore*. He hadn't for years.

"But, just between us young man, I'm *not* here. The university is technically closed. Nearly everyone has gone home. I'm just picking up some things."

"Dr. Einstein," Katrine extended her hand, "I'm Katrine Adelman. You don't know me, but my father was a great fan of yours. Dr. Adleman, of the University of Berlin. He was the head of the Mathematics Department."

Dr. Einstein's eyes widened in recognition of the name. "You are Chaim's daughter! How is your father? Why, I have not seen him in nearly ten years."

"You knew him?" Katrine was shocked.

"Your father is a very fine mathematician. Very fine indeed. Who does not know of Chaim Adelman?"

Katrine's eyes welled up against her will.

"Ah," Dr. Einstein answered, his face saddening. "He was unable to leave Berlin, I take it."

It was so gently said, so understanding.

"Yes," she answered, maintaining her composure.

"These are dark times we live in. But for the young people like you, and—" He turned to Harry and asked, "What's your name, young man?"

"Harry Stenetsky, Dr. Einstein." Harry shook the genius's hand, surprised by his iron grip.

Dr. Einstein pointed towards the math building. "That's my office there, the one on the second story with the rather nice triangles in the stone beneath it." His voice took on a playful tone as he continued, "I bet you cannot guess what those triangles mean?"

Katrine and Harry squinted at the triangles. The angles, the curve… It was a pretty enough design, but what could it mean?"

Suddenly, it hit Katrine, "Why it's E equals MC squared! The Theory of Relativity!"

"Very good, Miss Katrine!" Dr. Einstein looked enormously pleased. "I couldn't believe it when the architect added that detail."

Harry scratched his chin. "Imagine thinking to put the formula for the speed of light in a vacuum being independent of the motion of those observing the vacuum on the outside of the math department. That's cute."

"And that, young man, is a very astute and simplified explanation of my theory. Maybe *you* should have won the Nobel Prize." Dr. Einstein was genuinely surprised. "You rarely meet two such handsome and intelligent young people. Maybe there is hope after all. How long have you been married?"

Katrine's cheeks flushed beet red. "Oh, Dr. Einstein! We aren't—"

"We're just friends," Harry interjected.

"Exactly," Katrine added.

"If that's the case, then I think you both need to go back and study the basics. I think that Newton's law of universal gravitation is the place to start."

"You'll have to refresh my memory on that one, Professor," Katrine said, still looking at Harry.

Dr. Einstein patted Harry on the shoulder. "It is simple really. It states that 'every body attracts every other body with a force proportional to the product of their masses and inversely proportional to the square of the distance between their centers.'"

Katrine and Harry stared at him, confused.

"In other words," Dr. Einstein explained, "sometimes you just need to reduce the distance between two bodies." He held his hands out and moved them closer together until he clasped them firmly. "My lecture is over now. You both have your homework assignments."

He chuckled and then turned serious. "But really, I was never here, you understand."

Harry nodded, locked in Dr. Einstein's penetrating gaze. The scientist was here on secret business, like everyone these days.

"Right, we never saw you. We just saw the view, which is where we are going now." Harry took Katrine's arm and pulled her down the path.

"It was lovely to meet you, Dr. Einstein!" she said over her shoulder.

"You never met me, Miss Adleman, remember? But I will say you were the pleasantest person I never met."

By now, the sun was just hanging over the horizon. The trees cast long shadows along the path leading to the outdoor amphitheater. Katrine and Harry stood on the top step. She gasped. So *this* was the view.

The amphitheater was built on the edge on Mount Scopus. It seemed to plunge over the edge, the forest disappearing into a vast expanse of barrenness.

"What is it?" Katrine asked as the wind picked up, blowing firmly in their faces.

"That is the Judean Desert."

"It's beautiful." She was overwhelmed with it, how big it was, so empty, harsh, and uncompromising. Not waiting for Harry, she carefully walked down the steps towards the platform at the bottom. Standing on the very edge, she felt her heart heave a great sigh of relief. Here, she thought, there was space to breathe. A terrifying, scary sort of space but space she desperately needed. She inhaled again and again. She felt like she was breathing for the first time in months, years really, if she was honest with herself.

Harry was behind her now. "Amazing how different the terrain is. Behind us is the forest. Then the city. And here, the desert."

"It seems lonely," she said. "But I like it."

"There are more people down there than you think," Harry answered.

"Who could possibly live there?" she cried out.

"Oh, there's a kibbutz or two. And the Bedouins have lived there for hundreds of years. And happily too."

Before Katrine could answer, two figures appeared at the top of the amphitheater. One began to wave his arms emphatically, motioning for them to come up.

"Looks like Professor Hildesheimer," Harry said.

"He looks rather excited." Katrine secured her hat and began to ascend the steep steps back up to the top.

~

PROFESSOR WEINBERGER WAS Professor Hildesheimer's direct opposite. Stout, pasty, and in need of a haircut. That said, their excitement was nearly equal. Both men couldn't sit down and paced back and forth in Professor Hildesheimer's office, speaking quickly.

"Like I said, we can't be sure!" Professor Hildesheimer spoke first.

"We can't be sure?!" Professor Weinberger repeated. "Oh, we can be sure! I am dead positive."

"Positive, yes. I suppose we are." Hildesheimer rubbed his hands together. "But you know what this means, don't you?"

"No," Katrine shook her head, "we don't know what this means."

"It means," Professor Weinberger stopped for a moment, gathering himself, "that we now have irrefutable proof that the Hebrews were in the Jezreel Valley in 600 BC." Beads of sweat had formed on his brow.

"I thought we already knew that," Harry said.

"Sure, we know that. But many people would have it so that the Jews were never here at all." Professor Weinberger stated matter-of-factly.

"If we were never here," Hildesheimer added, "then we don't have any right to be here *now*. Don't you see?"

Weinberger jumped back in. "Which means we may have no right to be anywhere, given the state of things, if you get my meaning?"

Harry and Katrine looked at one another. "So are you going to tell us what it is?"

"Oh yes! Of course." Professor Weinberger mopped his sweating brow with the back of his hand. "It's the seal of Baruch."

"Baruch?" Katrine asked.

"The scribe of the prophet Jeremiah."

"And you're sure about this?"

"As sure as an archeologist can be." Professor Hildesheimer finally sat back down. "It's not an exact science. But given its age and the location you found it in, we believe it is not only authentic but one of the most important finds of the 20th century."

"So then, we proceed as planned?" Harry asked.

"Indeed." The professor's voice took on a strange, eerie tone. "But the Lord said to me, 'Do not say, 'I am too young.' You must go to everyone I send you to and say whatever I command you. Do not be afraid of them, for I am with you and will rescue you,' declares the Lord. Then the Lord reached out his hand and touched my mouth and said to me, I have put my words in your mouth. See, today I appoint you over nations and kingdoms to uproot and tear down, to destroy and overthrow, to build and to plant." He looked at Katrine, "God's word to Jeremiah. As written by Baruch.'"

Professor Weinberger exhaled. "And the Jewish Agency's word to you both. We've already placed the call. Everything's set in motion. Your passage is already secured."

"They're fast, as usual." Harry gave a sigh. "And I was looking forward to showing Katrine around the town."

"You'll have to show her around New York instead." With that, Professor Hildesheimer took the seal wrapped in paper, placed it in a little wooden box, and pressed it into Katrine's hand. "Use it wisely, young lady."

"I don't understand?" She felt like there was a live flame in her hand.

"Harry will explain it all to you. Now, you better go get packed. The boat leaves at five in the morning. That gives you just enough time to make it to Tel Aviv." He turned to Harry. "You understand, this is a Smith operation."

"Yes." Harry nodded. "Dr. Herring told me."

"Tel Aviv! New York! Boat!" Katrine cried out. "Harry, what's going on?"

Harry looked at her. "Sorry babe, looks like the King David's going to have to wait. You and are I taking a little trip. We've been assigned to sell the seal back in the States, among other things. Operation Jeremiah meets Operation Smith."

"Sell it?" She felt her heart beating faster than usual. "How? There are strict rules for selling antiquities."

"Not on the black market," Professor Weinberger said quietly.

"The black market?" she repeated slowly. "Harry, what have you gotten me into now?"

"You're always asking me that," he said with a laugh.

Professor Hildesheimer took her hand. "Katrine, the money you raise will save many lives. You don't have to help, but you are smart, and you have plenty of free time, am I right?"

She nodded.

"We would appreciate your assistance." His look was so earnest, she had to look away. "You've seen what is going on in Europe. Americans must know what is happening. They need to hear your verbal testimony."

Things were moving much too fast. She had not even given Lorelei a proper goodbye. And Grace had expected her to be gone for only a few days at most. "What about the girls?" she asked.

"They're grownups. Stop worrying so much." Harry stood up. "They won't even have time to miss you."

THE DAY CONTINUES

~

"Oh look," Peter stopped reading. There's a note here from your aunt." From the page, he removed a small note Edie had paper-clipped to the page.

"Dear Piper," he read, "I'm sure at this point you must be dying of curiosity to discover what on earth Grace was doing all this time… So, I'm going to abruptly switch gears and take you right back to Kibbutz Kinneret. I know, jarring. Do you have any suggestions of how to smooth it out?" He looked up and chuckled. "That sounds like Edie."

"Dying of curiosity," I repeated. Arching my back, I stretched out on the floor in front of the fire. I was still in my flannel pajamas. So was Peter. For crying out loud, I thought to myself, I wish Grace would just tell us what happened herself.

"You know what's jarring?" He put the manuscript down and carefully walked over to the fire, easing onto the ground beside me. "All those men are out there, risking their lives. And I'm here, reading out loud in my pajama pants and eating lobster pie for lunch."

I nodded. Being back in America was strange. Life here hadn't seemed to change at all. "I know," I said, sitting up and crossing my legs. "No more air raids. No sugar shortages. No men in uniform."

Suddenly, the front door blew open, and Grace appeared in the study, her cheeks bright pink with the cold. "You'll never guess what I found!" she exclaimed.

That's when I noticed that her coat was sort of lumpy. And the lump was moving and making a strange whimpering sound.

"Is that a— " Peter started.

"Yes! It is!" She held out a small puppy and immediately dumped him (or her) in Peter's lap. "She was limping on the side of the road." The puppy had matted hair so dirty that it was nearly impossible to tell what color it was and mournful brown eyes. It was shivering and wet and licking Peter's hand. "Someone probably abandoned her. It's a girl. I found her about a mile up the coast."

"We can't keep it!" Peter held the dog out at arms-length and passed her to me.

"Oh, certainly you can!" Grace said. "You don't have kids, so you can handle a dog."

"Great logic," Peter said.

The little creature's heart pounded against my hand. "You found her, maybe you should keep her."

"But I'm only in the country temporarily." Grace looked at me. "You need a dog." She looked at Peter. "You can practice walking together. I thought it was perfect, in a strange way."

Peter groaned. "Piper doesn't need two invalids to take care of!"

"You are not an invalid," I said (with much more force than I intended). I looked down at the little paws. "Founder. We'll call her Founder. Because Grace found her. Get it?" I smiled at my cleverness.

"We can't handle a dog!" Peter reiterated.

"Why not?" Taking Founder's face in my hands, I continued,

"Looks like you need a bath, kiddo." The puppy barked at me, a pitiful weak little bark. I looked at Peter, my heart melting. "Have you ever seen anything cuter?"

"I'll do the honors of giving Founder her first bath," Grace volunteered, scooping the dog up and tromping upstairs to the bathroom.

Once she was out of earshot, Peter looked at me and shook his head. "Piper, we can't have a dog. Not right now."

"Why ever not?"

"Because... because... Oh, I don't know." He picked the manuscript back up. "We'll discuss it later."

"Chicken."

"What do you mean, chicken?"

"How hard can a little puppy be?"

"It's like having a baby. You have to wash it and feed it and play with it."

"That doesn't sound that bad." Then, leaning in, I said softly, "Please, it will be fun! We need to take care of something, a little creature. It will be good for us. It will get our minds off of ourselves." I started walking to the kitchen, "We've got some milk and cold chicken—I should think that will be alright, don't you?"

He shook his head. "He, I mean, *she* is too little to handle chicken yet. She could choke. Do we have any oatmeal?"

"Oh yes, that's just the thing!"

"Poor baby," I cooed as Grace examined the puppy's leg closer. Freshly bathed, dried, brushed, and fed, Founder was a fluff ball the color of honey, with a paunchy belly. "Do you think it's broken?"

Grace shook her head. "I wish Lorelei was here."

Peter held the squirming critter still. "That's right. I'd forgotten Lorelei was a nurse now."

"Oh yes," Grace said. "You should hear her talk about disinfectants and anesthetics. And because the course she took was in partnership with the British Military, she even knows about how to deal with things like field sanitation and defense against air, chemical, and mechanized attacks. She is very bright, you know, and catches on quickly."

The puppy yelped as Grace touched a tender spot. "I'm afraid it is broken. *My* expertise is limited to first aid, but I do know how to make a splint. I just need..." she looked around the kitchen. "How about a ruler? And some gauze or an old rag?"

I jumped up and found a wooden ruler in my aunt's 'catch-all' drawer and a clean dish towel which I proceeded to rip into strips. Carefully, Grace took Founder's leg and began to stabilize the bone on the makeshift splint as Peter held her still. The puppy growled and bit his hand from the pain, but Founder was so weak and small, it didn't hurt.

"You should have heard Lorelei in those letters she sent to me at first. I think she felt out of her league. She had to study Arabic and Hebrew on top of everything else. Thankfully, she already spoke passable French and English. Most of the educated Arabs speak French." She examined the splint, visibly pleased with her handiwork. "And of course, Becky was there by her side the whole time."

"It must be helpful to have your teacher also be your roommate," I said.

"Lorelei certainly thought so." She took Founder out of Peter's arms and set her on all fours. She slid to her belly and refused to move.

Grace sat down and looked at the puppy. "Lorelei was always a deep thinker. She always wanted to know more. I sometimes don't understand her."

Peter reached down, putting his finger in Founder's mouth. "She's so little, it doesn't hurt," he laughed. "We ought to buy her a toy to chew on. I don't want her to find my shoes."

"Does this mean you want to keep her?" I asked, trying to keep the excitement out of my voice.

"Well," he floundered, "it's not like we could just send her out in the snow."

"And Mr. Henderson already has a dog," I reasoned. "So it's not like we could give her away. And you could teach her to play fetch and bring you your slippers and sit and all the wonderful things you can train dogs to do!"

"But what about when we go to Boston?"

"I'll need someone to keep me company while you are in class!" I took Founder in my arms again, and she wriggled to get free.

"But if you get a job, what then?"

"I'll take Founder with me. Or I'll work at home and edit books, just like I'm doing now!" I imagined curling up with a new manuscript, a beautiful golden dog keeping my feet warm and looking up at me with adoring brown eyes. That would be much, *much* more fun than selling leather gloves or perfume at a department store.

Peter looked at the puppy. The ruler stuck out at an odd angle, and you could tell the puppy was not happy. "How about we all go into town and get Founder professionally patched up by Dr. Johnson?"

"Dr. Johnson?" Grace asked.

"He's the vet in town."

"We'll also need a wooden crate, a leash... maybe a tennis ball..." I stood up. "And as long as we are going into town, we need to run by the grocery store as well. We are almost out of everything."

Peter looked at Grace. "If you have any letters to post, bring them. The postman doesn't come out this far."

She shook her head and cried out, "Oh no! I have absolutely no letters to post! No letters at all!"

∾

"How's it coming?" I asked, stepping back into Dr. Johnson's surgery where he was putting the finishing touches on the plaster cast wrapped around Founder's leg.

"No offense to your ruler and rag method, but I think this will do a bit better for the little girl." He'd given Founder a sedative, and the puppy's eyes were only half-open.

"Oh, good." I rubbed my hands together, trying to warm them up. Peter and Grace waited on two chairs pushed up against the wall. "Was it a bad break?" I glanced at the vet.

Dr. Johnson didn't look up from Founder. "To be honest, it was more than a break. Little Founder here had a bit of a birth defect. It caused the muscle to be underdeveloped. Probably why the leg broke in the first place. Might also be why she was abandoned."

"Why, that's awful!" I exclaimed.

"I've been a vet in these parts for nearly 40 years. Still can't believe people would throw a puppy out on the side of the road like that. You don't throw a life away just because it may be a little broken."

"Tell that to the Nazis," Grace answered bitterly.

The vet was surprised. "I read in the papers what's rumored to be going on over there in Europe. Heard the Nazis don't like to have anyone around who's a little slow…"

"Or old, or deaf, or Jewish, or black, or Gypsy…" She stopped herself.

Dr. Johnson's eyes narrowed as though he were observing one of his patients. "Thought they were just rumors."

"Most people do. Until they see it for themselves."

"And you've seen for yourself, I take it?"

She looked down at the floor, unable to speak. Dr. Johnson exhaled sadly and picked Founder up off the table, carefully put her in my arms. "I'll give you enough sedatives for the week. It'll be best if she doesn't move around too much. Come back in two weeks, and we'll see if she's ready for the cast to come off. Puppies tend to heal up pretty fast, faster than old dogs certainly. Their bones are less brittle. There's more give and take, if you understand."

I nodded. "And in the in-between time?"

"Love her. Dogs who are abandoned early in life and are not socialized enough can become aggressive. It's important to make sure she knows she's safe. And of course, she'll need to learn how to walk with the cast on and then again once the cast comes off."

"How will she do that?" Peter interjected.

"Just by being herself." The vet laughed a short laugh. "Dogs aren't like people. They don't forget what they were born to do. They just do it."

"Do you think she'll limp forever?" He looked at the cast.

"Only time will answer that question. The important thing is that she gets lots of rest and doesn't move that leg. It will be difficult, but true healing in this instance will only come from keeping still." He smiled. "Not only will she heal, but she'll heal up stronger than before."

With that, the vet leaned up against the examination table and crossed his arms. "So all three of you were in Europe. At least, that's the gossip about town."

We all nodded.

"Is it as bad as they say over there?"

"Truthfully," Peter looked straight into Dr. Johnson's eyes, "it's worse."

"That's too bad," he paused. "I'm glad you made it home safe and sound."

All of Peter's conflicted emotions about being home and safe flickered across his face momentarily, and then, he stood. "I'll be in the truck. Thanks, Doc."

With that, Grace and I lifted Founder into her new crate and carried her outside. All three of us, (well, four counting Founder) crammed into the bucket seat. Silently, Peter started the engine. Thankfully, he could move his ankle well enough now to work the gas and brake pedals, and he slowly drove one block to the post office. I jumped out wordlessly and darted inside, the bell jingling merrily as I opened the door. The postmistress had already hung a Christmas wreath on the door.

"Why hello, Miss Agatha!" She beamed at me from behind the counter. I was pretty sure she was the only person (besides my parents) who insisted on calling me by my given name these days.

"Anything for me and Peter?"

Disappearing into the back, she emerged a moment later with three letters. "Looks like your Mother's handwriting." She smiled knowingly. "And another newspaper subscription for Peter."

"You could work for the FBI if you wanted to." I took the letters, wondering if she had also opened them, read them, and then resealed them as I'd seen in the movies.

"I just have a memory for handwriting, that's all." She reddened a bit, embarrassed. "But this one," she held up the third letter, "I've no idea who it's from. It's got your post box number, to be sure. However, it is not addressed to you or Peter."

I took it and examined the blocky handwriting. "Grace Adleman."

"You know her?"

"She's my cousin." I looked back up. "She's staying with us for a while."

"Oh," she nodded her head, as though all was clear. "Well, it came registered mail. All the way from Egypt."

I looked at the letter once more. Lorelei was in Egypt, but this was certainly not Lorelei's handwriting. Curiously, I took the letters and wished the nosy woman a good day without offering her any more information.

Back in the car, I passed Grace the letter.

The moment she saw it, she blanched.

"Don't you want to open it?" I asked.

She shook her head no vehemently.

"Do you know who it's from?" Peter shot her a look as he navigated the truck back onto the main road leading to the lighthouse.

"Amos."

Peter and I looked at each other and an awkward silence continued the rest of the drive back home. Almost before he'd put the truck into park, she had jumped out and raced up the walk towards the front door. She spent the rest of the afternoon and evening in her room pacing back and forth. I could tell because her footsteps echoed through the whole house and only abated when she emerged to grab a sandwich around dinner time.

"Like a bird in a cage," Peter remarked, looking up at the ceiling bitterly. "I'm starting to feel that way in this place. I just can't move as fast as her." He gritted his teeth together and muttered, "Not that it matters."

"Why wouldn't it matter?"

"I don't know where to go. Not really…"

"We are going to Boston, remember?"

"It feels a little pointless right now. Going back to study business when we know what's going on out there." He looked out the kitchen window, across the black swirling waves, and I knew he was seeing all the way to Europe and the men he'd left behind.

"I know God has a plan, Piper," he sighed. "I just don't know what it is. And I don't know why he allowed me to get injured. And more than anything," he stood up with the force of a great gale, "I don't know why he sent me back here! I'm a sailor, Piper! I belong on the sea! *Not* on the shore."

He charged out of the kitchen, leaving me all alone with Founder in the crate, sleeping away, her poor little leg all bound up. Between the sea of his dark mood and Grace's emotional tempest, it was stormier inside than outside.

"Where are you going?" I called after him.

"To find something productive to do!"

That productive thing was listening to the radio. In the study, the voice of a CBS news operative said, "As of today, conscription in the United Kingdom includes all men between 18 and 50. Women's participation in fire brigades and women's auxiliary groups is strongly encouraged."

All men between 18 and 50... And women too? Things must be getting very bad, very bad indeed.

Abruptly, I heard Peter stand up and switch the radio off. I could only wonder what he thought of the news. He was sitting in the leather chair, his head in his hands, when I came in a moment later.

"Shall I read to you?" I asked quietly.

He looked up, a faint glimmer of moisture in his eyes. He shrugged as if he didn't care, and I wanted him to hold me in his arms and tell me everything would be okay, and he would be happy again. But he did not. He just sat there, staring at the radio.

"Right then." I swallowed. "You stay right there and get comfortable."

I ran back into the kitchen and brought back Founder in her crate, placing her gently at Peter's feet. Then, I ran back to the kitchen for two cups of tea, one of which I pressed into Peter's hand. Finally, I picked up the manuscript, saying under my breath, "Where were we?"

CHAPTER 9

AND MEANWHILE, ON THE KIBBUTZ

For the first time in her young life, Grace found herself completely alone despite the kibbutz being filled with people. There were the Herrings, of course. And all the youngsters. But this was the first time Grace was on her own. When her parents had been arrested, she'd had Lorelei and Katrine looking over her shoulder like hawks. It'd been the three of them, Katrine, Lorelei, and Grace, ever since. And now, it was just Grace.

She didn't know what to do with herself. The first morning, she slept in late because Lorelei was not there to wake her up. Then, she came to the strange realization that she had never poured herself a cup of coffee because Katrine had always filled the cup for her.

The first night in the bungalow was heaven. This is the life! Grace thought. No one harping on me to pick my dress up off the floor. No one snoring and waking me up at three in the morning. No one telling me my shorts are too short. Oh yes, she thought, this is the life.

The second night was not quite as pleasant. There were clothes all over the floor, and the bungalow looked like a tornado had hit it. It was so quiet; she couldn't sleep. She'd worn her shortest of shorts that day and gotten a sunburn.

The third night was a nightmare. She was so tired from not sleeping the night before that she was abnormally alert. Every noise outside was the Arab sniper coming back to kill her. To make matters worse, her legs were peeling and blistered, and she felt like she had a fever.

On the morning after the fourth night, she'd had enough. Grace marched her sunburned legs right to the Herring's table at breakfast. Without a word, she poured herself a cup of coffee (which irked her, because she had to do it herself) and sat down.

Dr. Herring took one look at her red-rimmed eyes and frowned.

"Grace, are you feeling alright?" he asked, looking at his wife with concern.

In response, Grace held her head in her hands, crumpled over the table, and began to cry.

Mrs. Herring looked at Dr. Herring. They nodded at one another as Mrs. Herring scooched her chair next to Grace's and began to rub her back. "Grace, tell me what's wrong." Mrs. Herring said it as a command, not a question.

Grace's head popped up. "Oh, Mrs. Herring!" She choked back a sob. "I am so lonely."

"We have a prescription for that," Dr. Herring said with a chuckle. "In fact, Mrs. Herring and I were just discussing it."

"You were!?"

"With Dafna gone on her honeymoon, we've realized that we are understaffed in the girl's dormitory."

"Understaffed?"

"It's more like *un*staffed," Mrs. Herring clarified.

"What are you saying?" Grace wrapped her fingers around the coffee cup and drew it close to her chest, like a teddy bear.

"Dafna and Uri need their own space once they come back from Haifa. Of course, he'll be stationed at the RAF base in Tel Aviv, but when he comes back on leave…" Dr. Herring trailed off. "Would you be willing, Grace?"

"To take Dafna's place and head up the girl's dormitory?" she asked, hope blossoming in her chest.

"It's a lot of work." Mrs. Herring refilled her coffee cup.

"Oh, please give the bungalow to Uri and Dafna!" Grace begged. "I can handle a bunch of teenagers! Just don't make me stay alone anymore."

"You have a deal." Dr. Herring extended his hand and Grace shook it vigorously. "And start wearing longer shorts. You don't have Lorelei's complexion. You'll just burn." He added, "Besides, it's April. The sun may be out, but look at those clouds. Springtime in the Galilee can be brutally wet."

In answer to his statement, a thunderclap shook the building violently.

"I know."

With that, Grace ran out of the dining room. The rain was coming down in sheets. Grace quickly stuffed the clothes scattered all over the bungalow into her valise. Everything else she scooped into an empty crate. Two trips to the dormitory later, she was officially the new woman in charge.

Oblivious to the wet pile she was making on the rough wooden floor, Grace surveyed her new territory. It was a large long room. Twelve bunk beds on one side, twelve on the other. Enough beds for 48 girls. Under each bed were two drawers. One drawer per girl. Each held the exact same items: khaki shorts and pants (for winter), one nice dress for Shabbat and holidays and weddings, a sweater, and two pairs of socks. There were two hooks by each bunk for each girl's towel. It was all very organized and precise. All very egalitarian. All very… bland. Grace frowned. The room needed some color. And it needed it very badly.

At the end of the room was a twin bed. She remembered it as having been Dafna's. Now, it was hers! She smiled to herself and put the crate and the suitcase on the bed.

The sound of 48 teenage girls squealing and laughing burst into the dorm. The females of Kibbutz Kinneret were drenched. And they loved it. Thunder clapped again, and the raindrops hit the tin roof with such force that the sound of the girl's chatter was drowned out. The girls stopped and stared at Grace, instantly quieting down.

Grace sat down on the edge of the bed and surveyed her new wards. At 21, Grace was barely older than the handful of fourteen to sixteen-year-olds. But, older was older.

A tall girl with long braids that hung all the way to her low back saw Grace. She was soaked through.

"Got caught out there?" Grace smiled.

"We were all in the north field." The girl extended her hand and said, "I'm Sadie, and you're Grace, aren't you? One of the sisters?"

"I'm taking over for Dafna."

All the girls were listening closely. So this intruder was going to be their new 'superior officer.'

Sadie took a towel from the hook nearest Grace's bed. "I was wondering who was going to fill that spot," Sadie spoke very decisively.

Grace smiled. "Dafna and Uri are taking the bungalow. Now that my sisters are gone, I thought some company might be nice."

"Well, you'll certainly get it in here," Sadie answered. She was very decisive indeed. Grace could imagine her as a little six-year-old. She had probably been decisive since the day she was born.

Another clap of lightning shook the building, and the lights flickered off. As it was only about 10:30 in the morning and the room was full of windows, the girls were not plunged into darkness. However, it was a very, very bad storm. And the black clouds nearly blocked out the morning sun.

Sadie began to squeeze the water from her braids.

"I'm voting no one will be going back to the fields today," Grace said, taking a glance out the window.

The girl who slept above Sadie had slipped out of her wet blouse and was pulling her sweater over her head. It was not pretty in the least, but the sort of knotty, soft thing that never gets thrown away. Her hair was cropped very short, nearly to her skull. Grace made a mental note to ask what had happened.

"And your name is?" Grace stood up off the bed, extending her hand to the young woman.

"Cecelia."

Cecilia was very thin. Her blue veins showed through her skin, so pale it was practically translucent.

Another clap of lightning was followed by the low rumblings of thunder. Cecilia moved over to the window. "We had storms in Germany, but nothing like this."

So, Cecilia was from Germany.

Sadie pulled off her sandals. Her feet were covered in mud. "This is my second year here. I've never seen storms like the ones in the Galilee. The flooding in Tiberias is fierce. They have to shut down the bus station nearly every year. It floods right up to the platform."

Grace stood behind Cecilia at the window. The courtyard was now a sea of mud. "I hope we don't have the same problems here."

"Do you hear that?" Cecilia said, suddenly cocking her head to the right, listening closely.

"It's just the thunder," Sadie answered, unconcerned.

Ignoring her, Cecilia opened the window and leaned out, listening very hard. Rain and wind poured into the room, and a host of young voices demanded she close the window, but she was undeterred. Months on the run and weeks of living in mortal fear for her life had heightened her senses. She heard something, and it was not thunder.

Grace hunched next to the young woman, their heads close together. Suddenly, she heard it too. It sounded almost like thunder but more mechanical. She turned back into the room, nose dripping, and loudly shushed the girls. Now, all 49 girls, Grace included, listened intently.

There it was, that mechanical rumbling. It was getting louder now. It almost sounded like a—

"No! It couldn't be! What sort of idiot would fly on a day like this?" Grace asked to no one in particular.

Another flash of lightning revealed the outline of a small plane coming in for a landing. It was moving fast. Too fast.

Sadie's jaw dropped, "The same sort of idiot who would try to land it on a day like today!"

The plane was very low now. It was so low, they could make out the wheels and the words 'Bombay Baby' scrawled on the side.

"Looks like he's headed for the north field,"

Cecilia said as the plane roared over the dormitory.

"It will be a wet landing. The field was nearly flooded when we left it!" Sadie said with finality as the girls raced out of the dorm and slogged their way to the field. The rain kept coming down, even thicker than a few moments before, Grace thought. She hoped that they were not all on their way to view a plane crash.

The idiot, whoever he was, was a very fine pilot. He landed effortlessly. And from what Grace could tell as he got out of the plane, he was very fine looking to boot. Just as the girls arrived on the scene, he jumped from the cockpit into seven inches of mud. His aviator sunglasses, of no use in the dark storm, were pushed back onto the top of his head, revealing dark brown eyes. His hair was auburn, nearly as auburn as Dafna's.

Something clicked in Grace's mind. Could this possibly be the famous Amos Herring, son of Dr. and Mrs. Herring, brother of Dafna, new brother-in-law of Uri? Amos the pilot?

Grace squinted through the rain and pushed past her wards.

"Are you Amos Herring?" she asked boldly.

A flash of lightning illuminated the pilot's strong jaw. Big fat drops of water rolled off his leather bomber jacket.

"How'd you know?"

Grace didn't answer. "Are you alright? Is your plane okay?"

Amos shook his head, un-sticking his feet from

the mud and moving towards her. "Are you kidding? This is a Bristol Bombay."

"A what?"

"The new monoplane. It can transform into a bomber or a transport plane on a dime. And it flies like a dream. New government issue."

"British?"

He gave a sharp nod.

Grace felt Sadie on her shoulder. "Were you bombing somebody?"

"No. I was transporting somebody. Myself mainly. Am I too late?"

"For what?" Grace asked. Another clap of thunder. Though it was possible, the storm was getting worse.

"My sis's wedding."

The girls glanced at one another.

"I take it I didn't make it."

"You're nearly a week late," Sadie declared.

Amos shrugged. "Better late than never."

Grace eyed him warily. He knew he was late. He just wasn't about to tell 48 (49 with Grace included) young women why he had risked life and limb to fly to the kibbutz and land in the north field during the first and worst storm of the season.

Looking Grace squarely in the eye, the young man asked, "Are you in charge?"

"I guess I am," Grace said, after considering the question.

"Where are all the boys?"

"Tying up the date palms. Though I assume by now, they are all safe indoors."

"Or sandbagging the dining room," Sadie threw in.

"Then you all will have to do." He was moving towards the back of the plane when he threw over his shoulder, "Tell your girls to line up. We've some wedding gifts to unload."

"Wedding gifts?"

Amos smiled. "And we have to work quickly. These particular gifts can't get wet."

THE WEDDING GIFTS happened to be 30 British Air Force Issue Browning M1918 light machine guns. They had never been used… brand new so to speak. Or they would have been if they hadn't been nearly two decades old.

Amos, now dry and wearing some of his father's clothes, eased down next to his mother. The power was still out, and the water levels outside were still rising. A few candles on the table provided dim light in the quickly darkening dining room.

"Orde thought the whole thing up," he explained to his mother and father.

Orde Wingate? That British officer who was at the bonfire, Grace concluded silently.

"Very nice gifts, if you need guns." Dr. Herring looked slightly defeated. "Useful too. If they don't blow up in our faces."

"They are better than nothing. A gun from the Great War is better than no gun at all. Besides, if I took anything newer, my superiors would have noticed."

"And they won't notice you took a plane?" Grace arched her eyebrows.

Amos smiled in her direction. "Oh, they know. I came from the action in Egypt. I already made my deliveries to the base in Cyprus. I had permission to stop in Palestine for fuel and a quick leave for my sister's wedding. They'll just never know I made a quick stop here with the plane. Of course, if they ask, the storm was the perfect cover."

Mrs. Herring looked extremely concerned. "Then you're leaving already?"

"Afraid so, Mother, now that the worst of the storm is over."

"Dafna will be so sad she missed you."

"Give her a kiss for me, will you?"

His eyes lingered on Grace for a second before he stood up. She felt a warm flush crawl up her cheeks. He was even more handsome than she'd originally thought.

"I'm coming back though. I'm due for a *real* leave around Pesach."

"Another Wingate assignment?" Dr. Herring asked his son.

"Yeah. Everything's changing, Dad. You'll get instructions soon enough."

"So there really is going to be more violence?"

"I pray to God that's not the case. But it will be over my dead body if I allow the Arabs to do here what the Nazis are doing in Europe."

"I don't like it when you speak like that, Amos. The Arabs around these parts are our friends, our neighbors. You know these people,

Amos," Dr. Herring pleaded with his son. It was as though he had forgotten the shot that had been fired at Dafna's wedding.

"Father, I can't argue with you about this. Not now. Not here. It's a different world than it was. You must learn to defend the kibbutz. If you cannot, someone else will be brought in who can. I'm not saying this as your son but as a commanding officer in the Haganah."

Grace stared at Cecelia's chopped hair. She'd learned over the course of the afternoon that she'd been forced into a labor camp in Poland. The Nazis had shaved her hair off and taken everything from her. Her family, her life, everything but the young woman's dignity. Somehow, she'd escaped and made her way to Palestine several months before. The details of the story were hazy, but her thin little arms and short locks were an awful reminder of how necessary, and how terribly insufficient, 20 ancient guns were.

Dr. Herring followed his son outside. From the window, Grace saw the son embrace the father. Both, from the looks of it, were crying.

Twenty minutes later, the mechanical rumble roared overhead, and Amos Herring was gone as quickly as he'd appeared.

That night, as Grace lay in bed, a million questions went through her mind. But in the safety of her 48 wards, she slept better than she had in four nights.

Dear God, she prayed, if it's possible, I never want to sleep alone again.

~

AND SO, as Lorelei dove into her studies, memorizing the difference between pulmonary and systemic veins, Grace dove into her new role as the leader of 48 teenage girls. In all honesty, the learning curve there was quite a bit steeper. No amount of science, math, and foreign languages could have prepared Grace for the constant barrage of what those young ladies threw at her.

She was, at once, thrust into the role of mediator, counselor, confidante, and babysitter. When Cecelia woke up with nightmares from her time in the camp, it was Grace who was there to comfort her back to sleep. When Sadie's hair knotted itself into a hundred tangles, it was Grace who took the time to unknot it, one knot at a time. When little cat fights and petty arguments broke out, which seemed a daily occurrence, it was Grace's job to decide who was right and even dish out punishments (the worst of which was extra laundry duty).

Practically overnight, she became a mother to girls just barely younger than she was. Grace made it up as she went along, her creativity and ingenuity sparking laughter among the older members of the kibbutz, all the while increasing their respect for her.

"She's a born leader," Dr. Herring remarked to his wife. "Which is good, because according to Amos, we are going to need people who can give orders."

Grace would have scoffed at this if she had

heard it. She was not the 'order giver.' That was Katrine's job.

But in that, she would have been wrong. At this particular moment in time, Katrine was far from giving any orders. Rather, she was learning how to take them.

CHAPTER 10

THE SMITH'S REUNION

The *Aquitania Doria* left the port with a loud blare of the ship's horn, carrying her usual cargo for the last time. It was 9 in the morning. The ship was nearly 15 years old and boasted 770 first-class cabins, 784 cabin-class cabins, and 570 tourist rooms. Perhaps even more impressive were its two sparkling swimming pools, three beauty salons, music studio, lecture hall, outdoor paddle and tennis courts, and a dog kennel.

The main dining room spanned three stories in height and served the best that the British Empire had to offer. It was the last voyage the ship would make before returning to London, where it's 6 miles of carpet, 220 cases of china, crystal, and silver, and innumerable paintings and tapestries would be removed to storage and the ship would be outfitted to carry troops, up to 15,000 at a time.

But for now, everything was still lovely on board. It was almost as though there was no war. The enormous floating hotel was so large, you could barely discern the pitch and roll of the sea. The 500 crew members worked without tiring to ensure the 2,000 passengers had their every need under the sun met.

"Here," Harry said as he looked at the room number. "Room 412. In you go, *Mrs. Smith*."

Safe inside, Harry put their suitcases down and looked around the suite. The small bedroom was through a door to the right. At the moment, they were in a tiny sitting room with a little couch and a chair and a porthole looking out to the ocean. He stuck his head into the bedroom. "Looks like the bathroom is behind the closet."

"Harry, I agreed to travel incognito as Mrs. Smith because those were the orders from the Agency. I understand that for reasons undisclosed to my person, us posing as a married couple is for the greater good." Her voice was calm but gaining intensity. "I understand that you've had trouble with the British authorities in the past, and we don't want to make any waves that might, um, delay our little mission. This is a British ship. I get it. Your name is on lists. It draws attention in the wrong circles. I even sort of enjoy having yet another set of false documents. Not only am I an adopted teenager to a Scottish lobster baron, but now I am also the wife of an American millionaire, celebrating our 10th wedding anniversary. Don't try to do the math, it's disturbing. But I put my foot down to actually sharing a suite!"

"Of course you do, dear," Harry said, unfazed. "We've been married a while, at least five hours. I know you pretty well, and that's why," he whipped out a key, "I booked a double suite." Next to the small settee in the mahogany wall was a narrow door. Harry inserted the key, and the door swung open, revealing an identical sitting room. "Rooms 412 and 413. Take your pick, dear."

"Oh, this one I guess." Katrine exhaled with relief. This trip was turning out quite differently than she had expected. The ship's horn blared. They were out of the harbor now and on the move. And then, as an afterthought, she asked, "But won't it hurt our cover?"

He shook his head. "Nah. All the rich Mr. and Mrs. Smiths returning home to New York from world tours who couldn't secure a first-class suite because they had to cut the trip short due to the war," he took a breath, "take the next best thing: two middle-class suites."

"Sensible."

"I know, dear."

Katrine looked out the porthole. "I'll make a deal with you. You can call me 'dear' all you want outside this room, but in here, you can refer to me without the little sweet nothings."

"Have it your way." He tossed her a small gold wedding band. "And put that on. We've got dinner reservations at eight o'clock in the main dining room. It's fancy. We're celebrating, remember?"

"I didn't pack anything appropriate." Katrine frowned. "Come to think of it, I barely packed anything at all. Just a change of clothes… I thought we would only spend a night or two in Jerusalem."

"There's a boutique or two on the main deck. I've got a line of credit from the Agency. How about we get unpacked and go explore a bit? You can buy whatever you need. It's important you look the part."

"All right." An almost indiscernible trace of fear flickered across Katrine's features and then disappeared. Holding her hands together, eyes not leaving the band, she asked, "Is it really so dangerous that we *have* to be Mr. and Mrs. Smith."

Gravely, he nodded. "Yes, dear."

By now it was mid-morning, and Katrine and Harry had stopped to look out at the water. Anyone would have guessed they were a happy couple. Harry carried several packages from the boutique that held Katrine's new evening gown and a suit that was on sale. They found their roles surprisingly, or perhaps not so surprisingly, easy to play.

"Nothing's happened since the Nazis attacked Poland last September. Nothing at all! It's almost like there isn't a war." Katrine gave a heavy sigh. Like everyone else on the *Aquitania Doria*, they spoke of nothing except the war.

"Well, except for the sinking of the *Athenia*." Harry paused and looked out at the ocean.[1]

"Oh yes, of course." Katrine swallowed. The *Athenia* had been a British passenger ship that a

Nazi submarine, a U-boat, had sunk several months before. 112 passengers died.

"But don't worry, honey." He put his arm around her. "The *Aquitania Doria* is going at a very high speed, and I heard the captain say he was zig-zagging, which makes it virtually impossible for the U-boats to catch us."

"Comforting." She gently pushed his arm away. "Look, we may be fake-married, but that doesn't mean you can take liberties, young man."

He smiled down at her and was rather surprised to see her smiling back up at him. They were having a real conversation, and he liked it.

With that, the two began to walk once more. An old man wearing very dark sunglasses and a red knit winter cap pulled down over his ears stopped abruptly and stared. Katrine stared back. She saw the nose, the lips, the mustache. It looked almost like Dr. Einstein, or rather, a Dr. Einstein who did not want to be recognized.

She squeezed Harry's arm. "Why look," she said loudly, "it's Dr. Einstein!"

Harry tried to 'shh' her. Obviously, if Einstein was in disguise, he did not want any attention. But discretion was not one of Katrine's strong suits. "But we just met! Certainly you remember me?" she called out to the old man.

"Young woman," a voice that sounded decidedly like Dr. Einstein's said, "you must be mistaken. We've never met before."

"Are you sure?" She asked, quite confused.

"Quite sure, I am not doctor-whoever-you-said. I am Mr. Smith."

"No." Katrine, uncharacteristically dense, pushed Harry's arm away which was gently pulling her aside, "*This* is Mr. Smith, and I'm Mrs. Smith."

Urgently, Harry whispered in her ear, "This business really does not come naturally to you, does it?"

All pretense suddenly vanished. Dr. Einstein lifted the sunglasses up and squinted at Harry and Katrine. "You mean, you two *have* gotten married?"

"No. I mean, Mr. and Mrs. Smith got married." Katrine groped for an explanation but found none. And now, quite positive that he was, in fact, the famous scientist, she exclaimed, "But you are—"

Harry stopped her, saying forcefully, "Katrine!"

The lightbulb finally turned on. "Of course," she said, backtracking awkwardly and hoping no one else on deck had heard them. "We've never met."

Dr. Einstein chuckled and then whispered, "The Smith family reunion on the *Aquitania Doria*, of course! So, could I ask my 'cousins' to do a little favor?"

Katrine nodded. "Anything."

"Could you find me some breakfast and deliver it to my stateroom? The telephone in my room isn't working, and I couldn't find a porter. And it looks like my," his voice dropped to a whisper, "disguise is not going to fool anyone. Everyone will recognize me, which is exactly what I do not want to happen."

"No problem. Eggs okay?" Harry asked. He looked at his watch. "But it will be more like lunch, you know."

"I'd even eat bacon but don't tell my rabbi." He looked at a smiling Katrine and Harry and added, "No one for a moment would ever doubt you were married."

"We're celebrating our tenth anniversary," Harry said proudly, putting his arm around Katrine.

Katrine turned beet red. "Anything else, Mr. Smith?"

"Yes, coffee, and lots of it."

"What's your room number."

"414."

Harry blinked and exclaimed, "That's two doors down from us!"

"Good. That will make mealtimes much more discreet. If you don't mind…"

"Of course we don't mind, Dr. Ei—I mean, Mr. Smith," Katrine gushed.

"You are the nicest couple I never met before," he laughed.

As Dr. Einstein disappeared back inside, Harry and Katrine glanced at one another. "What do you think he's doing here? And why is he incognito?" Katrine whispered.

"I've no idea. No one told me about it."

CHAPTER 11

ON TROUBLED SEAS

*A*rmed with a full English breakfast consisting of beans, eggs, ham, and tomatoes covered by a silver-dome, Harry and Katrine stood outside Dr. Einstein's door. It opened before Harry could knock.

"Room service!" Harry quipped cheerily, feigning a British accent.

"Why, if it isn't Mr. and Mrs. Smith… again." Dr. Einstein once more looked like himself. He wore a wrinkled shirt under a thick sweater. His hair, always wild, was strangely pressed down where the wool hat had been.

"We brought sustenance, Mr. Smith." Katrine stepped inside.

Furtively, Dr. Einstein looked down the corridor left and then right. Satisfied that there were no listening ears or spying eyes, the scientist shut the door behind them and bolted it shut.

"Call me 'Albert,' dear," he said, taking the dome off and inhaling the aroma of bacon and eggs. Motioning with his fork, he offered them chairs.

"All right, Albert." Katrine sat down and unpinned her hat.

"Now, why is it that you let him call you 'dear?'" Harry smirked at her and put his feet up on the tiny ottoman, looking around the room. It was a suite exactly like theirs. Dark burgundy carpet. A little couch. Two chairs. The door to the tiny berth that served as a bedroom. And a porthole looking out onto the main deck.

Katrine ignored him and poured three cups of coffee.

"Now tell me, how long have you two *not* been married?" Albert chomped down on his toast, heavily buttered.

"Since before we boarded," Harry gave a short laugh, "though I wish it was longer."

"Haganah business? The Jewish Agency, perhaps?"

In unison, Harry and Katrine nodded. She hugged her purse containing the seal even closer. Harry explained, "We are on a fundraising tour."

The old man's eyes widened in understanding.

"And you?" Katrine asked after a minute. "Also Haganah business?"

"No," Albert put his toast down, "American business."

Katrine and Harry shot each other a questioning look.

Albert shrugged. "I like you both, and I

assume you're trustworthy. That said, what I am about to tell you must stay in the room, you understand?"

They nodded again. Harry took his feet off the ottoman and leaned in. The scientist's face had taken on a dark seriousness that made Katrine and Harry feel cold on the inside.

"I was consulting with some scientist friends of mine at the university, physicists like me." He paused and then continued, "Have you heard of nuclear fission?"

"I'm afraid not," Harry answered.

"It will take me too long to fully explain it to you, but it is enough for you to know that last January, we discovered that neutron-driven fission of heavy atoms can create a chain reaction in a large mass of uranium. Do you follow?"

"Sure," Harry said unconvincingly.

"This chain reaction could, in theory, create a massive bomb more terrible than anything ever witnessed on earth." He inhaled and then said softly, "My fear is that in the wrong hands, such information could prove disastrous."

"Is it in the wrong hands?" Katrine bit her lip.

"That is the problem, according to my friends at the university—"

"And Ben Gurion, I assume," Harry interjected.

Nodding almost imperceptibly, Albert continued, "The Germans have stopped the sale of uranium from the Czechoslovakian mines."[2]

"Which they forcibly took over," Harry said.

Albert nodded again. "This makes us think that similar studies are being carried out in Berlin.

It is possible that they are very close to discovering what we already know!"

He took another bite and chewed thoughtfully. "And now? Now I must contact the American president, President Roosevelt."

"But the Germans may not be successful, they may never create such a bomb," Katrine said.

"Oh, they will, my dear Katrine. They will. My goal is to make sure that we develop it first."

Harry sighed heavily. "In the words of Sun Tzu, 'To know your enemy, you must become your enemy.'"[3]

But Albert shook his head. "I think the more accurate quotation would be, 'Victorious warriors win first and then go to war, while defeated warriors go to war first and then seek to win.' In other words, 'The greatest victory is that which requires no battle.'"[4]

At that moment, the captain's voice sounded over the ship's intercom speaker in the hall outside their room, drowning out all thoughts of the ancient Chinese military strategist. "Attention all passengers! Attention all passengers!"

Harry was instantly up on his feet, Albert and Katrine close behind him. He unlocked the deadbolt and stepped into the hall. The voice continued, "This is your captain speaking, Captain Thomas Eldridge." Captain Eldridge's voice was unnaturally high and tense. "We just received a wire from the mainland." (What mainland he referred to was up for discussion.) "Apparently, the Germans have attacked France and the Low Countries. The Danish and Norwegians are completely overrun." The voice cracked a bit and then continued, "The Fins are fighting for their lives."

"That doesn't sound good, does it?" Albert frowned.

Katrine twirled her hat around and around nervously, staring at the back of Dr. Einstein and Harry's heads. One was a wild mane of premature white. The other, perfect dark curls.

Harry turned towards her and held his arm out. In a moment, she felt his strong grip on her hand. He was, without words, telling her to be strong, as though he knew she was crumbling behind him. If he can be strong, she told herself, I can be strong too.

She squared her shoulders and brushed his hand away, crossing her arms across her chest, like a shield against whatever news would come next.

Captain Eldridge sniffed loudly before saying, "Now this is a British ship, of course, and most of you on board are carrying British or American passports. You should know that Prime Minister Chamberlain, or rather, the former Prime Minister, resigned this morning. King George VI has appointed Winston Churchill as the new Prime Minister. This concludes the bulletin for this morning. God save the King." With that, a recording of the British National Anthem crackled down the halls of the *Aquitania Doria*.

Dr. Einstein shook his head. "Hitler has been one busy little man." A quick two steps back to the couch later, and he was once again at his breakfast. After stuffing an entire slice of bacon into his mouth, he looked at Katrin. "Now is as good a time as any to start reading, Mrs.

Smith. We all ought to refresh ourselves on Chinese military strategy."

"Yeah, that will be really helpful, won't it?" Harry's sarcasm was directed more towards himself than anyone else.

Dr. Einstein shrugged. "Never argue with Master Sun, Mr. Smith. Here's what I suggest." He buttered another slice of toast before saying, "For the next three days, take your lovely wife all over this enormous ship and enjoy it. Bring me a meal every now and again and any gossip you can pick up that might be interesting. And then, the moment this ship touches American soil, you two lovebirds raise as much money as you can. God knows we'll need it in Palestine. If the Nazis continue… Well, let's not even discuss it."

"And what about you?" Harry asked the scientist.

"I will spend the next four days enjoying the tidbits of gossip you give me."

"And then? Once we land?"

"I am going to apply for American citizenship."

WHAT WOULD NORMALLY HAVE BEEN an exuberant crowd of travelers enjoying the expertly prepared food, formal attire, and snobbish service, was instead quite subdued. The worry and fear in the air were so thick you could cut it with a butter knife. Sure, the dance floor was jam-packed, and the band was swinging away, but it was all a cover, a last-ditch effort to drown out the doom and gloom of war.

"You look very nice tonight, Mrs. Smith. Nice dress." It was dinner time, and Harry had been waiting in the dining room for Katrine for 20 minutes.

Katrine adjusted the bow on her gown. Black velvet with big shoulder pads. She had on a simple strand of pearls. "Thanks. You don't look half bad yourself," she said, looking up from the menu for a moment. "White dinner jacket? Very elegant."

Out of nowhere, a steward came over and presented Katrine with a lovely corsage of red carnations. "For you, Mrs. Smith!" he said, beaming. "Congratulations!"

She held the flowers. A note was attached that read, *Carnation, the symbol of heartache and undying love.*

"We love helping our passengers celebrate life's little joys. Ten years is something to be proud of! And, if I can add, you are both obviously still so in love."

"I… don't know what to say," she stuttered, slightly stunned as Harry took the corsage and pinned it on her shoulder.

Harry passed the man a tip and sat back down.

"You didn't have to do that," she said.

"It *is* our anniversary. I wouldn't want you holding this over my head later." His voice went up a few notches as he imitated a woman's voice, "Oh, Harry! That time you forgot our anniversary! And it was our tenth!"

"People are staring." Katrine was blushing.

"Your order, sir?"

Both Katrine and Harry looked up. Their waiter was there.

"Two tomato juices on ice." Harry looked at Katrine. "You don't mind if I order for you, do you?"

She shook her head and said, "Why not? You know what I like, don't you, Mr. Smith?"

"Of course, dear." He smiled as he emphasized the word 'dear.' His attention back on the waiter, he continued, "Two Terrines de Fois Gras Truffle, then the Turtle Soup with Sherry. For the fish, Supreme of Halibut with lobster sauce, and we'll take the Poularde braisee Demidoff for our main."

"Your sides, sir?"

"Peas and potatoes."

Katrine sipped her water. "Those are the only two things I think I've ever eaten before."

"Salade de saison?" the waiter asked.

"Of course," Harry answered, putting the menu down. "And the Fresh Peaches Cardinal for dessert."

"You have an excellent palate, sir."

Harry winked at Katrine. "Everyone's always complimenting me on my palate."

Once the waiter was out of earshot, Katrine stared at Harry. "Well, Mr. Smith, this is the best anniversary I've never had. For one thing, I think I might starve. I don't think you ordered one thing that's kosher."

"Oh cut it out." He gave her a smile and said, "I already know you don't keep kosher. You're just being difficult. Now, you'll be a good little girl and eat all your peas and potatoes like the all-American girl I know is in there somewhere."

"Only if I get a pass on the Poularde braisee Demidoff, or whatever that is."

"Capon stuffed with chestnuts."

"Capon?"

"Wartime measures. Chickens are scarce. It's practically chicken."

With that, the waiter reappeared with two tomato juices on the rocks.

"Like it?" Harry asked, clinking his glass with hers.

Katrine took a sip and put it down. "It's salty."

"Drink it up. It's good for you."

"So what are you now, my husband or my mother?" The band began playing a samba. Katrine was unconsciously swaying back and forth. "I'll cut you a deal, I'll dance with you if you drink mine."

"Why, Mrs. Smith, you have yourself a deal."

"You are getting an inordinate amount of pleasure from this arrangement, aren't you?" Katrine chuckled as Harry helped her out of her seat.

With that, Mr. and Mrs. Smith stood up and walked to the crowded dance floor.

"I don't like the way those guys at that table are looking at you." Harry shot a table full of the ship's officers a death stare. "They don't know you're an old married woman."

Katrine rolled her eyes as Harry swept her off her feet, literally and figuratively.

"You are a better dancer than I thought you

would be," Katrine managed to say after a few moments. "You've surprised me!"

"It wouldn't be the first time." Harry grinned at her. "And you ain't seen nothing yet, young lady." With that, they went from doing the basic steps to a Side Samba Walk. For Katrine, this was kid's stuff.

"You up for a challenge?" he asked.

"If you are asking if I can keep up—" she began to say, but before she could finish, Harry was off. Criss Cross Bota Fogos, and then Solo Voltas and Foot Changes. Reverse turns, Shadow Samba Walks, and a resounding finish with a Closed Rocks.

The song ended, and Katrine looked up at Harry with newfound respect. Was it even possible? Could Harry be a better dancer than her?

She wasn't the only one. The dance floor had cleared, and the whole dining room was applauding, not for the band, but for her and Harry.

The band began to play again. This time, it was a rumba.

She felt a tap on her shoulder and turned around. An officer, a rather handsome officer, wanted to cut in.

Katrine smiled and was about to agree when Harry abruptly took her arm and shot back at the man, "My wife's drink just arrived."

"Oh, sorry," the officer said. "I didn't know you were married."

Katrine, vaguely annoyed, looked at their table as Harry led her away from the offending officer. There were no drinks on it.

"Harry!" She looked back at the officer and

said cheekily, "I wanted to dance with him. Who knows? He might have been *the one*!"

"Dance with him when you're not Mrs. Smith."

"Technically, I'm not Mrs. Smith."

"I think he was a Nazi."

"He is *not* a Nazi."

"You don't know that. I could have just saved your life."

"He was a good dancer. I like dancing. I like dancing with people who ask me to dance."

Harry's eyes were intently focused on Katrine's hand. He couldn't look at her. "I'm a good dancer. Dance with me."

It was too much. A pit of fear formed in her stomach. Afraid to commit, afraid to risk… she retreated as quickly as she could. "Well… I guess you are a very good dancer. But just remember, we are simply business associates. All right? That's all."

When she looked at Harry's face, it was frozen. She couldn't read what was going on behind his eyes. Suddenly, the steward appeared yet again, this time with a remarkably tall chocolate soufflé in both hands.

"Oh Harry, you shouldn't have."

"I didn't," Harry answered.

"With compliments from your uncle." The waiter smiled and set the dessert down between them. "Congratulations, by the way."

"My uncle?" Harry looked at the waiter.

"Yes, your 'Uncle Al' in room 414." He handed each a long spoon and nodded to the band leader, who cut the rumba short and started to play "A Fine Romance."[5]

"Uncle Albert?" Katrine groaned.

"Let me guess, he asked you to have the band play our song." Harry looked at the singer making her way to the mic. The waiter nodded. "He said you play it every year on your anniversary."

The singer smiled in their direction and bowed. She was a seasoned performer and immediately drew the attention of the audience. Her smoky voice filled the dining room, telling the sad, if witty, tale of a couple whose love affair is as stale as an old loaf of bread when it should be quite the opposite.

Harry stuffed his spoon into the puffy soufflé and watched it instantly deflate. He could practically hear Albert laughing in his suite.

Katrine wanted to crawl under the table and die.

CHAPTER 12

PASSOVER IN PALESTINE

*M*rs. Herring had spent all week preparing for tonight. For one thing, Amos was due back, which in and of itself would have necessitated a cleaning frenzy. But it was also Passover, which meant that any good Jewish mother had to rid the house of all possible chametz, or leaven. There must not be any bread anywhere! It was a formidable task for any regular housewife. But for a woman who ran a whole kibbutz? It was gargantuan. All dishes were rewashed, so no crumbs remained. Every dish towel, tablecloth, and napkin was put through the wringer. Even with the help of a few hundred teenagers, Mrs. Herring was on the verge of collapse. She hadn't slept in two nights.

And because Amos was coming back, she had taken over the preparation for the meal as well. It was to be a magnificent feast, the kind of Passover to remember. Of this, Mrs. Herring was

utterly and completely determined. The gold
standard was, of course, matzah ball soup; a
clear delicious broth with carrots and chicken
and something resembling a dumpling but much,
much heavier and made of matzah meal. Then there
was Mrs. Herring's brisket, a recipe passed down
from her mother and a much-guarded secret
(except to Cecilia and the twins, who were on
brisket duty). Mrs. Herring took special pride
in her crispy potato kugel, which was a crowd
favorite and made its appearance every Passover
at her table.

It had been a long time since Grace had celebrated a real Passover. Of course, growing up,
her parents had always hosted a rather crazy
affair. Students, both Gentile and Jewish, would
crowd from their dining room all the way out
into the living room, sitting on every chair
available. The last few years, there had always
been a handful of young men who were interested
in Grace more than the actual feast. She was the
sort who got on well with boys, but she never
settled on one. She was young and free and could
choose whoever she wanted when she was good and
ready. And she wasn't ready yet. There was still
much too much fun to be had!

Mother had always made an enormous roast lamb,
potatoes, and her chopped liver, taking special
care with the setting of the table and Seder
plate. It was really the only time of year her
parents had embraced their Judaism, that, and at
Yom Kippur, the holiest day of the year. But
Passover was much nicer, in Grace's opinion.
Fasting leaven for a week was infinitely easier

than fasting food and water for a whole day. And celebrating the Jewish people's deliverance from the bonds of Pharaoh was also much more pleasant than acknowledging one's sins, for that matter.

Besides, her mother had always come up with the most inventive ways to use matzah in place of regular bread for the week. Without yeast, the flat, cardboard-like bread substitute was dipped in chocolate for desserts and snacks. It was broken and mixed into scrambled eggs and sprinkled with cinnamon and sugar for breakfast. And of course, there was matzah ball soup, the Passover staple. The list went on and on.

As a child, Grace had been sure that Passover was all about the food. The whole week centered on a special plate with herbs and hard-boiled eggs and bones… So it seemed appropriate that she and Morris, the Polish rabbi's son, were on kitchen duty, peeling dozens of hard boiled eggs for the Seder plates.

"So, wiseguy," Grace was struggling with her egg, "why are there eggs on the Seder plate?"

"Well, everything on the plate represents something from our deliverance from Egypt." Morris pushed his glasses up on his nose. A lecture was coming. Grace thought it was funny how he said, "our deliverance," as though they had been slaves in Egypt thousands of years ago.

"First, there's the karpas."

"I know," Grace replied, "the bitter herbs."

"In our case, it's parsley. Back home in Poland, we didn't really have green herbs, so we used potato. Anyhow, we dip it in salt water to represent our bitter tears from the hard labor and years of oppression and slavery." He continued, "The charoset—"

"The apples and honey."

"Yes. That's brown and pasty, and it sort of looks like the mortar Pharaoh forced us to make for all the bricks we used to build the pyramids."

"*We* didn't build the pyramids."

"How do you know?"

"Because we didn't." Grace was emphatic.

"What, you think the Egyptians were lugging all those rocks around? No. That's what the slaves were for. And what were the Jews in Egypt?"

"Slaves."

"See. We built the pyramids. My father was a rabbi. You can trust me."

Grace shrugged. There was no arguing with Morris.

"Moving on," Morris was referring to the Seder plate, where all these symbolic foods would be placed in neat little bowls, "we come to the maror, the other bitter herbs. Horseradish."

Grace finished her egg and began on another, muttering under her breath, "So much bitterness."

Morris didn't hear her. "And the lamb shank bone, which is kind of the point of everything, right? I mean, the sacrificial lamb's blood spread on the door frames is what saved us from the worst plague of all, the angel of death! The plague that finally scared Pharaoh into letting us go to the Promised Land."

"Until he thought better of it and chased us into the desert."

"God knew what he was doing, Grace. I think God lured Pharaoh's army out there so he could destroy them, you know, with the sea crashing down on them after the water parted, and we crossed over."

"Morris," Grace grabbed yet another egg, surprised at the wave of emotion that was welling up inside of her, "it was not us who crossed over. It was our ancestors. Our ancestors!"

"Tut, tut." Morris looked at Grace disapprovingly. "Oh, ye of little faith."

"Morris, where was God when my parents were thrown into that camp? When my sister's fiancé was beaten to—" She didn't continue for a moment. "Where was the parting of *that* sea?"

"Grace, my parents aren't here anymore either." He put down his egg and gently put his hand on her arm. "I think there is a parting of the sea here that we can't see. You and I are here. And all these others. That's a miracle. Maybe even more so then that crossing so long ago. My father would have given everything for this. And in a way, he did."

My parents didn't ever think about it, Grace thought. But she said nothing.

Morris was still talking. "It's like what we say at the end of every Seder, 'next year in Jerusalem.' Well, we're there, practically. God brought us back, Grace."

"And how do our parents and what's happening

in Europe fit into all this?" She chucked the growing egg-shell pile into the garbage.

"I don't know. I'm not God. But I know he is good, and he promised that he would bring us back. And here we are."

"And where does that bring us?"

"To the egg." He picked up two eggs, one for Grace and one for himself.

Grace looked at him, "So, Rabbi, what does the egg stand for?"

"I'm glad you asked." He smiled. "New Beginnings. In the most painful of times, my father always said, there is always hope for a new beginning. Some of the sages say that the egg represents the final redemption."

"What's that?"

"The coming of Messiah! May it be speedily in our days."

"I don't understand."

He held it up. "It's just an egg, right?"

She nodded.

"No. It's not. It's a chicken in preparation. Same with the Exodus. It's preparation for the coming of Messiah. It appears like an end unto itself, but it is much, much more."

"That's a little too deep for me, Rabbi." Grace laughed softly, but though she did not fully understand, her heart was comforted. "But, if that's the case, I'm glad we are on egg duty."

"Much more pleasant than peeling the horse-radish, that's for sure."

With that, the two continued to peel in silence for several minutes until the peace of the kitchen was broken by the arrival of a frantic Mrs. Herring. In she came, carrying a stack of matzah nearly a foot and a half tall.

She looked at Grace through red-rimmed eyes. "Do you think we'll have enough?"

Grace dropped the egg she was working on and rushed to take the stack of matzah out of the woman's arms. "Mrs. Herring, you've done enough. You need to go lie down. Morris and I can handle it from here."

Still protesting, Mrs. Herring replied, "But Amos will be here any minute, and I still haven't made the matzah balls for the soup!"

Dafna's voice rang out into the kitchen, calling, "Everyone! Look who I've got!"

"Mama!" a masculine voice exclaimed.

Grace looked over the stack of matzah in her arms. It was Amos, wearing his pilot's uniform just like last time. Funny, she thought. She hadn't heard a plane.

"Amos!" Morris exclaimed. "You're back!"

Amos didn't see anyone in the room except for his mother. He pulled her in for a hug, saw her exhausted face, and demanded she go and rest before the evening. Mrs. Herring, after patting his face and assuring herself that Amos was once more safe at home, surrendered and went to take a nap.

Dafna glanced at Grace. "Hey, any chance you can leave kitchen duty and help me with the flower arrangements? I'm hopeless with that sort of thing, and you are so artistic!"

"What about the matzah balls?" Grace asked, eyeing the young man.

"Morris and I know how to make matzah balls," Amos said, looking at her for the first time.

"But it's your vacation! You ought to be sitting right there," Dafna pointed to a chair, "drinking coffee and telling us all your hero stories."

Morris looked up, very concerned. "Look, I know this is a kibbutz, and all the men and women are all equal and everything, but I don't know if we can make matzah balls…"

Amos did not hear the teenager. He was focused totally on his sister as he slipped off his bomber jacket. "I'm too tired to tell stories."

"Then you should be sitting in that chair drinking coffee and listening to me tell you all about my wedding, which you missed, in case you need reminding."

Grace carefully put the matzah on the counter.

"I don't." Amos was putting on an apron. "You need to do flower arrangements, correct? Besides, you already told me all about the wedding in your letters. Mama sent photographs. They were nice."

"That means a lot. I'll remember that when *you* get married." Dafna was as upset as she could be at Amos, which wasn't saying much. "But I'll let it go *this* time because you're on leave."

With that, she grabbed Grace's hand and skipped out, yelling behind her that Morris and Amos better hurry. It was already three in the afternoon!

∾

"Do you really think they can make matzah balls?" Grace asked doubtfully.

"Well," Dafna took a bunch of greenery and stuck it forcefully into a vase, "look at it this way, imagine how they would do arranging flowers."

Grace frowned. "I'm not sure I agree."

Dafna looked at the vase and grimaced. "It was the lesser of two evils." She paused before adding, "I think."

"I didn't hear the plane. How'd Amos get here?"

"It's an actual leave this time. No 'fake forced landing' because of a storm or engine trouble. The plane's at the RAF base in Petah Tiqva. Uri took the truck and picked him up."

"So, no special deliveries?"

"Amos never comes back here unless there is a purpose. Not since he and Orde Wingate became close. Something is up. He'll tell us when he's ready."

"Speaking of the RAF… when does Uri report for duty in Tel Aviv?" Grace took the vase Dafna was working on and began to rearrange the roses.

The young bride didn't have a chance to answer. Uri had snuck up behind her and lifted her off her feet. She squealed in protest.

"Aren't you two finished yet? It's almost time!" He was laughing, but also serious.

The girls looked at the dining room. Each of the tables was covered in a gleaming white linen cloth. The Seder plates were prepared. There enough matzah. The sun was sinking low.

Dafna pushed her hair back behind her ear. "I

guess I ought to go get cleaned up. Mama and I are the only married ladies here. We've got a lot of candles to light once the sun sets, which looks like will happen in about 20 minutes. I have to hurry!" She smacked a kiss on Uri's lips and bolted.

"I guess I should go get cleaned up too," Grace said, putting the last vase of greenery and roses on the last table. Her artist's eyes approved. The room was ready. It was going to be a beautiful night, she could feel it. "Bye, Uri." She waved and pushed her way out the door and almost barreled headfirst into a large crate of sweet Passover wine held by none other than Amos.

"I brought wine." Amos smiled. "Special delivery. From our friends at the commissary."

Morris's head appeared from behind Amos. He had a comical expression on his face. "Amos said they won't ever know it's missing!"

"You stole it?"

"No." Amos adjusted the heavy box. "Seriously? What do you think all those Gentiles would want with this? It's Manischewitz. Practically fruit punch. A special present from Orde." Grace had no idea if he had stolen them or not. He was confusing.

Grace, quite tall, looked up at the even taller pilot. Her feet wouldn't move. It was something about his freckles. Or his smile. She wasn't sure. Something about him was slightly stun-worthy, especially from this angle. "Oh," was all she could think to say.

"Would you mind holding the door open?" he said. "This is heavy."

Her mind snapped back into gear. She stepped aside and opened the door. Amos did not turn around and look at her. Strange, she thought. She usually had that effect. He was totally focused on distributing the bottles on the tables. Hmm. She'd get his attention all right, she thought to herself. Challenge accepted!

In the midst of dozens of girls brushing their hair and fastening dresses while the men went to evening prayers, she was suddenly completely dissatisfied with every single article of clothing in the drawer. There was the dress she'd worn to the wedding. It was pretty, but she was bored with it. She groaned. Back home, they'd always bought new clothes for Passover. It had been a long time since she'd bought a new dress. All of these thoughts only made her feel worse. Not only did she hate what she had, but she was also awfully materialistic, which made her an awful kibbutznik. She was supposed to fill her mind with higher thoughts, like the good of the community and how to strengthen her mind.

Then she remembered that Katrine had left most of her clothing in the bungalow before she'd left. Uri and Dafna had left it all in a box under their bed. She raced across the courtyard and knocked on the door vigorously. No one answered. She pushed the door open. Dafna was just spritzing herself with some perfume.

"You're not ready yet?" she asked.

"I need Katrine's stuff."

"Under the bed." Dafna pointed with her eyes. "I've got to go." With that, she jogged out, leaving Grace all alone.

Like a maniac, Grace dove into the box. There it was, Katrine's good dress, the dark green one with a sweetheart neckline. Just the thing, she thought. She quickly pulled off her blouse and shorts and fastened the dress up. A quick look in the mirror. Yes! It was perfect.

Back in the dorm 30 seconds later, she went to war with her hair.

"My! What a pretty dress!" Cecilia said, touching the fabric. "Where'd you get it?"

"Borrowing it. It's my big sister's."

"Isn't she a lot shorter?" Sadie asked, braiding her hair carefully.

"On her, it's a full length. On me," she looked down, "it's tea-length, which is better for spring anyway."

The brushing was growing painfully vigorous. Cecilia and Sadie were concerned. "Grace," Sadie began cautiously, "what are you doing? Your hair is going to fall out!"

"It's Passover," Grace stated. "We have to look our best!"

The girls looked at one another, eyebrows arched.

"We think you look fine," Sadie said decidedly.

"Fine is as fine does."

Fine might be as fine does, but by the time Grace appeared in the dining room, she was looking more like mighty fine. And she knew it.

Heads turned. Dafna told her she'd never

looked so radiant. Everyone was impressed. Everyone except for her target. Amos looked at her as he would look at anyone coming in the door. After a glance, he went back to his, apparently very deep, discussion with his father. He was completely absorbed.

Grace sat down in her chair with a huff. All that work for nothing. Her skull was bruised. But at least her hair looked really good. There was some vindication in that at least!

Mrs. Herring looked all refreshed and had a satisfied expression on her face. All her children were under her roof for Passover. Life could not be sweeter.

The dining room filled, and everyone looked to Dr. Herring to start the proceedings. At each place was a small booklet, the Haggadah, that they would follow as the story of the Exodus was retold. Expectancy hung in the air.

Finally, the doctor stood up and said loudly, "Dear children, Pesach Sameach! Happy Passover!"

Young voices responded with 'Pesach Sameach' and cheers and laughter. Then, he blessed the first cup of wine, the first of four, to sanctify the feast day.

Amos stood up and took his father's place at the head of the table. "Kibbutz Kinneret," he began. All eyes were riveted on the handsome airman. "Before we begin our service, I want to say what many of you already know. Our people once more need a deliverer. Like the Jews in Egypt, we once again face annihilation."

The festive mood instantly died. No one moved.

"Let us take a moment of silence for our

brothers and sisters, and our mothers and fathers, who are unable to celebrate the feast. We all know their reasons, whether they be in hiding, or in labor camps, or—" He did not finish. Instead, he bowed his head.

Kibbutz Kinneret followed suit.

A few of the teenagers stifled back tears.

The heaviness remained through the entirety of the Seder, all the way until the point when the soup was served. The matzah balls were as heavy as lead.

"Well, I think you were right about the soup," Dafna whispered, pushing the dense dumpling aside. "The flowers might have been a better bet."

"They must have forgotten the eggs," Mrs. Herring was saying loudly. "A light matzah ball must have eggs!"

Eggs.

Grace glared at the Seder plate. Amos had definitely forgotten something. Like looking at her. The hard-boiled egg seemed to stare right back. Usually, she had more success when it came to getting boys to notice her. In fact, if she was honest, she usually had one hundred percent success. But Amos was different. He wasn't like other boys. His mind was full of important things. He was busy saving lives not noticing girls. This irked her for two reasons. First, because she had apparently lost her touch, and secondly, because Amos was a better man than she'd met in a long time. He wouldn't be impressed by the usual methods. He was too good for that.

Grace suddenly felt very foolish in her sister's dress.

Morris stood up to read his portion from the Haggadah. "He who did all these miracles for our fathers and for us. He took us out from slavery to freedom, and from mourning to festivity."

He added, "And may the Messiah come soon and deliver us again."

The room resounded in an echo of 'amens.'

With that, Grace concluded, it was time to grow up. She would become the most focused woman on the kibbutz. She would show everyone—the Nazis, Amos, and everyone else —just what an Adleman was made of!

IN THE MIDDLE OF THE NIGHT

~

It was a convoluted dream. Peter and I were on a sailboat. A small one, just right for two. We'd made it through some sort of gale and were dripping wet. The mast had broken, and Peter was trying to fix it. And then, on the horizon, the most enormous black cloud appeared. I cried out to Peter, but he couldn't hear me. The cloud came closer and closer and closer. My eyes fluttered open, and I awoke with my heart pounding in my chest.

We'd already made it through the war, I told myself. It was over. We were safe now.

I was breathing heavily, trying to calm down.

I could hear Founder shuffling around in her crate. Maybe she needed to go out?

I checked the clock on the side table. It was 3:30 in the morning. The sacrifices of motherhood. Quietly, I tiptoed out of bed, to not wake Peter, and scooped Founder up, carrying her outside. The puppy nestled her head into my shoulder.

"Alright little girl," I said as I walked back inside a few minutes later, slipping Peter's shoes off my feet.

"How about we add another log to the fire?" I asked, walking into the study and switching on the lamp on the desk. There was Edie's manuscript. Beside it, my old pocket Bible. It was open to the Psalms, and I wondered who had been reading it the night before. I usually left it on the side table by the chair. The little ribbon lay across Psalm 23. My eyes stuck on the words "He makes me lie down in green pastures."

That was us, I thought. Peter and I had been made to lie down. We were out of commission, that was for sure. Out of commission, for now anyway. But of course, the song did not end there. "He leads me beside quiet waters; He refreshes my soul; He guides me along the right paths for his namesake."[6]

A flash from my nightmare passed through my mind. And I felt an ominous shiver.

"I will fear no evil," I was reading the Psalm out loud now, "for you are with me."

I inhaled the comfort of the words. God knew when we would be ready to journey again. The cast would eventually come off, I looked at Founder, and then he would lead us to whatever was coming next. The *right* path. For his name's sake.

"Now what?" The puppy gnawed at my hair and yawned. But unlike Founder, I was wide awake. My eyes caught the manuscript once more.

Founder's eyes were drooping, and as soon as I sat down behind the desk, she curled up into a tight ball and fell fast asleep. "Right then," I sighed. "Back to work. No time like the present." And I picked up my pencil and opened up to where Peter and I had left off the day before.

CHAPTER 13

THIS YEAR IN JERUSALEM

*I*f Passover on the kibbutz inspired Grace to think more mature and deep thoughts, Passover in Jerusalem turned Lorelei into a true philosopher. But in all honesty, Lorelei had always been a sensitive, introspective girl. It's what drew her to music, the piano specifically because it was individual and private. The loss of her parents and Rolf's untimely death had only made her silent periods more intense and frequent. Becky, the Christian nurse and roommate, watched her nervously, worried over her, and loved her as well as she could, or rather, as well as Lorelei would let her. But a wall had formed in Lorelei's heart, one she would let no one cross, one built by harsh reality and loss. She saw the world for what it was. And she didn't like what she saw. Her only escape was class and work and flashcards of the pulmonary system and the names of all 206 bones in the human body.

That, and letters from Grace, Katrine and, of course, Aunt Rose, Edie, and cousin Piper. It was one of these that she was reading now.

"What does she say?" Becky asked. "It's from Katrine, yes?"

Lorelei's eyes swept over the airgraph that had been delivered earlier that morning. It was the first one she had ever received. An airgraph was a letter that had been photographed and sent as a negative on rolls of microfilm to reduce weight. Once it reached the proper destination, the negatives were printed on photographic paper and delivered as usual. It was also a rather brilliant way that His Royal Majesty's Government could keep tabs on what the Commonwealth was saying and make sure no one was inadvertently sharing any government secrets.[7]

"Katrine says she and Harry made it to New York safe and sound."

"And how are the talks going?"

"Don't know. She sent this the day the boat docked."

"Does she say anything else?" Becky rubbed some rouge on her cheek and looked at Lorelei through the open door of the bathroom.

"No, not really. Just something sort of cryptic about meeting up with Uncle Albert onboard the *Doria Aquitania* and she and Harry's 10th anniversary."

"10th anniversary of what?"

"I have no idea. But that's not what's strange."

"What then?"

"We don't have an Uncle Albert." Lorelei sniffed and stared at the letter.

"Mysterious." Becky emerged from the bathroom, a smile on her lips. She had on her Sunday dress. It was mint green with thin white stripes and a Peter Pan collar. A perky white grosgrain ribbon tie hung from where the collar closed down to the slim waist. "I'm finished. We can go."

"You really think it's all right?" Lorelei asked as she put the letter down on the side table by the couch and smoothed out her black skirt. "For us to go, I mean." Her creamy silk blouse, spotless, was buttoned at the wrist with tiny pearl buttons, and her hair was swept back in a low bun at the nape of her neck, which was becoming her trademark.

"Oh yes. It's tradition to have a gentile at the Seder."

"I know," Lorelei smiled, "but me coming too?"

"Mrs. Finkelstein was adamant we *both* come. She wouldn't dream of leaving you here by yourself for the evening. And we are going to have a good time. They are a lovely family."

Lorelei braced herself for the evening. Passover. Her first without her parents or sisters or friends. A lovely family, Becky had said. She'd had a lovely family… once.

"Lorelei?"

She didn't want to go. She didn't want to celebrate. But Becky wouldn't let her get out of it.

Lorelei followed Becky out the door and waited

while she locked it behind her. It took less than a minute to walk down the stairs to the apartment directly below. Before Becky could knock, the door opened.

Both young women were surprised to find that their welcomer was none other than a tiny little boy in a perfect black suit; his best for Passover. He must have been no more than three years old, with white creamy skin, rosy red fat cheeks, and perfect golden curls under a tiny skull cap.

"Shalom," the little boy said with a big grin.

"Why hello!" Becky said and knelt down. He extended his chubby little hand like a man, and she shook it.

"Who's this?" Lorelei asked, suppressing a smile.

Another, taller version of the boy appeared in the doorframe. In perfect English, he said, "This is my brother Benjamin."

"Benji," the child corrected, putting a stubby hand on his hip.

The taller of the two extended his hand. "And I am David."

"Yes, David, I remember you." Becky gave a laugh. She knew all the Rabbi's children.

"But you and I have not formally met," Lorelei said, shaking his hand. She recognized him. Often the sound of his voice carried through her open window when she studied. He was one of a handful of neighborhood children who played ball outside every afternoon, rain or shine, though it was nearly always shine in Jerusalem.

There were seven Finkelstein children, all

between the ages of two and twelve: Ruth, Joseph, David, identical twins Elizabeth and Martha, Benjamin, and baby Michael, in that order. That meant, with Becky and Lorelei and Rabbi and Mrs. Finkelstein, there were 11 places set at the table, and of course, the one place reserved for Elijah. A very proper twelve, Mrs. Finkelstein said.

The Finkelstein household was obviously a creative one. Paintings, toys, and books filled the room. The children were industrious and energetic.

Ethel Finkelstein was very tall with very black hair, which made her skin look that much whiter. The angles of her face were severe and dramatic, and if she hadn't the biggest smile ever planted on a woman's face, she would have been quite intimidating. Two children ran past, the twin girls, in matching dresses with big bows around their hair.

Ethel stepped over a pile of blocks. "I'm sorry about the mess! Trust me, there is no yeast anywhere in the house, but I can't stop the building projects—David would kill me." Lorelei could not trace the accent. It was extremely slight. Her clothes were well-worn but clean. Her eyes were wide and big. Balancing the baby, she extended her hand to Lorelei. "I am terribly sorry for not inviting you over sooner. I lose track of time."

"Please, don't worry, Mrs. Finkelstein. I probably couldn't have come even if I'd wanted to. Becky's been keeping me busy."

"Call me Ethel, like everyone else." Becky and

Lorelei stepped into the apartment and followed Ethel towards the living room. "We are so proud of our Becky and all the work she's doing at the hospital."

Before Lorelei could respond, she came to a dead stop. The living room was not like any she had ever seen. Instead of a couch and chairs, there was an enormous nine-and-a-half-foot grand piano sitting right in the middle of the room. Pushed up against one wall was a line of desks ranging in size from that for a tiny child to moderate child to grown-up. The other wall was lined with bookshelves so full that they bent from the weight of them all. That was the wall nearest Lorelei. Her eyes caught titles in Lithuanian, French, English, German, Polish, Yiddish, and Hebrew. She gasped.

"I know, I know." Ethel looked a bit embarrassed. "We need to get organized. Everyone says it. I'm a terrible housekeeper."

"That's not why I married you," a deep voice said from behind them.

"And here he is," Ethel smiled, "the man himself. Aron, this is Lorelei, Becky's new roommate. Lorelei Adleman."

Unconsciously, Lorelei's hand reached out and touched the piano. It had been months since she'd played.

"Adleman?"

Lorelei nodded.

"Where are you from, Lorelei Adleman?" David and Benji began to swing on their father's strong, long arms like monkeys from trees.

"Kibbutz Kinneret."

His eyebrows raised a slight bit. "Before that?"

"Berlin."

"A good Jewish girl, Papa," Ethel said.

"A good Jewish girl," he repeated, "who likes pianos?"

She nodded.

"It's a Bluthner," Ethel said proudly. "The only Bluthner in Palestine."

Aron, a bear-like man in his early 40s, put his arm around his wife. His kippah was slightly off-kilter. The lips under the light brown beard smiled. "Ethel goes nowhere without her piano."

She laughed. "Who needs furniture when you can have music?"

"Indeed!" Lorelei smiled.

In bits and pieces, the couple told of how Aron, the young rabbi with a Ph.D. in Biblical Languages had fallen in love with the young concert pianist studying at the Prague Conservatory. Both were Lithuanian. Both had moved to Prague. Both were lonely. And brilliant. They'd met at a circumcision for a mutual friend's baby, and everyone thought it was about time they start having babies too. So they got married on the single condition that wherever Ethel went, so would her beloved piano.

"But why Palestine?" Lorelei asked towards the end of the story.

"Why not?" Aron laughed. "But seriously," his accent was heavier than his wife's, "the University offered me a chair. And the way things were going in Europe… I knew it was time to go."

"And Jews were slowly being eliminated from

the Philharmonic. I never would have made the cut," Ethel added. "We opted out early. Adventure and helping build a Jewish homeland. It all sounded very romantic in our first year of marriage."

They began taking their places at the table. Becky was intrigued and asked, "And how has it been?"

"Still romantic. But a lot more hectic. I had seven babies in ten years. Peace is hard to come by these days."

Ethel looked around the table. Two children were missing, and she shouted for the twins, who were hiding somewhere. Instantly, they bounded from a bedroom and appeared at their places.

"Well, as they say, it's showtime!" Ethel clapped her hands together. The children snapped to attention. The seven Finkelstein children took their places around the table. Ethel had set it with their special dishes reserved only for this time of year. The Seder began.

THE FINKELSTEIN HOUSEHOLD ran on interruptions and questions. Every thought was worth deep consideration, no matter how small a brain it came from. One hour stretched into two. Everyone grew hungry. But it was like this every year. It was practically tradition.

Great excitement came with the hiding of the afikomen. Aron took three squares of Matzoh, hundreds of piercings in the dough made room for the candlelight to gleam through. The middle piece was broken and then put in a special bundle and passed on to Ethel, who disappeared momentarily to hide it. Every child knew that if they found it, something wonderful would happen to them.

Aron settled back in his chair and waited for his wife to return. A moment later, she reappeared, winking at him conspiratorially as she pulled her chair back in. "Okay, story time."

"Story time." He rubbed his hands together. "A long, long time ago..." His resonant voice carried over the table and into Lorelei's heart. He didn't need to look at the Haggadah. He had memorized the entire Torah by the time he was 12. He knew every word of the Exodus by heart. With stunning drama, he wove the story of Moses leading his people out of slavery into something that would forever be etched in the memories of his children. They watched him, wide-eyed. Aron was all teacher. All showman. A genius. Becky was enthralled. And even Lorelei, skeptical and slightly bitter, could not help but smile.

Finally, it was Benji's time to shine. The four questions were up for grabs, and Michael couldn't speak yet. Ethel whispered the lines in his ear. "On all nights we need not dip once, on this night, we do so twice?"

Aron looked from child to child. "We dip because we are free. The poor do not dip. Slaves do not dip. We are free."

David looked confused. "But Dad, I don't get what dipping has to do with freedom. Why can't a slave dip?"

"Slaves didn't have salt probably," Ruth answered.

"So what? Why couldn't they dip?"

Ethel whispered again to Benji, who then also whispered, "On all nights we eat yeast, but on this night we eat only matzah?"

"Matzah commemorates the bread that could not rise when our ancestors so hastily fled the Egyptians."

Once more, Ethel whispered in Benji's ear, but the toddler was losing patience. He didn't want to repeat anymore. Ethel took over, "Why do we eat the maror, Papa? The bitter herbs?"

Aron smiled with a self-satisfied expression. "The bitterness of slavery must be remembered."

"Don't look so smug. Of course *you* know the answer. You're a rabbi." Ethel shushd her husband and nodded at Benji. "Last question. Come on, Benji! Make Mama proud!" Ethel prodded the child.

He pursed his lips together.

Ruth was bored and hungry. She was the oldest and ready to eat. She blurted out, "On all nights we eat sitting upright, but on this night we all recline. Why?"

"Only people in freedom can recline on cushions. Slaves eat on the run, right, Dad?" Joseph asked.

"Yes. You've been listening, haven't you?" Aron smiled at his son and then looked at Ethel. "Who's hungry?"

~

196

THE FINKELSTEIN'S spoke seven languages at home, a different one each day of the week. Mondays, English. Tuesdays, French. Wednesdays, German. Thursdays, Yiddish. Fridays, Lithuanian. Saturdays (Shabbat), Hebrew, of course. And Sundays were reserved for Spanish. The children did everything and anything they wanted to, within reason. There was no room on the walls for any more artwork. Lorelei and Becky would have been very uncomfortable in the midst of such genius, except that it was a messy, disorganized sort of genius that made everyone feel completely at home.

Aron and Ethel were figuring it out as they went. As far as discipline went, well, they had room for growth. Tantrums happened, right at the dinner table. There was a lot of passion in that apartment. Lorelei vaguely suspected it could get pretty noisy.

"What's the prize?" Lorelei asked after the children were released to find the afikomen.

Ethel smirked. "A bar of chocolate I've been saving. It's getting harder to find good chocolate these days. It's expensive."

"My mother used to take whoever found it shopping," Lorelei said, looking over from the dining room to the piano.

Ethel caught the look. "Really, you should come down and play it." From the back of the house, a childish scream pierced the evening. The afikomen had been found!

"That's my cue." Ethel stood up. "Tea and almond cake is on the way. You two make yourselves comfortable." She stood and began to clear the table.

Becky was immediately on her feet helping. Lorelei was about to help as well, but both women urged her to stay.

Awkwardly, Lorelei took a sip of water and looked at Aron.

"So, Ms. Adleman, what did you think of our Seder?"

She grinned. "I thought it was refreshing and untraditional."

"You are not a fan of doing things traditionally, so to speak?"

Lorelei thought a second. "No. I guess not."

"Tradition has its place, Ms. Adleman. And religion."

It was as though he had read her thoughts. Unconsciously, she shook her head. Where had religious tradition gotten so many of her people? Where had the tradition of her grandparents and great-grandparents gotten her parents? It had labeled them. Trapped them. Killed them, she thought.

Somehow, the rabbi understood what was passing through her mind.

"It was not Judaism that killed your friends and family. It was the Nazis."

She looked down and then back up, her eyes meeting the rabbi's defiantly. "I don't see the point of much of anything anymore. Being Jewish or otherwise."

He did not answer, prodding her to continue by his silence.

"I'm not religious. Neither were my parents.

But then again, all the families who went to synagogue every week and wore black died too. God did not save them for keeping the tradition. He didn't save my parents for not keeping it. Why would he save us from Pharaoh only for this to happen?"

"I have wondered such things myself."

"You have? But you are a rabbi!" She stared at Aron, her mouth slightly open. This was not what she had expected from him at all.

"Indeed." He let the weight of his words sink in. "It is not such a bad thing to ask questions, as long as you are willing to receive the answer God gives you. But I think this is a conversation for another time, perhaps. Dessert is almost ready, from the sounds of it. Isn't that right, Ethel?" he shouted into the kitchen.

"What?" she shouted back.

"The almond cake?"

"Two seconds!" she yelled back.

Once more, he turned his attention to Lorelei. "You really are welcome here, Ms. Adleman, anytime. If you want to borrow a book, play the piano… Ethel and I love visitors. And the children like you." His kind eyes twinkled sadly.

CHAPTER 14

BUSINESS ASSOCIATES

*W*hile Grace grappled with adulthood and Lorelei wrestled with God, the past, and the future, Katrine fought against the question arising in her own heart. It was a simple question but one that had to be answered: What *were* she and Harry, exactly? She didn't know, and she was too scared to ask.

Katrine dabbed her lipstick. It was the exact same shade as the burgundy suit she wore under the light coat that fit her petite frame as flawlessly as the set of pearls hanging around her neck. It didn't really feel like Passover.

For one thing, they were in New York. Katrine loved the city but it was nothing like Berlin at all. New York was all lights and colors and music, a completely different sort of city.

Harry had knocked on the door of Katrine's room in the dingy hotel they were staying in and informed her they were going to spend Passover at his mother's.

"When is Pesach?" Katrine had asked, surprised.

"Tonight is the first night."

"Oh my." She'd completely forgotten. They'd only been off the boat for a week, seven frantic days spent making appointments and running all over the city pitching the cause of the Jews in Europe to ladies luncheons, boardrooms, and synagogues. They'd moved so quickly, they had barely had any time to talk or sleep or eat. The seal remained in her purse, at all times, waiting until they could find the right buyer at the right price.

"I forgot too." Harry sighed.

And now, three hours later, there they were, on the fifth floor of Harry's mother's apartment building on Delancey in the Lower East Side. The cab had driven them past the Bowery, Chinatown (which Harry promised to take Katrine to if they had time), barber shops, tattoo shops, and pushcarts.

"There's Yiddish on those signs," Katrine had remarked, curiously. "They speak Yiddish here?"

"And German, Italian, Polish, Ukrainian, and Irish. This is America, Katrine. They don't call it 'the melting pot' for nothing. And the Lower East Side is the melting-est part of the pot."

"Isn't Irish English?" she'd asked, taking his hand as he helped her out of the cab.

"Nope. You ever heard of Gaelic?" He held in his hands a small bouquet of bright red flowers they'd bought on the way over from a street vendor.

The street was dirty but strangely sort of cozy too. So this was where Harry grew up. She smiled.

A father and two boys, each wearing a yarmulke and prayer shawl, passed them, obviously on their way back from the synagogue. It reminded her of her childhood before it had become dangerous to celebrate Passover. She liked it. It felt homey.

Harry watched the father and his boys round the corner. "Mother's not going to be happy that I didn't make it to shul." He took a yarmulke out of his pocket and put it on his head. "Don't say anything, okay?"

"I wouldn't have said anything anyway but sure."

Katrine followed Harry up the five flights of stairs and down the hall to his mother's apartment. The hall had garish wallpaper and ugly electric bulbs swinging from the ceiling. It was clean enough but smelled strongly of stale cigarette smoke. She could hear music coming from behind the wall as well as raucous laughter.

Harry looked at her apologetically and said, "Noisy neighbors." Then, a second later, he stopped in front of a door and knocked, remarking, "This is it."

A voice from behind the door exclaimed, "Harry! Harry! You're here!"

"She's excited to see you." Katrine inhaled, feeling nervous for no reason in particular. No reason, except that she was about to meet Harry's mother.

The door swung open, revealing a very short and plump matronly woman impeccably dressed. From her silver hair swept up on top of her head, to the emerald brooch pinned on the silk blouse, everything was exactly 'just so.'

Harry's mother's jaw dropped slightly at the sight of Katrine, her sharp eyes taking in every detail of Katrine's dress and face in a millisecond.

"Oh Harry," she said slowly. "You didn't. You didn't!"

"I didn't what?" He looked concerned.

"You went and got married."

Katrine felt her face burn.

"Oh no, Mama! This is Katrine Adleman. She's a business associate."

"Well, you should've told me you were bringing a friend!"

"Yes," Katrine shot Harry a look, "you should have told your mother you were bringing a friend."

"I wanted to surprise you." He passed her the flowers.

"Just the surprise every mother wants, her adult son to bring home 'a friend.' I'm not getting any younger, young man."

He pecked his mother on the cheek. "And hello to you too."

Harry's mother swatted him away, casting her penetrating gaze again on Katrine as she took her hand. "I'm Bertha Stenetsky. And I want to apologize for my son's rudeness. It comes from my side of the family."

"It's nice to meet you, Mrs. Stenetsky."

"Call me Bertha." She stepped aside for Katrine to enter. "Is that a German accent I hear?"

"Katrine's from Berlin," Harry said with a nod.

"Ah." As though it was possible, she seemed to look down on Katrine, though she was a solid four inches shorter. "My people are from Austria."

"By way of Russia." Harry chuckled wryly.

"These are lovely Amaryllis. Did you get them from John on Seventh?"

"I did."

"Your father sold to him. Your father grew the most magnificent Amaryllis. Worth beyond beauty, isn't that right dear? That's the symbol of Amaryllis? Are you sending me a secret message? I'm looking old, aren't I?"

"You couldn't be prettier." He took off his hat and helped Katrine off with her light coat.

Inside the apartment now, Katrine observed her surroundings. There were wonderful smells emanating from the kitchen to the left. Some sort of roast, definitely. Soft music, Chopin, played on a record player. On her right was the living room. One wall was lined with books, the other, an upright piano. And two small windows. Bertha Stenetsky was a lover of fine antiques, evidenced by the settee and chairs. Beautiful dark mahogany and needlepoint. In the corner, by the fire, was a small table with a jigsaw puzzle scattered across it. It was a lovely room. The sort of room Katrine would love to spend hours and hours in.

"You approve?" Bertha asked.

"Oh yes."

Katrine was immediately drawn to the mantle. She pointed to a photograph. "Is this your husband?"

"Yes. That's Harry's father. His name was Israel."

Katrine stepped closer and examined it. "He looks just like Harry!"

"He was wonderful. Everything good about Harry comes from him. Including the green thumb."

"I have to ask, wherever did your husband garden?"

"He had the whole roof. It was a veritable paradise. Now I'm afraid it's gone to ruins. Someone keeps homing pigeons there now, in the old greenhouses. They fly back and forth all day long."

"You loved him very much."

"You've no idea, Ms. Adleman."

"I think I do," she whispered, almost afraid to look in Harry's direction.

"Who wants a glass of seltzer? Mama? Katrine?" Harry asked as he moved towards a brass rolling bar cart. His mother stopped him before he got more than a step away, whispering fiercely, "You remember Judy Rosemblum who lived downstairs?"

Oh yes. Harry remembered Judy. "Bucktoothed Judy?"

"I invited her to the Seder."

"You didn't!"

"I thought you would come *alone*!"

A knock on the door.

"That's her." Bertha braced herself and shot Katrine an apologetic look. "If I'd known Harry was bringing a friend—"

By then, the door opened, and there stood Judy. It was obvious to all that she was no longer a buck-toother. No. She was gorgeous.

"Judy," Harry faltered. "You've grown up."

"It's good to see you too, Harry." She stepped in and gave him a friendly kiss on the cheek. Gorgeous, with a very strong Brooklyn accent. She rested her hazel eyes on Bertha. "Thanks for inviting me, Mrs. Stenetsky."

"Judy, this is my business associate, Katrine. We are in town on… business." Harry blushed slightly, and a terrible ball of something formed in Katrine's stomach. Harry had just introduced her as his business associate, as requested, for the second time in five minutes, and she didn't like it one bit. Nevertheless, Katrine put on her warmest smile and extended her hand.

Judy took one look at Katrine and froze. The night was not going to plan at all. In fact, it was going south. Storm clouds were brewing in Bertha Stenetsky's apartment.

Bertha brushed past Katrine. "I'll set an extra place at the table. Why don't the three of you young people get to know one another?"

"Don't worry about me, Mrs. Stenetsky. I'll just sit in Elijah's chair." Katrine tried to laugh.

~

BERTHA, Harry, Katrine, and Judy Rosenblum sat around the dining room table making their way through the Seder. Judy, who didn't like feeling invisible, was wondering why she had been invited. Mrs. Stenetsky had been very clear that her son was single. But he obviously liked his business associate so much that he couldn't stop looking at her.

For Katrine, the night was even more awkward.

Harry had introduced her as a business associate. He hadn't even used the word friend! But then, that's what Katrine had said she wanted, wasn't it? She wondered why it all was making her so upset.

And then, somewhere between the matzah ball soup and the fourth question, Katrine admitted to herself that what she really wanted was to be something else altogether, and that was terrifying, especially sitting across from beautiful Judy.

"My father owns the kosher meat market downstairs," Judy said, batting her eyelashes flirtatiously. Normally that got their attention.

"That's nice." Harry's smile was flat.

"It's a great place." Her accent was thick. "Great Bratwurst."

"Bratwurst. How nice."

"What kind of work are you in, Harry?"

"Oh…" he exhaled. "Uh, public policy of sorts." He looked at Katrine and grimaced. Judy caught the look. "For the Jewish Agency."

"We are raising money for the Jews in Palestine," Katrine explained.

"You should hear her speak! Katrine's something else."

"Is she?" Bertha asked.

"Oh yes. Tomorrow we are going to be meeting with the American Jewish Committee. They have a lot of money; money we need. And political connections."

"That's nice," Judy said, her eyes narrowing. Her charming wiles were not working on Harry. He was too far gone. Like any smart woman, she decided to cut her losses and bail before she suffered any more humiliation.

"It's not easy. Yesterday, we went to a Daughters of the American Revolution meeting.[8] We were speaking about current events. They bring a new speaker every Tuesday."

Bertha raised her eyebrows. "The DAR? What will the Agency think of next!"

"Some of the women were very polite and kind. One even teared up," Katrine said. "But another approached me after the talk and told me that I was a liar and just spreading preposterous Zionist propaganda. She said that the Germans would never do anything like what they did to my parents!"

"Probably a member of the Bund," Bertha said.

"The Bund?"

"American Nazi Party."

"Oh." Katrine blanched slightly.

"And then," Harry put his elbow on the table, "I told her that the Germans won't let the Red Cross behind the occupied territory lines, and

she told me I was an idiot and was about to
slap me—"

"The Nazis are outrageous liars." Katrine
dabbed her lips with her napkin. "The problem
is, they are good at it. And people don't verify
facts. They just believe what they hear on the
news."

"You can't believe anyone these days." Judy
managed a tight smile and tapped her fingers on
the table impatiently. "Let's get this show on
the road, shall we?"

"Right, sorry." Harry picked the Seder back up
and plunged once again into the service.

Before the hiding of the afikoman, Judy looked
at her watch and said, "I'm so sorry to leave
the party, but I've got a terrible headache."

Harry saw her out.

"Judy, I'm sorry. I feel you were brought here
under false pretenses," he said, opening the
door.

"Don't worry about it. I've had bad setups
before. Usually, they don't bring the other
woman though."

"Other woman?"

"Don't play dumb with me, Mr. Jewish Agency.
For business associates, you two seem awfully
close."

"You have no idea," Harry said.

She gently patted Harry's face. "Advice to the
wise; he who hesitates perishes in the wilder-
ness. She seems very nice."

When Harry came back into the dining room,
minus Judy, he found that Bertha and Katrine
had cleared away the dinner dishes and were in

the kitchen preparing tea and dessert. He could overhear their voices, chatting away pleasantly. Now that Judy was gone, everyone had relaxed.

"I completely agree with you, Bertha. Harry is not getting any younger. It would be wonderful for him to settle down, that is, when he finds that special someone."

Harry stopped and listened closely. "And you like New York?" his mother said.

"Oh!" Katrine's voice was jubilant. "I just love it. I love America. I had no idea I would like it so much."

"If you are as good a friend as he says, you should tell him to settle down back at home where he belongs. He never listens to me. I'm just his mother. He would make a wonderful father. I so want to be a grandmother."

"Would you hand me that cup, dear," Bertha said. She paused for a moment before softly exclaiming, "Oh! You're married, I had no idea."

"I'm not married."

"But you're wearing a wedding ring."

"Oh my. Harry gave it to me to wear!"

Harry's heart was pounding loudly in his chest.

"My son gave you a wedding band?" Bertha sounded tense.

"No! Yes. We were married once, sort of. I forgot to take it off!"

"Sort of?"

"Oh, don't worry, Bertha." Katrine's voice sounded panicked. She tried to backtrack but was doing a terrible job. Harry could feel her squirming. "It was only for a week on a ship. It was a temporary arrangement. It wasn't real!"

"Temporary? Are you trying to tell me that my son married you, and now you are not married?"

"Um, something like that. Oh dear."

Time for intervention, Harry thought, stepping into the kitchen. "Mother, it was for work. We weren't really married!"

"That's what I meant to say!" Katrine breathed a sigh of relief. "We could never be really married because we are only friends, if that."

"Business associates," Harry clarified.

"Right," Bertha looked from Katrine to Harry, "business associates."

"Business associates," Katrine repeated.

"Well then, would you two business associates take the coconut macaroons and flourless chocolate cake to the living room?"

"I THINK MY MOTHER LIKES YOU." Harry sighed as he shut the door behind them. His tie was loosened, his jacket slung over his arm.

"I like your mother."

"Good… good."

They hadn't said a word to one another during the long walk down the stairs and out of the apartment building. The street was busy, even though it was nearly 11 at night. It was warm and noisy. They began to work their way down the street, side by side.

"I hope Judy is all right," Katrine finally said.

"I'm sure Judy's headache left the minute the door shut."

"Still." Katrine stopped for a moment before plunging ahead. "I'm sorry. I didn't want to spoil things."

"You didn't spoil anything."

"I think Judy liked you."

They turned and began to walk down Delancey Street. The sound of families singing the Nirtzah, or the special songs reserved for Passover, floated over their heads.

"I don't care." He looked up at the skyscrapers. "She's not my type."

Very quickly, Katrine looked up at Harry and then stared straight ahead. "Well, you should care. You want a future, don't you?"

He ran his hands through his hair. He was angry at Katrine for saying that, but he couldn't quite put his finger on why. "I can't believe you told my mother we had been married. I think she's still confused."

"It did get out of hand, I'll admit." She let out a nervous laugh and then added, much to her own distress, "You told your mother - and that Judy woman - that I was *a business associate*. You couldn't even use the word friend!"

"Your words, Katrine. Not mine."

She stopped walking. Harry felt his heart start beating very loudly again.

Harry looked down at Katrine. He could see the moon reflecting in her blue eyes. "We were never married," he whispered.

She took the ring off her finger and handed it to him.

"And we're not just business associates," she added.

"So, Katrine, if we are not married, and we are not business associates, what are we?"

A cab pulled over, but neither Harry nor Katrine moved to open the door. The cabbie rolled down the window and shouted, "You need a ride?"

"No." Harry didn't look away from Katrine's face. He spoke his next words slowly. "I think we'll walk home. Hotel's only five blocks away."

The cab pulled away, and Harry paused before repeating his question, "So, Katrine, what are we?"

"Hi."

Startled, I looked up. There was Peter, leaning up against the door. His hair was messy and growing long, like when I'd first met him. He stuffed his hands into the pockets of his flannel robe.

"What are you doing up?" I asked.

"I could ask you the same thing."

"I didn't wake you, did I? What time is it?"

"No…" he stopped. "It's nearly 5:00."

I'd been working for almost two hours. I realized I hadn't moved in who knew how long, and I stretched my back slightly as I asked, "Is it your leg?"

He didn't answer but still came into the study, and his eye caught on the manuscript. "How's it going?"

I put the pencil down. I didn't know exactly what to say. "You want my honest opinion?"

"Of course!"

Struggling to come up with an opinion, I finally blurted out, "How about you read it yourself and then we'll talk."

"That bad?"

"She's trying something new," I tried to explain. "No main character. No plot. It's sort of avant-garde."

"Avant-garde?"

Founder stirred in my arms, and I looked down at my lap and then back up at Peter. "Are you going back to bed?"

"No. It's too hard to sleep without my girls." He chuckled, and I felt a bit of a blush creep up my neck. It was funny, when he looked at me a certain way, I still blushed after all this time. "Why don't you catch me up. Tell me what's going on in the story."

"I'll catch you up later." I pushed the manuscript towards him and stood up."What would be very, very helpful to me is if you read it to me while I put on the coffee and make us something fancy for breakfast. How does that sound?"

I rounded the corner of the desk and passed the sleeping puppy into his arms. "What do you want? French toast?"

"Heavy on the French."

I wondered what he meant as I answered, "Deal."

Extra 'French?' Maybe that meant he wanted more butter. Or soggier toast than I usually made? But then again, I'd only made French toast once since we got married.

As I rummaged through the pantry for cinnamon, I could faintly hear Peter's voice in the study talking to Founder. "Well, darling, what do you say to a bedtime story? I guess it's actually more of a wake-up story because it's morning."

When I looked back up, Peter was in the kitchen, Founder in his arms. He pulled out a chair and sat down. "I forgot to ask what your mother wrote. How's everyone in Scotland?"

Pulling the milk out from the ice-box, I answered, "They're all right. She sends her love. She was writing primarily to ask how Grace is doing. I could feel her concern inbetween the lines." I heard footsteps up above and glanced at the ceiling. "Is it possible she's still pacing?"

He opened the pages of the manuscript, also looking up for a moment. "I bet she has walked nearly 20 miles. Listen up, Founder," he continued. "Maybe Edie's left us a clue as to why Grace can't sleep!"

CHAPTER 15

UP, UP, AND AWAY

*G*race was, by nature, a bold and adventurous type of girl. She was the first to try daring new trends amongst the sisters. When hemlines went up, she whipped out her scissors and snipped away. When permanent waves were all the rage, her golden locks were the first to be twisted and forced into the chemical curl. She wasn't afraid to hop onto the back of her friend Hans' motorcycle and fly down the crowded streets of Berlin, something that her father put a stop to immediately once he found out how she was traveling to and from school.

Grace was fearless, and when she put her mind to something, she always—and I mean always—did it. So when she decided to become the most focused woman on the kibbutz, the most dedicated of dedicated young Palmach leaders, that's exactly what she did.

Dr. and Mrs. Herring noticed the change right away. Of course, they had already known she had leadership abilities but now? *Here* was a girl who took things seriously. *Here* was a girl who was focused.

They could often hear her in the courtyard, holding a pole above her head (a poor substitute for a rifle) and shouting at the girls in her dormitory to run through the drill again, again, again! If the Arabs or the Nazis were to invade the hallowed boundaries of their little communal home, they WOULD be ready, she shouted. The girl's dormitory of Kibbutz Kinneret would be on the front lines. Grace took it upon herself to make sure that they would run the fastest, think the clearest, and shoot the straightest; even if they could not actually practice the shooting part.

And if Amos was ever to wander back onto the kibbutz and notice how focused she was, how deep thinking and philosophical, what an effective and passionate leader she was, well, she would be too focused and passionate and deep thinking to notice back. Maybe. For a while anyway.

If it hadn't been for her quick wit and a ready smile, Grace could have quickly become the most resented person on the kibbutz, but as it was, her cheerful approach to her new way of life was inspiring. So when the letter came from the Palmach, it was obvious to Dr. and Mrs. Herring what should be done.

"Certainly you need me here though!" Grace exclaimed. "What about the girls?"

"We need you where you will be the most effective," Mrs. Herring answered sadly. "And right now, that is *not* here."

"But you want me to volunteer?" Grace's voice struggled. She had been working terribly hard with her girls. Her blood, sweat, and tears were in the kibbutz. She couldn't imagine doing something else. "With the British Air Force? Whatever for? But why not Uri?"

Dr. Herring switched on the lamp. They sat in the Herrings private sitting room attached to his office. The sun was nearly set. Dinner was over, and the kibbutz was slowly winding down for the night.

"No one married is allowed on the mission. Besides, between us, Uri is afraid of flying. My son-in-law is brave, except when it comes to heights." He coughed behind his hand. "Didn't you ever wonder why he was stuck at a desk job at the base in Tel Aviv?"

"How do you know *I'm* not afraid of heights?"

"Are you?" He returned to his seat and sat down, leaning forward towards Grace who sat next to his wife.

Grace shrugged and ran her hand through her hair. "Well, I guess not." She looked at her fingernails and exhaled. "I guess it just seems like the moment I get used to something, it all changes."

"These are unusual days, dear. It will, God-willing, be different for your children." Mrs. Herring took Grace's hand gently and gave it a squeeze.

"But this is my home. I finally am used to it," Grace said quietly. "Besides, it's all I have left."

"All the more reason for you to volunteer on this mission. You must fight for what you love."

Grace looked up, thinking through what Mrs. Herring said. After a moment's silence, she finally asked, "What's the mission?"

"That was not specified. Secret missions usually are secret."

"So," Grace spoke slowly, "I've been chosen to go on a secret mission with the British Air Force. And you really think I'm cut out for this?"

"We do. You are the best this kibbutz has to offer. We know that you will make us proud."

"When do I leave?"

Dr. Herring didn't answer. Instead, he said, "We also want you to take Cecilia and Morris."

"Cecilia and Morris?" Grace was shocked. "But Cecilia is barely 17 and Morris turned 15 just three days ago!"

"Yes, but they are special in a way. Cecilia has survived the camps, and Morris knows the ins and outs of Warsaw. The British need information that only they can give. They have our special permission to go," Dr. Herring answered.

"So then, when do *we* leave?" she clarified.

Who would have thought that she would ever be a member of His Royal Majesty's Air Force? And she'd never even been in a plane!

"First thing in the morning. I suggest you go talk to Cecilia and get packed up."

Grace nodded and stood up quickly. She barely knew where to start. "Does Morris know?"

"I'm on my way to talk to him now." Dr. Herring followed Grace to the door.

Before she left, Grace turned back and smiled. "You knew I would say yes, didn't you?"

Dr. Herring and his wife didn't answer.

"WHAT DO YOU MEAN? A secret mission?" It was the next morning, and Sadie's hands were on her hips, her lips were pursed together. She was jealous, and it showed. "Why Cecilia and not me?"

Grace stopped folding a blouse and put her hand gently on Sadie's shoulder. "Because someone has to take over for me. As of this moment, you are now officially in charge of the women's dormitory."

"Really?" Sadie answered, her ruffled feathers slightly soothed.

"Why yes, of course. I had to choose someone I trust. You are the perfect woman for the job. And I expect the girls to be whipped into shape by the time I come back."

"When will that be?"

"I…" she trailed off. She had no idea. "Come to think of it, I guess I don't know when I'm coming back. But believe me, this is my home. I will come back. And I expect you all to be able to do one hundred sit-ups when I do."

Sadie was still slightly miffed. "I did two hundred yesterday."

Both suitcases snapped shut, and a few moments later, the girls stood outside with Morris and the whole kibbutz. Everyone had turned out to say goodbye and wish them well. Mrs. Herring had tears in her eyes and pulled the three young people close and kissed their cheeks.

"Mrs. Herring," Morris pushed her back, secretly enjoying the attention, "please, none of that!"

"Now, the bus is here!" She sniffed and prodded them towards the old bus doors that creakily swung open. In they went. The door slammed shut, and the bus ambled away from the kibbutz and all Grace had grown to find familiar and safe.

GRACE AWOKE from an uncomfortable sleep to Morris's jab in her ribs. "Look. We're here." A sign outside the bus stop said in English, Hebrew, and Arabic the name of the small village of 'Lydda.'

Cecilia was already standing up, adjusting her shirt.

A British soldier poked his head through the open doors of the bus. "Are you the three recruits from Kibbutz Kinneret?"

"That's us." Morris raised his hand like a schoolboy, looking as worried as he felt.

"You're late." The soldier turned on his heel. "Come with me."

Out of the bus, another soldier waited behind the wheel of a military-issue jeep. He gave a low whistle when he saw the trio. "Girls? And kids? What are they going to think of next!"

Cecilia whispered in Grace's ear, "I'm nervous. What do you think they are going to have us do?"

Grace shrugged. "Just think of it as an adventure. It's going to be fun."

"I've had enough adventures to last me forever. I want to go back home."

"Come on now," Grace chided her. "We're doing this for the Palmach, and for the kibbutz, and for the Jews back in Europe— our family Cecilia! Buck up."

"Yeah and buckle up!" the driver added, gunning the idling engine.

The short ride to the Lydda airfield was bumpier than expected. The driver seemed to enjoy careening around curves, narrowly avoiding oncoming traffic, and plunging headfirst into potholes. When the jeep finally slowed at the base's front entrance, Cecilia was white, and Morris was green. But Grace looked fresh as a daisy. She tossed her hair and shot the driver a knowing glance. He couldn't scare her! Remember, she was fearless.

The young man chuckled and quickly saluted the guard. Immediately, the gate opened, and once more, the jeep's engine revved to life and sped through the gate. "All right," he swerved to the left and then killed the engine, "we're stopped."

"Where are we supposed to go?" Grace asked.

"See that building over there?" He pointed to

a squatty tin building that was half-tent and half-structure several feet away. "That's it."

"Delightful," Cecilia groaned.

Grace shrugged and hopped out of the jeep, helping both Cecilia and Morris after her. The second soldier threw their suitcases beside them and didn't look back as the driver roared back towards the gate.

Together, they marched towards the low building and pushed through the door. A young woman wearing a khaki uniform, a simple skirt, matching shirt, and low block heels, was waiting with a clipboard. Beyond her were roughly 200 chairs filled with young men, and, Grace breathed a sigh of relief, a handful of young women, albeit, a very small handful.

The woman with the clipboard stopped them. Her clipped accent carried over the gentle murmur of hushed voices, all wondering what they were doing there and why.

"Names?"

"Grace Adleman, Morris Greenburg, and Cecilia Haan." Grace's eyes were glued on the young men and women in the chairs. She recognized some from the bonfire, the one where Orde Wingate had told them all about the Palmach. That night felt like a very long time ago.

"Haan, Greenburg." The woman looked at Cecilia and Morris, "You're both starred as minors. You are under 18?"

They nodded.

"Do you have written permission from your parents to be here?"

Grace looked at the British woman as though

she were an idiot. "Their parents are dead," she said flatly. "They have special permission to be here from the Herrings, their legal guardians."

"Good enough, I suppose." She crossed off their names. "Adleman, Haan, you're both assigned to Barrack C. And Greenburg, you're in Barrack D." She checked a few boxes. "You've officially reported for duty."

They stood there, not knowing exactly what to do. Voice tinged with exasperation, the woman sniffed and said, "Well, go sit down! Put your things against the wall."

"She never asked to see the letter from Dr. Herring," Cecilia whispered.

"She doesn't care." Grace cleared her throat. A lot of the young people were smoking. It burned her eyes. "Do you think we are going to get the same uniforms?" She looked back at the woman, frowning. "It's a little dowdy, don't you think?"

"Why, look!" Morris said, setting his bag down beside the girls'. "It's Orde Wingate!"

Grace jerked her head to where Morris was looking. There on the platform was none other than the famous soldier. She followed Cecilia and sat down in the last row.

Orde Wingate commanded everyone's attention. He was that sort of man. The room quieted.

"I'm here unofficially," he began, coughing slightly. "Obviously, I'm an army man. But I was a big part of planning the ground part of this operation, which you don't know about yet. What I am about to tell you does not leave the room. Understood?"

Everyone nodded.

"Your brothers and sisters in Europe are desperate for help." He looked deeply into the eyes of the men and women seated in front of him. "And you have been chosen to help organize local resistance and rescue operations among your old communities."

Morris, Cecilia, and Grace looked at each other questioningly. Each thought the same thing with a slight shudder… *our old communities?*" For the majority of those in the room, that meant Nazi-occupied Europe.

He continued, "Now, the British have agreed to train a few units of our top Palmach leaders and those in the Youth Aliyah—that's you," he looked slowly from face to face, "And deploy you as volunteers to infiltrate certain countries that shall remain nameless."[9]

"What do you mean?" someone asked from the middle of the room.

"I mean that out of the 200 of you who volunteered, 110 will be chosen for special training in Cairo. I'm not at liberty to say more."

"Cairo?" Grace whispered.

"It's in Egypt," Morris whispered back.

"I know where Cairo is!" she huffed. Morris was always such a know-it-all.

"There are three selection phases. Each one builds upon the next. By tomorrow night, you will either be on the plane to Cairo or on the bus back to your kibbutzim." Orde clapped his hands together. "Testing starts in the morning."

∾

"I'M GOING to be on the plane to Cairo if it's the last thing I do." Later that night, Grace clenched her teeth together as she and Cecilia walked to their barracks. It was a chilly night, and she chided herself for forgetting to pack her sweater.

"Why are you so determined?" Cecilia asked, her voice quiet.

"Determined?"

"You know what I'm talking about, Grace. Ever since Pesach, you've changed. You've become. . . different."

Grace stopped and looked out at the desert. "It was something that Amos said, I think."

"What was it?"

She thought back. "He said something about our families back in Europe and all the reasons they could not celebrate the Passover as we did. And I thought about it and thought about it." She paused and then said, "I want to make the Germans pay for what they did to me. To my family. To yours. You understand that, don't you, Cecilia?"

"I understand, perhaps more than you."

"I guess you do." She smiled sadly. They walked silently for a few steps before Grace continued, "But it's more than that too."

"What is it then?"

She thought, but couldn't answer. "I really don't think I know."

They stood outside their barracks. "I feel as though going in is the point of no return," Cecilia's voice cracked with fear.

"But it will be worth it, whatever it is, if

it helps our families." Grace gently prodded Cecilia through the door. "Come along then. We'd best get to sleep! It sounds like Orde has something up his sleeve for us tomorrow, and we want to be at our best!"

~

WHEN ORDE SAID FIRST THING, he meant it. The ten mile run through the desert began at '0300,' as they said in the armed forces. By the end of the run, forty of the recruits had been eliminated, but Grace kept up with the best of them.

Still heaving and sweating, the remaining recruits were ushered into a brightly lit room filled with long narrow tables. It was exam time. Grace sat down next to a pretty young woman with light brown hair who gave her a gentle smile and extended her hand. "Hannah Senesh. Kibbutz Caesarea."[10]

"Grace Adleman, Kibbutz Kinneret." Grace smiled back. "Good luck."

"You too."

Grace paged through the test and tapped her pencil on the table. It appeared to be primarily math.

Her shirt was stuck to her back, and she longed for a cool bath. She tried not to concentrate on how hungry she was or how thirsty. The blisters on her feet from the run were raw and bleeding. A voice from the back of the room groaned. "Oh dear. I'm sunk! I hate math!"

Stick to the problem at hand, Grace told herself. One problem at a time.

"The lengths of the sides of a triangle in the ratio are 4:3:5. If the perimeter is 18 inches, what are the lengths of the sides?"

Inwardly, Grace breathed a sigh of relief that her father had taken such pains to make sure she understood trigonometry and algebra. The test would be a breeze. She looked up and locked eyes with Morris. He obviously found the test as easy as she did.

Cecilia was having a slightly more difficult time. She crossed her eyes and stuck her tongue out in Grace's direction. She'd handled the run with difficulty but had still finished with enough time to spare to make it to the second phase. Her pale skin looked even more translucent, if such a thing was possible.

Twenty minutes passed. Then forty-five. Each time they finished their booklet of problems, they handed it to the proctor who replenished the recruit with a new set of problems.

The test went on and on. Three hours went by. Grace began to feel dizzy, but still, she pressed through. Several recruits excused themselves, complaining of headaches and the need for water. They'd had no water or food since the middle of the night. Those who left never returned.

Morris raised his hand, "Um… when does the test end?"

"When it's over," the proctor responded sternly.

Without any warning, the door to the room flew open. A crazed soldier wielding a gun brandished it high above his head and began shouting incoherently. One shot was fired, then another.

Many of the recruits dove beneath their desks. In all the confusion, the proctor disappeared.

Grace was rooted to her chair, observing the proceedings as though in slow motion. The gunman opened the window and jumped out, shouting wildly. She saw that he carried the rank of captain on his insignia. His hair was so blonde, it was almost white.

No one moved. A young man whimpered. Two of the women were crying. But not Grace or Cecilia.

Morris, instantly on his feet, shouted, "Somebody's got to go after that guy!" Then, lunging towards the window, he added, "He could shoot someone!" He had one foot out the window and was looking in the direction the crazy man had gone in when Orde Wingate once more appeared.

"That won't be necessary, young man." He looked at the recruits cowering under their desks. "Back in your seats, please." His voice was completely unemotional and flat. "You will wait here until you are called." With that, Orde spun on his heel and left.

For an hour, the recruits waited nervously. Finally, one by one, each young man and woman was called into the hall where the proctor and Orde sat behind a folding table.

By the time Grace's turn came, the surge of adrenaline that came with the gunman's appearance had given way to a wave of exhaustion.

The proctor looked at his list. "Adleman, Grace."

"Yes?"

Orde was looking at a map spread out on the table. He appeared to be unaware of Grace's presence.

"How many shots did the gunman fire?"

"Two," she answered simply.

"And his hair color?"

"Aren't these rather silly questions?" she asked, thinking that they all ought to be out searching for the nut with the gun.

"Just answer the question, Ms. Adleman." The proctor frowned. "We don't have all day."

"Blonde," Grace said decisively.

"Any other details you can remember?"

"I'm guessing he was nearly five foot seven. Small build but agile. And he was a captain."

"Excellent work, Ms. Adleman." Orde looked up from the map, his eyes glowing. "You passed the test."

"I did?"

"You can go eat your breakfast now." He checked a box off a list beside the proctor. "And you will be on the plane to Cairo tonight."

"Really?" she exclaimed.

"Really." Orde smiled and looked back down at the map. "And just between us, Ms. Adleman, you passed the test with flying colors. Not only did you receive higher marks on your exam than any other man or woman recruited for this mission, but you did so while sleep-deprived, dehydrated, hungry, and physically spent. To top it off, when put under extreme stress, you were able to remember not only how many shots the gunman fired but also his rank and hair color. For the record, you are the only recruit, man or woman, who thought to look for the rank."

Grace was stunned.

"Well, off with you then," he chuckled. "And welcome to the RAF."

CHAPTER 16

LIFE, LIBERTY, AND THE PURSUIT OF HAPPINESS

The bookstall on the busy street corner overflowed with newspapers, dime-store novels, magazines, and two types of gum: cinnamon and mint.

Harry picked up one paper, *The New York Times*, and angrily pointed at the headline '*The American Jewish Congress Rally to Show they are Anti-Nazi.*' Then, he huffed under his breath, "No wonder we've been so darned ineffective!"

"What?" Katrine was looking through a small stack of pocket-sized books stacked up against the fashion magazines. "I don't know what 'darned' means, but I have a feeling you shouldn't say it." She looked directly at him. "If we are meeting with Jonas what's-his-name, I expect you to watch your language. He's a politician. We have to be diplomatic about this."

"Jonas Hoffman drinks and swears like a sailor."

"Good heavens."

"But don't worry," he stopped and looked at the newspaper stand for a moment, scanning the headlines, "he'll watch the lingo around you." Then, he looked back at the paper and frowned. "The Jewish Labor Committee refuses to deal with the Nazis at all. The American Jewish Community wants behind-the-scenes diplomacy with Nazi officials, and we all know how that plays out in the long run." He made an ugly face and continued, "And then we have the American Jewish Congress, who holds rallies and boycotts and demonstrations all over the country to show they are anti-Nazi, much good it does actually helping the Jews in Europe who are dying by the minute."[11]

"Harry, please." Katrine glanced at him sideways and then went back to perusing the magazines and little books. One title caught her eye, *Flowers and Their Secret Meanings*.

"And don't get me started on the American Jews who couldn't care less about a Jewish state. Oh sure, they are okay with the Brits opening up Palestine for all 'those poor European Jews' as long as they aren't inconvenienced in the process. And *then*," he dramatically emphasized the word 'then,' "there are others so anti-Zionist that they stage their own demonstrations to show how 'anti-Jewish state' in Palestine they really are. How many crazies are there around here?"

Katrine rubbed her temples. She felt a

headache coming on. There were two at least; Harry and her. Their work was starting to feel futile. Over the two weeks she had been in America, speaking here and speaking there, she too had noticed how divided the Jewish community was. In fact, she had concluded that there was no 'American Jewish community' at all but rather many different communities strung together by the fragile thread of simply being Jews, and, for most of them, new immigrants.

When it came to actually rescuing the Jews in Europe, each group had their own idea of how to best go about it… or not go about it. They had too much to worry about right there on American soil. Best not to rock the boat! Oh yes, best not to rock the boat.

Harry put the paper back on the stand and looked at his watch, "Come on, we've got to get moving. Jonas is going to meet us at Carnegie's in 20 minutes. It's down a little street, 7th Avenue, between 54th and 55th. A new place. I've never been, but Jonas says the pastrami is great." He glanced up at the street sign. "And we're on 52nd. We've got to truck it, young lady."

Katrine inwardly groaned. They had walked all the way from 15th. It had taken two-and-a-half-hours, but it was cheaper than a cab, and the busses were on strike.

"Wait, I want to buy this." She pulled a dime out of her purse and thrust it into the old seller's hand.

"What?"

She pushed the book deep into her purse,

235

brushing up against the seal. It was still there. She touched it reassuringly. "Just some light reading," she flushed slightly, "for when I can't sleep."

Harry scratched his chin and took off walking. "If only we could get everybody to come together, we might get some leverage! Hopefully, we'll be more successful with Jonas than the others." He saw the sign on the street corner. "Make a left turn."

They rounded the corner and were thrust into an enormous crowd of Manhattaners.

"Have you ever noticed how fast everyone walks here?" Katrine said, breathing quickly. She always felt that she and Harry jogged everywhere in New York. Fast, fast, fast! They even talked fast. Sometimes, she had to ask people to slow down to understand them.

"Here we are!" Harry said looking up at a cheerful yellow sign with glowing neon letters that spelled out *Carnegie's* in a dramatic cursive script.[12] Beside it, in blue letters, read *Delicatessen and Restaurant*. "Are you ready to do some politicizing?"

"Obviously." Katrine shrugged "Why else would I be here?"

Harry feigned hurt. "Because a friend offered to take you to lunch."

"Oh yes," she laughed, "I nearly forgot." She could smell the pastrami from the street, along with the brine of pickles and freshly baked rye bread. Her stomach rumbled, and she suddenly realized she was very hungry indeed.

~

OVER A BOWL of sweet and sour cabbage soup, the variety with plump raisins and delicious chunks of brisket, Katrine examined Jonas Hoffman, the secretary to the Secretary of the Treasury, who was none other than Henry Morgenthau.[13] He appeared in his late thirties, was prematurely balding, and wore thin wire glasses. He was the intense sort who didn't seem to ever get enough sleep or eat right.

"Thanks for meeting us again, Jonas," Harry said, plowing into his sandwich stacked with nearly a mile of the deli's famous pastrami.

Jonas didn't touch his 'Giant Homemade Knish,' a dome of golden pastry that was deep fried and filled with potato and pastrami. It was nearly as large as a softball and as heavy as a bowling ball. "When I got your wire that you wanted to come to the Treasury Office in DC, I thought I'd save you the trip. My wife and I are here to visit her sister—she lives off of Broadway. She just had a baby."

"That's nice." Katrine smiled.

"Anything for the Jewish Agency. I really believe in what you guys are doing, Mr. and Mrs. Smith," he smirked at Harry.

"Then you can arrange a meeting with Morgenthau?" Harry said hopefully.

"That," he sighed and began to methodically cut into the knish, "I sadly cannot do."

"Why ever not?" Katrine asked, putting her soup-spoon down. The restaurant buzzed with the midday rush.

Jonas looked at Katrine. "Let me guess. You've got an accent. You're from Austria, or Germany, or Hungary, or Poland, or somewhere like that. The Nazis did terrible things. To you. To your brothers. Your parents. You escaped by the hair of your chinny-chin-chin. Right?"

Katrine's eyes narrowed, and she shook her head yes.

The secretary to the Secretary nodded knowingly. "You and every other nice kid fresh off the boat." Jonas ran his hand over his bald spot. "You all want me to talk to Morgenthau so he can talk to the President. Well, let me tell you something. Morgenthau knows. He knows more than the three of us put together. Roosevelt is stuck between his Congress and his conscience."

Without giving any time for a reply, Jonas plowed ahead. "I've met four others just like you in the last month. They all want me to get my boss to talk to Roosevelt and get him to do something. To open up the border here… which, I can tell you now, will *not* happen. America is determined to stay strictly neutral."

"And you don't think there is any hope that he might change his mind?" Katrine asked. She looked down at her soup. She'd lost her appetite.

"Do you know how hard Roosevelt had to fight Congress to get them to change the neutrality laws enough to sell arms to the *Allies*? They flat-out refused to raise immigration quotas to allow Jewish children from Germany to immigrate last year. Twenty-thousand Jewish children denied entry. The borders are closed."

"We know all of that," Harry said. "Look, the Jews in Palestine know not to depend on American politics. Even if your people could push some sort of solution, temporary housing, escape scenarios, diplomacy, anything through Congress, it would be too little, too late."

"That's true," Jonas said sadly. "And don't I know it." He sighed deeply. "The truth is, the real reason that most Jewish politicians in America won't stand up and demand our government step in is that they are scared of the anti-Semitism in the States. Henry Ford, America's top car manufacturer, rails against what he says is 'the Jewish plan to take over the world,' which is a boatload of hogwash over 1,000 years old, to whoever will listen. Charles Coughlin, a creepy priest on the radio, has an underground army that attacks elderly Jews in the streets of Brooklyn."[14]

"We've heard of them," Harry interjected. "I'm an American too, remember."

"But I bet you haven't heard of Breckinridge Long."[15] He waited for the name to sink in. "The former ambassador to Italy. The guy idolizes Mussolini."

"So what?"

"So what?" Jonas grew red in the face. "He's now the US State Department's man in charge of helping Europe's Jews. He is deliberately creating obstacles for refugees who need visas. And, in my opinion, he's behind many of the walls that have gone up for humanitarian efforts to up immigration quotas. You can tell that to

Ben Gurion. Complements of the US State Department."

"That's abominable." Katrine felt sick.

"That's America, Ms.-? What was your name again?"

"Adleman."

"Right. Adleman. Life, liberty, and the pursuit of happiness apply to all, even those who don't think everyone should have access to those things. It's a blessing and a curse."

Katrine felt her eyes water. They'd been working so hard. She'd told her story to everyone who would listen. Everyone agreed that what was happening was terrible, just terrible, but no one really wanted to do anything about it. They were too scared. Too busy.

"But certainly if people would just listen to us, to what we've seen," Katrine protested.

"Like your boyfriend said," Jonas answered, "it would be too little, too late. Every Jew in America couldn't get Congress to change their minds on immigration because they will never agree on how to go about doing it. My goodness, Congress is practically trying to disband the army, and then we'd be in a real mess. The president is in a bind. But that's not why we are meeting, is it?" Jonas asked, his eyes honing in on Harry.

"Nope." Harry smiled a cocky smile.

Katrine looked at Harry and then Jonas, her face downcast. "So, what's the point of all this? If we can't change the Americans' minds?"

Jonas pushed his plate back. "Hope is not necessarily lost. Not every Jew, but a good many of them have come together. And we've raised a lot of money." He leaned over and whispered across his knish that was, by now, lukewarm. "One hundred and twenty-seven million dollars."

Katrine's jaw dropped. "We can shelter thousands of Jews making their way to neutral countries in Europe and Palestine, isn't that right, Harry?"

"As the good book says," Harry nodded, "if you want something done, stay out of politics."

"And as the good book also says," Jonas chuckled, "'getting that kind of dough out of the country is going to take some finesse.'"

"That's where we come in." Harry looked at Katrine. "You and I, my pretty little bird, are about to be transformed into carrier pigeons."

Katrine blinked several times as this sunk in. She had known they were in America to raise money. That was obvious. Money and support. It had not occurred to her to ask how they were going to get that support back to the Agency. But certainly, they could not just walk out with hundreds of millions of dollars. It was absurd.

"We can't 'carry' that sort of money! What about customs!"

"Keep your voice down, kiddo," Harry shushed her. "It won't be in cash. And it won't be all of it."

"It will just be a couple of million," Jonas clarified. "You two aren't the only Mr. and Mrs. Smith in America."

She glanced around the restaurant nervously. "Aren't you worried about people hearing us?"

Her voice lowered, and she asked, "How are we supposed to accomplish this?"

"We have ways." Jonas drummed his fingers together. "You are one of them. And I'm not worried. Crowds are always the best place to have private conversations."

"I see." Katrine inhaled deeply. Harry patted her hand, as though to say that all of this was quite normal.

Jonas addressed Harry now. "I believe you have a rather nice antiquity on the market? Am I correct in deciphering that cryptic message you sent?"

"It's an important find. Specifically when it comes to public relations." Harry nodded at Katrine.

She took the lead, explaining, "It's the Seal of Baruch, the scribe of Jeremiah. Quite authentic. Priceless." She pulled it out of her purse and unwrapped it, passing it to Jonas.

He held it lightly. "Fascinating. To think that the Prophet Jeremiah might have held this?"

"Baruch definitely held it." Harry smiled.

Katrine took the seal back and carefully wrapped it back up and put it in her purse. "More importantly, it could have been the very seal that was used on the original copies of Jeremiah's texts."

"I know who you need to take it to." Jonas looked a bit nervous as he said softly, "It's all very hush-hush. You have to go to the MET tomorrow." (Katrine did not know what the MET was, but she knew not to ask.) "You won't get what it's worth, that's quite sure. But my friend will make sure it is seen by the public, where it will do the most good. All of New York will know that our ancestors were in the Jezreel Valley long before the British, the French, the Ottomans, the Arabs, or even the Crusaders for that matter."

"Thanks, Jonas." Harry shook the man's hand. "We really appreciate this.

"I only wish I could do more," he answered, pulling a pen out of his pocket and writing out an address on a paper napkin. "I've gone ahead and taken the liberty of buying your 'wife' a birthday present. Here's the address." He pushed the napkin towards Katrine and Harry. "You can pick it up at this address tomorrow night and look over a little order I placed for you."

Harry's eyes narrowed as though he understood, but his voice held a question as he said, "Oh."

"We're not married," Katrine said, an air of tiredness tingeing her voice. The joke was getting old, but Harry didn't seem to mind.

CHAPTER 17

THE COURTYARD CAFE

"You've been doing nothing but study for two months!" Becky shook Lorelei's shoulder. "You have not gone out once. You never get together with the other girls."

Lorelei looked up from her notes. "You, as my teacher, should know how difficult the material is. I have to memorize all of this by tomorrow!"

Becky swooped up the notebook. She was in her bathrobe. It was Friday morning (there were no classes on Friday) and Becky had spent the morning luxuriating on her one day off. She'd washed her hair, and her blond ringlets were hanging loosely from the hand towel she'd swept it up in to dry. She'd made scrambled eggs and toast, which was saying something because on a normal day she barely had time for a cup of coffee. She'd even painted her nails red. And now she was ready for some fun.

"What is the typical symptom of pneumonia?"

"Coarse crackles."

"What is the correct way to use a spirometer?"

"The patient inhales slowly from the spirometer until she can't anymore. And then she holds her breath for six seconds before she exhales."

"Your patient has been diagnosed with pneumonia, and the sputum cultures show that she is infected with a gram-positive bacterium. She's allergic to Penicillin. What do you prescribe?"

"Macrolide?"

"Yes, good." She then asked, "You are prepared to hang a bag of intravenous Vancomycin for your patient who has severe pneumonia. You will *not* hang the bag and will run to find a doctor if the patient—"

"Complains that her mouth tastes like metal… Wait no! It's when they say their ears are ringing."

Becky was exasperated. "You know this stuff inside and out! You will *undoubtedly* ace Pneumonia 101. That's it!" She pulled Lorelei, who was still in her pajamas, to her feet. Pushing her into the bathroom, she demanded that Lorelei get dressed. "We are going to have a real day off. I'm taking you to the Old City. You haven't been yet, have you?"

From behind the door, Lorelei shouted that she had not.

"Good. Because I'm going to take you. And we are going to get dressed up and drink coffee and shop for cheese and pastries and have a wonderful time."

An hour later, Becky and Lorelei, strolled arm in arm through Damascus Gate, an enormous stone structure flanked by two towers. The two blondes, one rather petite, the other taller than average, in their fashionable suits and hats tilted just so, stuck out like the outsiders they were in the strange world of the Muslim Quarter that had changed so little over the centuries.

Young boys pulled wheelbarrows filled precariously with piles of bread or melons. They shouted dramatically for everyone in their path to get out of their way as they raced down the narrow corridors. Lorelei barely escaped being run over by a runaway donkey cart, its owner padding after it breathlessly, yelling in Arabic for it to stop.

To Lorelei, everyone was dressed like they were out of the Bible days. If it was not for the radios in several of the stalls blaring modern music, she would have sworn they'd stepped back in time.

"Let's see," Becky stopped and looked to her left and her right, "I want to get to Jaffa Street. I think it's that way!"

The stones they walked on were slippery, and Lorelei had to concentrate so as not to trip or slip. Her neat little shoes had very little tread.

Becky smiled at Lorelei and said, "Hold on to your purse! We are diving in!" And off they went. A baker covered in flour shouted from a stall for the girls to step inside. The smell of the hot bread baking in the giant open wood-fire oven was enormously tempting. As Becky pulled Lorelei onward, the baker took pity on Lorelei and threw her a small roll covered in sesame seeds and winked at her. She blushed down to her toes and nodded her thanks. She passed a chunk to Becky, who munched on it approvingly, brushing the crumbs away with her gloved hand.

Becky was moving quickly through the narrow streets, barely six feet across in some places.

The skinned goats hanging outside the butchers whizzed past, along with the flies. Long dresses and bangles and linens blurred into a colorful jumbled quilt. It was all a blur: ornately carved boxes inlaid with mother-of-pearl, antique dealers, and men selling pomegranate juice squeezed with a clever device that seemed to crush all life from the ruby red seeds in an instant.

They narrowly avoided the water-men, with their large copper pots of water and cups hanging from a poll balanced across their shoulders—a drink for a penny—and wheelbarrows of muddy produce pushed by barefoot boys clanging precariously across the cobblestones. Lorelei imagined how dangerous it would be to be caught in a riot in the corridors linking the narrow streets together, all bound up by the 16th-century wall, built by the Crusaders, like a belt. You could easily be trapped with nowhere to go. That was saying nothing of how easy it would be to get lost!

At noon, a loud gong began to ring. And then,

a Muezzin from the Dome of the Rock sounded out the call to prayer. A procession of priests passed them, each carrying a large wooden cross while chanting, scattering a gang of street urchins. Some British soldiers pushed through, nodding politely at Lorelei and Becky. It was an utter clash of worlds, old and new. Lorelei's senses threatened to explode.

Becky rounded a corner, and there was peace, utter and complete.

"We made it!" she announced triumphantly. "The Courtyard Cafe!"

"Where are we?" Lorelei's eyes swept over what appeared to be a walled garden. There were about 10 tables, each occupied by Europeans by the looks of it. There were several British officers, who looked in their direction the moment that they entered, and an elderly woman and her daughter. The hubbub of the city outside was drowned out by a fountain.

"It belongs to a church, Christ Church. That's it," she pointed across the courtyard, "right there."

"It doesn't look like a church," Lorelei answered. "It looks more like a synagogue."

Becky crossed the courtyard quickly and walked up the steps of the church. "Come see this," she said, beckoning Lorelei to follow. She pushed the heavy wooden door open. "Look." Becky stepped inside the church's cool stone interior.

Inside the courtyard, it had been quiet. Inside the church, it was silent. They could practically hear their breath echoing off the stone walls.

"What do you see, Lorelei?"

Lorelei looked and looked, and then she saw it; there was Hebrew scripture inscribed all over the building. By all shapes *and* appearances, it was a synagogue.

"The bishop who built the church, oh, nearly 80 years ago, was a Jewish convert to Christianity and an Englishman by birth, Michael Solomon Alexander.[16] He lectured on Hebrew and Rabbinic literature at King's College in London," Becky said simply.

"Why in the world did he come here?" She had never been in a church like this! Though in all honesty, Lorelei wasn't sure she had ever been in a church before.

"He was chosen to be the first Anglican Bishop in the Middle East. I think he wanted other Jews who met the Messiah to feel at home."

"Jews who met the Messiah?"

"Well, yes. That's who Jesus—or Yeshua, as he is called in Hebrew—is. He's the Messiah!" Becky exclaimed. "Anyway, Bishop Alexander came here when Jerusalem was still a dirty backwater town in the Ottoman Empire. They say he was convinced that the children of Israel would return to the Promised Land. And then," she paused.

"And then what?" Lorelei asked, looking at the engraved Hebrew letters surrounding what appeared to be the bema. She was still thinking about what Becky had said about Jesus being the Messiah. For Becky, and for the man who had built this place, Christianity was simply a continuation of Judaism. She had never heard anyone talk about it like that. It made her feel strange and uncomfortable, though, in truth, she knew very little about either faith.

"And that then God would pour out his Spirit on them and all mankind. I never really gave those prophecies much thought, but now…" She looked at Lorelei. "Well, here you are."

"Here I am," Lorelei answered, not at all sure of what Becky was talking about. She decided not to ask.

"And more of you keep coming!"

Becky pushed the door back open, and the women stepped into the sunlight. "He built the first modern hospital in the region. Everyone came to it. The Jewish community in Palestine at the time had no money at all, and the Muslims had even less. He also set up a college. It's just behind the cafe."

"You know a lot about this place," Lorelei said, looking back at the building.

"I worship here when I've got a Sunday off." Becky selected a table and sat down. "It's always an adventure getting here." She took off her gloves and adjusted her hat. Then, she leaned her head back, absorbing the sun. She relished life, every moment of it.

Lorelei studied her closely. Becky was a mystery to her, always moving with such energy, such purpose. She always thought about others and never seemed to think of herself. And yet, she was genuinely happy. Happiness was a mystery to Lorelei, come to think of it.

"Tea," Becky told the waiter. "The whole works." He nodded wordlessly and left the young women alone.

"They have the best tea in Jerusalem. When I get lonely for home, I come here." Becky inhaled and exhaled. The air was sweet from the flowers hanging in baskets. It was a paradise, a true oasis in a city that was constantly wild and strange to a country girl from Ireland.

"Are you lonely for home?"

Becky nodded wistfully. "Something about spring I guess. Ireland in springtime."

"Yes," Lorelei answered. "I suppose there is something about spring that makes you miss things."

"Or people."

"Yes," Lorelei repeated. Against her will, the thought of Rolf surfaced, along with a fresh wave of grief. She missed him. Oh, how she missed him. She fingered her bracelet.

The table of British officers stood and prepared to leave. "Ladies," they each said, bowing slightly as they passed the girls' table.

"Hello," Becky answered. She wasn't unkind, but she was not interested in any future conversation either. Lorelei didn't bother to say hello.

"He liked you, I think," Lorelei said when the young men had left. "The one with bright blue eyes."

"I'm waiting for someone very specific." Becky looked down at her hands. "God's timing matters. It's not my time yet." She smiled playfully and added, "You could have been a little friendlier yourself, you know. He *was* kind of cute."

Lorelei shrugged. She hadn't noticed.

"Oh, I see how it is. Do you have a friend in the corner?"

"What?"

"You know, a special someone?"

She shook her head. "No. I mean, uh, I did."

Becky didn't press. "I see," was all she said, and rather quietly at that. "Gone, I take it?"

Dead. Along with everything else she'd ever cared about, Lorelei thought. But instead, she just said, "Becky, I'm not interested in finding love. I had it once and lost it. I don't think I can ever go through anything like that ever again. A part of me died the day—" She stopped abruptly.

The waiter appeared and set an elaborate silver tea service down. As he poured, another waiter carried a tiered tray filled with little sandwiches and cakes.

Becky poured two cups and handed one to Lorelei. "Here's what you need, dear." She began to distribute the treats. "Ooh, there's some brown bread and butter, oh, and gingerbread, and a potted salmon sandwich."

She slid a few little fish onto the plate. "I think these are fried herrings."

"That will fix everything, won't it?" Lorelei smiled cynically at the little oily fish.

"No," Becky answered, "but this damson cheese might."

"That looks nothing like cheese."

"That's because it's actually a paste made of damson plums and sugar." She looked straight into Lorelei's eyes. "Really though, you're too

young for that sort of attitude. I should know."
She stirred her tea gently. "Trust me, you'll
find love again. Just give your heart time to
heal."

"I don't understand you," Lorelei said after a
moment, watching Becky.

"How so?"

Lorelei paused, dipping her fork in and out of
the little pot of plummy spread, not knowing
where to begin. "When I was a little girl, my
mother took my sisters and me to a pet shop in
Berlin. They had fish and kittens and puppies,
all very fluffy, very cute. It was my sister
Grace's birthday. She was turning 8 and her
present was to be a kitten. We got one, a pretty
black one with white socks, and we named it
Flomar."

"Flomar?"

"Yes, Ramolf backward. Ramolf was a friend of
my father's who we loved to pick on."

"I see," Becky said, trying to follow.

"Anyway, as Grace and Katrine oohed and awed
over the kittens and tried to choose just the
right one, I wandered the store and came across
the hamsters."

"The hamsters."

"Yes. The hamsters." Lorelei's eyes took on a
distant look. She was back in that pet store.
"There were two little hamsters in a cage. One
was running on the hamster wheel, and I was
mesmerized. I'd never seen anything like it. All
that running, and yet, going absolutely nowhere.
All of a sudden, the hamster's foot got caught

in the wire. It was stuck, you see, and my heart was terrified for it. It was so light, that the wheel kept spinning, and the little hamster was dangling for its life."

"This is horrific."

"It gets worse. The other hamster jumped on the wheel and began to run, jumping over the stuck hamster every time the wheel came around."

Becky put her cup down, her mouth slightly open.

"Oh, it turned out alright. Hamster number one eventually became unstuck and stumbled out of the wheel. I was pressed up close to the glass, very concerned over its paw. But it was fine. The little creature shook itself off, jumped right back on, and began to run nowhere once more."

"And which hamster are you Lorelei? Number one or number two?"

"Both. Neither." Lorelei shrugged. "It doesn't matter. I was once going somewhere, and then Hitler came, and I got stuck. And hurt. And now I feel that I am running, running, running. And I will be, the rest of my life."

"You know, the hamster was all right. He brushed himself off and kept going."

"Yes," Lorelei nodded. "And I've done that. But sometimes it still feels like I'm going nowhere."

"You don't have to keep running, you know," Becky said slowly.

Lorelei did not answer.

Becky waited and then said, "What I meant was,

you don't have to run nowhere. You need a purpose."

"I thought nursing would be that purpose. But it's not working. I still feel like I'm going around and around."

"Of course you do!" Becky was not surprised.

Lorelei leveled her gaze on Becky. Her roommate was totally unflustered.

"A profession is never a direction."

"What then?"

"People. Or rather, one person in particular."

"But he's dead."

"No. I don't mean him. I mean Yeshua."

"I know you are a Christian." Lorelei met Becky's gaze. Jesus was a name that brought pain and suffering and the threat of mobs and violence towards the Jews who 'had killed the savior.' She could never understand how her Aunt Rose had ever converted to become one of them. It was something the Adleman family never discussed.

"But you don't know what that means to me." Becky continued. "It doesn't mean tradition or history, though that's a part of it. It means relationship. It means the end of loneliness."

Lorelei didn't answer.

"And because of Yeshua, I have a reason to keep going. Not around and around, but forward."

"What does that even mean?"

"It means that everything has a purpose, because he suffered and died, and I believe he rose again. And it means at the end of the road, there is hope, joy, and freedom."

If it had been anyone else, Lorelei would have

laughed out loud. But she could not. Becky was deadly serious.

"Don't you want those things?" Becky pressed.

Lorelei felt crushed by the weight of her pain, "Of course I want them! But Becky, sometimes I miss Rolf so much! How can there be more to my life? I can't imagine a happy future without him. I can't imagine a future at all."

"I am going to pray for you if you don't mind?"

"Pray away."

"Father God," Becky prayed, her Irish shining through, "Thank you for sending me your dear daughter. And I pray that she would learn just how dear of a daughter she is to you, and how much you love her and care for her." Becky waited silently, her eyes still shut.

At first, this made Lorelei feel awkward. But as she was beginning to squirm, a strange, warm peace seemed to envelop her. The courtyard and all the other people dining on caramel cake and drinking out of fine hand painted porcelain drifted away, as though in a dream. She felt her heartbeat, one beat at a time, and for the first time in her life, Lorelei was at rest.

Becky opened her eyes that looked, if possible, even more brilliantly blue. "Oh, Lorelei," she reached out and grabbed her friend's hand, "God has a purpose for your life, *still*. Just as he has for me. And it is wonderful and mysterious and precious. Don't throw it away running nowhere just to fill the time. Run to God. Run to Yeshua."

"How?" Lorelei breathed.

"Ask and he'll show you. He didn't bring you here for nothing. He brought you here for something."

From her seat, Lorelei watched all of Jerusalem pass by and she shook her head slowly. She didn't understand. But she wanted to. She really, really wanted to.

CHAPTER 18

MAKING THE JUMP

"Oh my goodness," Cecilia said over and over again, "I don't like this at all! Not one bit!"

The plane jostled its passengers terribly. Several had become sick.

"It's just turbulence," Morris said. "Chaotic changes in pressure and flow. There's no danger at all. Usually."

"How would you know?"

"I read about it. I read about things," he responded.

Hannah sat across the aisle. She looked at Morris approvingly. "You like to read Morris?" The pensive, thoughtful woman watched Grace, who was glued to the window.

When she turned back towards Morris and Cecilia, Grace's eyes shone, "I absolutely love flying! Can you believe it? Look down there! Did you ever think you would see such a thing!"

"I could write a poem," Hannah agreed, turning out to look through her own window. "It's very inspiring!"

"I can't look," Cecilia shut her eyes and leaned her head against the wall. It had been a very difficult flight for the young girl. "All I want is to be on solid ground again. And I thought being sea-sick was bad." She groaned, "Why are we doing this again?"

Hannah leaned over and held her hand, "We were called, so we went."[17]

"That's pretty," Morris said. "Very poetic."

"I write poetry." She grinned, "I wrote a lot of poems when I moved to the kibbutz at Caesarea."

She began once more, her voice taking on an eerie, philosophical tone. "We've all lost those we love. We've cried for our loss. And now, we are going to do something about it."

The four friends did not speak, the engine drowning out their thoughts.

Cecilia squeezed Hannah's hand, sending her a silent thank you through her eyes.

The plane pitched forward slightly and from the window, a great gleaming white city rose out of the desert. "Nine out of ten, that's Cairo!" Grace paused, "Oh my, Cecilia, you have to look! It's the pyramids!"

Grace was right, it was the pyramids. Enormous triangles loomed behind the enormous city. Everything was glowing white in the midday sun. It was late May, but the heat was felt by everyone in the plane. It penetrated the cabin.

Slowly, the plane turned and descended. The

wind from the desert was picking up. It threw the plane this way and that. Morris, clenching his fist together shouted, "It's totally safe everyone, I did read about it!"

"Shut up!" Someone shouted from the back of the plane.

Moments later, the plane touched down, bounced for a brief second of terror, and then touched down again, stayed down and rolled to a stop.

Grace beamed. "Wow. That was invigorating! Don't you think so?" She turned to Cecilia and Morris. But Morris had his eyes closed and his head bowed, "Baruch Ha'Shem," he uttered beneath his breath. Cecilia was staring straight ahead and refused to look at her back.

She locked eyes with Hannah, and the two of them broke out laughing. Only 10 women had made the final cut to go to Egypt; she, Hannah, and Cecilia were among them. They were Palestine's finest. And they were officially on Egyptian soil.

"I'LL TELL you all right now, you won't have any time to visit the pyramids. You kids are going to be too busy in this outfit, we've got too much to do in too little time." Captain O'Rourke stroked his handlebar mustache and looked penetratingly into the faces of the new Jewish Unit of volunteers. His strong Yorkshire accent tempted Grace to smile, but she knew it would have been terribly rude. This was a serious moment.

"You are all wearing your new uniforms." He bellowed. "You all have been cleared by the air surgeon. You are young. Eager. Smart. The best your people have to offer. But I am going to make you better."

Captain O'Rourke stood under a strange wooden structure out in the desert, about a mile from the Cairo RAF Base. "And it begins right here!"

He pointed his cane upwards, "This is *trainasium*." Smiling at the structure proudly, he struck one of the wooden beams with a thump, thump, thump. "A 60-ft high aerial assault course."

"It looks like a jungle gym," one young man snickered.

Captain O'Rourke's look silenced him, "I'll pretend I didn't hear that." He looked lovingly back at the structure, "This 'jungle gym' is going to test you to the limit. By running, crawling, and jumping off of it, it simulates the exit phase of a parachute jump out of a plane."

Cecilia whispered in Grace's ear, her voice tinged with panic, "And I thought it was bad enough riding in a plane. Now they want us to jump out of one, and willingly!"

"Quiet young lady!" O'Rourke shouted. "It's a process that builds bodies and spirits. Now, move, move, move!"

Move, move, move! Move, move, move!

They were words Grace would dream about for the next two weeks. It seems they were the only words Captain O'Rourke knew how to say, that is, except for, "faster, faster, faster!"

"I wish you could see him Lorelei," she wrote in the first letter she was able to send to her sister in Jerusalem, "He is rather pompous and, dare I say it, foolish, in his bearing. But, endearing all at the same time."

She paused, not knowing what to write next. She couldn't say where she was, that was a secret. She tapped her pencil on the small desk in the tent that Hannah, Cecilia, and she shared.

"The training has gotten a lot harder. They have us jumping from 60-foot-tall towers to simulate jumping from an airplane. They strap us into these leather harnesses and we slide very quickly from the tower to ground. It really feels like we are flying, if just for a moment. Yesterday, they had us stand in front of a giant wind machine so we can learn how to handle a parachute on the ground after landing. How you would have laughed! It took Cecilia and me an hour to brush the tangles out of our hair after all of that. The boys have it easier. And tomorrow, they are going to drop us from a 200-foot-tall tower in a parachute chair. It's supposed to give us the sensation of 'coming down quickly.' Sounds like fun, don't you think?"

Grace read over what she'd written and crossed out all the parts about the parachute and the tower. It was too much information if the enemy were to intercept it.

Poor Lorelei, she would have a very difficult time making sense of this letter.

Oh well, Grace shrugged. Some information was

better than none. She'd learned enough information at the Cairo Base to last her forever, she concluded. She knew her parachute inside and out. Every fold, piece by piece, cord by cord. Next week, they would have their first real jump.

"And Lorelei, you remember Cecilia, don't you? Well, she complains all the time of being afraid, but just between us, she's one of the bravest of the bunch. She grits her teeth and plunges in like some sort of heroine from the novels Katrine used to read to us. Sometimes, she can barely keep up. But still, she hangs on. I wouldn't be surprised if she is selected to be among the 32 at the end of all this. Oh yes, that's right, I didn't tell you. Not all of us will be going to wherever they are sending us. Out of the 110 here, only a handful will actually be selected. I want to be selected so badly I could cry."

She looked out her tent flap at the open desert. She could see the outline of Cairo on the horizon, and the pyramids behind it.

"It's very beautiful here." She wrote and stared at it. The Germans couldn't get anything out of that, could they? "And historic. Morris is very excited by all the history. You should hear him talk!"

Cecilia popped her head into the tent. Her RAF issue trousers were too big for her tiny waist, and she had an oversized men's sweater pushed up over her elbows. She looked like a little girl dressed up in her older brother's clothing, "You coming to dinner?"

Looking up, "Yeah. Just let me finish this letter."

"I'll save you a seat." Cecilia turned on her heel and disappeared while Grace looked back down at the sheet of paper.

"Well," she wrote, "I have no idea where Katrine is in America, so I can't write her. But can you tell her I'm just fine and not to worry about me. I know she worries over us so. I love you forever, Grace."

Grace folded the letter, addressed it, and stamped it. Then, she quickly rolled down the sleeves to her khaki shirt and tied the laces to her boots. She carefully put the letter in her pocket and dropped it in the mail slot next to the mess tent. There was a great deal of talk coming from inside the tent, along with the clatter of tin forks against tin plates.

"Here!" Cecilia shouted over the din when she saw Grace's form appear in the tent's opening. "Over here, Grace!"

Grace spotted her and waved, taking her tray of tinned vegetable hash and a glass of milk (powdered, of course), and made her way to the table at the back.

"Did you see the paper today?" Cecilia asked eagerly. "Everyone's talking about it!"

"No." Grace shook her head. "I was out on the trainasium all day taking my harness on and off and on again. I've got it down to 60 seconds."

"Not bad," Morris looked up, "But you've got to get it down to 30."

"Thanks, wise-guy." Grace's eyes traveled to the paper that was spread out between her friends. She began to read and let out a low whistle. "Wow, while we've been climbing around jungle gyms in the desert, these guys have been…" she let out another whistle. And then said, her eyes wide, "Why look! It's Peter! It's Peter!"

She stared at the picture of a tall handsome man on a little fishing boat. He was being awarded a medal of some sort.

Hannah leaned over her shoulder. "Who's Peter?"

"Why, he's my cousin's fiancé! He's gone and made himself a hero!"

Grace looked closer, "And if it isn't Horatio! And Frank! They were there! At the battle!"

The newspaper told the whole story, of how the British War Office made the decision to evacuate the British forces trapped on the beach of Dunkirk in France on May 25. In a herculean feat of ingenuity, a fleet of British sailboats, fishing vessels, and motorboats successfully helped over 300,000 men escape the oncoming Germans.

Grace carefully tore the photograph of her future cousin-in-law, Horatio, and Frank, the rough around the edges, good as gold, dearest type of friend. Seeing their faces in the picture pricked her heart with a homesickness she hadn't felt in a very long time. "I've got to send this to my cousin, Piper. She'll flip out when she sees that Peter's photograph made it all the way to Cairo."

"I think she'll flip out when she finds out

you're going to be hurdling yourself out of a plane," Hannah added.

"Yeah," she sighed and looked at Morris, who was shoveling the tasteless goo into his mouth, "It's too bad I can't tell her."

"That's the problem with secret missions. You can't tell anyone. Not that I have anyone to tell." Morris sighed sadly and kept eating. "Cecilia here already knows all my secrets. I can't impress her with anything."

"You've been trying to impress me?" She looked at Morris, slightly surprised.

"Couldn't you tell?"

Morris looked at Grace and shrugged, "See what I mean?"

~

O'Rourke's mustache looked extra red if such a thing was possible. The plane was ready, and so were his men, and "uh," he coughed, "women."

"In you go! You know where your objective landing is. A truck will pick you up and drive you back to base once you complete your first jump. I'm not going to lie to you. We have lost some people doing this. Your emergency cord is there for a reason!" He frowned, "Load up!"

"I'll see you when you come back. I'm in the next group." Cecilia raced up and gave Grace a quick hug.

"What about Morris?"

"I'm with you," he said, coming up behind her. "So? What do you think?"

"I'm impressed, I'm impressed." Cecilia

laughed nervously. "Just promise me you'll both come down in one piece."

"Amen to that," Morris said. He wore his skull cap under his helmet.

Grace and the rest of the first time jumpers loaded into the plane as the engine roared to life. For the second time in her life, she found herself by some miraculous power hovering above the earth. Her helmet felt very tight, and the goggles were uncomfortable. The jumpsuit was wildly hot, but she supposed it would be handy later on. Europe was colder than the North African desert.

The jump-master stood near the opening in the back of the plane. It was so loud, he had to yell, "Stand up!" And a second later, "Hook static lines!"

All twenty stood. Each one helped the one next to them with their last-minute checkup. Tensely, they waited for the order. Then, the order came. "Jump!"

Within 10 seconds, all 20 recruits were out of the plane. A rush of hot air. The elation of free falling. For Grace, it was over almost before it began. The jolt as her parachute opened. And then, a strange peaceful silence. Skillfully, she worked the lines of her parachute to guide her to the target. Then, the earth coming closer and closer and closer. Her feet were moving, running, and suddenly, she made contact. Within a minute she had the chute off and was ready for action with her rifle and mock demolition kit. In the words of O'Rourke, a paratrooper must be able to handle just about anything. In their spare time, each of the Jewish recruits had been studying everything from breaking codes to how to survive in the jungle. It would take the ability to withstand overwhelming odds if they were going to come back from behind enemy lines alive.

Several yards away, Morris came in for landing.

"Morris!" Grace called out, "You're going too fast!"

"I can't slow down!"

It was too late. "Incoming!" He shouted as he crashed painfully upon the hardened desert sand. Writing and twisting on the ground in pain, he moaned over and over, "My ankle. Ah!"

She examined it quickly, "Not broken. Bad sprain though. Looks like you are getting a couple of days off." Grace helped him get the chute off and let him lean on her as they made their way to the truck. "Count your blessings, at least it wasn't your head."

"Baruch Hashem." Then, limping, "Do you think Cecilia will be impressed?"

"Morris, do you have a crush on Cecilia?"

He stopped walking and answered thoughtfully, "Well, yes. I suppose I do." He blushed, "I know. She's an older woman."

Grace chuckled, "Well, I don't know if she will be impressed, but I certainly am. It's not everyone who will just throw themselves out of a plane." Then she added, "But didn't you just love it?"

"I hated every minute." Morris groaned. "If

God wanted men to fly, he would have given them wings."

"Oh, but he did Morris! He did." She looked up at the plane of the second group hovering above their heads. A fresh wave of white parachutes opened and began to flutter towards them. "Look! Look at them! It's the most beautiful thing I've ever seen."

"If you ask me," Morris said as he climbed into the truck, carefully avoiding putting weight on his ankle, "I think if you like being up there so much, you ought to learn how to fly."

"Learn to fly?" Grace stopped before throwing her parachute into the truck. "I never thought of that!" A wave of excitement rushed over her. "Why, do you think they would let me learn to fly?"

GRACE EMERGES

～

"She stopped," I said. The thump, thump, thump of Grace's feet on the ceiling had slowed and finally silenced.

The remains of uneaten French toast and cold coffee sat lifelessly on the table. Peter looked out to the sea from his seat which faced the kitchen window. It was a beautiful, clear morning.

"Did you ever jump out of an airplane, Peter?" I asked, not moving to begin clearing the dishes. I had Founder in my arms now, and she was teething on my finger.

He looked at me, a funny smile on his mouth. "I was in the Navy, remember? Boats?"

"Well, I know *that*." I shrugged. "I was just wondering... You were in the war. Things happen."

"I never jumped out of a plane." He drummed his fingers on the table and looked at me with an expression I had not seen in a long, long time. "Piper, I don't think we are supposed to go to Boston."

I was shocked. "Whatever do you mean?"

"Just that." He looked back out the window. "I don't think we are supposed to go."

I felt a little miffed. "Don't you think we should discuss this?"

"That's what we are doing right now."

Gently, I put Founder back in her box. "What's all this about? What happened?"

"It's something I've been feeling the last day or two. A feeling I can't seem to shake. I can't see us in Boston. Not yet. Maybe one day…" His eyes met mine. "But I was reading last night before I went to sleep."

I remembered I'd found my pocket Bible open to Psalm 23.

"God brought us here. And he hasn't told us to leave yet." He paused, and then continued, "I'm not going to fight him anymore on how I think my future should look. I've raised my flag of surrender."

"But," I struggled, "there's nothing for us to do here."

"Not yet. But I think something is coming." He pointed at the manuscript. "Edie wrote in the chapter before the last one we read that Lorelei felt like a hamster on a wheel. I think us going to Boston is us getting right back on that wheel. A profession is not a calling, she said. I need my calling before I get started in a profession. I'm not ready yet Piper. I'm not strong enough yet." He stretched his leg out carefully. "But I will be, by and by. Just you wait."

My throat constricted. Is this what God had been trying to tell me the night before? That we might be spending more time in the green pastures of the lighthouse than I had anticipated?

It's not that I didn't like the lighthouse… Though it was dawning on me that I had been banking on Boston to solve so many of our problems. It would cure the boredom, the need to 'do something.' And now my husband was telling me he wanted to wait on God!

"Of course, I want to wait on God too, but can't we wait on him in Boston?" I said.

"I think he wants us to wait *here*." He had that decisive look I'd grown not to argue with.

Swallowing and looking about the kitchen, I choked out, "But what are we supposed to *do* here? What about school?"

"Harvard has an extension program," he replied. "And I was thinking I might build a sailboat or something."

"A sailboat?"

"Yeah." He smiled. "Can't you see it, me, you, and Founder? The wind blowing through our hair?"

I was about to add, "And how are we supposed to live on the 'wind blowing through our hair,'" when Grace appeared.

Peter looked at her and pronounced, "You look terrible!"

I shot him a silencing look and turned to Grace. She was pale, had dark circles, and her hair was a wreck. She was in the flannel night dress I'd loaned her and had on two pairs of thick socks. In her hand was the mystery letter—*opened*.

"It's all right, Piper," she said. "He's right. I must look as bad as I feel."

I was standing up now, pressing my hand to her forehead. She didn't have a fever, which was a good sign. She obviously had not slept all night. I pulled her down into one of the kitchen chairs and poured a large glass of milk and set it in front of her. "We just read all about you jumping out of planes."

"Yeah." She didn't crack a smile.

"You were very brave to do that."

"Yeah," she repeated.

Peter looked at me, worried.

Before I could say anything else, she threw the letter on the table. "I can't talk to Katrine! She's up on the top of Masada in the middle of some crazy archeological dig, and she only lectures me because she thinks she's always right. And Lorelei—" she stopped suddenly before plunging back in, "Well, she's one of you now."

"One of us now?" I asked, confused.

"Yes." She didn't explain. "I feel uncomfortable talking with her."

"Do you feel uncomfortable talking to us?" I looked at Peter.

"Well... no." She rubbed her eyes that were starting to moisten. "I guess not. I just don't understand so much. And," she looked towards the door, "how can you just 'settle down' when there's so much world out there?"

"Grace," Peter took her hand from across the table, "you are not making any sense."

"I guess I'm not." She glared at the milk and gave Peter the letter with her other hand. "Read this."

Peter cautiously took the letter and read slowly, "Grace, I'm worried you didn't hear me when you jumped out over Hungary. I've been sending letters everywhere and only just heard from Katrine that you are in Maine. So, I'm asking you again, will you marry me?" He paused and said, "Ummm... he didn't sign it."

"Didn't need to. It's from Amos."

"The guy from the kibbutz?"

She nodded.

"Is this a bad thing?" Peter asked, holding the letter.

"No." She shook her head. "No, of course not. It's just... well, my friends are dying behind enemy lines. It seems to me a pretty stupid time to just go and get married." Peter and I looked at one another and Grace stopped and said, "No offense."

"None taken." Peter looked back at her. "This is why you are here, isn't it?"

"I admit it. I'm a coward. I can't tell the poor guy 'yes'... and I can't tell him 'no' either." She inhaled sharply. "I've got to get back in the war," she said firmly. "I can't do that as a married woman."

"But what if," I said quietly, "you can do more good together than apart?"

"Now you're sounding like Lorelei."

"Is that such a bad thing?" I asked.

Her face showed her inner conflict. "I... I don't want to talk about it." Nervously, her lips twitched, and she reached for the manuscript. "Here, how about I read to you both?"

"I thought you didn't want to read it 'because you lived it.'" I began to clear the dishes.

She ignored me and plowed in, choosing not to see the knowing glance Peter and I shared as I began to start yet another fresh pot of coffee.

CHAPTER 19

KATRINE'S MISTAKE

"It certainly appears to be authentic." Stewart Greenspan held the seal in his bony fingers. He was an older gentleman with a soft British accent. "If not, it is the best forgery I've ever seen."

"It's not a forgery," Harry looked at Katrine, "you have my word."

"Oh," Stewart looked up, "I was not implying it was a forgery. Between the report from your friends at the Hebrew University in Jerusalem and my own analysis, I am satisfied the piece is genuine. At least, as to the date. The seal is certainly a contemporary of the Biblical prophet Jeremiah's scribe, Baruch. Whether it is the same Baruch… well, we'll never know." His eyes sparkled slightly and returned to the seal.

"How much can you give us for it?" Harry asked bluntly.

Stewart was a smart sort. The old man turned

his sharp eyes on Harry and Katrine. The museum had had its fair share of those like 'Mr. and Mrs. Smith.' He knew that the seal was probably smuggled into the country, that Harry and Katrine, or whoever they were, were middlemen to those who had found it or traded for it covertly. But like museums all over the world, they had a 'don't ask, don't tell' policy when it came to buying new pieces for the collection.

"Of course, of course." The old man wrote a number on a piece of paper and pushed it towards Harry and Katrine. Katrine's eyes saw the number: $10,000. So much and so little simultaneously. "It will do?"

Harry frowned. "$15,000 and you have a deal."

The man shook his head. "The Metropolitan Museum of Art is only prepared to offer $10,000. I am not authorized to pay you anymore." *This* was the mysterious 'MET' Jonas had mentioned at the deli, Katrine deduced.

Harry was firm. "We won't take less than $15,000."

Steward sniffed and put the seal carefully back on his desk. "I'll write you a check now for $12,500. Take it or leave it."

"We'll take it." Harry nodded. "You can make it out to my wife and me, Mr. and Mrs. Smith."

"Of course." Stewart pulled out his checkbook. "Mr. and Mrs. Smith."

He folded the check carefully in half and gave it to Katrine. "I hope you enjoy your time in New York."

"Thank you," she said, putting the check into her purse as Harry helped her up from her chair.

Their next stop was the bank so the check could be wired to their joint account in a bank in Switzerland. Which, unknown to Katrine, yet another Mrs. Smith would draw on to pay bribes to German soldiers at the border.

Stewart showed them to the door of the small office on the upper level of the museum and pointed to the left. "The most straightforward way out of this maze is down those stairs and through the European Arms and Armor exhibit."

Katrine nodded tersely as the door shut, leaving her and Harry in the cavernous hall. "Right," Harry said. "That way!"

Katrine's heels clicked across the marble floor and down the steps in rhythm with Harry's duller thud of rubber soles. She was shaking her head in disbelief as they made their way through the museum.

"What a strange morning," she sighed. Her purse felt rather light now that the seal was gone.

"A lot of money is going to be flowing in and out of that account, Mrs. Smith. Your country thanks you." Harry smiled kindly. They were the only two in the whole museum, or so it seemed.

"I don't have a country, remember?" From Germany to Scotland, to Palestine, to America… who knew where she would end up.

Rounding the corner, they were met by a magnificent model of a horse wearing a full suit of armor, a knight perched on its back. The armor appeared to be quite old. Katrine paused, sensing something was not quite right.

"What is it?" Harry asked.

She leaned over and read the small inscription, sighing, "That explains it."

"Explains what?"

She pointed at the helmet. "See those markings? They are quite unusual really. Apparently, these are pre-15th century. They found it on the Greek island of Euboea when the Venetian fortress at Chalcis fell to the Turks." She spun on her heel, walking away. "Not long ago, I would have given anything to visit this exhibit and perhaps spend three or four months doing research. It's a historian's dream."[1]

"And now?"

"I have the distinct feeling I've moved from studying history to becoming a part of it." A thought struck her, and she looked at Harry. "You know, I'm not sure I like the idea of the seal in this place."

"What do you mean?"

"It belongs in Palestine," she said firmly.

"It belongs where it can save the most lives. We were tasked to sell the seal, and we did."

"But we can't let our treasures just slip out of hands like that." She snapped her fingers on the last word. "One day, our children will need to know that—" She stopped, embarrassed by how much her heart hurt to let the little clay object go.

"Our children will need to know what?" Harry smirked.

"Oh stop it. You know what I'm saying." She began walking again. "Our national treasures belong in our nation."

"Technically, we don't have one yet, as you so aptly just reminded me.

"Well, when we get one," she rubbed her temples, "I'm going to get the seal back. Maybe even open up my own museum."

"That's very industrious of you." He chuckled. "I can see it now, 'The Mrs. Smith Wing.'" He glanced around. "Do you want to look through any of the exhibits? I heard there's a great new one on Ancient Egyptian stuff. King Tut."

"I don't think so," Katrine answered slowly.

"Really?" Harry was surprised.

"Really." She shrugged. "I've had enough old things for a while. Let's do something *new*. That is, if we have some 'minutes to die,' as you Americans say."

"I think you mean 'time to kill.' And yes, we have the rest of the day. Our last appointment is not until later tonight, nine o'clock to be precise."

"Then let's go and have some real fun!"

"Real fun?"

"Yes." Katrine looked up into his eyes. "Some real fun. Heaven knows how long we are going to live to enjoy ourselves."

"The New York World's 1939 Fair, Coney Island." Katrine glanced at her ticket and then looked up. "But it's 1940, Harry." The whole entrance was decked out in red, white, and blue bunting.

It was a Saturday, and it seemed the whole world had come to the World's Fair; kids, teenagers, families, couples on dates eating cotton candy and walking arm in arm. Loud music from various side shows blared onto the midway. In the distance, she could hear the roar of rollercoasters and the terrified screams of the passengers.

"Oh, it'll go for a year or two. They put a lot into it. Four years of planning. It covers nearly twelve hundred acres. Looks like they are all ready for the Fourth of July celebrations tomorrow. You asked for fun, kiddo. And when Harry delivers, Harry delivers."

Katrine read the sign over the entrance gate. "'Dawn of a New Day, the World of Tomorrow.'" Look, they're advertising Albert Einstein. He's speaking next week on the 'diversity of America.'"[2]

"Maybe we should come back and check in on how old Uncle Al is doing?" Harry tapped the brochure in his hands. "So, what do you want to do first?"

"What is there to do?"

He opened the brochure. "Well… there are some great exhibits. Scentovision, nylon fabric, the streamlined pencil sharpener. General Motors built a car-based futuristic city."

Katrine was stuck on scentovision. "You mean, you can smell a movie?"

Harry shrugged. "Don't know. Haven't been to that one."

"What else is there to do?"

"How about a roller coaster?"

"Oh no, no, no." Katrine shook her head. "I've never been on one."

"IBM's got an electric typewriter," Harry offered.

She shook her head. "Boring."

He kept reading the small brochure. "The Government Zone sounds interesting. Over 60 foreign governments have set up miniature versions of their countries."

"Do they have a miniature version of the war going on too?"

"I'm guessing that's a 'no.'"

She pointed over his shoulder to a billboard that caught her eye. "Now that looks fun!"

"The Aquacade?"

"It's only 80 cents." She poked him in the ribs. "And we're old millionaires, remember."

Harry smirked. "Look, if I'm going to go watch some ballet dancers swimming around in a pool for 80 cents, you gotta cut me a deal. One ride."

"You have a deal!" She shook his hand firmly.

"*Any* ride I say."

"Any ride."

And that is how Katrine found herself standing below the Parachute Jump looking up, up, up, at an enormous tower in the amusement zone. A man standing near the long line for the ride bellowed, "Eleven gaily colored parachutes! From the top of the 250-foot tower, you will be able to experience all the thrills of 'bailing out' without the hazard or discomfort of jumping from a moving airplane!"[3]

"Oh no, Harry!" Katrine shrunk back, "I just couldn't! I think I'm afraid of heights."

"You have no idea what you're afraid of."

Harry pulled her forward and got in line. Immediately, five people were behind them. Katrine was stuck. Harry was adamant. "Don't worry, it's perfectly safe." He pointed up. "See? Each parachute has a double seat suspended from it. That will be me and you." He smiled down at her. "A cable pulls it to the summit of the tower. An automatic release starts the drop, and then we float gently to the ground."

She felt dizzy thinking about it. But they were already in line.

"This parachute jump is similar to what real fellows in the army use." The little boy in front of them said to his friend loudly.

Katrine squeezed Harry's hand. "Really, I don't think I want to do this."

"You made a deal, remember?"

She pursed her lips and watched as the next batch of passengers rode up the cable. She couldn't look. It was too terrible.

And suddenly, it was their turn. The attendant harnessed them in while Katrine shut her eyes.

The minute riding up was torture, and the moment the drop began was sheer terror. Her hat flew off her head, and her hair blew every which way. A blood-curdling scream came out of her mouth, and then the chute opened, and they began their peaceful slow descent back to earth.

She turned to Harry, who was laughing his head off, and punched his arm.

"It's fun, right?"

"Actually, you know, it was sort of exciting. Not that I would ever do it again, mind you." She looked straight ahead.

They were at the bottom now. The attendant was helping them take the harness off. She put her hand on her head, "Oh dear, my hat!"

"That was quite a scream, lady," the attendant said, taking her hand as she got out of the chair. "You got a nice set of pipes."

"She's a singer," Harry offered, "in a trio with her sisters."

Walking towards the midway, Katrine tripped over her feet. She was still dizzy from the drop. "Can you imagine if Lorelei and Grace knew I just parachuted from a tower like that! What would they say?"

"They would say you need a new hat." He scanned the midway and pointed to a stand where you won prizes by throwing baseballs at a stack of bowling pins. Among the prizes were women's hats.

"Allow me," he bowed to her before taking aim.

He was a good shot and won a hat after only two rounds. It was a straw hat with little cherries on it.

"Thanks, Harry," she said taking it in her hands. She rather liked it, even though it was sort of cheap.

"My pleasure."

Harry looked at his watch and clapped his hands together. "We've still got some minutes to die" he winked, "before picking up Jonas's birthday present from the Jews of America. You hungry yet? Want a corny-dog?"

"Dog?"

"It's a sausage dipped in cornbread and deep-fried."

"Sounds… American."

"It is. You'll love it." Harry smiled and pulled her towards a small corny-dog stand. Katrine's eyes were riveted on Harry's face as he ordered two dogs and two lemonades. He carried them to a small bench overlooking the Canals of Venice Gondola Ride. They sat down and watched as one couple after another rode by, leaning back in the fake little canal. The sun was starting to set, and it cast the park in a haze of soft blues and pinks.

"What do you think?"

"I think they are very cute. But it is not at all like the real Venice. It smells like chlorine."

"I meant the food."

She put her corny-dog down and picked up the hat Harry had won for her. Carefully, she put it on. "We ought to be going, don't you think?"

Harry looked a little disappointed. "I didn't have time to take you to the main lagoon. They have a submarine ride that's pretty great. Mermaids and stuff…" Then he stopped and said, "Look, I want you to know something." He stood up and looked down at her.

"What?"

"I want to take you on a real date."

"You do?"

"What do you say?"

The moment she had been waiting for had arrived. Harry was asking for something more than friendship. The excitement that this reve-lation elicited, however, was quickly replaced

by a wave of fear much worse than what she had
felt before going on the parachute ride.

What if he really *was* like the others? What if
it would end the way it had always ended before?
What if she opened her heart, loved him, and
then he left her? Like the others? All of these
thoughts went through her mind in less than a
second, but in that second, Harry seemed to
understand what was going on in her heart.

It was simple, she couldn't make the jump.
Harry's face went from hopeful ,to confused, to
hurt.

Deep hurt.

What had begun as sweetly romantic instantly
turned increasingly horrible and awkward as
Katrine refused to move or speak.

"I… I thought," Harry paused, "I thought you
felt differently. I'm sorry."

"Oh, Harry." The words came out choppy and
strange. "Once we cross that line, there's no
going back."

"Is that such a bad thing?"

"It won't work. It *couldn't* work." she looked
down.

"Why not?"

"Because it never works." She swallowed and
looked down.

"One day, Katrine, you are going to be brave
enough to make the jump."

She looked back up. His eyes were filled with
pain, even anger. "And you are going to love him
so much you won't even know you're diving out of
the plane. I'm sorry I brought it up. I won't
ever bring it up again. You have my word."

Stunned, her mouth opened just a bit. The corny-dog sat like a rock in her stomach.

He looked away, and when he looked back, he was himself again. Just Harry. "All right, we should be going. I think the exit is this way."

CHAPTER 20

THE SPAFFORD BABY HOME

"*L*orelei," Becky read off a list, "you've been posted to the Spafford Baby Home in the Old City." She looked up. "Can you manage getting there?"

"I think so." Lorelei nodded.

"Good," Becky smiled, "they'll be expecting you."

They'll be expecting me, Lorelei thought to herself as she stood outside the gate of the stone house in the Old City an hour later. She had managed to get there just fine, speaking to the bus driver in Hebrew, navigating the twisting passageways of the Old City with only two wrong turns. All in all, she felt rather accomplished.

The sign above a little bell read, "Spafford Baby Home." Quickly, she rang it and waited. A moment later, a pleasant-looking woman, in her late 40s or early 50s, appeared.

"You must be Lorelei Adleman. You have that nurse's look about you." The woman's softly greying blond hair was cut in an old-fashioned bob. She moved with purpose and a slight, almost indiscernible limp. But Lorelei caught it.

She unlocked the gate, and Lorelei stepped inside, looking about the clean courtyard. A line of young women holding babies and toddlers were up against one wall. A group of young children played in a corner with blocks and a rocking horse.

"I'm not a nurse yet," Lorelei said, following the woman inside the building, "but I'll be certified next month."

"I know. Henrietta told me."

"Henrietta Szold?"

"Of course. We've had several from her programs intern here. Now, we won't have you doing anything too exciting. Just weighing the babies and such. But we are so short of staff, who knows, we might have to have you do more!"

The woman rounded a corner and beckoned Lorelei to follow her up a small staircase. At the top was a row of doors facing the courtyard below. The first one was cracked open slightly. "Do come inside," the woman said kindly, "and we'll talk a bit before putting you to work."

Lorelei took the chair offered her, a straight-backed wooden chair.

"Thank you." She paused. "Forgive me, I don't know your name," Lorelei asked, unfastening her smart blue hat and slipping off her gloves.

"Oh, dear me. I forgot to introduce myself!" Her cheeks reddened slightly with embarrassment.

"Spafford." She sat down behind the simple wooden desk across from Lorelei. "I'm Mrs. Spafford.[4] Welcome to my home."

"Your home?"

From outside the open window, she could hear the children playing and laughing and the soft murmur of the mothers talking. It was a taste of heaven almost, set apart from the bustle of the city and filled with a peace Lorelei was unfamiliar with. It was lovely.

"Yes, this is my home. These are my children. Well, our children, to be precise. My husband's and mine." When Lorelei looked into Mrs. Spafford's eyes, she was stunned by their piercing blueness. "Now, Ms. Adleman, I know you are a Jewish girl. So I'm going to tell you bluntly that at my house, everyone is welcome. People of all faiths, do you understand?"

Nodding, Lorelei said, "I'm here to learn… But I thought this was a clinic, not an orphanage."

"Actually, it's both. We've 60 beds in the building next door. And a new surgical wing if you can believe it. Sometimes, I can't." She stood up abruptly. "Come along, I'll show you around."

Suddenly, a beautiful young Arab girl, dressed in a pretty floral dress and saddle shoes, crashed into the office. "Mother, I—" she saw Lorelei and froze. "Sorry, Mom. I thought you were alone."

"This is Lorelei, a fresh recruit from Henrietta's nursing training program."

The young woman extended her hand. "Oh, good.

I'm sure Mother told you how short-handed we are. I'm Noel."

"She's my first," Mrs. Spafford said, a soft smile gracing her lips.

"Your first?"

"My first baby."

"Noel." Lorelei took the girl's hand in her own. "That's a very unusual name."

Noel grinned from ear to ear. "She hasn't told you the story?"

Lorelei shook her head, smiling at the girl's exuberance. "I've only been here for about ten minutes."

"She found me on Christmas Eve,"

"We were on our way to Bethlehem to sing Christmas carols," Mrs. Spafford interjected. "Twelve years ago."

"Let me tell it, Mother." She put her chin down. "You saw some bedouins on a donkey. The wife was very sick, and she was holding a newborn baby. That was me."

"They'd been traveling for six hours to get to the hospital, and it was so cold. They looked just like Mary and Joseph." She looked at Lorelei, "You know the Christmas story, don't you, dear?"

Without waiting for an answer, she kept on. "When we finally got to the hospital, it was closed for the Christmas feast. Well, needless to say, we didn't go caroling. I nearly beat down the doors of the hospital to get the mother admitted. But it was too late. She died by morning."

Lorelei was looking from the woman to the

girl. They'd told this story hundreds of times before. It was well-rehearsed, and yet, she could tell it still held much meaning for the two of them.

"The Bedouin begged me to take his child. He told me he lived in a cave, and he feared he could not keep you alive alone." Mrs. Spafford turned and looked at Noel. "A cave. Just like the Lord Jesus. Of course, I couldn't say no."

"Within a week, she was asked to take in two more orphan babies," Noel added.

"And so, the Spafford Baby Home was born." Mrs. Spafford looked up at the clock on the wall. It was nearly ten o'clock. "Oh! I lost track of time. The clinic will be opening up soon. There'll be a line out the door. Come along, Ms. Adleman. We'd best get you to work!"

"ALL RIGHT," Lorelei said, looking out the door of the baby clinic. "Next please!"

A young woman with large brown eyes and curly dark hair cut just above her shoulder stepped inside. In her arms was a baby boy, nearly a year old by the looks of it.

"Put your baby on the scale, please," Lorelei said. In just the few hours she'd spent in the clinic, she had the system down to a science. Weight. Temperature. Check the baby's skin for any discolorations or rashes, etc. It was all standard procedure and came naturally to Lorelei. She would be able to quickly check pediatric nursing off the list if it continued as well as it was going.

"It's not my baby," the young woman said. "It's my mother's baby. He's my brother."

"Oh," Lorelei said.

"You're new, aren't you?" The young woman looked at her.

"I am, yes." Lorelei checked the scale. The baby was a healthy 24 pounds.

"Are you raising the child?" Lorelei asked.

"His name is Nick. And no, I'm not. My father is a jeweler in the Old City, and my mother helps him with the accounts this day every week."

"So you babysit?" Lorelei began to examine the baby's arms and legs and listened to his heart.

"Exactly…" The young woman was the curious sort. "Where are you from?"

Lorelei looked at the young woman. She caught the look of loneliness peeking out from the brown eyes.

"I am from Germany."

"What's it like?"

Lorelei laughed. "Very, very different from here."

"I've never been outside Jerusalem." The girl sighed with longing. "But I want to go everywhere! Yosef, he's been to France. He went to school there."

Lorelei went back to checking the baby. "And who is Yosef?"

"My fiance."

"That's nice." She looked up suddenly. "Wait a minute. How old are you?"

"Fifteen."

"That's a little young to be engaged, don't you think?"

"We won't get married for a while yet. Yosef wants me to finish school."

Lorelei breathed a sigh of relief. "I'm glad to hear it."

"Yosef is very wise."

Lorelei looked down and smiled to herself. This girl was so innocent and so talkative.

"So," the girl asked, pushing a rogue curl away from her face, "how's Nick?"

"He's just fine. You can tell your parents that they have a healthy baby boy."

The girl frowned.

"What? That's not good news?"

"Well, I was hoping he was just a little sick."

"Whatever for?"

"So I could come back tomorrow or the next day for another checkup."

It was quite clear something else was at hand. Lorelei put her hand on her hip and lowered her chin. "What's this really about, young lady?"

"Well, to get here, I have to pass through the Arab quarter, and I can see Yosef!"

"Why can't you go see him anyway if he is your fiancé?"

"Oh, he's an Arab!"

Lorelei looked at her, confused. "And you are?"

"I'm an Armenian. My father would die if he knew I was seeing Yosef! Or kill me. Or kill Yosef. Or both of us!"

How melodramatic she was. "Armenian?" Lorelei tried to remember what Becky had told her about the Armenians. They were Christians.

"My family came here after—" she stopped. "I met Yosef at the market, by chance. It was love at first sight."

Lorelei tried to follow. "Is it because Yosef is a Muslim?"

"No. He is Catholic. But that doesn't matter to my father. He wants me to marry an Armenian boy. He is very old-fashioned that way. But we'll change his mind, me and Yosef. He is so good, you see. And so kind. It's just not the right time yet." She looked wistfully out the window.

"And you are only 15."

"And that." She looked back at Lorelei. "So, perhaps, you could say that Nick is just the teensiest, weensiest bit sick?"

"I won't lie—"

"Paulina," she answered, "my name is Paulina."

"And I'm only here once a week."

Paulina's hopeful face caved. Her plan had failed. A prick of remorse hit Lorelei's heart. Rolf's face flickered in her mind, and the bracelet he'd given her shimmered for a brief second on her wrist. "But," she paused, "I think I have an idea…"

"YOU INVITED HER OVER FOR DINNER?" Becky flipped an egg in the pan and waited while it sizzled. The girls seemed to eat fried eggs and toast nearly every night for supper. After a full day of teaching, working at the hospital, or studying, it was about all they could handle.

Lorelei already had her plate and was tucked up on the couch in her bathrobe. "It was all I could think of. She seemed lonely."

"Well, what night is she coming over?"

"I told her Wednesday night."

"That's tomorrow." Becky slid her egg onto the plate and salted it generously. "I guess that works with me." Her slippered feet padded into the living room, and she eased herself onto the floor. "And she wants to cook for us?"

"She said she loves cooking."

"Well, that's good because between you and me all we can cook is fried eggs and oatmeal."

"Makes a girl healthy, wealthy, and wise." Lorelei laughed.

"Anything for young love, I guess." Becky took a bite of her toast. She had dark circles under her eyes.

"Once upon a time, I could make a pretty good Bernaise." Seeing the question in Becky's eyes, she clarified, "That's a sauce for steak."

"Ah."

It had been a long day. For the next few minutes, both girls concentrated on their dinner.

"I forgot to ask," Becky said suddenly, "what do you think of the Spafford Baby Home? Do you think it's a good fit?"

"Not to be rude, but it is quite a bit more pleasant than the hospital. Everyone is so cheerful and kind. They made me feel right at home." Lorelei took a sip of milk.

Knowingly, Becky nodded her head. "Mrs. Spafford takes the Bible seriously. 'A joyful heart is good medicine.' Mrs. Spafford would say it is the *best* medicine. She reminds me of a nun sometimes, except that she isn't Catholic and has a husband and more children than you can count. Did she tell you about how she adopted Noel?"

Lorelei nodded. "Does the Bible really say that? About good medicine?"

"'A joyful heart is good medicine, but a broken spirit dries up the bones.' It's in Proverbs, I think."[5]

"Where is Mrs. Spafford from? I couldn't place her accent, and I forgot to ask."

"Bertie?" Becky put her plate down. "I guess you could say she's from here. She's lived here since she was a very little child. I doubt she remembers much of America at all."

"Why did her parents leave America? They aren't Jewish!" Lorelei was surprised. Palestine seemed like the last place on earth anyone would want to go.

"You haven't heard of the Spaffords, have you?" Becky said. It was more of a statement than a question. She leaned her head back against the chair. "Oh, it must have been nearly 50 years ago. Horatio Spafford was a very wealthy man. I forget if he was a lawyer or a businessman, but it was something like that. There was a terrible fire in Chicago. It destroyed much of their property. The Spaffords were a very devout couple, and they devoted themselves to helping people who had lost their homes in the fire."[6]

"But how did they get here?" Lorelei pressed.

"It's a sad story. They were going on vacation with friends to Europe. Horatio had to stay back in Chicago for a few days for business. His wife and four daughters went on ahead. There was some horrible accident at sea. Their steamship collided with another ship mid-ocean. Anna was saved alone. All the children perished."

It was an awful story, and Lorelei's brow furrowed thinking of it.

"Horatio was a poet."

Horatio, Lorelei tilted her head to the side. The same name as Edie's husband.

"And when he received news of the tragedy," Becky continued, "he wrote the words, 'When peace like a river, attendeth my way, when sorrows like sea billows roll, whatever my lot, thou hast taught me to say, it is well, it is well, with my soul.'[7] Someone put it to music, and it's now a very famous Christian hymn." And with that, Becky proceeded to sing.

The poignant words hung in the air.

"How could he say that?" Lorelei finally said. "How could he say it was well with his soul?"

She couldn't imagine after all that had happened to her being well with her soul. "Whatever his lot?"

"That's the power of God's healing, Lorelei. He can heal hearts." Becky said gently.

Lorelei looked down. She wasn't ready to go there yet. The pain was still too fresh.

Quickly, she said, "But you haven't told me yet how her parents got here."

Becky sighed. "Anna and Horatio were blessed with several more children. Mrs. Spafford is one of them. They felt led by God to come to Jerusalem with several other Americans who loved God. They settled in a little house, the one where the Baby House is now, and determined to share all they had with others. The American Colony, they called it. A place where all were welcome, Jews, Christians, and Muslims. As they grew, they bought another property just around the corner from here. An old Arab Pasha's home. Very grand. It's been used for everything under the sun since then. A soup kitchen, a first-aid station during the Great War. . . It's an inn of sorts now."

"And their daughter runs the Baby House?"

"Yes." Becky stood up and took her plate back to the kitchen. "See, it is a good ending after all."

"A good ending after all," Lorelei repeated thoughtfully to herself. She leaned her head back against the couch and shut her eyes. These Christians were very different from what she had thought. Very different indeed. They seemed to run on a different sort of energy, as though they drew from a deeper well that made them unafraid of the future. More thoughts like this went through her head for the rest of the night and continued for days.

CHAPTER 21

GRACE GETS HER WINGS

"Well, in answer to your question, Ms. Adleman, no, we cannot allow you to learn to fly combat planes."

"Why ever not?" Grace protested.

O'Rourke didn't answer her and instead turned to the door and called, "Flight Sergeant Herring, come in, please!"

Flight Sergeant Herring strode in, eyes locked on O'Rourke. Only when Grace cried out, "Amos!" did he turn and look at her.

"You're that girl from the kibbutz!" Amos said after a minute, recognizing Grace.

"You don't remember my name?" Grace's jaw dropped a bit. Her pride was stung.

Amos shrugged. "Mother and Father always have new people at kibbutz. It's too hard to remember all of their names."

"I see you two sort of know each other," O'Rourke said, taken aback.

"Barely," Grace answered quickly, trying to regain her dignity.

"Well then, I'll let you know that Amos is one of our ace pilots, and he's one of your people."

"You know, you still haven't even told us what our secret mission is yet," Grace said, refusing to look at Amos. Hand on her hip, she continued, "So if you won't let me learn to fly officially, what's this all about?"

"I said we would not let you learn to fly combat. We do want you to learn to fly, but women in the RAF are only permitted to fly transport."

"That works for me," Grace exhaled, relieved. "Flying is flying."

"Once you complete your training, you will receive a civilian license."

"*If* she completes her training," Amos corrected the captain.

Grace ignored the jibe, focusing on O'Rourke. "How long will it take?"

"Twenty hours on the ground. Twenty hours up in the air." He coughed behind his hand awkwardly. "Amos is going to be your instructor. And I'm relieving you of your duties with the others until Amos clears you for solo flights."

Amos groaned. "This is a terrible idea. Twenty hours? It takes most people eighty."

"Well, I'm *not* most people." Grace glared at him before focusing her most winning smile on the captain, shaking his hand vigorously. "You won't be sorry, sir."

"I certainly hope not, Aircraftwoman First

Class Adleman." He was surprised by her strong grip.

"Aircraftwoman First Class?" she asked.

"Your new rank." O'Rourke clasped his hands together. "All right. You two are dismissed."

Grace followed Amos out of the captain's office. Amos was walking quickly, huffing under his breath, "Just what I need, training some teenager how to fly. Didn't anyone tell those idiots there's a war on? I've better things to do than train some girl to fly a plane she'll never need to fly. What a waste of time!"

"I'm 21 years old!" Grace called after him. But he didn't turn around. She ran to catch up to him. "Wait a second!"

He looked over his shoulder. "What *more* do you want?"

"Well..." A terrible sinking feeling came over Grace, a mixture of shame and righteous indignation all mixed together. And to think, she had actually tried to impress him with a dress! She would show him who was *not* a waste of time! "If we only have a limited training period, we better get going early, don't you think?"

"0500. Sharp. Classroom C. You know where that is, don't you?"

"Five in the morning. Classroom C. I'll be there." She tilted her chin up at him, her voice taking on an extra measure of politeness. She would show him just what a woman could do! Oh yes, she would, and she would do it with poise, dignity, and grace. Yes, grace. That was her name, wasn't it?

∽

THE NEXT MORNING, Amos was waiting for her. There was no 'good morning' or 'how did you sleep?' Oh no. No pleasantries whatsoever. She walked in, and he pointed to a desk on the front row. There were a bunch of figures on the blackboard.

"Look," Amos said, "it takes a normal pilot in the RAF 150 hours, minimum, and that's before they get in the air. Initial training is eight weeks. Elementary Flying Training School, ten weeks. Service Flying Training School, sixteen weeks. That is what it takes to get your wings. This forty hours business is dumb and, in my opinion, a serious risk."

"I like risks." Grace said, crossing her arms.

"Not when it could put other people's lives in danger." Amos crossed his arms and stared back.

"What if the danger is not having me learn at all?" Grace countered. "Look, someone on this mission is going to need to know how to get a plane up and a plane down. It might as well be me."

"Or me." Amos looked directly at her.

"Except, you aren't going on the mission. And I am."

His mouth twitched. "We'll see about that." He turned to the board. "I'm assuming you know the basics of arithmetic and algebra. If you don't, then this is pointless. That said, I want to do a little refresh on your calculus and geometry. You will use math constantly while in flight. You have to be able to calculate angles for takeoff and landing. If you are coming in too steep and too fast, you'll crash. Understand?"

She nodded.

"And you'll need to be able to determine flight times between distances based on how fast you're going, or you may end up somewhere you never intended to be. Along those lines, you have to be able to read your directional compass and calculate how many degrees to turn your aircraft during flight. That's how you actually pilot your plane."

Again, she nodded, staring at the equations on the board.

"So," he pointed at the board. "In this equation-"

"It's 124 degrees," she answered before he could finish.

He stopped and checked the answer key, surprised. "Yeah. That was an easy one." He pointed at the next problem. "And this one—"

"Four hours."

His eyes opened a little wider. "Correct."

"And the next one, the answer is 'D,' and after that, 'Angle C.'"

Amos reddened slightly. "I guess we'll move on from mathematics to morse code."

"Already learned it. It was a part of our basic training."

"Okay." He swallowed. "Navigation then."

"I think that would be a much better use of time," Grace agreed.

He stopped. "How'd you get so quick at the figures?"

"My father knew a little bit about math. He

was a famous mathematician, actually."

"Oh, I see…" He took a textbook from the desk and tossed it to Grace. He was trying to maintain the illusion that he was in total control, but inwardly, he was worried that he might have underestimated the young woman sitting in front of him. "That being the case, open up to Chapter Four: 'Route Planning.'"

Grace looked at the cover. Embossed in gold letters was the title, 'Basics of Flight.' 'Amos Herring' was written in light pencil on the first page. Turning to Chapter Four, she noticed multiple sections had been underlined and circled in the same steady light hand.

"Read the opening paragraph, and we'll jump right in."

Her eyes scanned the page, "The first step in navigation is to decide where you want to go." She looked up. "Makes sense."

Amos had unfurled a large aeronautical chart hanging from the wall over the blackboard. "Once you choose a route, you plot it on the map. That's called a track. The aim of all subsequent navigation is to follow that track as closely as you can. Now, normally you will have a navigator on board. But every pilot needs to know how to do it for himself, just in case."

"What if I don't have time to choose a route?"

"You can cheat and follow a railway track, a river, a highway, or even a coastline. But this is a lot harder than it looks."

"Why?"

"Wind."

He sat down in the chair behind the desk and

put his feet up. "Your main job as a pilot will be to compensate for wind. There is almost never 'no' wind. And wind will always be trying to push you off course. You will need to calculate each leg of your journey according to the wind forecast, and you will have to make constant adjustments in flight." Swinging his feet off the desk, he stood up, "You can read the rest of the chapter tonight on your own time."

Grace swallowed. "Okay."

He was marching out the door. "Are you coming? What was your name again?"

"Grace Adleman!" she jumped up and jogged after him. "My name is Grace Adleman!"

"My, you're back late." It was 10:30 at night. Cecilia was already on her cot, reading out loud to Hannah, who was sitting on the floor painting her toenails.

"How's *The Yearling*?" Grace looked exhausted. She sat down on the edge of her own cot and took off her boots.

Cecilia shut the book and sat up, drawing her knees up to her chest. "Jody's parents allowed him to adopt the fawn." She sighed. "It's all the rage in America. A bestseller, they call it."

"That's nice." Grace yawned loudly.

"Well?" Hannah didn't look up from her toes.

"Well what?"

"Well, you've been gone all day learning how to fly like a bird! With a very handsome pilot, who shall remain nameless. Aren't you going to tell us all about it?"

Grace threw herself back on her cot and moaned. "Well, first off, he's *not* so handsome."

Hannah shot Cecilia a glance, "Debatable, but please, continue."

"And second," she answered, exasperated, "I haven't been learning to fly like a bird at all. I've been sitting behind a flight simulator for hours and hours without a break, learning how to use something called a magnetic compass which," she sat up again, "does NOT correspond with true north but with magnetic north, so I, the pilot, have to allow for something called magnetic variation."

"I don't understand."

"Me neither. Not really. And let's not even talk about cruising speeds and headwinds and dead reckoning, which is how you calculate your current position based on your first position and how fast you estimate you're going."

"Oh come on." Cecilia turned over on her side and propped her head up on her hand. "We want to know about Amos! We don't need to learn to fly a plane."

Grace folded her arms. "Trust me, you absolutely do *not* want to know about Amos."

"That bad?" Hannah stretched her legs out.

"It's like I'm not even there. He spits out information faster than I can catch it, and he doesn't care. He is just 'following orders' because he has too," she groaned. "I've got the world's worst headache. But I am going to learn to fly a plane if it's the last thing I do."

She stood up and began to brush out her hair. "And what about you? How was your day?"

Hannah shrugged. "I had kitchen clean-up duty. It was disgusting, as usual."

"Morris and I spent six hours helping a cartographer create a route for the mission. I learned that means someone who makes maps," Cecilia answered.

"You know so much about geography?"

Cecilia nodded. "I escaped the concentration camp on foot."

"But you remember?"

"I long to forget." Cecilia took her book back and began to read once more. "You ought to get some sleep. You look tired."

"Yeah, and Amos has me scheduled at 0400 tomorrow. An hour earlier than today!"

"Early riser, huh?"

"I think he's trying to prove something to me. Make me pay for suggesting this hair-brained scheme." She looked straight up at the ceiling. "Little does he know I *like* waking up early!"

∼

GRACE LOOKED DOWN at the desert below. She wore her flight overalls, goggles, and helmet, her ringlets sticking out of it. This was it, she told herself. She was in heaven. She loved it so much she could almost ignore the man sitting beside her.

"Keep your eyes on the instruments!" Amos said harshly.

"Sorry." Reluctantly, she turned her attention back to the instrument panel.

The plane was a Blackburn B2. A side-by-side trainer. So far, Grace and Amos had spent nearly six hours in the air. She had taking off down pat. It was far easier than landing, but she had pulled that off too, twice, without Amos having to grab the control panels.

When he was with Grace, Amos never once deviated from lecture mode, but privately, he begrudgingly admitted to O'Rourke that she had 'good instincts.'

"All flying on the front is done by the seat of your pants," Amos glanced over at his pupil, "without an airspeed indicator."

"Then how do you know what to do?"

"You fly by the feel of things." He took the control wheel in both hands and rolled the plane over.

Grace laughed out loud, not quite the response Amos had expected. "That's called a roll." He then pulled back, and the plane made an enormous loop. A wave of euphoria rushed over Grace as they hung suspended in the air.

She grinned from ear to ear. "That was wonderful!"

"It's called a loop." He pulled out, leveling the plane once again, and rubbed his hands together. "Aerobatics 101. This is how you become one with your ship. The better you know what flying feels like, the better you'll fly."

"Makes sense," she agreed, eagerly adding, "How do I do it?"

"You don't scare easy, do you?" For the first

time, a little grin escaped Amos's serious demeanor.

"I am choosing not to answer that question." She looked at the instrument panel. "Now tell me how to do it."

"Well," Amos scratched his chin, "it's simple, really. You decrease the lift on one wing while increasing it on the other. That's what causes the plane to roll left or right."

Grace put her hands firmly on the wheel and, without waiting, followed Amos's instructions, mimicking his actions identically. The plane gently rolled over and righted itself.

"How was that?"

"Good. Good." Amos swallowed. She was good! Too good. It was almost embarrassing. "I think we can move on."

He adjusted a dial and pushed a red button. Instantly, the engine sputtered and died.

The plane was falling fast. Grace shot him a stare. "I think there's something wrong with the engine."

"Are you scared now?" he challenged.

"No!" she answered. With only the slightest twinge of panic, she added, "What do I do?"

"You're the student. What did you read you are supposed to do in the case of an engine failure?"

Grace clenched her teeth, trying to remember, as the plane lost altitude. "I glide to an emergency landing spot, like a field, while troubleshooting and making radio calls."

"Good."

"So…"

"So do it!" he exclaimed.

Right. Got it. I can do this, Grace coached herself. She grabbed the radio and spoke calmly, "Mayday, Mayday. Engine failure. Request emergency landing."

Her hands firmly on the wheel, she took the plane steadily down on a gentle incline. She saw the runway and began to prepare for landing. All of a sudden, Amos fiddled with a switch, and the engine revved to life once more. "Take it up another 1000 feet."

"All right," she answered. "What then?"

"We do it again." She was too focused to notice that he was watching more than her performance. For the first time since meeting her, Amos was watching her.

And he was impressed. He had never met a girl like Grace before. He didn't know girls like that existed. Sure, his sister Dafna was brave and beautiful, but Grace was something else. She was fearless.

It was sunset when Amos finally said the lesson was over. Grace landed the plane for the 7th time and exhaled a sigh of relief.

She jumped out of the plane without Amos's help and, without saying goodbye or thank you, began to walk off the runway and towards her tent.

"Hey, Grace!" he called after her.

"You finally know my name, huh?" She kept walking.

He ran to catch up with her. "Wait up!"

She stopped and faced him. "What is it?"

Amos flushed slightly. "I just wanted to say, you did all right up there."

"Oh," Grace answered, taken aback. "Thanks."

THE DAY GOES ON

~

With that, Grace quickly slammed the manuscript on the table and stood up. "Well," she said, "Edie certainly captured him. I'll give her that!"

"The guy who couldn't remember your name is asking you to marry him?" I asked, laughing.

She glared at me. "I told you, I don't want to talk about anything that has to do with that boy." Storming out of the kitchen, she added, "I've got to lie down. I feel dizzy."

"Wow," Peter said quietly. "That girl definitely needs to lie down."

"She definitely needs *something*," I agreed.

"What do you think she meant," Peter asked, "about Lorelei being one of us?"

I shrugged. "Your guess is as good as mine. I haven't heard from Lorelei in a few months. You know how it is with the mail over there. It's a miracle if we get anything from the front at all. Especially the North African front." I paused. "Peter, you are really sure about this... us staying in Maine?"

"Quite sure. We are not done here... yet."

"But technically, we *aren't* doing anything."

"Just pray about it, for me."

"Where are you going?" I asked.

"Mr. Henderson asked me to help him with some cabinets he's working on this afternoon. I thought it would be nice to do some real woodworking again."

I pursed my lips together and groaned.

Peter stood up and kissed the top of my head. "How about you keep working on the manuscript, and when I get home, you can tell me all about Amos, and we'll poke fun at Grace."

"That sounds like a terrible idea."

He laughed, his old, honest, real laugh, and I looked up into his face. It was, for the first time since he'd come back from the war, confident.

With that, he went upstairs and came back a few minutes later with his old jeans on and a worn flannel shirt and sweater. He flung his coat over his shoulders and winked at me as the front door blew shut. I noticed that as he walked, his limp was less perceptible.

Upstairs, Grace was quiet, and I assumed she had fallen asleep, which was good. The strain and lack of sleep were making her loopy. I had never taken Grace for the type who would have such trouble committing, but then, people do surprise you. She was adventurous and loved her freedom. Sort of like Edie...

I was instantly transported back to two years before. I could see Edie pacing back and forth, quite sure that her marriage to Horatio would be the end of her freedom. But she was wrong, it was just the beginning.

My chin resting on my hands, I looked out at the sea. More time at the lighthouse? What was Peter thinking? What was God thinking? It was so... lonely here. I had planned on so much in Boston. New friends... new adventures... a new beginning.

A new beginning... right back from where we started. Could any good come of this?

Well, at least I had a puppy. I looked at Founder, sleeping peacefully at my feet. Her golden fluffy puppy fur flattened out on the floor by my toes. There was a comfort in that. Maybe I would take up the violin or something... something more industrious than knitting.

With these thoughts swirling in my head, I took a bath and washed my hair and put on real clothes, a rather smart grey wool skirt, and structured blouse. Then, I sat behind Edie's desk like a real editor and got to work. I may not have had a real job, but I needed to *feel* professional. And so, my red pencil in hand, I set to work, pushing all thoughts of the future away, doing my best to concentrate on the task at hand.

CHAPTER 22

THE ARMENIAN GIRL

"What time did you say she was coming again?" Becky pushed the sleeves to her blue cardigan up over her elbows and moved to open the door of the balcony. "It's warm, don't you think? Hopefully, this isn't a precursor to what summer is going to be like."

Lorelei grabbed a blouse slung over a chair and straightened a stack of magazines. "I told her to come around six-thirty. That gives us half an hour." Looking around the room, she spotted a rogue sock and scooped it up. "Eh, it's clear enough, probably."

Becky frowned. "You know, we really ought to set aside a day to actually clean this place. I can't remember the last time we mopped. And we are nurses! We're supposed to be sanitary."

"Or at the very least neat and tidy. I can't remember the last time I made my bed when I woke up," Lorelei agreed.

"It's because we work too hard and are too tired. It's the most we can do to keep *ourselves* tidy. Between all the time I spend teaching and working and your studying and working—"

A rapid knocking on the door caused them both to look up. "She's early," Lorelei said, tossing her load of clothes through the bedroom door and shutting it firmly before jogging over to open it.

"Hello, Paulina—" Lorelei stopped. Behind the beautiful girl was a young man in his early twenties holding two very full paper bags.

"I brought Yosef!" she exclaimed cheerily. "I thought you wouldn't mind."

Becky stood behind Lorelei and stared at the young couple. "Oh no," she faltered, "we don't mind. We don't mind at all. Come in, come in, please. Both of you."

Yosef said nothing. He gave a shy nervous smile and nodded politely.

"Nice to meet you, Yosef." Lorelei extended her hand and then withdrew it quickly. His hands were full. Pointing behind her, she said, "The kitchen is that way."

"We've bought the most marvelous things for dinner, and I don't want you or your roommate to lift a finger." Paulina looked at Becky, "What was your name again?"

"Becky."

"Right. Well, we want to thank you so much for letting me come, us come, I mean. I know I sprang this on you, but Yosef's mother was at home, and it's awkward just sitting in the living room staring at one another. And it's not like we could walk in the market because one of my cousins might see us and then where would we be? The only thing to do was to tell him to meet me here! How else could we see one another?"

"How else?" Becky said, her mouth slightly open.

Paulina and Yosef were in the kitchen now, and she was taking mysterious wrapped packages out one by one and looking in the various drawers for pots and pans. "Now, you two go and talk, and Yosef and I will make you the most delicious meal you have ever eaten because we are ever so grateful."

Yosef looked over at Becky and Lorelei standing in the doorway of the kitchen, smiled, and nodded.

With that, Paulina took the curtain, which served as a door separating the kitchen from the living room, and shut it forcefully.

"Ah. All right then," Becky said.

From behind the curtain Paulina said, "We'll call you when it's ready!"

Lorelei and Becky moved to the couch and sat down.

"Do you think it's okay to let them alone back there?"

"Oh come on. What are they going to do? Jump out the window and elope?" Lorelei laughed nervously. "I'm sorry, Becky. I had no idea she was going to bring Yosef."

"He seems sweet enough. Paulina certainly likes him."

"And apparently," the smell of garlic and

onions frying in a pan wafted out from behind the curtain, "he's a good cook."

~

THE TABLE WAS ARRAYED with dish after dish. "That's Pasus Tolma. It's pickled cabbage leaves stuffed with chickpeas, lentils, and spices. And there's lavosh bread, and lamb, and cracked wheat with fresh herbs. And this is a soft salty cheese, I think you will like very much," Paulina explained.

"Certainly beats eggs and toast." Becky grinned.

"And for dessert, I had Yosef bring his mother's baklava. It is the best in all of Jerusalem!"

Yosef reddened slightly and said, "It is true. She is very famous for them." (These were also his first words of the evening.)

All four sat down at the table out on the patio. It was nearly dark, but the light from inside the living room was bright enough to allow them to see their plates, and Becky had lit several candles, giving the whole space a romantic feel.

"Eat! Eat, please!" Paulina urged.

Lorelei took a bite of the lamb. It was delicious. "You two are very talented! You should open a restaurant."

"We did meet in the market, you know." Paulina grinned over at Yosef. "He was picking up nuts for his mother's baklava. He was home from school for vacation. He is an engineer now." She looked proud.

The young man nodded. "Yes. I just graduated from La Sorbonne."

"That's wonderful," Lorelei exclaimed, quite surprised. She had not expected Yosef to be so accomplished.

Becky caught the look and explained, "Many of the affluent Arab Christian families send their children to school in France." She faced Yosef and asked, "So, now that you are an engineer, what do you want to do?"

"To be honest," he gave a pleasant smile as he spoke softly, "I don't know. There is not much need for a mechanical engineer in Jerusalem."

"Not yet anyway." Paulina looked down.

"What do you mean?" Lorelei asked.

"My people are like your people," Yosef sighed. "They don't have a country. And like your people, my people also have a promise from the British Government. A promise that we can have a country too. Right here."

"What promise?" Lorelei asked.

"You have your letter from Balfour. We have our letters from McMahon, the British High Commissioner to Egypt, to Hussein Bin Ali, the Sharif of Mecca. Both promises are over a decade old. Both of our people have been biding their time, preparing for whatever will come."

"The Arab Muslims and the Christians, they are unified in this?" Lorelei asked.

"Yes," he spread his hands out, as though to say, 'of course.' "It is a matter of national-ism, not religion, you see. The West has not been good to the Arabs. Colonialism," he spat the word out vehemently, "is not compatible with a dignified, independent people. And the Arab nations are determined to be independent."[8]

"I don't think that everyone would see it so simply." Becky took a sip of her water warily.

"A Jewish state in Palestine defeats your purposes rather drastically," Lorelei observed him, cooly.

Yosef smiled sadly. "That is true. But don't think I do not understand the complexities. I've heard the rumors. I am also not one of those uneducated fools who refuses to believe the Jews were not ever in Palestine. I know the Jews were in this land thousands of years ago. As a devoted Christian, I also believe that my Lord and Savior is Jewish. I wish… I wish things were different between us."

Innocently, Paulina reached out and grabbed Yosef's hand. "I just don't understand why we can't all live in peace together."

"It's for the same reason your father won't let me come and see you." They stared into one another's eyes. Yosef looked back up. "I'm here for a reason. You are Jewish, and I suppose you know people to talk to, people who know people."

"People, who know people?" Lorelei watched them, wondering why they were really there and what they really wanted.

"You'll understand in a minute. Hear me out. A few of the Mufti's people, he is in charge of the Arab Nationalists in Palestine, approached me yesterday. They want to send me to Germany."

Lorelei and Becky stared at him blankly.

"Don't you understand? They want me to receive more training. For war machines. They are learning from the Nazis."

Lorelei felt a chill sweep through her. "I see… Why are you telling me this?"

"Because we *know* about the Nazis." He frowned and looked at Paulina.

The young girl nodded. "My family is from Armenia. We were ruled by the Ottomans, the Turks… and beginning in, oh, when was it, 1915, they began to eliminate my people. Forced labor, deportations, toxic gas. Even worse things I will not tell you of. But you must know that the Nazis were inspired by these evils. It went on for almost ten years. My parents barely escaped with the clothes on their backs and made it here to the Old City. I think they will never want to leave now that they are safe behind its walls. So many died. Not many are left. I think this is why my father hates Yosef so."[9]

Yosef looked out over the balcony. "They say that Hitler was inspired by the Turks. He is not original. But he does build on what has been done before. The camps. The gas."

Lorelei shook her head. "What is this you speak of, gas?"

He looked at her. "They are gassing those they deem undesirable. Euthanasia, they call it. I learned of it in France. I'm surprised you haven't heard of it."

Lorelei had been so busy with work and school, she had not been listening to the news or reading the paper as she should. Well, to be honest, she was never very up with current events. Katrine always told her everything she needed to know, and they had been separated for months.

Yosef stood up. "Perhaps we can go inside. You are all finished with your food, yes?"

The girls nodded, and they followed the young man back into their living room and tensely sat on the couch. Yosef shut the door, pulled up a chair, and leaned forward. "Some of the key leaders of the Palestinian Arab Party live in the neighborhood. They won't like what I have to say."

"And what do you have to say, young man?" Becky asked, folding her hands gently and laying them on her lap.

"I want a country as much as anyone else, but I won't participate by joining with those who are taking their cues from the Nazis. Not all Arab Christians feel the same way as I, but then, they do not know Paulina. They do not understand how much blood may be shed." He looked at Paulina. "I love her too much to be a part of more violence."[10]

"What will happen if you tell them no?" Becky asked, still looking at the young man.

"Oh, they will put the pressure on. They always do. But I will resist them. You'll see!"

Lorelei digested this information slowly. "For someone who I thought didn't talk very much, you sure have a lot to say." A slight chuckle escaped her lips. Lowering her voice, she said, "You've trusted us a great deal. And you are right, I think I know who to talk to. But to be honest, they probably already know.

It's no secret that many of your people and mine do not get along. And that the tension will get worse. Our conflicting interests will only increase as more of us show up from Europe. And we will."

"I do not wish the death of anyone," Yosef said quietly. "Not your people or mine."

Paulina stood up and went to the kitchen. "You have a teapot, don't you? I brought tea." She didn't wait for an answer and disappeared back into the kitchen. Yosef stood up, bowed slightly to the two nurses, and followed her. "And I will help you."

The girls waited until they were out of earshot and looked at each other. Becky raised one eyebrow. "What do you think all this is about? They did not come just to make us dinner and talk over politics."

"I'm not sure yet." Lorelei stared at the curtain. She could hear them speaking softly to one another in Arabic. The whistle of the kettle came on, and they returned. In Yosef's hands was a box of his mother's pastries, layers and layers of paper-thin dough stuffed with nuts and soaked in honey. He passed the box around as Paulina poured tea.

Becky and Lorelei each took a bite, exclaiming that it was indeed the best they'd had in Jerusalem. Neither Paulina nor Yosef spoke, looking at one another nervously.

"All right," Lorelei put her tea down, "you might as well spill it. What is our part in all this? You must need something, or you wouldn't have come and told us all of this, right?"

Paulina exhaled. "We need help with visas. We want to go to America."

"America!" Becky exclaimed. "You might as well want to go to the moon! The borders are closed to everyone."

"Even if you were to write us a letter of recommendation?" Her face still held hope.

Lorelei thought of her forged adoption papers, and her lips twisted into a smirk. "My American citizenship is shaky at best."

"And I'm Irish, so there's no help for you there," Becky added.

"Well, it is more important for Yosef to go. Perhaps, it would be easier for you to just get one visa instead of two?" Paulina said. "He will send for me once he's settled, yes?"

"If only it were that easy." Lorelei looked at the girl. "But at least it would give you a chance to grow up. Fifteen is much too young to get married."

Yosef nodded. "But this we have discussed. Paulina must finish school, of course! Why she may even want to go to college. But not here; in America."

"Can't you just say you no longer want to be an engineer?" Lorelei asked. "Maybe you and Paulina could open a restaurant. You are quite good cooks."

That got a slight laugh and lightened the mood.

"Have you thought of joining the British Army, the Palestine Regiment, perhaps?" Becky suggested. "It seems like a viable way out of your little predicament."

"After he's been targeted to go join the Nazis? He'd be viewed as a traitor. Who knows what they would do to him!" Paulina said fiercely.

Becky sighed. "I guess it doesn't hurt to ask around. God does still do miracles."

Lorelei wasn't so sure about that, but she held her tongue.

"So," Paulina said slowly, her hope growing, "you will see what you can do?"

Becky nodded. "Yes. You have my word."

With that, Paulina hopped up and kissed Becky's cheek and then Lorelei's. "I knew it! I just knew it!" She looked into Lorelei's eyes. "When I saw you… I just knew it."

"You two ought to head home," Lorelei said. "It's almost curfew."

"I'll see you tomorrow," Paulina replied as Yosef helped her on with her sweater. "I think Nick is not doing so well. He had a little fever."

"I won't be in the clinic tomorrow. It's not Monday."

"Right. How forgetful of me."

Becky stepped in. "Any other symptoms?"

Lorelei laughed. "Nick is as healthy as a horse. Imagined fevers let these two lovebirds visit one another."

"Oh!" Paulina exclaimed. "It's not imaginary this time. He really did feel warm. And he was crying an awful lot. And he has a rash that isn't going away."

"Bring him to the hospital tomorrow instead of

the clinic." Becky sounded concerned. "I'll take a look at him myself."

"All right." Paulina nodded. "I will."

"And I'll meet you there," Yosef said.

She pecked him on the cheek. "Wonderful."

After the couple left, Becky and Lorelei collapsed on the couch and looked at each other. "I'm sorry for whatever I just got us into," Lorelei said solemnly. "Those two are quite the pair!"

"Oh, I don't think it was you," Becky said, smiling. "I'm voting that it was the hand of God that pushed Paulina and Yosef into our apartment. What he wants to do with them here is another matter altogether."

CHAPTER 23

THE FOURTH OF JULY

*A*fter a tense walk to the entrance of the park, Harry hailed a cab and passed the driver the napkin with the address that Jonas had written at the deli the day before. An unspoken agreement between Harry and Katrine said they would not address the fact that he had just asked her out, and she had said nothing. They would ignore it. Press on. Be the good soldiers they pretended to be and finish their mission as soon as possible so they could get on with their lives.

The cab driver looked at the address and then at his watch. "Seriously, you're gonna take that dame there? At this time of night?"

"Yes?" Harry answered. "Is there a reason why I shouldn't?"

"That part of the harbor is under the control of the Gambino family."

"Who's that?" Katrine asked.

"One of the five families. Mafia," the cabbie answered. "They run the coast of New York and the Eastern Seaboard all the way to California."

Harry exhaled, trying to hide his nerves. "Yeah. That's where we are going."

The cabbie shrugged. "Whatever you say." He eyed them warily. "You a member of the mob or something?"

"Ask me no questions and I'll tell you no lies," Harry said, a twinkle in his eye.

"Yeah, yeah, wise guy. Get in. I'll take you. But I don't want any trouble, you got it?"

Katrine held her breath and got in the cab. Harry looked over at her. "Are you scared?"

"Nothing can scare me after the parachute ride."

"I'm scared." He looked straight ahead. "I don't know what Jason was thinking. The Gambino's have their toes in everything from racketeering, pier thefts, gambling, loan sharks… not to mention the darker side to the underworld."

"Darker side?" Katrine's eyebrows went up.

It was a short drive to the docks. Only a couple of blocks.

The cab wove through the streets of New York headed directly to the dockyard.

A guard stopped them at a gate. He wore a long wool coat and a fedora.

Harry unrolled his window, "Um, Jason Hoffman sent us."

"You two Mr. and Mrs. Smith?"

Katrine jerked her head up and down.

"You're expected. Dock Five."

"Dock Five. Right. Thanks." Harry rolled up

the window, and the cabbie rolled forward. Slowly, the vehicle inched towards Dock Five.

"My, it is dark down here," Katrine said as she slid out after Harry.

"Wait for us, okay?" Harry said to the cabbie.

"The meter is running."

"You'll get a big tip, I promise."

A man appeared on the dock, wearing the same long wool coat and fedora as the guard at the gate. It must be some sort of uniform, Katrine thought. The man flagged them down, motioning them towards the entrance of a large cargo ship. Light from the open door poured out onto the dock.

"Mr. and Mrs. Smith?" the man said, extending his hand as they drew closer. "We've been expecting you."

"So we've heard," Harry said. "And you are?"

"No names, please."

"Sure thing." Harry looked sideways at Katrine and allowed her to step onboard first.

Inside were two more men. Both wore very expensive pinstripe suits. It looked like they were in the middle of a card game. "It's the Smiths," the one without a name announced, following them inside.

"Good." The man sitting closest to the door put his cards down and stood up. "We've got your birthday present ready for inspection. We've been holding onto it for a quite a while, and I'm happy to get it off of our hands. Follow me, yes?" Then, as though he had forgotten his manners, he said, "I'm so sorry, can I offer you both a drink?"

"Later," Harry said. "I want to see the merchandise."

"Sure, sure," the man said appreciatively. "And would your wife like to come too?"

There was no way Katrine was going to wait in that room. With more enthusiasm than she'd planned, she exclaimed, "Oh yes. You promised me I could see it, didn't you, dear!"

The man shrugged. "I wasn't sure if you wanted to surprise her or not."

With that, Harry and Katrine followed the man deep into the recesses of the cargo ship, passing box after box of cognac, bananas, and cigarettes. Finally, they reached a crate that was padlocked. The man took out a key, unlocked it, and pulled the door open. Inside were five unmarked wooden boxes roughly two by six feet long and a foot high. Motioning for Harry to hold a flashlight, he took a crowbar leaning against the crate and pried one open. Inside was a row of rifles. They looked old. Katrine assumed there were several hundred guns.

"WWI, I take it?" Harry frowned.

"I know. Not great. But better than no guns, right?"

"And expensive."

"It's what we've got."

Harry's shoulders slumped. "We'll take them. How do you plan on delivering them?"

"This boat goes to Cuba. Strictly kosher business, if you get my meaning. It's up to your people to get the guns to wherever you want them from there. We don't deal with the British."

"And how am I supposed to get this stuff from Cuba to Palestine?

"We work with another, uh, company. Your stuff will be loaded on a British freighter, unknown to the boat's owners. The guy doing the loading and unloading has been well paid by your people. Trust me, no one will open the crate." The man went to the back of the crate and motioned for Katrine and Harry to follow him. He pointed to a stack of rugs piled up. Large Persian rugs. At the moment, he seemed like the most untrustworthy character either one of them had ever met.

"Carpets?" Harry asked.

"Inside the carpets, if you get my meaning. Rolled up inside are all the pieces to two machine guns. *Not* WWI, if you can believe it."

"I'll believe it when and if someone manages to put them together." Harry paused and then asked, "How can you assure me that this stuff will reach the freighter in Cuba?"

The man didn't answer and looked at Harry like he was an idiot, ignoring him.

"Final item of business," the man said, pulling out a beautiful mink coat. "He wanted you to pick up a little birthday present for your wife. Tax-free, duty-free, and worth more than its weight in gold."

Katrine held the coat. It was heavy… very heavy.

"What's in this coat?" she asked.

"Don't ask." The man began putting the covers on the crates again and locking them up. "And don't lose it. Let's just say, it is the traveler's most cost-effective way of getting a large sum of petty cash to… say Poland, or Palestine, or wherever you two kids are spending your vacation."

"Why are you helping us?" Katrine asked.

"We pay him to help, Katrine. We pay him a lot."

The guy shot Harry a menacing stare. "My father may be a Gambino, but my mother is a Gamburg."[11]

Gamburg? Katrine thought. He had a Jewish mother?

"And for your information," he went on, "those machine guns are my personal donation to the cause if you get my meaning."

Harry reddened. "I'm sorry."

The man softened. "I get it. It's hard to know who to trust these days."

Harry extended his hand towards the mobster. "I appreciate your help, Mr. Gambino. Please, forget I said that."

"Sure. Sure." He took Harry's hand and shook it. "Go show those Nazis a thing or two. Give em' the old one-two," he did a quick jab and a hook in the air, "for me!"

HARRY AND KATRINE did not say goodnight when they went to their hotel rooms after the tense drive back from the dock. And it was too warm to wear mink. Katrine felt hot and claustrophobic. It had to weigh nearly 40 pounds, she thought as she eased it off of her arms and locked it away in a new trunk under the bed.

The night wore on and on. Katrine couldn't sleep.

Why hadn't she said yes to Harry? Why, oh why, oh why! It was just a date? Just a silly little date!

She tossed and turned and finally sat up and turned the light on. She had wanted to say yes, but she hadn't. Why not? What was she so scared of? Was she really so afraid of what falling in love might do to her? Was she really so afraid of jumping out of the plane?

Her fear had not only destroyed her chances of something more with Harry, but it had destroyed the friendship they already had. Something must be the matter with my tongue, she thought. It's always moving when I don't want it to, and then, when I want it to, it stops working or says utterly the wrong thing.

Her feet skimmed the cool wood floor, and her hands reached for her robe. Maybe there was some buttermilk in the icebox? The woman who ran the little hotel left the kitchen open at night for the guests. There were always cheese sandwiches and a couple of apples on hand for midnight snackers. Yes, she told herself, all she needed was some buttermilk. That would calm her down and help her sleep. Buttermilk would push Harry out of her mind.

She made her way into the kitchen.

No use crying, she told herself, wiping a rogue tear out of her eyes and looking into the icebox. She spied the jar of buttermilk and took it out.

No use crying over what you can't have. Steady on, Katrine. Steady on, she said inwardly. No use crying over what you threw away.

But the tears came anyway, flowing hot and strong down her cheeks. She'd lost her chance, and she knew it. There had been something in that final look before she stood up off the bench. He wouldn't ask her again. She had been too tough a nut to crack after all. Her shell was impenetrable. And at that moment, the milk undrunk, the single bulb swinging from the dingy kitchen ceiling, Katrine hated herself.

"You're not going to give up that easily, are you?" a kindly voice said from behind her.

Katrine swung around. It was the hotel's night janitor making his way round the ground floor with his mop. The old man's dark skin around his mouth opened to reveal two rows of perfectly white shiny teeth. His hair, tight white curls, was cropped close to his head. And tiny wrinkles around his bright black eyes crinkled compassionately down on Katrine.

"Who are you?"

"I'm Timmy. I clean up around here. And who are you?"

"I don't know anymore." She looked up at him, surprised. "How did you know I've given up?"

"I've worked in this here hotel for over 40 years. Every girl or boy who comes down in the middle of the night and sits at that table crying, not drinking their buttermilk, normally has given up or lost something important."

edld be right on both
accounts."

He leaned his mop up against the wall and
sat down in the chair across from Katrine.
"Well, 40 years of wisdom rarely prove me
wrong."

She looked down, the tears welling up again.

"So, are you going to tell me what happened?"

She shook her head no. "It's too terrible."
Then, a slight choke in the back of her throat,
she forced out, "I haven't been very kind. I
made a terrible mistake."

"What made you do it?"

"I was afraid."

"Nothing a good ol 'I'm sorry' can't fix, I
bet."

She thought of Harry's face. "We are beyond
talking, I'm afraid."

"Then if you can't say you're sorry, show it.
Actions speak louder than words, as the saying
goes."

She blinked once or twice.

The old man eased out of the chair and once
more took up his mop, saying in a sing-song
voice as he disappeared out the kitchen and down
the hall, "My 40 years of wisdom, they ain't
proved me wrong yet."

∾

"WHERE'S KATRINE?" Bertha peered out in the
hallway.

"She slid a note under my door early this
morning. Told me she had a couple of errands to

36

run." Harry took off his hat and stepped inside. "She'll be here before the fireworks."

"You are going to let that beautiful girl go around New York by herself! I raised you better than that!"

"If Katrine wants to go around alone, that's her business, Mama. Katrine is a big girl."

He was inside his mother's apartment now, sitting down on the couch. His eyes lingered on the photograph of his parents on their wedding day.

"Not so big a girl, I think." Bertha shut the door firmly and sat down next to her son, studying his face.

"What did that girl go and do to you? She hurt you, didn't she! And I thought she was such a nice girl. I liked her!"

"I liked her too. That's the problem."

Bertha frowned. "What happened?"

"She's like a scared cat. I got too close. The claws came out, and I got a scratch. Nothing permanent. The bleeding will stop."

"Leave a scar?"

"I don't scar, Mama, you know that." He stood up and began to look through his mother's records. He chose a Benny Goodman and put it on the player, carefully adjusting the needle. A moment later, soft jazz swirled out of the horn.

She made an 'mm-hmm' sound and narrowed her gaze on her son. "I can see right through you, Harry, even if you are a trained spy. I'm your mother."

"I don't want to talk about it anymore."

"That girl needs a good talking to!"

337

"You are going to be nice to her. Understand?"
He picked up the newspaper and sat back down in
an armchair, away from Bertha, and tried to
change the subject. "What'd you make for the
potluck tonight on the roof?"

She sighed. "Something very American. I got
the recipe from a magazine. It's called 'Independence Day Cake.' It's got pink frosting.
Judy's father is providing the weenies, as
usual. And Mrs. Ichler is making something very
exciting, 'Sparkler Punch.' It's made with
pineapples and grapefruit and a lot of ginger-
ale."

Harry was only half-listening and looked over
the paper. "You read this yet?"

"Yes." Bertha crossed her legs and leaned
back. "The French signed an Armistice with the
Germans. Now France is split in two; the quasi-
sovereign French state and the German-occupied
zone. Those poor French. The pathetic Maginot
Line! All I can say is that I'm glad your father
chose to come here instead of France. It sounds
very bad over there." She looked at him fondly.
"It warms my heart to have you home, you know
that?"

Harry smiled and then said, "I didn't know
that you and dad thought of going to France?"

"It was only for a moment. Who could choose
Paris over New York?"

With that, there was a soft knock at the door.
"Must be Katrine," Harry exhaled.

"I'll get it!" Bertha sprung up. "And I am
going to give that girl a piece of my mind!"

"I told you to be nice to her, Mama."

Bertha unlocked the door, and Katrine burst inside. She seemed jumpy and very nervous, unable to stay still. She started with, "I'm ever so sorry I'm late! I hate being tardy more than just about anything." Then, she pushed a small bouquet of purple irises into Bertha's hands. "These are for you, Mrs. Stenetsky. They reminded me of you."

"The flower of wisdom and respect?"

"You have much of one and deserve much of the other."

Now, Bertha was speechless. She had been preparing an epistle of sharp words for the young German woman, but all she could do was stand there, confused.

Katrine kept moving. She was afraid she would lose her courage if she stopped.

"And these are for you." She pulled out from behind her back another bouquet. "It's for the fourth of July. And I know it is not exactly *usual* to buy men flowers but given how you appreciate them so…"

"Blue, white, and red?" He looked at them curiously. "It's very patriotic." Thoughtfully, he said, "Hyacinth, jasmine, and camellia. If I didn't know better, I would almost think you were trying to tell me something."

"I am Harry." She breathed.

For the moment, both forgot that Bertha was in the room.

He touched the blue hyacinth first. "Please forgive me?"

"Yes," Katrine said. "I—" she willed her mouth to move. "I'm ever so sorry, Harry. I wanted to tell you yes at Coney Island. I really did. I was afraid, afraid to love you. But then the thought of not having you to love was much, much worse."

He didn't move. "Much worse?"

"Ever so much worse. So, that's the white jasmine. It means love, yes?" Katrine asked.

"Yes. It does."

"I ran all over town to find those. And the red camellias." Katrine blushed and gripped the chair beside her for support. "'My destiny is in your hands.' I looked it up."

"You're a good researcher."

"I've always been an 'A' student." She stepped towards him.

Harry stood there, stunned. He was completely and totally surprised.

Exasperated, Bertha pushed him towards her murmuring, "So kiss her, you idiot!"

The moment their lips touched, a burst of blue and red fire exploded out their window.

Katrine went weak in the knees, and Harry held her up. "I think," she said after a minute, "I mean, I always wondered if when you had the kiss of true love, you would hear bells or music or something. I never thought it would be a full-blown explosion. I must have it bad!"

Harry started laughing. "That was the beginning of the fireworks show."

"Oh," she was smiling up at him, "I see."

"And we are going to miss the rest of it if we don't get up to the roof right now!" Bertha interjected. She was beaming from ear to ear.

Harry and Katrine didn't move, gazing steadily into each other's eyes.

Bertha was at the front door now, holding the pink cake. "Come on, you two!" The woman couldn't contain her grin. "We have much to celebrate!"

Right then, Judy and a tall young man in a Navy uniform came up the stairs on their way to the roof and peeked inside the apartment. "Why, if it isn't Harry and his business associate!"

"Who's this?" Bertha pointed her chin at the sailor.

"My new business associate." She laughed gaily. She turned to Harry and Katrine, both standing very close to one another. "Tommy, meet some old friends of mine. They're business associates too."

"WE NEED to talk about what happened back there," Katrine said quietly as they walked hand in hand back to the hotel. She had never felt so happy in all her life. The world was new and young and fresh. America was wonderful. Life was wonderful. And the Fourth of July was the most wonderful holiday of all! But still, there were decisions to make. Things to discuss.

"We do?"

"You kissed me."

"I'm pretty sure you were the one who kissed me."

"Harry, really, be serious. We need to talk

this through like two grown-ups. We must decide what to do!"

"I'll admit, we did get a little carried away. In front of my mother no less."

Suddenly, a man stepped out of the shadows. He was dressed as a workman, in coveralls with a small little cap. He was completely unmemorable, the kind who could disappear in any crowd. In a low voice, he said, "Shalom Chaverim."

Harry stopped and protectively put his arm in front of Katrine. "Who are you?"

"Haganah. I've been waiting for you for three hours." The man stuck out his hand. Katrine could tell that there was a small scar right above his eyebrow. "Ma Nishtana."

"Ma Nishtana?" Katrine asked. "Why is this night different from all other nights?" The phrase referred to the four questions asked at every Passover.

"It's the password," Harry said softly to Katrine.

"We can't talk here." The man whispered.

Harry frowned. "What's the matter?"

"You are to come with me. Plans have changed."

Harry took Katrine's arm, preparing to follow. "All right. Let's go."

The man stopped her. "Not the girl."

"She's one of us!" Harry exclaimed.

"Orders."

He pulled a note out of his pocket and passed it to Harry. He scanned it quickly, his face falling by the minute. He shot the man a glare. "Give us a minute, okay?"

The man nodded, and Harry pulled Katrine away.

"Wait for me, okay? I'll be back in the morning. See you at breakfast. Usual table."

"All right." Katrine's voice had an edge of panic. She was afraid to ask what would happen if he wasn't there.

CHAPTER 24

A MATTER OF FAITH

"Have you thought of what to do about Yosef yet?" Paulina asked Becky. Lorelei was shadowing her roommate today and stood by the table where Becky was carefully examining Nick.

"No." Becky looked at Paulina. "I haven't had time to go to the consulate."

"You are both very busy women, did you know that?"

Becky acted as though she had not heard Paulina. "I hate to say it, but this isn't the first baby who has come in today with this rash."

"What do you mean?"

"It's measles." Becky pointed to the little red hives around the toddler's mouth. "They also call it rubeola. See this? The large, flat blotches that seem to flow into one another? And the tiny white spots inside of his mouth?"

"But couldn't it be something else? Perhaps a reaction to his baby soap or something?" Paulina stepped forward, growing concerned. "He's never had anything serious before!"

"I'm afraid he has all the symptoms. Fever. Dry cough. Runny nose. His eyes are inflamed, see?" She looked straight at Paulina. "Have you had measles before?"

Paulina shook her head no, and Becky swallowed.

"All right, I want you to go to our apartment. You remember where it is, don't you?"

The young girl nodded. "You are going to stay with us until Nick's better. Measles can be very dangerous. Once you've had it, you won't ever get it again. But in your case, I don't want any risks. The Old City is too cramped… it's not safe."

"What about Nick?"

"He's going to stay right here at the hospital." Becky was very serious. "I want you to take off every piece of clothing you have and leave them outside on the porch. We'll boil them later. And then, get in the tub and scrub, and I mean scrub, every part of you with the white medical soap. You'll know it because the regular soap is pink. All right?"

"All right," Paulina repeated.

"What is it, Becky?" Lorelei pressed. "Why are you looking like that?"

"I'm worried about an epidemic, Lorelei. This is the 10th child to come in with the same symptoms. We don't have enough beds." She took the thermometer, and her frown deepened.

"Is it really so bad?"

Becky nodded. "His temperature is 103. Measles is highly contagious and life-threatening, especially if you are little, like this one." Becky bit her lip. "The complications can be terrible. Ear infections that lead to deafness. Bronchitis or croup. Pneumonia. And in the case of high fevers, brain swelling."

Lorelei dug in her purse and pulled out her spare key, which she gave to Paulina. Paulina took the key, her fingers lightly brushing up against Lorelei's. "I'll see you at your home then?"

Lorelei nodded. She wasn't worried about herself; she'd had measles as a child.

"I can call my parents from the phone in your apartment, yes?"

"Of course," Lorelei answered.

"I'm sure my mother will be here soon!"

"Has she had it?"

Paulina nodded her head yes. "I am pretty sure they have both had it, my mother and father."

"Tell them not to come on any account. Nick will be just fine here. I'll watch him like he is my own," Becky said firmly. "We can't have too many parents hanging about, you see. There will just be too many for the hospital staff to handle."

Once Paulina left, Nick was deposited into the darkened children's ward. There was no medicine to treat measles, only rest, hydration, and, strangely enough, darkness. It was not unusual for those ill to find bright light uncomfortable.

Lorelei and Becky braced for the worst. The madness had begun.

Measles swept across the city without regard to age, wealth, or religion. Jew, Christian, and Muslim lay side by side in the hospital and various clinics across the city. Lorelei split her time between the children's ward at the hospital and the Spafford Baby Home. It seemed to hit the young the hardest. Paulina proved a Godsend. She kept her hosts well-fed and cleaned their apartment from stem to stern.

After the first week, Lorelei stumbled into the apartment. Her eyes were red from tiredness. She couldn't remember the last time she'd had a proper night's rest. As was their habit, she dropped her nurses uniform outside to be boiled and then lowered herself into the scalding bath prepared by Paulina. She rubbed her skin till she was nearly raw and then, out of the tub once more, put on an old worn sweater and some khaki slacks.

Paulina was waiting for her in the living room with a cup of tea. "You saw Nick today? My parents have asked."

Lorelei nodded.

"They also said to thank you for letting me stay here."

Lorelei managed a small smile.

"I held Nick for two hours." Lorelei sighed and took the tea. "He's strong, Paulina. He seems to be coming through much better than some of the others." She didn't add how they had lost four, just that morning. They had over 300 in the hospital now, and the Baby House was close to bursting.

"How is Becky?"

Becky? Lorelei didn't know how to answer. Physically, Becky was tired. But she was also, somehow, peaceful, even joyful. It was baffling. When Lorelei had asked why, she'd answered simply, "Why Lorelei, I'm casting my cares."

"Casting your cares?"

"On God, of course. He promises to sustain me through any trouble if I trust him."

Trust him? How did Becky do it? It was still a mystery to Lorelei, one she pondered while taking temperatures and distributing aspirin. Her head had become so full of questions since that day at the Courtyard Cafe that she sometimes thought it would burst.

A quick knock on the door jolted Lorelei's attention. It was Yosef, holding a large sack of groceries in his hands. It was not safe for Paulina to venture to the market. The risk of catching the germs was too high. Yosef, who also had already had the measles, had (conveniently for the lovebirds) become their errand boy.

"I brought you something." Yosef blushed and gave Paulina a small box from behind his back. "Halva."

Wrapping her arms around Yosef in the doorframe, paper sack and all, she exclaimed, "My favorite!" and dragged him inside, opening the package of sweetened sesame paste studded with nuts and dried fruit.

Lorelei chuckled. Young love… they were still

in the candy and flowers phase. It pricked her heart, and she had to turn away.

"I had him bring everything I need for my famous chicken soup." Paulina noticed how tired Lorelei looked. "I think you need it."

Standing up abruptly, Lorelei replied, "I think what I need is a little walk." She didn't know what to do. All she could see in her mind's eye was row after row of beautiful children, their tiny bodies shaking with fevers, their soft skin mottled with hives. She was having trouble breathing evenly.

"You're leaving us here, alone?" Paulina asked, shocked.

"I trust you not to do anything foolish."

"We were just going to make soup."

"That's what I thought."

Once the door was shut, Lorelei stood in the hall, not knowing where to go or what to do. She honestly had no desire to go for a walk. But the apartment felt claustrophobic. Before she knew it, her feet carried her to the Finkelstein's door. And before she could stop herself, she was knocking on it.

Ethel opened the door almost as soon as she knocked. "Lorelei! I didn't expect you!"

"I didn't expect myself. Do you mind if I come in?"

"Of course not." She stepped aside and looked curiously at Lorelei.

Lorelei stood in the entryway, not knowing exactly what to say. Almost as an afterthought, she asked, "All your children are alright?"

"They're steering clear of the measles if

that's what you're asking. No symptoms, any of them." Ethel's voice was tense. She had trouble hiding her fear for her children.

The apartment was strangely quiet.

"Where are they?"

"Aron and I sent them to some friends on a kibbutz in the south until the city is no longer quarantined."

"That was wise."

"We are lucky to have friends."

Ethel Finkelstein swallowed. "I'll make us some tea."

"Oh no! Please don't. I just had a cup." Lorelei saw the piano and stopped. "I was wondering…" she trailed off.

"Yes?"

"If you and Aron wouldn't mind—"

"Yes?" Ethel's eyebrows raised slightly.

"Could I possibly play your piano?"

Ethel exhaled and smiled. "I've been waiting for you to ask. It's perfect timing. Aron is at the University, and I am working in the kitchen. It's all yours, my dear. The music is on the fourth bookshelf. If you need me, call."

And so, the concert pianist with the palest of skin and the blackest of hair, the mother of seven and the wife to Aron, the rabbi with questions, left Lorelei to her most prized of possessions. Her piano. Her beautiful Bluthner. Worth more than wedding dishes or clothes or furniture but not more than books.

Lorelei scanned the music library and selected a Chopin collection. Nocturne in C. Her fingers touched the keys tenuously. Her eyes saw the

familiar notes. And then came the music. In a
wave, it all came back. Every bit of it. The
laughter of days gone by. The pain of them never
coming back, never ever. She played, and she
played, and she played. And when she was done,
she felt as though she could sleep for a very
long time.

"That was very beautiful. I've never heard
that song played quite like that before, and
I've heard a lot of people play it." Ethel had
been listening in the doorway for quite some
time.

Lorelei didn't look up. "Thank you, Mrs.
Finklestein. That means a lot coming from
someone like you."

"Aron is coming home in a minute. Maybe you'll
join us for dinner?"

"I can't, but thank you." She stood up and
smoothed out her slacks. "I've two youngsters in
the apartment who need looking after."

"In my opinion, you look like you could use
some looking after."

"When I play, I feel like I can breathe. Do
you know what I mean?"

"I'm probably one of the few women who does
know what you mean."

LORELEI RETURNED to the Finkelstein's the next
evening and the evening after that. It was on
the fourth evening that it was obvious to Ethel
that the young woman was in some sort of deep
inner turmoil. When Aron returned from work,

351

Ethel pulled him aside and whispered, "She's been playing for almost three hours. No stops at all! Her hands must be awfully tired." The Finkelstein's peered into their living room where Lorelei sat behind the Bluthner. She had made it through all of Chopin's preludes and was starting on the etudes.

"She's working something out inside." Ethel poked Aron in the ribs. "You need to talk to her."

The rabbi did not speak. Slowly, he walked into the living room.

Lorelei looked up, feeling Aron's presence.

"Hello, Mr. Finkelstein," she said quietly, lifting her hands off the keys. "Home from the university so early?"

"So early?" he repeated.

She looked at the clock, shocked that it was already past seven. She'd had no idea she'd been playing for so long. "Oh my, I am so sorry."

"Don't apologize. You'll stay for dinner this time, won't you?"

She shook her head. "I don't want to impose. Besides, Paulina will be making something time-consuming, and I don't want to have all that effort go to waste." She was standing now, rolling down the sleeves to her blouse.

Aron put one hand on the piano and looked at Lorelei. "I think you didn't come here just to practice the piano, no?"

"Sometimes it is easier than thinking."

"Indeed."

Lorelei pushed the bench in and gently placed the cover over the keys. As an afterthought, she suddenly looked the rabbi straight in the eye.

"You said at Passover that my questions were for another time. Well, it's another time."

"And you want to ask me a question?" he finished for her. "As a rabbi," she replied.

He nodded, contemplating the troubled young woman standing behind his wife's piano.

"What's the point?" Lorelei said bluntly.

"The point of what, Ms. Adleman?"

Lorelei decided to say exactly what she was thinking, even if it might offend Aron. She didn't care, she had to say it. She had to have answers. "I live with a Christian nurse who confuses me to no end because she has faith and trusts that God works things out for our good and thinks Jesus is *our* Messiah, and I do not, and from what I can tell, there is no end to suffering. I spend hours every day in a chil-dren's ward with dying babies. Sometimes I feel as though I cannot breathe! But she is stable and happy. I'm almost jealous of her. And yet, she tells me that it is important that I am Jewish. She says it is a gift!" She was rambling on and on, and she stopped herself as suddenly as she began. She waited, wondering how Aron would respond. "I think being Jewish is getting old. It's the same thing. Over and over and over again. It's not working. And I don't know if it's worth it." She choked out her last words. "Sometimes I think it is a death sentence."

Surprised at her forthrightness, she caught herself and began to apologize. "I am so sorry, Aron. I'm not making any sense, am I? I'm not religious myself. I celebrate Passover and fast on Yom Kippur, and that's about it. I have to be honest, I'm not sure what being Jewish means for someone like me. My parents are dead, and heaven knows where my sisters are."

"Ms. Adleman," the rabbi stroked his beard, "I think you are asking me something else."

"What?"

"I don't think you are asking me what I think the point of being Jewish is. I think you are asking me what I think of God. Because you are disappointed."

She looked at him, surprised.

He smiled sadly. "But first, I will answer your question. For I too had many such questions when I was your age. I come from Vilna."

Vilna, Lorelei knew, was the 'Jerusalem of Europe.' It was the heart of Judaism, the cultural and religious core of the diaspora. "My family was very, very religious. My father studied at the Lithuanian Yeshivot."

"I've heard of it." Lorelei was impressed. Even as a secular Jew, she knew of the famous yeshiva that had been founded in the 18th century by the Great Gaon of Vilnius, Elijah ben Shlomo Zalman. The rabbi was recognized throughout the world as one of history's greatest thinkers.[12]

"Then you know that I understand tradition. More than most."

Lorelei looked at Aron.

"At first, I played the game. But after a while, I started asking questions. Why could we not write, erase, or tear paper on the Sabbath?

Why were the girls taught only prayers and basic texts?"

"And then what?" Lorelei asked, rather surprised at Aron's frank confession.

"I asked more questions. Why did we spend so much time reading the Talmud, the rabbinical law and commentaries, and so little time reading the Torah—the actual Scripture? Why couldn't we study other subjects? Why was it against the law to go to a public library? My education was so narrow, there was no way I would ever be prepared for the outside world. But you see, Ms. Adleman, there was no outside world. We had everything we needed. No one left the fold."

"You did though, didn't you? Obviously."

"I had to find answers or die, Ms. Adleman. I could not turn my brain off. It was much too active. I found no evil in tearing paper on the Sabbath, you see. And when I read the Torah for myself, without the parameters set by the Talmudic scholars, I found little to support my white stockings and black coat."

"And I still have questions. About all of this." He swept his hand over the table. "About the Mashiach, the Messiah, you spoke of."

Lorelei felt nervous. What in the world was this man about to say?

"But you are still Jewish, aren't you?"

"As Jewish as you, Ms. Adleman. I am still a rabbi!" He paused. "I have great pride in my heritage. Even in the traditions. As you can see, I still carry most of them on and teach them to my children. It is a great blessing to be one of the chosen."

"Both a blessing and a curse, it would seem." Lorelei frowned.

The rabbi chose not to answer and said instead, "Have you ever read the 53rd Chapter of Isaiah?"

"I'm not sure." Lorelei's eyes narrowed. She chose not to express that she had spent little time, if any, reading scripture.

"You probably have not. It has not been read out loud in synagogues for several hundred years."

Not that Lorelei would have known the significance of this, as she never went to synagogue, but she intuitively understood that it was a weighty revelation.

"Apparently, the chapter caused arguments and great confusion."

He answered her questioning stare. "The Jewish sages of ancient times, the Targum Jonathan, the Book of Zohar, the Midrash Konan, and a dozen other rabbinical texts and commentaries all connect the chapter to the coming of the Messiah."

"What does it say about him?"

"It says that he will be rejected by his people, that he will suffer in agony, and that God will see his suffering and subsequent death as atonement for the sins of the world."

To Lorelei, it sounded an awful lot like Becky's description of Yeshua. I.e., Jesus.

"The mystery deepens. You look at the words used in this chapter, and all the 'traditions' we practice day in and day out take on new significance. They suddenly become less 'point-less,' to use your word."

"I don't understand." She frowned.

"Think back to the Passover traditions, the matzah bread. Unleavened, Ms. Adleman. Without sin, as the Messiah was said to be. And look, it is pierced through with stripes, as was his body. Hidden from view, like the matzah inside the Afikomen. Just as in this chapter. It goes on and on, Ms. Adleman."

He seemed to look past Lorelei, out the window into the darkening sky over the Old City. "Think of the bone on the seder plate. It's representa-tive of the sacrificial lamb; the spotless lamb's blood that preserved the lives of our people when the angel of death hovered over Egypt. The same language is used to describe Yeshua in the Christian scriptures, the 'Brit Hadashah' as they called it, the 'New Covenant.' The same language used in the forbidden chapter of our own scriptures. The Lamb of God whose shed blood preserves those who believe."

A pit formed in Lorelei's stomach. What was this rabbi trying to say? If the community found out what he might be considering, he would quickly be ostracized and declared anathema, or worse, a traitor. Was it possible that he thought this Jesus might be the Messiah? Lorelei stared at him, her mouth slightly open. Her questions and inner troubles had opened up a discussion that she was completely unprepared for. She had never expected *this* from Aron.

Rather, she was expecting a fatherly reprove for her doubts, a comforting word about suffering in the world being a part of life, and an encouragement to hold on to faith. Instead, he was opening the door to the possibility that maybe, just maybe…

"Are you telling me that you think Yeshua is —?" She couldn't finish.

"I've asked hard questions before, Ms. Adleman. And you see, I am still asking them. And that is my answer to your real question, I think."

"I don't understand." Her mind spun. Was it possible that Becky was right? Was Yeshua the Messiah?

"God, Ms. Adleman, and his ways. They are higher than ours. It *is* possible we've been blind. And that is why you and I, and others who value truth over tradition, ask."

Wordlessly, Aron went to the shelf and pulled out a small red letter book. "This is the Tanakh, the complete Hebrew Bible. Read it and ask God to give you the answers you seek."

Lorelei paged through the small book. "It includes the Christian scriptures. The," she looked up and said the Hebrew words, "Brit Hadashah?"

"If you are curious about the Christians, you must satisfy your curiosity."

CHAPTER 25

THE POINT OF NO RETURN

*G*race faced Hannah and Cecilia at their usual table in the back of the dining room over dinner.

"What do you mean you can't come?" Cecilia exclaimed. "It's the *Pyramids*."

"It may be the Pyramids, but I'm not on leave like the rest of you." Grace pushed her goggles down around her neck and shook out her hair. She'd been up two hours earlier than the rest of them that morning, and Amos had her scheduled doing air maneuvers for the rest of the day.

"It's only a one day leave. Amos can't let you off the hook for one day? You may never get another chance like this again!" Hannah said.

Grace sighed. "It's not to say I don't envy you. If not for the adventure of it, then for the thought of having a whole day off with no saluting or uniforms." Smiling, she began to butter her bread liberally with margarine. "You know, if I could have my way, there is nothing I'd rather do today than go to the Pyramids. That is, except maybe flying over them. Take plenty of pictures for me, won't you?"

"A picture is a poor substitute for riding a camel." Cecilia sighed.

"I've ridden a camel."

"But not in the shadow of the Pyramids." The young girl was emphatic.

"Well, right now finishing up my flight hours is more important. I need my wings as soon as possible. Preferably before we are scattered all over the skies of Europe." She took a bite of her bread. It was dry and crumbled in her mouth. "I haven't seen you two much lately. How's the paratrooper training been going?"

"They've whittled us down to 38 if you can believe it. And only 36 are going to be selected for the actual mission."

"How's Morris?" she asked, and then quickly clarified, *"Where's* Morris?"

"About that." Cecilia leaned in. "Grace, he's been acting sort of funny. He's told me things I don't like."

"What do you mean?"

"He said that the British aren't doing anything to help us."

"That's not true, completely. Look, they are training us, aren't they?"

"Only because it serves them to serve us. You heard what happened to the *St. Louis*! Turned down at every port. All those people, 900 Jews, sent back to concentration camps."[13]

"There were a lot more countries at fault there than just the UK."

"Still," Cecilia kept going, "the British don't want to help us. They just want to beat the Nazis, and they are using us to help them." She stopped abruptly. "Anyway, those are the things he is talking about. He isn't even going to see the Pyramids because he's got some meeting in Cairo."

"In Cairo?"

"Yeah. And he didn't even invite me!"

"*Us,*" Hannah corrected her roommate.

"That's pretty odd," Grace agreed. But before she could dwell on it any longer, she noticed the time. Gulping down her powdered milk mixed with water, she grabbed her flight jacket from the back of the chair and walked quickly towards the exit. There was never enough time for a square meal these days. Her stomach grumbled slightly.

"You haven't finished your lunch!" Hannah called after her.

"Don't have time!"

IF HE WAS REALLY honest with himself, which he was not, Amos would have admitted that he liked spending time with Grace alone up in the air. That's why he had (secretly) insisted on person-ally finishing up her instructor hours instead of assigning her to some less important pilot with more time on his hands.

They had been up there for over an hour, and he was still lecturing.

"The point of no return is exactly what it sounds like. It's that point when a plane has just enough fuel to return to the airfield you left from. Once you make it past that point, there's no return. Hence, 'the point of no return.' Once you cross it, you have to go somewhere else."

"Got it." Grace nodded tersely.

"Try another roll," Amos commanded.

"Yes, sir!" Grace smiled and rolled the plane to the left. For good measure, she did it once more after the plane leveled out.

"Now, come in real low. Like we are going to take out their guns." He stopped himself. "Not that you are ever going to be in combat, mind you. But just in case."

Grace nodded and brought the plane down gently. They were roughly 400 feet above the ground of the base, and she spied her friends gathered around the trucks like little miniatures. They were loading tents, sleeping bags, and ration packs.

"Looks like fun, don't you think?" She hadn't meant to say it. She was determined to say no more than was necessary to Amos, but there it was, out in the open.

"If you like camping I guess." He shrugged. "Bring the plane back up to a thousand feet."

The plane gained altitude.

"You wish you were down there, don't you?" Amos said.

"Well, yes, I do," she answered honestly. "I

may never get the chance to see the Pyramids again."

Amos felt a prick of guilt. "Okay, we are going to loop the base a couple of times. Get your hours checked off. Today is just about flying. No more lectures."

"Okay." Grace heaved a sigh. It was a little boring getting flight hours in with nowhere to go. But at least they were in the air. There was some fun in that. And they had hours and hours to go. Both settled in for the flight.

The minutes ticked by, and Amos (who was also slightly bored) began to read.

"You're reading the comics!" Grace exclaimed when her eyes caught sight of Amos's choice of literature. "What kind of flight instructor are you?"

"The kind who likes to pass the time productively." He tried to maintain his serious air of professionalism, but he had been found out. It was too late.

"You know, I took you for a news-only type. You are so serious all the time." The plane banked a moment, and she adjusted the wings. She glanced at the cover of his comic. It read, 'The Masked Marvel! Keen Detective Funnies. Introducing Air Man.'[14]

"Air Man?" She asked skeptically. Air Man, apparently, was half-bird, half-man. He wore a yellow mask with feathers pointing down and had yellow and red wings sprouting from his back. His red boots had talons on the ends, like a hawk. This creature hovered above a green ocean and, safely secured in his arms, was a beautiful girl with strawberry blonde hair, who, she assumed, he had just rescued.

She read the caption out loud. "After saving the girl, Air Man made quick work of the Pirate's Boat with one of his secret pellets!"[15] She looked up at Amos. "What in the world is that supposed to mean?"

"Beats me. These never make any sense, but they're harmless fun. Makes me feel like a kid."

"American?"

"Who else would write something like that. The Americans have a hero complex."

"I'm not so sure it's just the Americans, but yes, I do agree that only an American would write about secret pellets."

Both stopped talking for a moment, simultaneously surprised that they had spoken to each other like two human beings for nearly a minute.

Grace was coming in back over the base. As per Amos's instructions, she swooped in low and began to fly over the desert. Nonchalantly, she gazed below.

All of a sudden, she jerked her head towards the window and looked down. "What's he doing!" she exclaimed suddenly.

"Who?"

"Look! That's Morris, isn't it?" Grace could make out the cova tembel (his distinctive kibbutz hat) even from 100 feet above.

"Hand me the binoculars." He peered through and nodded. "Looks like he's hiking out into the desert, with two others by the looks of it. They have an old jeep too."

"No. That can't be it. Cecilia told me he

had a meeting in Cairo. That's why he wasn't going to the Pyramids." The plane soared beyond the small group on the desert floor below.

"Maybe he missed his bus?"

Her women's intuition told her that wasn't it either. "I'm bringing the plane down." She paused. "Permission to bring the plane down, sir?"

"I'm sure nothing is wrong," Amos said.

"I really feel it, Amos. We need to go down there!"

Reluctantly, Amos acquiesced. What was there to lose? "Permission granted. Bring her down."

GRACE BROUGHT the plane in for an easy landing, and quickly, they jumped out of the plane and jogged towards the place where Morris stood with the unidentified men.

"Morris!" Grace shouted towards him.

Morris waved and yelled, "Grace? What are you doing here?"

Amos, a pace or two behind Grace, observed Morris carefully. Grace was right. Something was wrong. Something felt… off. "What are you doing here, Greenburg?"

Morris licked his lips nervously. He looked up to Amos, hating to disappoint him.

Grace looked at the two men behind Morris. Both wore white linen suits. "And you two are?"

The first one bowed his head and said in a soft German accent, "I am Walter Brunsky, and this is Milton, my brother. We run a bookshop in Cairo."

"You aren't in Cairo or at the Pyramids. Now spill!" Amos looked like he was ready to pummel the young man into telling the truth. Grace pulled him back. "Morris, we need you to tell us what you're doing. No one just goes out into the desert. You could get lost. Or worse."

"They invited me here," Morris said quietly. "They said they had a way to speed up getting the Jews out of Europe. They wanted to meet somewhere secret."

"Obviously, the desert was not deserted enough," Milton said, speaking for the first time. The brothers looked at each other nervously. They gave Grace a creepy feeling. She addressed Morris, ignoring Milton. "How did you meet these men?"

"I rode into Cairo last week on a delivery convoy. I had the afternoon off, so I stopped by the synagogue, and they were there having a meeting in the basement."

"He stayed to listen and was interested in what we had to say." Walter said.

The sun beat down mercilessly on them, causing beads of sweat to roll down their cheeks.

Morris nodded. "They are determined to evict the British authorities. They want unrestricted immigration of Jews to Palestine. And I think that's a good thing."

"We do too," Grace agreed. "That's why we are working with the British to defeat the Nazis, and we are working with the Palmach to bring in as many Jewish refugees under British noses as we can, illegally, of course."

Walter stepped in. "Stern, our leader, thinks there is a better way to accomplish this mutual goal."

Amos stepped back, his eyes hardening. "You are members of the Stern Gang!"[16]

"The Stern Gang?" Grace asked, confused.

Amos shot her a look. "They will do anything to get the British out, even if it means hurting innocent women and children. They are terrorists who call themselves freedom fighters. They give Jews a bad name."

He looked at Morris. "What were they going to have you do, Morris? Destroy everything we've worked so hard to build? Do you know what we had to do to get the British to allow us to train you on this base for this mission? A mission that could save thousands! These men are traitors!"

"We could save thousands too," Milton retorted. "We are not traitors. We just have different views on how to win this war."

"Different views!" Amos was appalled. "Stern says we should be willing to go to Fascist Italy and Nazi Germany. He thinks we should offer to fight alongside *them* against the British."

"Fight alongside the Axis Powers?" Grace looked at the brothers in shock.

"In exchange for the transfer of the Jews from occupied Europe to Palestine," Walter answered.

"Men like you have no honor!" Amos shook his head. Disgust was written all over his face. "These guys are selling their soul to the devil.

It's not worth it." Amos looked down at young Morris.

"What are we going to do with them?" Grace whispered to Amos.

Without taking his eyes off the brothers, he shook his head, speaking quietly. "I don't know. If we tell the Brits that we've caught members of the Stern Gang, we might all be suspected of treason. They've put the whole mission in jeopardy." There really was nothing that Amos could do. The two men stood there, smirking.

Amos put his hand on the gun in his holster, addressing the men loudly. "I'm going to keep my eye on you. If one mishap happens, you will pay, do you understand? You talk to one more of my men—" Menacingly, he pointed at them. And then, looking at Morris, he spat out, "Go get in the plane, Morris. We're going back to the base. And I never want you to speak with these men again! Do you understand, Greenburg!"

"Really, Amos! I had no idea what they were about!"

"Do you hear me?"

"Yes, sir." Morris hung his shoulders. "Are you going to send me back to the kibbutz?"

"I don't know what I'm going to do with you yet." Amos sighed.

ALL THREE WERE silent during the short flight back to the base. When the plane finally rolled to the end of the runway, Grace breathed a sigh of relief. She felt very tired.

Morris grabbed Grace's jacket and pulled her back before she got out of the plane. "You won't tell Cecilia about this, will you?"

"I think she needs to know, don't you?"

"Please don't tell her! She won't speak to me again."

Grace put her hand on his back and steered him off the plane. "We'll discuss it later."

Amos was waiting below. "You can spend the rest of the day on your bunk. And if I hear you went *anywhere*, you'll spend tomorrow there too, do you understand me?"

"Then… you are not sending me back to the kibbutz?"

Amos's face softened slightly. "I get it. You want to do something. You want to help. But do it the right way. Not the fast way. Finish your training. Complete the mission you've been given. Shortcuts never work out in the long run. They'll just hurt you and others in the process."

Morris looked up at Amos, his face shining with relief and admiration. "Okay," he quickly caught himself and saluted, "I mean, yes, sir!"

"Off with you." Amos slapped him on the back. As Morris jogged off the runway, he turned to Grace. "I, um, you were right back there."

"About what?"

"You saw something on the ground, and you knew in your gut something was wrong. What I mean to say is," he stopped a second, "I underestimated you, Grace Adleman." Without waiting for her reply, he added, "Get some rest. Tomorrow morning is your first night flight. Be on the runway by 0400."

"Point of no return, right?"

Amos looked in Morris's direction. "He almost reached his today, that's for sure. And he would have if it wasn't for you."

"You were right there beside me. We were the superhero in your magazine, swooping in for the rescue."

He nodded and gave a small grin. "Just in the nick of time."

CHAPTER 26

TICKET FOR ONE

The busboy looked at Katrine with a compassionate expression. "Do you want some more coffee, miss?"

"No, thank you." She shook her head. "I've already had five cups. I don't think I could stomach anymore."

He looked at the clock. It was almost noon. Katrine had been waiting for four hours. "I don't think whoever you are waiting for is coming this morning."

"He'll come," she said firmly. "He told me he would come."

But an hour later, it was clear that Harry was *not* coming. Dejectedly, Katrine went back to her room, a sick feeling in her stomach. She grew afraid. What if Harry had been mugged? Or worse!

She went to the front desk and asked if Harry had left her a message. He had not, and, more than that, he had checked out late the night before.

"How late?"

"At two in the morning." The desk clerk looked at her pityingly.

Nervously, she walked away and back to her room. At the foot of the stairs, she turned left and walked past Harry's door. It was open slightly, and she glanced inside. A maid was cleaning it from stem to stern, and there was no evidence of Harry's things. It was true. He was gone. Really gone.

As minds do, Katrine's began to play harsh and cruel games. What if Harry had been playing her all along! What if he didn't love her after all? He'd never actually said he'd love her, had he?

Katrine frowned and continued on to her own room, several doors down, listening to the evil doubts her fears cast upon her shoulders.

Immediately, she noticed a note had been pushed under the door. Her eyes scanned it quickly. She must have missed it when she'd gone to breakfast earlier that morning.

Katrine, wear your new coat to Mother's. She's expecting you.

She sighed in relief. At least he was okay! He would explain everything soon enough, she told herself. Something must have come up with that man in the coveralls.

Quickly, Katrine unlocked the trunk and took out the coat. Then, she called for the bellboy to hail her a cab. Twenty minutes later, she had checked out of the little hotel and was en route to Delancey Street and Bertha Stenetsky's apartment.

~

THE LITTLE JEWISH woman from Austria certainly was expecting Katrine. Before she could knock, the door to the flat flew open, and Katrine found herself being wrapped in a tight embrace and dragged inside. Bertha locked the door and, for good measure, wedged a chair underneath the knob. "That will keep the Nazis out!" she muttered.

Katrine was breathing heavily. The coat was very, very heavy. She took it off and threw it on Bertha's couch. "Water, please, Bertha. This spy business is more physically taxing than you can imagine."

"I can imagine." Bertha nodded vigorously. "I've been too nervous to sit down since he left. Up down, left right! My feet won't stop moving."

"You saw him?" Katrine asked eagerly.

"Oh yes. He stopped by on his way to the harbor."

"The harbor!" Katrine could not hide her horror. "Why didn't he wake me up and tell me at the hotel?"

Bertha didn't answer her question. "Something happened. I don't know what. But they needed him to meet some sort of transport there to ensure the shipment arrives. He didn't tell me what the shipment was, mind you, even though I am his mother!"

"But why am I not going?"

"He wrote you a letter." She pulled it out of her pocket.

Katrine tore open the envelope.

"Our people have booked you a ticket on the HMS Dorina straight to Lisbon. Boat leaves tonight. In Lisbon, you'll be met at the port by someone you can trust. You'll know him by the blooms. Once you've passed the coat on to someone who needs it more than you, we'll get you back home.

Yours,

Harry

P.S. Sorry I didn't stop by to say goodbye. There wasn't time.

Katrine held the note and read it several times before Bertha interjected, "What did he say?"

"Looks like I'm going to Lisbon." She rubbed her hands through her hair. "I have a delivery to make."

Katrine stared at the note in her hand. No 'I love you.' No anything really. It was all business.

"My son is always leaving abruptly. You'll get used to it. It's his job."

Katrine looked up. "I won't get used to it."

"But you'll have to, now that you're…" Bertha smiled and nodded.

"Bertha, I don't know what you think about your son and I—" she struggled with her words, "—but there is no agreement between us."

"But last night?"

"Last night was last night."

"Oh, Katrine." Bertha's face fell. "He has not asked you to marry him?"

She thought back to the night before. What was it he had said? That they had gotten carried away?

"Isn't there some saying that goes something like, 'never do business with friends"? She crumpled the note in her hand. "I've been a fool, that's all. I'll be back to myself soon enough."

"My son's the one who has been a fool." Bertha blew out an exasperated breath. "So, when does your boat leave?"

"All the letter says is tonight."

"I'm going with you to the port," the old woman said determinedly. "Just let me put on some lipstick."

While she was gone, Katrine looked around the beautiful sitting room. There was the stupid bouquet she had given Harry last night. Bertha had put it in a crystal vase on the coffee table.

Gritting her teeth together, she took the bouquet out of the vase and went to the open window. There, five stories up, she tore the bouquet apart and watched the petals fall to the cracked pavement of Delancey Street. A little girl eating a pickle looked around her in wonder as red, white, and blue petals floated down around her. When she looked up to see the source of colorful rain, she saw Katrine. But Katrine didn't see her. She was looking out at some unknown point on the horizon.

~

"THE STATEROOM IS VERY SMALL," Bertha said, disapprovingly.

"It will do just fine. It's only a week. Well, ten days is more like it, given all the zigzagging we'll have to do to avoid the Nazi U-boats. Even if America is neutral, and this is an American boat, accidents happen."

Once more, Katrine eased off the heavy fur and sunk onto the bed.

Eyebrows raised, Bertha ran her finger along the bed. "I don't like this at all. I wish you and Harry were staying safe at home."

"I don't have a home, Mrs. Stenetsky. Not yet, anyway. That's why I have to go to wherever I'm going."

"Listen to me, Katrine," Bertha said, suddenly urgent. "Harry is a dope. He loves you! He would have told you, but he didn't have time. I'm his mother, I know these things!"

The ship's horn sounded, and Katrine looked away. "You better get off the boat, Bertha, or you'll be going to Lisbon too." Impulsively, she turned back and pulled the old woman in for a gentle hug. "I'll never forget you or your kindness to me. Being with you has felt more like home than I've felt in a very, very long time. I wish… Well, you would have liked my family very much."

"Maybe I'll meet them one day."

Shaking her head sadly, Katrine led Bertha towards the deck. She doubted Bertha would ever meet her family.

Out in the hall, a little man with beady blue eyes, a round bowler hat, and a cane glared in their direction. Just as Katrine and Bertha passed by he spat, in perfect German, to his stern-looking wife, "Genau das, was wir brauchen, zwei Jüdinnen nebenan," meaning, "Just what we need, two Jewesses next door."

Out of earshot, Bertha clung to Katrine's hand. "Promise me you'll be careful. I don't like you sleeping next door to those bigots!"

"Oh, them?" Katrine tried to laugh. "I could take those two on blindfolded."

THE JOURNEY to Lisbon was completely without any significant incident, at least, anything significant to Katrine. If something significant happened, she knew nothing of it. She couldn't stand the thought of people. She didn't want to deal with Nazis or sympathizers or anyone at all. Nothing sounded worse than sitting at a table with a bunch of inquisitive strangers, lying to them, telling them that she was (repulsively) Mrs. Smith, recently widowed, and on her way back home to Switzerland.

Instead, she told the porter she was seasick and refused to leave her stateroom. Oh, she was sure there were spies aplenty onboard. And the danger from Nazi U-boats was real indeed. She simply didn't care. All she wanted was to deliver the coat and go back to Palestine. She would figure out what came next when 'next' came.

Maybe, she thought, she would go back to Scotland. Horatio and Edie would need a nanny for the baby, wouldn't they? It was too bad she was terrible with children.

But she couldn't think these thoughts for too long at a time. She'd wind up crying, and that would make her feel even worse. She had wanted to be Mrs. Stenetsky, not a nanny in the far reaches of Scotland! The shame was nearly too intense to bear.

Thankfully, when the ship finally reached the port in Lisbon, she had pulled herself up by her bootstraps (or black heels, to be more precise) and was ready to do her part. If Harry could go and be a success all alone, so could she. She could be just as good of a spy (if that's what she was) as he was!

And so, her black hat tilted just so over her left eye, her red lipstick flawless, and her mink slung over her shoulder, Katrine descended the gangplank. If someone asked her why in the world she was wearing a mink in the middle of July, she would tell them that she was recovering from a terrible cold. Or, she thought, she would tell them she was a model from a mink manufacturer, and the company was paying her to wear it. Summer discounts, you see.

Her eyes scanned the crowd waiting below the gangplank. What was it Harry had said? *Someone you can trust. You'll know him by the blooms.*

Know him by the blooms? Oh, seriously. Why couldn't Harry be more forthright!

And then, she saw her; a gorgeous woman, probably in her early forties, wearing a hat covered in freesias. And in her arms was a large bouquet of freesias. Quickly, Katrine thumbed through her pocketbook of flowers. Yes, her hunch was right. Freesias were the flower of trust.

The woman was shouting out, "Mrs. Smith! Mrs. Smith!"

The hostile German man and his wife from next door glared in Katrine's direction. She felt a shiver run down her spine, and she quickly moved away, signaling the woman with her hand.

The woman's white suit nearly glowed in the sunlight. "Are you Mrs. Smith?" she asked, lowering her voice.

"It depends."

"You are." The woman gave a twinkling laugh. "You're wearing my coat. These are for you, compliments of your husband. I'll hold them for you though. It looks like you're carrying quite enough as it is."

"I'm not really married." Katrine frowned.

"None of them are," the woman said. "I've been a Mrs. Smith too."

"Pardon me?" Katrine asked, but the woman couldn't hear her. They were working their way through the crowd, pushing towards a limousine. The driver popped out and opened the door.

The two women slipped in, and the blonde threw the bouquet on the seat beside her and looked at Katrine. "Now, take that heavy thing off before you die of heatstroke." Her accent, a soft European one, was subtle.

The coat was off now, and Katrine examined the woman sitting next to her. "What's your real name?" Katrine asked her curiously.

"We won't use them, real names, that is, if you don't mind," the woman said not unkindly. "But right now, I'm the Countess Andreevna. I'm a simple refugee, just like the rest of the drifters in Lisbon."

Katrine nodded. "And I'm Bette Davis, the famous American film star."

The Countess smiled.

"You are the first other Mrs. Smith I've met. *Former* Mrs. Smith, I mean, Countess." Katrine was breathing easier now, and she dabbed her forehead with her handkerchief.

"Smithies are a special sort, aren't we?" She sighed, "We've had to get creative with getting all the money raised for aid out of the States. There are a few key bank accounts, all in the name of Mr. and Mrs. Smith. And other assets, you see, boats, cars, apartments; all in the same name. Some of us go and sell antiquities or jewels on the black market. Some of us carry cash across borders. It's not very organized. We've had to work fast. I find the work very interesting. Don't you?"

Katrine shrugged. Interesting was not the word she would choose to describe her feelings towards being 'Mrs. Smith.'

"Where are the rest of them?"

"Rest of who?"

"The other Smithies?"

"Scattered all over the globe. We've even got a set in China. Lots of money in jade."

"I see. And this all has to do with that 127 million dollars."

Nodding, the woman took the coat and spread it

over her lap. She ran the scissors along the inside seam. Out popped one gold bar, then two, three, four, and five.

She gave Katrine a grin as she exhaled with relief, putting the bars and scissors into her purse. "You did well, Mrs. Smith. They all made it."

"I've heard of jewels in music boxes, but this is quite different," Katrine exclaimed, thinking of the jewels her Aunt Rose had smuggled across the border for the Kindertransport. "Talk about worth its weight in gold. What are you going to do with them?"

"This money will be used specifically for bribes to get refugees across the Spanish border to Lisbon."

The limo wound its way through the crowd and turned onto a two-lane road that was heavily congested with cars, bikes, carts, and people.

"So, Bette Davis, welcome to the last comparatively free country in Europe."

"Thanks." Katrine sighed. The car passed cafe after street cafe, all crowded and bustling. It seemed that there were people everywhere.

"Hundreds come every day trying to escape the Germans. The consulates are swamped. There is barely anywhere to stay that's decent. The cafes never close. And interpreters cost real money."

"But why here? Why Lisbon?"

"If they can get here, which is a big if—" Seeing Katrine's curious look, the Countess stopped and explained, "They have a chance to leave Europe altogether, that is, if they can manage the bureaucracy and grease enough palms to get the necessary exit visas. It's a slim chance, but a chance nevertheless." She shook her head, "Many have spent everything they have to get here and now they're stuck."[17]

"And I suppose that money will help get some of them out?" She looked at the gold bars.

"It will. And it will help others get in. Lisbon is infinitely better than Nazi-occupied Europe."

"So, what do I do now?"

"Now? Now you go home, of course."

"But not before picking something else up to deliver, yes?"

"You *are* getting the hang of things."

Katrine leaned back in the seat and shut her eyes, relieved of a heavy burden in her mind but weighed down by the heavier one in her heart. "And I suppose I don't need to worry about exit visas or anything?"

"You're traveling as a millionaire American widow now, Mrs. Smith. Your papers will be expedited, and the Agency has seen to it that you will be well taken care of." She tapped her purse knowingly.

WHAT PETER SAW

~

I heard the rumble of the truck pulling up and watched out the window as Peter got out and walked up the drive. In his hand was his toolbox. It was true; the limp *was* discernibly less. I wondered what had happened.

I met him at the front door and kissed him lightly. His cheeks were red and cold, but he was happy. He looked up the stairs, a question in his eye. I shook my head no, wordlessly telling him that Grace had not come down.

"As I was driving up, I noticed that one of the glass panels in the tower is hanging loose. Mr. Henderson said another storm is coming tonight. I want to make sure it's tight so it doesn't blow off and cause any damage to the house."

"You want some help?"

He nodded and smiled. "Sure."

"Now?"

"It's as good a time as any."

Together, we trudged up the stairs to the second story and then up the second set of stairs that led to the lighthouse tower. We walked through the washroom (that held a strange assortment of supplies and fuel for the lighthouse keeper back when it was actually used as a lighthouse) and finally, up into the lantern room itself.

I looked out onto the sea. It was different every single day. The only constant was the taste of salt and wind. I sat on the small bench and watched as Peter looked through his toolkit for what he needed. "I haven't been up here for a long time. It's nice."

"It's cold too." He rubbed his hands together and located the panel that was loose. "Hey," he looked at me, "can you hold it here. He pointed, and I acquiesced, holding the panel as he replaced the missing screw in the hinge and began to tighten it with the screwdriver.

I observed him — his beard, his intense blue eyes. He had new little wrinkles around them. "How's the book coming along?" he asked, leaning slightly out the window. Unconsciously, I reached out and held onto the back of his shirt… It was a long way down. He laughed good-naturedly, and I grinned.

"They are different than I thought," I said after a moment, considering his question.

"Who?"

"My cousins. I always thought Katrine knew exactly what she was doing. She always seemed so sure, so determined. But really, she doesn't know what she is doing at all. And Lorelei? If I'd known that there was so much going on inside of her head, I would have—"

"You would have what?" He struggled to keep the screw in place.

"I don't know. I think I would have opened up more."

"You didn't have time."

I shrugged and stood back as he straightened up, examining his work. The panel was solidly back in place. "I suppose not."

We both looked out at the sea. "And Grace?" he asked.

"Grace?"

How to say it? Passionate, headstrong… her heart was in the right place, but she was moving so fast she barely had time to consider why she was doing what she was doing. Before I could answer, there she was.

"I heard something and found the stairs in your room," she said sheepishly. She was still in her pajamas and shivered slightly. "My! What a view!"

Peter looked over at her, smiled, and then looked out at the sea, the green and grey waves churning. Suddenly, he leaned forward and squinted.

"What is it?" I asked.

"I can't be sure." He was intensely focused on whatever he saw on the horizon. "If only I had my binoculars."

I frowned. "I think we might have left them in Scotland." But then, an idea hit me. "Wait a minute!"

I raced downstairs as quickly as I could and rummaged through the 'stuff box' I hadn't bothered to unpack in the base of my wardrobe. There it was! My camera! I had a semi-brand-new 50mm Leitz Elmar lens for the Leica that might just do the trick.

Back upstairs in less than three minutes, I passed the camera to Peter and watched as he adjusted the lens. "Wow," he said under his breath. And then, "It couldn't be. Certainly not." He snapped a photograph, adjusted the lens, and then snapped another.

"What is it?" I asked.

"Well," he put the camera down and looked at me, "it looked to me like the tower of a sub."

Grace wrapped her arms wrapped around her shoulders. "You mean... a submarine?"

He nodded and said, as though to himself, "But there shouldn't be any German submarine activity around here."

"German?" I asked, horrified.

"Maybe you ought to call the coast guard?" Grace added.

"Yeah," he frowned. "Maybe I should."

"Do we need to be worried?" Grace asked.

"Of course not!" I exclaimed. "We are in America, remember? We aren't at war! We are neutral. Why it's probably just an American sub doing maneuvers or something."

"It looked German to me," Peter said.

"How can you tell a German sub from an American sub," I responded, following him down the stairs. "They look the same!"

"What do you mean," Peter spoke into the receiver, "he'll call me back?"

Grace and I looked at one another.

"Okay, I guess that will have to do." He put the phone back on the hook and faced us. "The station only has two people who work there. One is out sick, and the other went into town to pick up some supplies."

"Who answered the phone?" I asked.

"The janitor. He said he'd leave a note. There's nothing else we can do, I guess." He looked at me after a second. "Maybe we ought to develop the film."

"Okay. But I don't have the proper chemicals."

"I'm going to run into town to get them. And a red light too. I have a feeling this could be important," he answered, standing up. "If the coast guard calls, you'll tell them what I saw, won't you?"

I nodded as he made his way out the door. "You won't be long, will you?"

"I'll be back before the storm breaks." He smiled.

Grace stood up again. "Wait!" she called out. "I'm going with you! I need a break from all the birds in the house. Every time I look at a wall, I hear them squawking at me."

She stopped and glared at one of Edie's darker paintings. On a glassy sea, pearl blue and grey, a storm petrel seemed to walk on water, its wings outstretched in a graceful dance. In the background, a storm hovered on the horizon.

"You okay by yourself?" Peter asked me, as the sound of Grace upstairs, wildly throwing on her clothes and clomping around in her fur-lined booties, drew our attention to the ceiling.

"I won't be by myself. I have Founder now, remember?"

"Right." He looked at the pup fondly. "I'm glad we kept her."

"Me too," I answered, heading towards the crate where Founder was beginning to stir. She gnawed at the cast, and I imagined how hard it must be for a puppy to hold still for so long. Actually, it wasn't so hard to imagine.

Grace emerged on the landing, dressed to a certain extent, her bedhead covered with the knit wool cap I'd made for her. It was a lavender color that clashed with the burnt orange coat she was borrowing. "I'm ready!"

"She's ready," I repeated, looking into Peter's eyes. "Do hurry. I don't want you caught out in that." I motioned towards the window where, on the horizon, black clouds were beginning to form.

And so, as the wind blew the door to the lighthouse shut, I picked up my puppy and sat back behind the desk. I would keep working while waiting for the call and Peter and Grace's return.

There was nothing to worry about! I told myself. Nothing at all. It was just Peter's imagination. Though, I couldn't deny that a feeling of dread seemed to hang over the house. I willed myself not to look out at the sea or listen to the howl of the wind and to instead focus on the words on the page.

CHAPTER 27

A JEWISH CHRISTIAN

*P*aulina and Yosef's soup was simmering away on the stove, and the two lovebirds were nestled next to one another on the couch, listening to the radio. It seemed that Yosef had spent every evening with the nurses and his fiancé since the beginning of the epidemic.

The announcer's polished voice calmly read, "The German Luftwaffe continues to pummel the United Kingdom from the air in large-scale attacks known as 'The Blitz.' In the last month, the Luftwaffe has primarily targeted our ports and shipping centers, but now, in a move to dominate the sky, the merciless bombings have moved on to the RAF airfields and areas of aircraft production…"

Lorelei was rooted by the front door of the apartment, listening.

The Germans had quickly overwhelmed France and the Low Countries. There was nothing separating

Britain from the Nazis but the sea. But at least there was the sea! And the British were 'the Lords of the Sea," weren't they? That's what Horatio had said, and he knew about such things. *As long as the British control the English Channel and the North Sea... there is hope.*

Lorelei did not move closer into the apartment. She was afraid to. Afraid of the news she bore and how Paulina would manage it.

Paulina's beautiful brother Nick had taken a turn for the worse, against all expectations. His fever had spiked, and if he made it through the night, he would no doubt have some sort of brain damage or hearing loss.

Becky had been there with her, looking at the toddler. The beads of sweat on his forehead, his troubled screams enough to try the strongest of hearts.

Becky had held the baby close, her lips barely moving. Then, Becky put Nick back in his bed. There was nothing they could do. It was up to God now, she said calmly.

"How can you trust the baby to God like that?" Lorelei had asked, her mouth open slightly.

"Lorelei," Becky looked straight into her eyes, "it is better to trust God and have the hope of help, then not trust him and have no hope at all."

Becky had checked her watch. "My shift is over. I'll meet you at home, all right?"

Lorelei nodded and went back to changing sheets. Her own shift ended an hour later, and she had opted to walk home, giving her time to gather her thoughts. She had to think!

"Oh! You are back," Paulina exclaimed, noticing Lorelei leaning in the doorframe, lost in her thoughts.

"Yes, I am back." Lorelei's face paled.

"Becky's already home."

"I know," Lorelei answered.

"I will pour you some soup, yes?"

Before waiting for an answer, Paulina was up off the couch and moving towards the kitchen.

"How are you, Ms. Adleman?" Yosef asked kindly, standing up and adjusting the radio dial.

"Between you and me, a little shaky. I've seen a lot of things over the last week I never thought I'd see. Life of a nurse, I suppose. I'll have to get used to it." But even as the words came out of her mouth, she didn't believe it. The smell of disinfectant, the darkened hospital wards, the huddles of anxious parents. It was so unjust. So evil… a little tiny germ slowly attacking the tiny and defenseless. It was almost like Hitler, except, in that case, at least there was a chance to stop him! She could point her finger and say, 'He's the one to blame for all of this.'

She wasn't like Becky. Lorelei just couldn't trust God the way she did. She didn't know how.

It was dark outside now, and Lorelei moved out of the doorframe and switched on a lamp as Becky emerged from her bedroom, dressed in her house dress and slippers. The two women looked at one another and said nothing.

Becky glanced towards the kitchen where Paulina was bustling and said quietly, "Say nothing of Nick. Not tonight. Let them enjoy their happiness."

Lorelei understood. Why take away from the couple's brief season of joy by giving them unfiltered reality.

From there, Lorelei went to take her sanitizing bath. Her fingers moved mechanically, scrubbing her hair and then dressing in slacks and a soft pink cotton blouse. She brushed her hair 100 times, counting under her breath, and then excused herself to the patio to let it dry. In her hands, was the little red Bible that Rabbi Finkelstein had given her several nights before.

From inside, she could hear Yosef speaking to Becky.

"Ms. Hampton," he said, "I know this may not be the time to ask, but have you had a chance to ask anyone about my situation?"

Becky's voice was tired. "I've been at the hospital 16 hours a day, Yosef. I'm sorry. I've not had the chance to talk to anyone about much of anything."

Paulina's voice chirped out, "All right, suppertime, friends! How about we sit on the floor? Yosef, turn up the music, I like this song." Frank Sinatra crooned out, "I'll never Smile Again" as Tommy Dorsey's band carried him along.[1] Lorelei didn't move from her spot on the patio.

"We need to do something else first. We need to pray," Becky said.

Lorelei turned her head and peered into their

living room. She saw Becky, Yosef, and Paulina bow their heads, holding hands lightly.

"Dear Lord Jesus," Becky began, "we come before you now, and we need your help. Yosef needs a way out. And we desperately need your strength and courage for what is coming. Help us to trust you." She paused for a moment before concluding with an "Amen."

A gentle peace seemed to fill the room, resting on the two girls and the boy standing on the worn carpet. The presence made Lorelei nervous.

Paulina and Yosef's voices echoed Becky's amen. All three lifted their heads and opened their eyes.

"It is a matter of faith, isn't it? We must trust him, but it is difficult to do when you do not understand what is happening." Yosef sighed.

"We'll help each other, Yosef," Becky answered. Turning towards the patio, she called out, "Lorelei! Come inside!"

But she wasn't ready to join them. The three shared a special connection that she didn't understand. They believed in something, in some- one, she did not. It made her feel apart and separate and awkward sometimes, as though she was imposing on something private and intimate, though that was certainly not their intention.

"I'll just be a minute." Lorelei held the book lightly in her hands and stared at it intensely. She had tried reading bits and pieces in her few moments of solitude, finding it to be filled with long lists of names and strange laws that had no application for modern life. She liked the psalms, certainly. They appealed to her artistic nature. But beyond that? She struggled to grasp what answers such a book could have for her. Randomly, she opened the book and read the first words that caught her eye.

"When Jesus had said these things, he departed and hid himself from them. Though he had done so many signs before them, they still did not believe in him, so that the word spoken by the prophet Isaiah might be fulfilled: 'Lord, who has believed what he heard from us, and to whom has the arm of the Lord been revealed?' Therefore they could not believe. For again Isaiah said, "He has blinded their eyes and hardened their heart, lest they see with their eyes, and understand with their heart, and turn, and I would heal them."[2]

Lorelei felt pinned against the wall. Holding her breath, she kept reading, "Isaiah said these things because he saw his glory and spoke of him. Nevertheless, many even of the authorities believed in him, but for fear of the Pharisees they did not confess it, so that they would not be put out of the synagogue; For they loved the glory that comes from man more than the glory that comes from God."[3]

"Your soup is getting cold!" Paulina yelled.

Lorelei put the book aside, her hands trembling for reasons she did not understand.

∾

THREE DAYS LATER, Ethel opened the door, her face showing her surprise. "It is a little late to play the piano, don't you think Lorelei?"

"That's not why I'm here." Her eyes searched behind Ethel. Aron was walking towards them, his face concerned.

"Is everything all right?" he asked, now standing behind his wife.

"Yes." Lorelei stopped, "Well, no. No, everything is not all right."

"You ought to come in," Aron said. And then, to Ethel, he murmured, "Make us some tea, Ethel, yes?"

Ethel nodded and locked the door behind Lorelei as Aron led her to the dining room table.

Lorelei nodded and held her breath, sitting across from the rabbi. She didn't know where to start. She put the little red Bible on the table.

"So?" Aron waited patiently. "You need to talk of something? More questions?"

She nodded. "I saw something today, and it frightened me."

"What did you see?"

"There's a baby, a friend's baby, his name is Nick. He has," she paused and corrected herself, "had, the measles, and he is at the children's ward in the hospital. He spiked a fever, a very high fever. He shouldn't have made it through the night, you understand. I've watched the disease play out now for nearly three weeks. When the fever gets that high they don't make it."

"And what happened?" Aron asked.

"Becky held that baby to her chest, and she prayed in Jesus's name that he would be healed."

"And then what happened?"

"For the last three days, he hovered between death and life. Then, the fever broke. No damage to his brain or hearing whatsoever." She leaned forward, "Don't you see? God healed him!"

"And it surprises you that God does miracles?"

Lorelei shook her head. "No. It's not that. Well, it is that, but it isn't that."

"So, what is it?"

"My Aunt Rose was healed. She almost died of tuberculosis last year. She prayed, and she recovered. The doctors said it was a miracle, and I chose not to think about it too much. How could I? It was a freak of nature or something. But now this?"

"Now what?"

"Don't you see? They are both Christians! They prayed in the name of Jesus!"

"Go on," he urged her. His face showed no emotion whatsoever.

Lorelei kept talking. "Last night, I cornered Becky. I asked her why God would do something like heal baby Nick and not the other children who died or protect my parents from the Nazis."

He motioned for her to continue.

"She said that we live in a fallen world."

"She's right." The rabbi nodded.

"And that sometimes God delivers on our timetable and sometimes he does not. But just because we suffer, or those we love suffer, does not mean God is not good. He will see us through our suffering if he does not deliver us from it."

She paused. "She said that I'll never find peace by trying to figure it all out. Peace is found only in Yeshua, *Jesus Christ*, and trusting him, even when he does not send help when I want it or how I want it. She said I have to believe that he helps me in the way that will bring me the most good and him the most glory, and sometimes that is very hard to understand."

Aron said nothing, looking at Lorelei intently, his eyes narrowing.

"What do I do?" she urged him.

"What do you think you should do?"

Lorelei was perturbed. "Rabbi, you are the one who gave me that book. That Bible! How can I deny what happened without denying who I am as a Jew? What if—" her hand shook, "what if Yeshua really rose from the dead as the Christians say?"

"Such things have happened before."

"What if Yeshua is the Messiah after all?"

Aron stroked his beard thoughtfully. "Let's say he is the Messiah, what would change? Our thinking of who the Messiah is *could* be wrong. What if it looks different than we thought? Does that change who you are as a Jew?" He folded his hands and exhaled. "Some say it certainly does."

"What do you say?" Lorelei implored the rabbi.

"Me? I have thought on this, and I have come to no conclusions." He stroked his beard thoughtfully and slightly raised his shoulders.

"What should I do!" she repeated, desperation in her voice.

"You must do what your heart says is true."

"My heart is at war with my mind, Rabbi." Nervously, she paged through the red book, her fingers gently touching the thin pages. Her eyes caught a passage that had been underlined in thin pencil by some previous reader long ago.

"*Then let your heart not be troubled, trust in God, and the peace of God that passes all under-standing will guard your hearts and minds in Christ Jesus.*"[4]

Her eyes rose and caught those of the rabbi. She swallowed heavily.

"You know what you must do, I think." The rabbi said as Ethel entered the dining room carrying a tray with a teapot and several teacups.

Lorelei stood up. "I have to go. I'm sorry, Ethel, about the tea. I need to think!" Was it possible? Her heart screamed out that yes, it was possible. It was more than possible. Yeshua was the Messiah… *is* the Messiah.

At the moment, being Jewish or not seemed to fade away. She had seen the hand of God, tasted his peace, felt his presence. It happened so quickly, it was barely perceptible. But she believed.

Ethel, completely oblivious to what was happening in Lorelei's heart and mind asked, "Do you know when the children can come home?"

"Another week, and we should be in the clear. We haven't had any new cases, which means we caught it before it spread beyond the city." Lorelei answered, only half-present. The peace that she had longed for was hers at last.

"That's good." Ethel's smile faded as she looked at her husband.

"Is everything all right Aron?"

Lorelei looked straight into the Rabbi's eyes. "Am I a Christian now?"

"Lorelei Adleman, you are you. Whether you call yourself Jewish or Christian or anything else is beside the point."

"Can one be both?"

Ethel put the tray on the table, looking down her long thin nose from Aron to Lorelei. "What's going on?"

Aron reached out and took his wife's hand. "What is it called when a Jew believes he has found the Messiah?"

"What Messiah?" Ethel looked confused. "The Messiah hasn't come! What are you two talking about?"

"Some would disagree with you, Ethel. Rumor has it that the Messiah is alive and active and healing babies at the hospital. What do you make of that?"

CHAPTER 28

TRUSTING YOUR INSTRUMENTS

*I*t was pitch-black and cold. The drastic change in temperature between day and night in the desert never ceased to amaze Grace, and she was grateful for her leather flight jacket.

Amos already had the engine running and waved to her from the cockpit. With a well-practiced swing, she thrust herself up into the small plane and settled into the pilot's seat.

"Long time no see." Amos glanced at her as they were cleared to take their place on the runway.

She didn't say anything. There was too much on her mind to make small talk.

"Okay." Amos looked straight ahead and rubbed his palms together, "So, let's talk night flying."

He held up two flashlights. "Very, very important. Don't attempt a night flight without one of these, preferably two. And extra batteries. These planes don't have interior lights, and if you want to see around the back or below your feet or anything else for that matter, like your map, you'll need a flashlight."

"Got it. Flashlights." Grace nodded and prepared for takeoff.

"Now, look at the runway. There are lights on both sides. Those lights at the end signal just that, the end of the runway."

"I'm not an idiot."

"I'm just doing my job!" Amos put his hands up defensively. "There are a lot of different lights you have to get used to when night flying. The lights of other aircraft, airport lights, approach lights… the lights for civilian, military, and seaplane landing strips. They all look different."

At the end of the runway, they were given the all-clear by one of the air traffic controllers.

"Now," he continued, "bring her up slow and gentle."

The plane lifted off the ground and soared upwards. The exhilarating sense of taking off never wore off for Grace.

"All the normal regulations apply. The 45-minute fuel reserve, approach procedures… You know the drill."

Amos looked at a map spread out on his lap and put his finger on a spot, giving Grace the coordinates. She lightly turned the plane, and they settled in for the flight.

Now Grace was ready to talk.

When she turned to Amos, she was surprised to

see that he had a thermos and two paper cups. He held one up. "Coffee?"

"Sure." She smiled. It smelled wonderful.

He pulled out two jelly donuts and a chocolate bar. "And breakfast."

"You know, you are different than I thought." She tried to think of what it was exactly. "*Younger*. Definitely younger. 'Air Man'" she said, referencing the comic, "and donuts and candy for breakfast."

"Thanks." He coughed on his coffee, "I think."

She took the donut and chewed thoughtfully. "Amos, I'm worried about what happened yesterday with Morris. What if those guys have already targeted others on the base? We got to Morris just in time, but who knows who else they've been talking to?"

"You mean there might be a possibility that there are members of the Stern Gang already among us, planning to sabotage our planes or something?"

"That's exactly what I'm saying."

"Don't think I haven't already thought of that." He swallowed and added, "I have. Grace, just between us, I've no idea how or what to do about it. We have a serious problem."

"There are about 40 of us left on the base, all of whom have made it this far in the training program. We could just ask each one if they know anything," she said.

"And they could lie."

"That's true." Grace sipped her coffee. Looking into the distance, she gasped. "Do you see that?"

Amos peered in the direction she was looking. "What?"

"It's like a horizon, but it shouldn't be there, right?"

"Good instincts, Grace. What you are looking at is a false horizon. It can happen when you are flying over a banked cloud or featureless terrain at night."

"Like the desert?"

He nodded. "There are a lot of things that will mess with your vision at night. Vections, that's when it feels like you are moving backward. And autokinetic illusions make it seem like a stationary object in front of you is moving. The worst is mistaking a star or a planet for a landing light."

"That's happened?"

"It's easy to get confused when you are flying. It's why you have to trust your instruments."

"Trust your instruments," Grace repeated. *Trust your instruments.*

"Amos!" she exclaimed.

Startled, he spilled his coffee and screeched as the scalding liquid burned his thigh.

"Sorry," she said, more calmly. "I know what to do!"

"For a burn?"

"No! About the Stern Gang."

Brushing the spot on his pants with a handkerchief, he waited for her to continue.

"We get Morris to make contact with those Brunsky brothers. He'll tell them that we, me and him, are interested in joining. We'll create an illusion, don't you see?"

Amos nodded, slowly seeing what Grace was trying to convey. "And then, once you and Morris infiltrate the group, you will find out if any in our unit on the base are involved."

"Exactly."

"It could take a while." He scratched his chin.

"But it's better than nothing."

"We need to know as soon as possible. Our mission is just three weeks away."

"But we won't know unless we try," she said determinedly.

"Then we have to try. Looks like you'll be making a trip to Cairo." Amos frowned. "But I don't want you doing anything stupid, you hear me? Those guys are crazy."

"I won't do anything you wouldn't do."

"That's what I'm afraid of."

"So, what do we do now?"

"We finish this flight, and as soon as we get back to the base, we wake Morris up and get to work. But Grace," he frowned, "I'm not kidding. Be careful. I have a bad feeling about those two."

"I'll trust my instruments," she assured him, staring ahead.

For the next hour, Grace circled the clear desert night sky above the base. Amos served as navigator, plotting one point to the next. Then, just as the sun was about to break on the horizon, Amos gave Grace completely new coordinates.

With a questioning shrug, Grace set the course and turned the wheel.

A minute passed, and the sun broke forth. From out of the earth, the silhouette of the Pyramids dominated the landscape. Like ancient giants, they loomed in front of the plane, their hard angles glowing with the fire of the burning star steadily rising behind them. Grace gasped and punched Amos's arm.

"I thought you should at least see the Pyramids after all the hard work you've been doing."

She had seen them, barely, on her first flight to Cairo. But this was totally different. She was flying right towards them. It was magnificent! She shook her head in disbelief. "This is much, much better than camping."

"I think so too."

And as Grace observed one of the Seven Wonders of the Ancient World, her face radiant with surprise and joy and the first morning light, Amos thought she must be one of the Seven Wonders of the Modern World. She was the most beautiful woman he had ever seen. And he wondered why he had never noticed it before.

"You want me to call those guys and tell them I want to join the Stern Gang?" Morris was appalled. "After everything you said back there in the desert?"

"We don't want you to *actually* join," Grace explained. "We need someone on the inside, two people actually. Me and you."

"So you can keep an eye on me?"

"Yes." Amos crossed his arms. "Exactly."

Grace quickly added, "And because two are always better than one. We need to know as quickly as possible if they have recruited any in our unit. It's imperative to the mission. There are too many lives at stake to risk not finding out."

The three stood crammed inside the one public telephone booth on the base. It was 6:00 in the morning and Morris was still in his pajamas after being rudely shaken awake by Amos and dragged outside to where Grace was waiting.

"For the sake of peace, and to save lives, I will tell this lie," Morris said seriously. "But I want you to know something. I would only do such a thing for the sake of peace. It is the only time telling a lie is permitted, according to the sages."

"We would never want you to do anything against the sages," Amos said, slightly sarcastically. "Let's not talk about how the Stern Gang would murder innocent people to get what they want."

Morris put his hands up. "I get it. I get it. You don't need to rub it in. So, do you have a penny?"

"That's more like it." Amos dug a couple of coins out of his pocket and thrust them into Morris's palm. A moment later, the operator put him through to the Brunsky Brother's Bookshop in the center of Cairo. As luck would have it, they were thrilled to meet with Grace and Morris. A meeting was set for 4:00 that very afternoon.

Amos clapped his hands together and patted Morris on the back. "I'll get you a jeep to drive into town."

"I can't drive," Morris answered.

"Grace will drive."

"I can't drive either," she said slowly.

Morris looked at her. "You mean, you can fly a plane, but you can't drive a car?"

She looked helplessly at Amos. "Maybe I should get some driving lessons next."

"That would be a very good idea." And then with an air of finality, he said, "I'll drive you."

~

GRACE AND MORRIS were both dressed in their civilian clothes. Grace hadn't worn a skirt and blouse in so long that it almost felt unfamiliar. The clean white blouse had a pretty bow around the neck, and the light blue A-line skirt fit around her slim waist perfectly. When Amos saw her, he had trouble concentrating for a second and had to look away. Then, he was silent and stared straight ahead the whole drive to Cairo.

He dropped Grace and Morris off two blocks from the bookshop, with instructions to meet him at the Barrel Room after they were finished.

Grace was thoroughly enjoying herself. "This is fun, isn't it?"

"If you enjoy espionage, I guess so." Morris shrugged and adjusted his glasses. "I personally do not."

The street was crowded with all manner of people. Smart, attractive, wealthy young Egyptians wearing the latest trends mixed in with those in more traditional Arab costumes. The bookstore was not far from the famous Cairo University. The smell of strong coffee mingled with cigarette smoke permeated the air. Horse-drawn buggies and camel caravans drove right alongside modern buses and private cars, all under the shade of the elegant buildings, of both European and Arab architecture, and tall palms.

They walked by Shepheard's Hotel, where a small plaque read: "On This Ground Napoleon Set Up His Headquarters After the Battle of the Pyramids."[5]

"Wow." Morris looked up at the grand hotel. "Napoleon made it all the way to Egypt."

Grace pulled him along. "Come on. We don't have much time!"

Morris looked around. "I don't know where the bookshop is. We should have been there by now." He looked at the address written on a small slip of paper.

The terrace of the hotel was filled with Europeans sitting in comfortable rattan chairs, drinking cool things, and looking out at the street. Across the street from the hotel, a group of Egyptian men in long flowy robes, Dragos they were called, waited for tourists who needed guides. It was against the law for them to solicit at the actual hotel, and yet, some still did. One of these men honed in on Morris and Grace, picking them out as foreigners, and approached them with a glint of determination.

"You need guide?" he asked in broken English.

"Actually we do," Morris said.

"You want to see Pyramids?"

"Already seen them. We want to go to Brunsky's Bookshop," he replied.

"But they are the biggest structures ever made by man!"

Morris was firm. "Brunsky's Bookshop."

The guide's eyes narrowed. "*Brunsky's Bookshop?*"

Morris handed him the address, and the man shrugged. "Well, I'll tell you now. This shop is nothing compared to Pyramids."

"But it is where we need to go."

"Come then, I will take you." And so, after much bartering for five pennies, the man led them across the street and around the corner. It took less than 45 seconds.

Grace put her hand on the doorknob of the grimy little shop and said under her breath, "That was the most expensive walk across the street I've ever taken."

WITH A DING of the bell above the door, Morris and Grace stepped into the dark and dusty interior of the musty bookshop.

From the back, the voice of one of the brother's shouted, "I'll be with you in a minute!"

Morris and Grace looked at one another and then glanced around the shop. It was nothing unusual. Nothing rare or expensive. Just a plain old bookshop that sold silly dime store novels and cheap tourist guides. It gave Grace a creepy feeling, but she pushed it aside. Don't be a scaredy cat, she chided herself.

Walter rounded the corner. "Milton! They're here!"

"Good," Milton called back. "Bring them back."

With a flick of his chin, Walter motioned for them to follow him into the back office where Milton waited. Walter locked the door behind them, and Grace tried to quell her nerves.

Milton leaned forward, and for the first time, Grace took a good look at him. Thinning light brown hair, dull eyes, paunchy. He had a distinctly disturbing look about him.

Patting Grace and Morris on the shoulder, Milton grinned. "What'd I tell you, Walter. We'd get some kids on the base who think the same way we do."

"Quiet, Milton." Walter silenced his brother with a death stare. But Grace had caught what Milton had said. They were the only ones at the RAF base with whom the Gang had made contact. The cat was out of the bag. Amos would be so relieved. Their mission was accomplished already! She almost wanted to laugh out loud. It had been so much easier than she'd thought.

"We need to find out if these kids are for real. We need some sort of proof," Walter said.

Morris answered quickly, "Proof? If anyone caught us with you guys, we'd probably be court-martialed. We've taken a big risk coming here. That should be enough."

Walter seemed to buy it and relaxed.

"Well, to show you are sincere," he paused, "you will do exactly as we say. Or else…" He trailed off menacingly.

"What do you mean?"

Milton looked at Walter and shook his head solemnly. "We have it from the high-ups that Admiral Wells is going to the Windsor Hotel."

The Windsor Hotel? That was where the Barrel Room was, where Amos waited.

"And?" Grace waited.

"We are going to do a little demonstration that will show those British snobs we mean business." Walter laughed dryly.

"And how do we come in?" Grace tried to maintain her composure. For good measure, she threw in, "I sure do hate that Admiral Wells, whoever he is."

From under the desk, Walter produced a shoebox that contained, for all intents and purposes, an extremely primitive explosive made of dynamite. "You are RAF. You can go into the officer's club and place this discreetly under the table where the admiral is."

"That's the best the Stern Gang can do?" Morris asked, looking at the bomb disdainfully.

"The Cairo office is a small one. We don't have many resources," Walter said apologetically.

Milton silenced his brother and continued, "And then, once you are out of the hotel, we will detonate the bomb."

"How?" Grace tried to keep her voice steady.

"It's on a timer. You'll have ten minutes to get in and get out."

"And if we refuse to participate?"

"You won't ever leave this office, my dear." He snickered. "But you won't refuse, will you?" He sneered evilly.

Grace suddenly got a sick feeling in her stomach. She had the distinct feeling she had been played. Perhaps these brothers were smarter than they looked. There had to be something they could do to get out of this mess! Oh, why hadn't she been more careful? Why hadn't she brought a gun or something? Why hadn't she trusted her instruments! She should have known something was wrong the minute they locked that door.

Milton pointed at Morris. "We are going to keep your friend Morris here with Walter. If this girl doesn't do her part for the war effort, you will feel it, my little friend. If Walter doesn't get my phone call that everything went according to plan at 5:30 precisely…"

Grace looked at Morris with a horrified expression on her face. How could they have been so stupid! They were trapped.

"Don't worry about me, Grace. I'll be just fine." Morris put on his bravest face and watched as the shoebox was placed carefully inside a large shopping bag.

She had to think of something. Anything!

GRACE SQUARED her shoulders and showed the guard her RAF identification card and asked where the Barrel

Room was. She could feel Milton's beady eyes watching her from the street. Over her shoulder, the bomb silently ticked. She had ten minutes. Ten short minutes to think of what to do.

She entered the Barrel Room, a beautiful dark wood lounge. He was there. They *both* were there, Amos and the admiral.

Amos's smile froze when he saw her face, white with fear. "What's up?" he asked, standing up and making room for her in the booth.

"Good news or bad news first?"

"Good."

"All right." She licked her lips. "There are no Stern Gang members on the base."

"That's great!" he exclaimed. "And the bad news?"

"I've got a ticking bomb in the bag aimed for Admiral Wells. If it's not detonated in the next," she glanced at her watch, "seven and a half minutes, they are going to kill Morris."

"You are kidding."

"If only I was!" She gulped down the remains of Amos's coke. "We underestimated them. They are a lot smarter than I gave them credit for!"

Amos went into command mode. "We've got to get everyone, especially the Admiral, out of here. And now!"

"There's not enough time. The hotel's too big." Grace was panicking.

"What's the bomb made of?" Amos asked suddenly.

"An ancient alarm clock and old dynamite," she answered, in a way that said, *'so what?'*.

"Okay," he mumbled. "Okay!" Amos took the

shopping bag and dashed out the back door. There had to be a swimming pool around here somewhere! He knew it! There it was. His legs ran faster, and he jumped the low fence surrounding the pool, shouting for everyone to get out of the pool immediately and for someone to call the bomb squad. With that, he tripped over a rock, let out an awful moan, and tossed the shopping bag into the pool as he collapsed onto a lounge chair. Wet dynamite, he knew, could still explode. But the water might stop the Brunsky Brother's crude timing mechanism. If anything, it would buy them some time.

Around the pool, a half-dozen officers in their swim trunks dripped on the side of the pool, looking at Amos with shocked expressions. "Another madman back from the front," one said with a sneer.

"I think we saved the admiral," he said, writhing in pain as Grace came up behind him.

They looked at the pool, relieved. The bomb should have gone off by now. It looked like the chlorinated water had done its job.

"Good. But now we've got to save Morris! Two more minutes until that phone call!" Grace took off back through the hotel as Amos limped behind her.

To her great surprise, a few moments later outside the hotel's grand entrance, she found Morris, three policemen, the guide who had brought them to the bookshop, and Walter and Milton, both in handcuffs!

Morris waved at Amos and Grace as though nothing had happened as two of the policemen led the brothers away. The guide bowed low, his long robes sweeping the dusty pavement. "Alli here saw us both go in and thought it was kind of funny that only you came out."

"So he called the police?"

Alli nodded. "Yes. I called the police."

The remaining officer (who spoke only Arabic) stood there, smiling.

"But why?"

The guide looked at Grace. "Because I am a father, and a good father always acts on his instincts."

"Yeah," Morris continued. "When the policemen came in, I started shouting that I was being held hostage, and my brother was a wealthy British soldier, and they were using you to blackmail him."

"That makes no sense at all," Grace said, her brow furrowing in confusion.

Morris shrugged.

"So, they are being arrested for kidnapping?" Grace asked.

"It pays to be young," the young man sighed.

Grace looked at the guide and extended her hand. "We are very grateful to you, sir."

"Next time, you listen to Alli. You go and see the Pyramids, yes?"

"Definitely." Grace nodded vigorously.

It was then that they noticed Amos. He was sitting on the stairs, his face white and his pant leg drenched with blood.

"There's a disabled bomb at the bottom of the pool." His voice was tight with pain, his words directed towards the remaining officer, who had no idea what he was saying. "Somebody ought to take care of it."

He looked like he was going to be sick.

"Grace," he groaned, "I don't think I'll be able to drive us back to the base." And then, he passed out.

CHAPTER 29

A PIECE OF CAKE

ountess Andreevna's driver wound through the colorful city of Lisbon. The sea was bright blue, and the buildings, white and yellow with red tile roofs. The air, still and warm. All of it gave the city a pleasant, almost peaceful atmosphere. At least, it would have if there hadn't been so many traumatized refugees wandering around.

"Before I take you to the airport, we have to make a quick stop in Bairro Alto."

"What is that?" Katrine asked.

"Lisbon is divided into five districts. It is one of the more lively of the five. I'm taking you out for lunch. It looks like you haven't eaten in a week. Was the food on the ship that bad?"

Katrine shook her head. "I just haven't felt like eating, I guess."

"Well, you'll feel like eating where I'm

taking you." The Countess smiled assuredly. "It's Salazar's favorite restaurant."

"Do you think we'll see him?" Katrine raised her eyebrow slightly.

"You never know. For a dictator, he's a shockingly good ruler. He's balanced the budget, built schools, torn down slums. Last month, he let 2,500 refugees from Gibraltar land in Madeira, the island that belongs to Portugal."

Katrine nodded disinterestedly, "How's he feel about Nazis?"

"He doesn't like them." She exhaled. "That said, he has no desire to provoke Hitler. He thinks the German Reich is a bastion against the spread of communism. He's determined to stay neutral."

"Just like the United States." Katrine looked out the window as the car went up a steep incline and rounded a corner.

"Here we are," the Countess' voice rang out cheerily as the limo stopped. "Out we go!"

Nestled beneath an apartment building and in between a nightclub (that was closed during the day) and a small grocery store, a small cafe, O Galito, welcomed the women with open arms.

The Countess fed Katrine Acorda, a stew made with bits of bread and garlic. Very, very Lisbon, she had said. On the side, there was carapauzinhos, a small mackerel served with tomato rice. Katrine assumed it was all very good, but in reality, she barely tasted any of it. The Countess talked on and on and on of absolutely nothing. Katrine had never known anyone who could say so much without saying anything of consequence at all; of Salazar and how he had sat 'just there' on Thursday night. Of the weather. Of her manicurist's poodle. She chatted and gossiped with the waiter. Katrine didn't even pretend to be interested. All she wanted was to get on with whatever she needed to get on with and be done with all this spy business.

The Countess, meanwhile, pretended not to notice the dark mood of her companion, but she saw all and understood more than Katrine could guess.

Finally, the woman pushed her plate aside, leaned in, and said bluntly, "Well, was it a man?"

Katrine sat back, stunned.

"It's always a man." The woman sipped her water.

Finally, regaining her composure, Katrine nodded grimly. "Is it so obvious?"

"Only to the well-trained, like myself." She paid the bill and stood up. "Look, you can mope around regarding the moron as long as you like, just don't let it get in the way of work. You get me?"

Katrine swallowed and followed her out of the restaurant. "Yes," she said, reddening. "I get you."

The Countess softened, "You know what you need?"

Katrine shook her head. "This is terribly embarrassing."

"Don't be embarrassed. We've all lost in love and war. What you need is chocolate. The best chocolate cake in Lisbon." She looked at the driver as he opened the door to the limo. "Paolo, take us to Landeau's. We want dessert!"

$$\sim$$

"So," the Countess pressed, "what do you think?"

Katrine put a bite of the cake into her mouth and took a sip of the strong coffee offered by the tiny pastry shop. The slender little cake was layered with thin, airy mousse and dusted lightly with cocoa powder. "It is quite indulgent," Katrine said, smiling at the Countess as they ate their cake at a delicate little table by the window. The store had a line nearly to the door.

"The best you've ever had, yes?"

Katrine knew the Countess would not take no for an answer. "I suppose it is."

"Good. Then you must take one back with you." She spoke to the young woman behind the counter, "We'll take one to go. And please wrap it up very carefully."

"Oh, I couldn't!" Katrine protested. "It'll get ruined. The mousse will melt."

"It'll be just fine. I've traveled with Landeau's cakes a million times. Besides, it's Joe's birthday, and I always give him a cake for his birthday from Landeau's."

"Joe?"

"Joe Miller. American Embassy, Cairo, Egypt. You have a slight layover before returning to Palestine."

Katrine leaned back in her chair. "Ah. I see."

"Good."

~

"Welcome aboard British Airways Airliner direct to Cairo." The petite British stewardess led Katrine to her seat. "Have you ever flown with us before?"

"I've never flown before, period," Katrine answered.

"You'll love it. Imagine, going from Lisbon to Cairo in 25 short hours. Cairo is one of the busiest airports in the world. Everyone goes through Cairo, whether you're destined for Europe, Africa, or Asia. It's practically the center of the world these days. Have you been to Cairo?"

Katrine shook her head no.

"This plane goes nearly 200 miles an hour." The stewardess smiled. "We've space for 32 passengers and three lavatories."

"I see."

"Under your seat is a bowl in case you get sick."

"Sick?"

"It's nothing to worry about. We go up very high, and you might get altitude sickness."

"I see," Katrine repeated.

"If the pressure does change drastically, we will distribute oxygen."

"Oxygen?" Katrine's voice rose a few notes.

"All of our airplanes are heated and air-conditioned, so no worries about getting cold or hot. And don't worry about noise," she took

Katrine's hat and jacket and hung them up in a closet across from her chair, "the walls are insulated. You won't even hear the engine."

Katrine eased into the roomy chair that had a small table in front of it. In a basket under the table was a stack of international newspapers and the latest issue of Vogue. All the fashions were American now. Hadn't been French since the Nazis had begun occupying Paris. Even the top fashion houses had been forced out. She settled in, holding the cake box on her lap.

The woman kept talking. "And if you get tired, we have several sleeping accommodations for passengers in the back of the plane. I can take that box for you if you like?"

"Thank you, but I'd rather hold on to it. It's a present for a friend of a friend."

"Of course." The stewardess's smile froze, but she'd learned that passengers could be peculiar. If this German woman wanted to hold a cake box for 25 hours, well, that was that. And so, she told Katrine when dinner would be served and moved on to the next passenger.

AFTER SURVIVING takeoff (Katrine gripped her seat so hard her knuckles turned white), and feeling quite positive that her end had come, she realized, despite the extreme turbulence, that the plane was not going down anytime soon. She would just have to endure this journey from hell until they reached French Algiers and touched down for refueling. Then, the whole thing would begin again and repeat itself in Zarzis, Tunisia.

By that point, she promised herself, she would never, NEVER, fly again, and she would never speak to Harry again either, for any reason whatsoever.

The cake on Katrine's lap jostled about precariously, but she refused to put it in the closet or let it out of her hands. When the stewardess offered her roasted beef tenderloin, roasted right there in the plane, and stewed tomatoes, she turned green and waved the stewardess away. Seltzer was the only thing she could possibly ingest at a time like this. Seltzer and a sleeping pill, please!

Katrine finally fell asleep for the last six hours of the journey, her hands tightly grasping the cardboard cake box, her head cradled against the window.

When she awoke, the stewardess was making her way up and down the aisle, gently informing the passengers from Lisbon to Cairo Direct, that they should look out their windows and observe the Nile River twisting lazily below, a wide strip of greyish blue, banked by the soft green of reeds and grass and fields, all of which gave way to the harsh orange of the desert.

It was two in the afternoon, and the overhead glare of the sun began to soften. Cairo gleamed in the distance.

Rattled, bruised, and sick to her stomach, a small suitcase in one hand and a less than pristine cake box in the other, "Landeau's" sprawled on the top in a fancy curly-cue script, Katrine emerged off the death trap and stumbled into one of the cabs that sat waiting for people just like her.

"The American Consulate," she huffed.

The cab driver, an older Egyptian with a thick mustache, looked at her through the rearview mirror. "No hotel?"

"All I want is to go to the consulate and get rid of this cake and get on with my life," she said through clenched teeth.

He turned his head and looked at her pale face and shrugged. "Okay. The American Consulate." Under his breath, he muttered with a frown, "Americans are so rude."

"I am *not* American!" She gritted her teeth.

The driver looked at her in amazement once more and took off directly to the consulate. He did not want to drive this unpleasant woman one minute longer than he had to. And whereas with other unsuspecting tourists he might have taken a longer route to make a few extra coins, this time he drove the quickest and most direct route from the airport to the consulate.

"I'M LOOKING FOR JOE." Katrine set the cake box down on the desk of the receptionist, who looked at her like she was crazy.

"Joe?"

"It's his birthday. I've brought him a present from Countess Andreevna."

Now, the receptionist *knew* she was crazy. "What's 'Joe's' last name?"

"Joe Miller."

"The aide to the ambassador?" she asked, her penciled eyebrows arching unnaturally high.

"I have no idea who he is. I'm just delivering a cake."

She looked disdainfully at the crushed cake box. "How about you leave it here, and I'll give it to him when he comes back from his lunch break?"

"No," Katrine clenched her fist, "I have to deliver it personally." She firmly believed (and rightly so) that Joseph Miller was not on his lunch break and was somewhere in the building.

"What, do you sing and dance too? Is this some sort of a birthday gram?" The woman threw her chin up.

"Would you please just call Joseph Miller and tell him I'm here!"

"Tell Joe who's here?" a strong male voice said from behind her.

The receptionist looked past Katrine, "Oh, Mr. Miller! This woman said that some *countess*—"

"A countess, huh?" the voice said playfully.

"Andreevna." Katrine wheeled around and faced the voice. It belonged to a handsome jovial face. The man was about 6'2 with black hair slicked back with some sort of pomade. Very, very American.

"The Countess, eh?" His eyes twinkled. "And my birthday cake from Landeau's! That woman! She never forgets." He chuckled. "And who might you be, ma'am?"

"Mrs. Smith."

"Mrs.?" He feigned disappointment. "I'm sorry to hear it."

"Technically, I'm widowed." Katrine put her suitcase down and frowned. She had no time to flirt, especially with another one of those American charmers. "All right, you have your cake. Happy birthday. Now, can you please direct me to a hotel?"

"Oh no," Joe Miller took the cake off the stunned receptionist's desk with one hand and Katrine's arm in the other, "not before you and I get more closely acquainted. I can't let you go without giving you some sort of tip for the delivery. And my wallet's in my office."

"Is that so?" Katrine asked archly.

They were walking down a long hall. "Most definitely." He answered.

Katrine's heels clicked along the sleek marble floor. The whole building was new and modern and square. Everywhere, there were angles.

He opened a door and stepped aside for Katrine to pass. Then, he shut the door and locked it. Katrine looked around the office. "Very sleek."

"The building's new. We just moved in a couple of weeks ago."

"I still smell the paint."

Joe Miller was totally focused on his cake. He set it on the table and opened the box, peering inside. The cake was squashed and dented. The frosting was all over the inside of the box.

"Want a piece?"

"I'll pass."

He smiled at her and opened a drawer under his desk, pulling out a small soup spoon. "I usually eat at my desk," he explained casually while he gently began to poke at the cake.

"Ah!" he exclaimed. "I struck gold." Using the spoon, he pushed the cake and mousse to the side, revealing a small round box. This he removed and wiped as clean as he could with a napkin. Finally, he lifted the box's lid to reveal a reel of film.

"Could be the most expensive cake ever *not* eaten, Mrs. Smith. A lot of lives were lost to get this to me."

"What is it?" Katrine asked, looking at him carefully. Joe Miller was not at all who he appeared to be.

"Solid proof that the Nazis are doing a lot more than just putting people into camps."

Katrine swallowed as Joe motioned for her to follow him to a room next door, which happened to be a deserted conference room with a small projector set up. "You'll want to see this, I'm sure. Your flight back to Palestine doesn't leave until tomorrow, right?"

She looked at him, surprised. How did he know when her flight left?

Joe had the reel in the projector now, and they both stared at the screen.

There, without warning, Joe and Katrine saw the most awful scene both had ever witnessed in their lives. "Turn it off, please! Please!" she cried out in disbelief. "It can't be!"

Not much shocked Joe Miller. And if it did, he didn't show it. But for a moment, a very brief moment, a flicker of horror crossed his features, and he quickly turned away from

Katrine to hide what he felt. This shocked him, shocked him deeply. He shut the automatic reel off, and the two sat in silence in the darkened conference room.

"They... there were women and—" She couldn't say it, but whoever had shot the film had somehow captured a troop of Nazis out in the woods systematically murdering row after row of men, women, and children. She felt sicker than she'd felt on the plane. All thoughts of personal injury, pain, and sadness regarding her future, or Harry, were instantly subjected to the seriousness of their mission.

"I'm sorry," Joe said suddenly, turning back towards her. Any shadow of what he was thinking was gone. He was once more the consummate gentleman, playing a host. "If I'd known how bad... I never would have played it in front of you."

"It could have been me or my sisters out there." She looked at him, trying to gather her thoughts. "Where was this filmed?"

"Poland."

"Who shot it?"

"Someone in the Underground. It was smuggled out."

"And what will you do with it?"

"I will get it to American Intelligence. Hopefully, it will inspire my government to do something, show them they can no longer remain neutral."

"They didn't believe my story, but who could deny this! It is sure to have an effect."

Katrine felt a tear running down her cheek. It was all too much.

"Exactly." Joe stood up and opened up the window shade. The dark room was now washed in light.

When he looked at Katrine once more, he realized how tired the beautiful young woman was.

"Oh, Mrs. Smith. How thoughtless of me. You've been traveling halfway around the world. You must want nothing more than a bath and a bed."

"You have no idea," Katrine said, sitting up a little straighter.

"I'll get you to Shepheard's. It's the nicest hotel in Cairo. You can rest up, put on a clean dress, and then, I'll show you the town. Cairo has the best nightlife in Africa. Hip music, exotic smells and tastes. What do you say, *Mrs. Smith?*"

She shook her head. "I'll gladly take you up on the first part of your offer. But I'll have to decline with the rest."

"Really?"

"*Really.*"

Joe, not used to being told no, shrugged. "Well, how about breakfast in the morning?"

"What for?"

"So I can give you what you need for your journey home."

"Oh," she said. "Of course. I'm still a courier."

"That you most certainly are." And then, as an afterthought, he added, "And one of the prettiest I've met yet."

CHAPTER 30

WING WOMEN

*S*hepheard's had everything a girl could want in a hotel. When Katrine arrived at her enormous room, dripping with oriental opulence (stained glass, Persian carpets, great giant pillars modeled after the ancient Egyptian temples… there was no restraint at Shepheard's when it came to decor), she sent out everything in her suitcase to the hotel's laundry. By the time it came back, neatly folded and smelling of lavender, she had made it out of the world's longest bath, in a tub the size of a swimming pool.

But no matter how hard she tried to sleep, every time she shut her eyes, all she saw were the images on the film she'd smuggled in from Landeau's. It was a strange, restless night. She felt lost in a world that she did not understand or particularly want to.

She arrived the next morning fully expecting

to be met by Joe on the patio, but instead, a porter let her know she had a telephone call from Joe instead.

"Joe?" she said into the receiver back in the lobby, recognizing the American's polished baritone.

"Sorry, Mrs. Smith," he said, "I'm going to have to postpone our little get-together till tonight. The guys need a little more time with the picture show I took you to last night if you understand me."

"I think I do."

"So, how about we meet up at the bar in the hotel? It's a hip joint. You'll like it."

"All right." She paused before asking, "And what am I supposed to do all day?"

"Whatever you want. This is Cairo. Go see the Pyramids. Put your feet in the Nile. I'd go with you, but I'm swamped at the office."

"Of course," she answered. "Then, tonight, the bar. Say, seven-thirty?"

"I'll be there. And go ahead and pack up. As soon as we take care of our business, I've got you booked on a flight to Palestine later tonight."

At 7:30 that evening on the dot, Katrine pushed her way through the crowded bar to where Joe was standing. She smiled apologetically. "I had no idea this was a formal place. I feel very underdressed!" All the women were in formal gowns, the men in their dress uniforms or tuxedos. "Really, you should have told me!"

"You're the prettiest girl here. We could

dance you know." He looked at the couples dancing cheek to cheek.

"I didn't come here to dance."

"Boy, you are one serious girl." He winked at her knowingly. "Whoever the guy is, he must be the luckiest guy in the world."

She flushed and looked down. "I have no idea what you're talking about."

"Yeah, sure," he answered, not believing a word she said.

Awkwardly, Katrine changed the subject. "My, this place is popular."

"The boys have nicknamed it the 'long bar.'" Then grimacing, he explained, "There's a joke around here that when the Germans get to Shepheard's, they'll finally be held up because the line is so long."

"But the Germans aren't anywhere near here," Katrine answered.

"They'll come, and they'll come through Libya to support the Italian troops stationed there. Just wait, Mrs. Smith. They'll come. North Africa will be a battleground, and they'll try for Cairo. They all do. Even Napoleon did, remember?"

"You mean, Mussolini and Hitler are now officially allies?" She was horrified.

"It's worse than that. Japan is thrown in there too. Where have you been the last week? Don't you read the papers?"

She shrugged. "I'll admit, I'm a little behind. I've been traveling more than any person ought to, and today I collapsed by the pool and finally fell asleep."

"Well, it did that pretty face a world of good. Look at all those freckles. Maybe even a touch of a burn." He smiled approvingly.

They had reached the bar by then, and Joe ordered a couple of cokes. Pushing their way through the dancing couples to a small dark table in the corner, they sat down and stared at the soldiers.

"Joe, you didn't ask me here to sit and wait."

"No, I didn't. But you are going to have to for a minute. I'm expecting a call. They should be finishing up with the film any minute. I thought they would be done by now, but they are taking extra precautionary measures. I want to give your people a solid answer on what they say. The information is much too sensitive to send any other way than by your lovely lips."

"You couldn't have just called me?"

"I thought you would enjoy a little fun! A pretty girl like you?"

"Oh, quit it with the flattery, would you? It's getting on my nerves."

He chuckled. "Have it your way. Most girls like a little flattery."

"Most girls are not Mrs. Smith." She frowned suddenly. "What about my flight?"

He looked at his watch. "We've got an hour. They'll call. Be patient."

She was patient. Fifteen minutes went by. Then thirty. Forty-five minutes. She drank two cokes and felt jittery. "Joe, they aren't calling."

Now Joe was serious. "You can't leave until I know the outcome."

"What about my flight?"

"You'll make it." He said with more gusto than he felt.

Another hour went by. Katrine's flight was long gone.

Katrine stood up. "I'm going to the front desk to tell them I'll be another night. We'll reconvene in the morning."

Joe nodded sadly. "Sorry about the delay. I'm sure you are ready to get back to that man of yours."

"There is no man, Joe. Not anymore."

"If that's the case, next time you're in Cairo, we'll take on the town. What do you say?"

"Joe, you are not Jewish. Why are you helping us?"

He stopped. "I'm a Christian, Mrs. Smith."

"That means little to me. Christians don't have a good track record in my book."

"Then you haven't met a real one yet. That is, before me. You kids have gotten a rotten deal, and I'll be hanged if I don't do something to stop it."

She blinked once or twice, stunned.

Joe took her hand, kissed it lightly, and said goodnight, leaving Katrine to walk back to her room alone.

THE CALL CAME at four in the morning, and it woke Katrine with a jolt. It was Joe.

"It's all decided." His voice was grim. "You've got to pack up and come downstairs. I'm waiting for you in the lobby."

"What's the matter?" she asked, sitting up groggily.

"It's not very good news, Mrs. Smith. I wish I was sending you home with a different message."

"I see," she said. "But did you need to tell me that at this hour?"

"Look, there are not any more commercial flights to Palestine out of Cairo for another two weeks."

"Oh no!" Her eyes were wide awake now.

"But I was able to swing it for you to get onto an RAF transport flight. Special cargo. I've a friend down at the base who owes me a favor."

"Oh, Joe, thanks!" Katrine exclaimed. "When do we leave?"

"One hour on the dot. So you've got to hustle. We'll talk on the drive, okay?"

Less than 10 minutes later, Katrine was in the passenger seat of Joe's convertible, racing down the streets of Cairo with the top down.

Katrine got right to the point. "What are the circumstances?"

"Not good." He made a sharp turn and acceler- ated. "Intelligence said the tape is a phony."

She gasped. "How so?"

"They are calling it 'Zionist propaganda' to get the States into the war. They said that the Germans are men like us. They wouldn't do such a thing, not to innocent women and children. The thing is, we already know they've gunned down innocent Poles trying to escape Warsaw. We don't need more proof! What more proof could we offer? Testimonies. Photographs. Now film. They are choosing to shut their eyes, to believe the lies they tell themselves."

Katrine braced herself. Joe drove like he was in a race against time, and she supposed that was essentially true.

"Tell the Agency the Americans are not moving. They are on their own, for now."

"But certainly, such footage could not be faked."

"You know the truth. I know the truth. That doesn't mean that they have to believe it."[6]

It was the same as when she was in America. She had learned this through personal experience.

"What do you think it will take for America to get in on the war?" Katrine asked.

"I think they will have to feel pain." His hands gripped the steering wheel as he drove along the barbed wire fence of the RAF Base. At the gate, he showed his diplomatic passport and name. It was, amazingly, on the list, as was Katrine's. "It's nice to have friends in high places," he said without a trace of joy.

He drove all the way to the runway, helping Katrine out of his little coup and then getting her suitcase out of the trunk. A small biplane was already on the runway; it's propellers whirling around and around. Before Katrine could make it to the door, he took both of her hands in his and said, "It was my deepest wish that what you brought would change the tide. I am very sorry. For you and for us."

"I'm sorry too." She paused, looking up into his earnest eyes. "You're a good man, Joe

Miller. And if I am ever back in Cairo, well, we should do something."

He smiled sadly and let her hands go. "I know a guy who gives great tours of the Nile."

"That would be nice."

She hesitated a moment more. "Joe, if the Germans come, stay safe."

"You too, Mrs. Smith."

The form of a pilot from inside the open door of the plane shouted, "Hurry up! We're on a schedule here!"

Something about the voice made Katrine stop. She peered into the darkness (the sun had yet to rise).

"Grace?" she asked, barely believing such a thing was possible, "Grace, is that you?"

Grace pulled her goggles off and jumped down out of the plane.

"Katrine?" she exclaimed. "What in the world are you doing here?"

The two sisters ran to one another and embraced.

"What in the world are *you* doing here?" Katrine answered.

"I'm flying the transport plane. Word is there's some precious cargo that needs to go on my Jerusalem run."

"I'm your cargo," Katrine said, fully rattled.

Joe frowned. "Who is this?"

"My kid sister." Katrine shot him a confused look.

"Your kid sister is flying the plane?" He looked at Grace. "Do you even have a pilot's license?"

"Do you have a license?" Katrine asked, suddenly quite concerned.

"Civilian but yes. Women are relegated in the RAF to civilian licenses and flying transport planes. No combat." She looked at Katrine. "Anyway, with all the activity going on with the front in North Africa, all the able-bodied men pilots are doing more important things. Dr. Herring's son, Amos is the regular pilot. You never met him… But he's in the hospital recovering from a leg wound. I'm the on-call pilot for emergency trips."

"How many flight hours do you have?" Joe asked.

"Enough." Grace stuck her chin out. "More than you, I should say."

Joe laughed nervously. "Well, now I see where your sister gets her sense of humor."

Grace looked at Katrine, concerned. "Where's Harry?"

"I… We'll talk about it later, okay, Grace?"

"Sure." Grace, a question still in her eye, took Katrine's suitcase. "Come on in. We've got to get going while the weather stays clear."

∽

"Don't you just love flying, Katrine? This will be the longest solo flight I've made, officially."

"You mean, you've never done what we are doing before?"

"Oh, stop worrying! I have my wings. His Royal

Majesty trusts me to carry some rather important things. You can trust me too."

"What happened to Amos?"

"He's laid up for a while. Hurt his leg saving an admiral."

Grace glanced at Katrine. She went white, then green, and then white again. She wasn't really listening. Instead, she watched as Grace adjusted a dial on the control panel. "Are you sure you're supposed to touch that?"

"Katrine, you don't know how to drive. Don't tell me how to fly a plane, even if you are my big sister."

"You can't drive either. Or can you?"

"No… But I can fly a plane. You are just going to have to trust me." Grace looked at her big sister. "So, let's talk about Harry now."

"I wish there was something to talk about," Katrine said without expression.

"That means something happened. You need to talk about it. A problem shared is a problem halved. That's what you always used to tell me."

"What is this? Are you the big sister now?"

"If I need to be." Grace turned the plane. "I was thinking, as long as you and I are both in town, we should find wherever it is they've been keeping Lorelei locked away, break her out, and go cause some trouble."

"What have they been teaching you, Grace?" Katrine laughed out loud.

"Of course, you are not the only delivery I have to make." Grace sighed. "I've a load of supplies from Cairo destined for the officers at the RAF Base in Jerusalem and a much smaller load for the Palmach, a load no one is to know about mind you, but I'm telling you because apparently, you are good at keeping secrets."

"You have no idea, Grace. I've carried just about everything there is to carry under the sun. Broken hearts. Gold. Antiquities. Cakes. Movies. And now, bad news."

"Really?" Grace asked.

"You have no idea. It's so bad they are sending me to Ben Gurion himself."

Grace looked at her sister. Katrine had said it with such heaviness, it made her hold her breath.

"Look, once we land, I'll drop off the stuff and then be your wing-woman for your meeting, as they say, and then, we'll rendezvous with Lorelei somewhere. Girls lunch. Just like the old days in Berlin. Remember?

"I remember," Katrine said sadly.

CHAPTER 31

LADIES WHO LUNCH

*L*orelei was stretched out on the sofa reading a letter from Aunt Rose. It was her first day off that she could remember. That is, the first day off since the epidemic. But now, the worst was most certainly over. Nick and Paulina were both back at home, safe and sound. And Lorelei had the apartment all to herself.

"The journey of faith," Aunt Rose wrote, *"is just that, a journey. We never reach the end, until heaven."*

After that fateful night in Rabbi Finkelstein's apartment, Lorelei had written her aunt a very important letter. Aunt Rose had converted many years before. Her parents had assumed it was so Rose could marry that gentile husband of hers, Uncle Nathan. But now, Lorelei wasn't so sure. She had to know the truth. Was it possible that Aunt Rose had truly found the Messiah too?

Lorelei scanned down several lines. This was the fourth time she'd read the letter since it had arrived the day before. *"To hear that you have come so far on your journey brought me no end of joy. In truth, it's something I've been praying for, for quite a long time..."*

"Edie's pregnancy is coming along beautifully, though you should know the doctor put her on bedrest. Piper sends you a kiss."

Lorelei put the letter down and put her feet up on the arm of the couch. September in Jerusalem always tended to be the hottest month, and she had pulled her kibbutz shorts out of the drawer and slipped them on. How her legs relished their freedom! She wouldn't dare wear them out of the apartment, but as long as she was inside, she was determined to be comfortable. The door to the patio was open, and the sweet smell of the last weeks of summer swept in on a gentle breeze. It was the smell of dust and horse sweat and diesel from the busses. The Finkelstein children, home from their forced exile to the kibbutz, played down below, and she heard their laughter. It filled her with joy...

This joy, however, was tempered with something else. Lorelei was restless.

There was a quick knock, knock, knock on the door, and she put the letter down on her chest, shouting, "Becky! The door's open!"

The knock repeated itself.

"I said the door is open!" she shouted again, swinging herself up from the couch. As the door creaked open, Lorelei screamed and jumped up and down and ran forward, pulling her sisters inside.

"How in the world did you two get here?" she asked, clinging to them both.

"It's a long story," Grace replied, looking over Lorelei's shoulder at the apartment. She nodded approvingly. It had a nice feel about it, very nice.

"And you are going to tell me absolutely every single little detail!" Lorelei exclaimed, speaking quickly. "Why! I almost can't believe it! Come in, come inside! Sit down. No, wait! I'm going to take you two out to lunch at the most lovely little cafe in the Old City. Are you hungry?"

"We had the same idea." Grace grinned.

Lorelei ran to her room and threw on one of her light cotton dresses, a grey one with white buttons up the front, "And it's my treat. I'm rich now!"

"Is that so?" Katrine asked.

"Oh yes." She buttoned the dress up the front. "Nurses make *real* money. None of this kibbutz business for you. When I want to eat out, I can. Which is never because I work quite a lot."

She came out of her room and looked at her two sisters, *really* looked at them.

Grace had grown if such a thing was possible. She was absolutely sure of it. The young woman had a fresh seriousness about her, made more so with the RAF uniform.

And then there was Katrine. She seemed, if possible, smaller than ever. She was thin, and her eyes were sad. That was not a good sign.

Even her suit had a sadness to it. It was beautiful and elegant to be sure but sad, nonetheless.

"Katrine," she asked, "is everything all right?"

In response, Katrine just shook her head. She didn't want to tell the girls about what she had spoken to Ben Gurion about. Didn't want to tell them about the film she had seen. She couldn't tell them about Harry. Instead, she put on the most cheerful face she could manage and bade Lorelei lead them to the cafe.

IT WAS Grace and Katrine's first trip to the Old City, and they wanted to see everything there was to see. Lorelei knew the city by now like the back of her hand. Proudly, she led her sisters up the narrow steps of the rampart wall encircling the city, pointing out the Dome of the Holy Sepulchre, the Dome of the Rock, and the Hurva Synagogue. The sisters carefully wound their way towards the Western Wall, huffing and wiping the sweat off their faces.

When they finally reached the wall, the sisters stood looking up at it, breathless. The rabbis in black. The married women, heads modestly covered. In all of Israel, this one wall was the greatest proof that the Jews indeed had had a homeland before, and perhaps, one day would have one again. Lorelei whipped out three small scraps of paper and three pencils and passed them out. "I came prepared."

"What do we do with them?" Grace asked.

"Write a prayer to God." She pointed at the deep cracks in the ancient structure, the foundations of the temple of their people. "Everyone does it. You roll it up and stick it in the cracks."

"But what will we write?" Grace asked.

"Anything you want God to do for you."

"Like a wish?"

"It's not a wish at all," Lorelei said firmly. "It's a prayer. He answers them. I've seen it."

Katrine took her pencil and scrap of paper. Before writing, she looked at Lorelei and said slowly, "You've changed, you know that?"

"Everybody changes, Katrine."

"But you seem different. More… secure."

A moment later, the girls walked solemnly up to the wall, spending a second or two in silence, and then left their prayers among the hundreds of rolls of paper already stuck in the ancient stones.

Away from the wall, Lorelei put one arm through Katrine's bent elbow and the other through Grace's. "It's just a quick walk back through the Arab Quarter, and then we'll be at the Courtyard Cafe. You'll just love it!"

OVER TEA AND SCONES, in the oasis of the Courtyard Cafe, the Adleman sisters felt almost like it was the old days. They could have been at their old haunt, the Cafe Kranzler on the Unter den Linden, after a morning at the zoo, eating

444

mohnkuchen (poppy seed cake) and drinking very strong coffee. They relaxed and laughed, and it was almost like they were those carefree girls of two-and-a-half years before, almost. But they had changed too much, too deeply, for it ever to be exactly the same.

"So, do you like spending all day holding babies and taking their temperatures?"

Lorelei nodded. "It's not forever. I'll be posted soon, who knows where. But the Spafford Baby Home has been quite an experience. They've taught me a lot about faith… and trust."

"Well, I'd like to go there after lunch and take a look around," Katrine said. "If you are up for it?"

"I'm sure Bertha wouldn't mind." She took a sip of her tea. "So, what's he like? Ben Gurion? What did he say? What did *you* say?"

"I didn't say anything he didn't know. He didn't particularly like what I had to say. Though thankfully, he didn't shoot the messenger. We all hoped that our efforts to spur the Americans to do something might work, be it through testimonies like mine or the film. But when Harry and I left for America, we knew it would be a hard sell. The real goal was to raise money and make sure the seal got into the right hands. I had a very small part to play, but it was a part." She sounded much older than Lorelei remembered.

"And what about Harry?" Lorelei asked, her elbows on the table.

The look on Katrine's face said it all.

Lorelei reached across the table and took her hand. "I'm so sorry. I really thought…"

Katrine tried to laugh it off. "I'm pretty sure I have a man allergy. I've sworn them off for my health."

"That bad?"

Katrine sighed. "Oh, I guess it could have been worse." She wasn't sure how exactly, but she was sure it could have been.

Lorelei turned to Grace. "And what about you? Any cute officers on the base?"

"Oh, Lorelei! How can you be so immature? There's a war on. I can't think about boys, not even ace pilots like Amos Herring, when they are about to throw me out of a plane somewhere over Europe." She clapped her hand over her mouth. "You aren't supposed to know that. Forget it right now! I never said anything!"

"You are going back to Europe!" Katrine was not pleased with this arrangement at all. "Oh, Grace, you can't!"

Grace ignored them both and said firmly, "Please, no one is supposed to know. It's top secret."

"Katrine's a professional at keeping secrets now, and I promise I won't say anything," Lorelei said. "Besides, who would I talk to?"

"I don't know," Grace smirked. "Maybe a cute doctor at the hospital."

Now, Lorelei frowned. "Grace, you know not to joke like that."

"You wouldn't be happier with someone though, really?"

Lorelei shook her head. "I'm happier than I've

been in as long as I can remember. I don't want to rock the boat if you get my meaning. I finally found *balance*. The last thing I need is a romantic complication."

"Amen." Katrine nodded and stood up. "Well, I don't know about you ladies, but I've hit the wall. I've had enough stimulation over the last few weeks to last me the rest of my life." She looked at Lorelei. "Any chance I can stay at your place tonight? I'll figure out what I'm doing with the rest of my life tomorrow."

"You can stay as long as you like if you don't mind the sofa." Lorelei stood as well. "Grace, are you staying the night too?"

"If you can handle one more. I have to get the plane back to Cairo early tomorrow morning."

Suddenly, a commotion outside the courtyard drew their attention towards the gate. It sounded like a crash, and several men were yelling.

"Do you hear that?" Katrine asked.

Lorelei tilted her head and listened as the shouting grew in intensity and number. Why, it sounded like there must have been 40 or 50 people, all of them shouting at once. She grabbed her purse. "Oh no. Come on! We'll need to make a run for it!"

"What is it?" Grace asked, jogging beside her. "What's going on?"

"It's a riot. If we get stuck in the streets, we could get hurt. They tend to get quite riled up sometimes! People get trampled or worse."

"Who?"

"The Arabs!"

Katrine chasing after Lorelei, panted, "But why are they rioting?"

"They want their own state. Just like us! The Brits will be here soon enough and shut the whole thing down. They might shoot some rounds into the air, but normally no one gets shot. Almost no one anyway."

They rounded a corner and came out of Jaffa Gate, running along the outside of the Old City wall until they reached the eastern side of the city and Lorelei's small, quiet neighborhood, untouched by the mobs. But even from the front of her building, they could hear the shouts and shots from inside the Old City.

~

As the girls came up the stairs to their apartment door, they noticed it was half-way open. Lorelei frowned. "I'm sure I locked it when we left!"

The answer to this conundrum met them an instant later. Stretched out on the sofa, blood soaking through his shirt, was Yosef. Paulina hovered over him, like a mother hen. Becky was in the kitchen digging out the first-aid kit from the under the sink.

"Oh my," Katrine whispered. "What in the world is going on?"

Becky shouted from inside the kitchen to come inside and shut the door and lock it. "No," she clarified, "barricade it!"

"The mob won't come in here, will it?" Katrine asked.

Lorelei took one look at Yosef and somehow

knew exactly what had happened. "It's not the riot she's worried about."

Becky emerged, the first-aid kit in hand. She took one look at Katrine and remembered immediately that she was Lorelei's big sister. She assumed the other girl must be Grace, the youngest of the Adleman trio. "Girls, take Paulina outside, would you? Lorelei and I need some space."

"Just when you thought it was safe to go out." Lorelei sighed and went to the bathroom, scrubbing her hands with the medical grade antiseptic soap. Silently, she began to pray.

Out on the patio, to the eldest and youngest Adleman, Paulina spilled the horrible story. She'd been at her parent's house, helping her mother clean the jewelry shop. She had a set date with Yosef at the market, like always. When she got to the market, Yosef was there. But he was afraid. He said there had been a threat nailed to his front door earlier that morning. *They* knew he wouldn't join them. And *they* would make him pay!

Paulina had noticed two men following them through the market. Yosef had noticed as well, and the couple had moved as quickly as they could back to Yosef's home. But they got caught in the middle of the mob as it surged through the narrow streets of the Muslim Quarter. Out of nowhere, the two young men following them emerged from the crowd. One of them had a knife. Paulina wasn't sure how it happened. They were separated by the mob, but when she was able to get back to Yosef, he was clutching his side, and there was blood.

"All I could think was that I had to get him somewhere safe," the young girl cried. "I thought about the Spafford Baby Home—they wouldn't dare go after him there. But nowhere in the Old City, in all of Jerusalem, is safe for Yosef anymore! And of course, it's not like I could bring him home. My father would have a heart attack. Not only am I not dating an Armenian, I'm dating a non-Armenian at odds with the Mufti's thugs."

Grace and Katrine shared a look.

"This wasn't a warning. They want him dead. He knows too much. They are worried he is going to tell the British, or the Zionists, their plans to work alongside the Nazis." She paused for breath. "I still had a key to the apartment. I could barely drag him up the stairs. He had lost all strength on the walk here. I was sure he would die!"

Katrine and Grace looked at one another throughout Paulina's monologue. Neither had any idea what to say or do.

"Something will work out," Grace finally said, patting her shoulder. "You were right to come here."

Paulina brushed the tears out of her eyes and tried to smile.

Meanwhile, Katrine stood up and took a few stray pins out of her hair that had fallen out in the mad rush back to the apartment, watching as Lorelei and Becky hovered over Yosef's body.

～

"How BAD IS IT?" Lorelei asked. "Should we get him to the hospital?"

"It's too dangerous. They know he's still alive, most likely. They'll be watching his house. They may even be watching the hospital." Becky blinked once or twice, "It's a miracle he's alive. It's a nasty flesh wound, but there's no damage to the tissue or organs. He'll heal, as long as there is no infection. And we'll have to put some stitches in." She turned her attention to Yosef. "This is going to hurt, worse than when you were stabbed. I don't have any sort of anesthesia here."

He nodded and bravely braced himself.

Immediately, Becky and Lorelei went to work cleaning the wound. Yosef clenched his jaw as a searing pain shot through his side, but thankfully, he didn't move. Several minutes later, Becky carefully sutured Yosef's skin back together. No one spoke.

She smiled as she put the finishing touch on the last stitch. "You'll be weak for a while, Yosef. You lost a lot of blood. But I think you'll be alright. God willing."

"Thank you," Yosef whispered and shut his eyes. He felt dizzy.

The nurses looked at one another, proud of their handiwork. "God willing." Lorelei nodded and exhaled. "Now we just have to figure out how to get him out of here."

～

"I've an idea," Katrine said carefully, "on how to get Yosef out. I've become a bit of an expert on unusual deliveries."

"Oh?" Becky asked looking at the wall clock. It was nearly midnight, but no one was asleep. (No one except for Yosef, that is.)

Katrine turned to Grace. "But it will take a little cooperation with the RAF."

"Ah," the lightbulb visibly went off in Grace's head. "You have a passenger who needs a ride to Cairo urgently."

"Yes, but my passenger has no transport visa."

Grace shook her head. "We don't have time to get him fake papers now! I've got to get back to the airport in a couple of hours."

"Don't worry about that. The papers will be waiting when you arrive. I've got a friend at the American Embassy. He'll take care of us."

"You mean that man who dropped you off?"

"What man?" Lorelei asked, intrigued.

"Joe Miller." Katrine was moving inside. "I'll call him now to let him know he has something coming special delivery via His Royal Majesty's Private Courier Service."

Becky smiled. "Joe Miller? I like him already!"

Katrine glanced at her. "You should meet him. He'd probably like you too. He is sort of the lonely type."

THE DARKENING STORM

~

"We're back!" Grace shouted as she came through the door. In her arms were a bunch of raw Eastman chemicals and photographic paper.

I let out a small startled scream. I was so focused on the manuscript, I hadn't heard the truck pull up or the door open. Founder, startled, began to yap in her crate.

"Oh, sorry," she said as I put down my pencil. "I didn't mean to scare you."

"I must be a little jittery, that's all." I looked outside. The sky was darkening quickly, more from the storm than from the sunset. They had gotten back just in the nick of time.

Peter was behind her now. "No phone call?"

"No." I stood up. "The coastguard did call. He said you must have been seeing things."

Peter shook his head. "I don't think so. I saw a sub out there. I know it!"

"I told him you thought it might be German."

"What'd he say?" Grace asked.

"He laughed at me. Said it was probably one of the wrecks on the reefs." He inhaled, "It wasn't a wreck. I know the wrecks around here, I know this coastline inside and out!"

"We haven't been here for a while," I said carefully. "It could be a new wreck you don't know about."

He was adamant. "I saw something." He took the chemicals out of Grace's hands. "I'm going to develop this film, and then you'll see!"

With that, he marched upstairs and shut the bathroom door forcefully. Grace looked at me and took her coat off, shivering slightly. Off came the hat, letting her hair fly every which way. She looked nervous.

"What are you doing?" she asked me.

"Reading."

"Hmm." She stood there, not knowing what to do. "I, uh… How about I make dinner?"

"Come to think of it, we didn't have lunch, did we?" My stomach rumbled.

"What shall I make?"

"Whatever you want… or rather, whatever you can find."

She nodded and walked slowly into the kitchen. I listened as she searched through the cupboard looking for something that might serve as dinner.

"I found some tinned beef. We could have that on toast?" Grace shouted from the kitchen.

"Sure. That's fine," I responded. It wasn't my favorite, but it was there.

I turned my attention back on the manuscript and hoped beyond hope that the photographs would reveal nothing at all, or at most, the remains of an old fishing vessel stuck on a reef.

CHAPTER 32

THE ONE THAT GOT AWAY

*L*orelei, Grace, and Katrine lay side by side in Lorelei's bed. There really wasn't room for all three of them, but they didn't care. Shoulder to shoulder, they stared at the ceiling, whispering like when they were little and their parents would come in and tell them to be quiet and go to bed, there would be plenty of time to talk tomorrow.

But, of course, there were no parents to come in and tell them to be quiet, and the truth was, they had no idea when they would all three be together and get to talk again. So they whispered away, as quietly as possible so as not to disturb Yosef, who slept in the living room under the anxious eye of Paulina, who had phoned her parents that she was spending the night with the nurses.

"I have to tell you girls something," Lorelei began tentatively, not knowing how to begin, but also knowing that she had to tell them what had happened. She started again. "Over the last few weeks, I've come to believe that…"

Katrine turned her face towards Lorelei. "What is it?"

"I'm not sure what you say when a Jew comes to accept that Yeshua, or Jesus, is the Messiah."

Katrine and Grace were silent. Finally, Katrine replied slowly, "You really believe this?"

In the dark, she could feel Lorelei moving her head up and down. "Just like Aunt Rose."

"Like Aunt Rose?" Grace repeated.

"I wanted you to know," Lorelei finished.

She waited for them to ask her why. Her heart longed to tell them of all she had seen and felt, of how believing in Yeshua had brought her more peace than she had ever felt possible. A minute went by and then another. But neither Grace nor Katrine spoke. Lorelei suddenly felt very nervous and worried over whether she should have said anything at all.

And then, Katrine said slowly, thinking it through as she spoke, "I don't understand why you've done this. I may not ever understand, but I'm glad you told me. And I respect your choice. If it helps you get through this terrible time…" she trailed off.

"Katrine," Lorelei stopped her, "it's not like that. It's not to cope or something silly. It's the truth. He's the truth. Don't you understand?"

Grace sat up. "I don't understand, and I'm not sure I want to understand. Lorelei! The

Christians are the ones who have done this to us!"

Lorelei kept her voice calm. "Grace, that's not true. There are those who call themselves Christians who are anything but. There are others, the ones who really know Yeshua, who are different. Look at Becky and Horatio and Edie! They all risked their lives to get us out of Germany. And Piper and Aunt Rose and Uncle Nathan? They are family! And they are Christians."

Katrine was sitting up now too. "That is true. Joe Miller is a Christian. He's risking his whole career doing what he's doing, helping us." Her voice was contemplative.

Lorelei added, "Not to mention Captain Orde Wingate. The whole reason he is helping the Haganah is *because* he is a Christian. And where would we be without him?" She paused. "Don't you see? Yeshua is *our* Messiah. He came for us, and the gentiles too, but he came for us first!"

Grace thought about this for a moment and then said with an air of finality, "All those people you mentioned are different, I'll give you that. And if you want to believe Jesus is the Messiah, okay. I won't hold it against you. We've all been through a lot. But I don't want to talk about it anymore." She lay back down and turned her back towards her sisters.

Lorelei felt tears spring to her eyes. "Grace," she said quietly.

"I *don't* want to talk about it!"

Lorelei felt Katrine squeeze her hand softly. It was just like in the old days, her big sister telling her it would be all right. But it wasn't. Nothing would ever be the same. And at that moment, she had never felt so apart from her sisters, though it had been months since they had been physically so close.

"Oh Lord," she prayed silently, "please show my sisters who you are. I want them to know you."

That was the sad end to the last slumber party. Each sister lay awake for a long time, not moving or speaking. Finally, when the alarm went off at 4:00 in the morning, they began to dress in silence, wondering if they had fallen asleep at all. No one mentioned the conversation from the night before. It was as though a chasm had been forged between them. None knew how to cross over to the other side. And it hurt.

UNDER THE COVER OF DARKNESS, a strange procession emerged from the apartment. By all shapes and appearances, it was an old woman supported by two younger women. Another woman led the charge, and another two took up the rear, looking furtively to the left and the right. In reality, it was Yosef with a scarf on his head and sunglasses and one of Becky's floral house-dresses thrown on over his clothes. Surrounded by his five female bodyguards, the wounded engineer was half-carried, half-dragged to the cab waiting on the road.

Once he was safe inside the cab, he took off the scarf and sunglasses, complaining it was so dark he couldn't see. Becky smiled. It was a good sign he could complain. And thankfully, he'd made it through the night without spiking a fever.

With all six of them crammed into the cab, the driver peeled off towards Atarot Airport where Grace's little plane waited.

Because Grace was a transport pilot, there was no need to go through the airport. Instead, she had the cab take her straight to the plane with her RAF identification papers and pilot's license. It was all that was required. And of course, her four friends and her mother wanted to see her off.

Paulina begged to be let aboard for a final goodbye while Becky made sure Yosef was comfortable.

For a moment, Katrine, Grace, and Lorelei were alone on the tarmac. They looked at one another, each feeling emotions too large to put into words. No one spoke.

Finally, Becky and Paulina's faces appeared from the plane door and Becky yelled, "You ought to be going, I think," and carefully climbed out.

Grace nodded and began to walk towards the plane. Abruptly, she turned and ran to Lorelei and threw her arms around her. "I'm sorry about last night," she said.

"Oh, Grace!" Lorelei held her close. "I'm not angry at you. I love you so much it hurts."

"And I love you. Even if I don't understand you, I love you. I want you to know that, you know, in case anything happens."

"Don't say that!" Lorelei chided her. "Nothing is going to happen." She looked up at the sky, willing her eyes not to shed tears, before cradling her sister's head between her hands. "And I am going to pray for you every single day."

Katrine was beside them both now, her arms wrapped around her two baby sisters who would always be smaller, even if they were both taller.

And so, as the plane roared down the runway and took off, soaring into the sky and finally out of sight. The Adleman sisters parted once again, none of them knowing the other as they had before, but loving each other more than ever.

$\sim$

IT WAS a gloomy group that returned to the apartment. Becky unlocked the door, and the four women shuffled in. All the effects of the day before and the awfully long night had begun to take hold.

"You girls go sit down. I'll make us some coffee," Katrine said tiredly.

"You don't know where anything is in the kitchen," Becky protested. "Let me."

"Now, now, I'm a big girl. I'll find the coffee pot." Katrine smiled, pushing Becky towards the couch. "Now, really, you go on."

With Katrine in the kitchen, Paulina, Becky, and Lorelei sat in stunned silence on the couch.

Suddenly, Paulina began to cry. "I should have gone with him. I should have gone with him!"

Becky was firm. "You have to trust him to God."

"But how can I?" Paulina was nearly inconsolable. "I hate goodbyes. What if we never get to see one another again?"

"Sometimes, dear," she ran her fingers through Paulina's curls, "there is a 'good' in 'goodbye.' When you let go of people or things and trust them to God, something miraculous happens. You give room for God to work."

Lorelei inhaled, struck by the wisdom of Becky's words. "Why, that is what I must do with my sisters."

Paulina looked up. "How so?"

"They don't know Yeshua. I have to let go and give God room to work. Just as Becky did with me."

Becky smiled. "We all have things… and people we must let go of in order to move forward and receive what God has for us *now*." She looked deeply into Lorelei's eyes as though to say, 'you know who I'm talking about.'

"I'm not sure I like what God has for me now." Paulina frowned.

Lorelei was only half-listening. She knew as soon as Becky said it that she had more to let go of than Grace and Katrine. She had to let go of Rolf. If she didn't, she would never be able to receive all of what God had for her. It was now or never. With a start, she stood up and went to the bedroom. When she returned, she had a small gold chain in her hand. Gently, she put it around Paulina's wrist.

Surprised, Paulina looked up questioningly.

"This belonged to someone I loved very much. Someone like Yosef. As long as Yosef is alive, and you are apart, it will remind you that there is still hope and to daily trust God."

"But," she paused, "you are giving it to me?"

"I… I'm letting go of it to see what God has for me now." She looked at her friend. "I want to allow God to heal my heart, *completely*."

Becky looked at Lorelei, pride beaming through her eyes. "You are quite a woman, Lorelei Adleman."

A crash came from the kitchen, followed by, "Come to think of it, I didn't want coffee anyway. How about tea?"

Lorelei grimaced. "She's not very good in the kitchen. I'll warn you now, she makes terrible messes and gets overwhelmed cleaning them up."

Paulina rushed into the kitchen. "Let me help. I'm practically a professional by now with all the cooking I've been doing for those nurses."

∼

"So," Joe Miller said eyeing the young man, "this is the precious cargo your sister phoned me about?"

Grace nodded her head.

Yosef extended his hand. "Sir, my name is Yosef Farachi. I speak English."

"All right, Yosef," Joe took his hand and shook it, "I'm going to give it to you plainly.

You are safer here than in Palestine, but the Arab Nationalists are as strong in Egypt as anywhere else in this part of the world. You get my meaning?"

Yosef nodded.

Joe continued, "The Egyptians got sick and tired of British rule about two decades ago. But the British still have a lot of clout. That's why this base is here at all."

"Yes," Yosef said quietly. "I know."

"So, here's the plan. You are no longer Yosef Faraci but instead Francis Marsafi, nationality Egyptian." He passed Yosef a small wallet. Inside was a new identity card. "First thing tomorrow, we get your photograph taken and put inside the passport."

"What then?"

"Once you heal up and grow a hefty beard to hide that baby face, you start work as my manservant until we find you something more suitable."

Yosef looked stunned. "You're giving me a job?"

"Like I said, until we find you something more suitable. I don't need someone bringing me coffee and pressing my suit. I like to do those things myself."

"I'm an engineer, but I think I can press a suit." He was beaming. "I don't know how to thank you."

"I'm sure you'll think of something, by and by." Joe chuckled. "Let's just hope for both of our sakes that you are as good of a man as Katrine said."

Yosef nodded and turned to Grace. Solemnly, he took both her hands in his and bowed his head. "If you ever need anything, you or your sisters or Becky, I am your man. I owe you my life." The way he said it gripped Grace's heart. "I will pray for you every day, that Jesus Christ protects you and guards you and gives you wisdom beyond your years."

Grace looked down, not knowing how to respond to his passionate outburst.

Awkwardly, she helped him into the open door of the convertible (the top was down) and shut the door, adding, "You remember what Becky and Lorelei told you? Watch for fevers and keep the wound clean."

Stopping Joe just as he was about to get into the driver's seat, Grace looked up into his face, searching for any trace of dishonesty. "Why are you helping him?"

"I owed your sister a favor. She brought me cake."

"You're doing this for cake?"

"I'm doing this because the kid needs a break."

"Is that all?" She poked her finger into his broad chest.

"You think there is some other sinister reason?"

"No." She caught herself. "I just don't understand why you would want to risk your position at the consulate by taking on a runaway Arab with a target on his back."

"Because everyone deserves a chance to live. That's why you're here, isn't it? So your people get a fighting chance to survive what the Nazis are doing?"

"But it doesn't explain what you are doing here."

"No, I guess it doesn't." He put his hand on the handle to the door of the convertible. "I consider it my duty to treat others the way I would want to be treated. If I was in his boat, I'd hope someone would do this for me."

"Your Christian duty? You are a Christian, aren't you?"

"Is that a crime?"

Grace didn't answer. She looked once more at Yosef in the backseat and then turned and walked towards her quarters.

She had a lot to think about, but she was much too tired to think. She would think later. For now, she had to concentrate. There were only ten days left to go before the mission commenced. Ten short days.

THE PHOTOGRAPH

~

The sound of a plate breaking in the kitchen distracted me and I looked up.

"Sorry!" Grace yelled.

I stood up and went to the kitchen. "You've been stirring that tinned beef over the stove for two hours. I'm not sure we will be able to eat it."

She gave me a funny half smile. "Yeah… I guess I got distracted."

"I don't blame you, not after everything I just read." I laughed.

"Well," she turned away from the stove, "what'd you think?"

Before I could answer what I thought, Peter burst into the room. "Piper, can you help me enlarge this even more?"

He passed me a still damp photograph. On the horizon of the image, there definitely was *something*. But it could have been anything.

"I can try, but it's pretty small, " I answered, turning to Grace. "You watch Founder, okay? This could take a while."

"I'll make something *else* for dinner," Grace answered, looking disdainfully at the canned beef that was beyond recognition.

I nodded and followed Peter upstairs.

Side by side, we worked in the red light of the darkened bathroom. It reminded me of our time onboard the *Goose*, that day after my birthday. Neither of us spoke, working in silence.

"So... you want to get a sailboat, huh?" I asked.

He looked at me and smiled. "Yeah."

We both looked down just as the enlargement became clear. I felt my husband's shoulders tighten.

All thoughts of sailboats were gone.

"Do you see what I see?" he asked.

"I wish I didn't, but... I do."

"We need to show Grace." He sighed, and I followed him out of the bathroom and down the stairs.

Grace had managed to pull together a few cheese sandwiches and was sitting at the table looking out the window into the dark. The wind was blowing very hard.

She looked up, a question in her eyes. "Well?"

"We have definite proof that it was a submarine in the waters behind the lighthouse." Peter held up the photograph. Whether it was German or American, who could tell... but it was, inarguably, a sub.

Grace pursed her lips, studying the print. "This can't be good."

I felt my hands shaking slightly, and my heart began to race. The weight of what was happening, or rather, what could happen, was almost overwhelming. I had to keep my head. Not panic. There was nothing to panic about, not yet. Technically, nothing could happen. Nothing except... except... Oh, what were the Germans thinking! Were they planning a large-scale attack against the shore? What were they spying on? We were neutral for crying out loud!

"Should we call the coast guard again?" Grace asked, urgency evident in her voice.

Peter nodded. "I'll call again right now. Hopefully, the officer in charge will pick up!"

Once more, Grace and I followed him into the living room. His voice took on his military tone. "Yes, sir. Quite sure. I've got photographs."

He put the receiver back and looked at us. "He's going to stop by to look at them first thing in the morning. Apparently, there was another sighting up the coast at Station Elizabeth."

"Why isn't he coming over immediately?" Grace replied, her voice rising. "If there was another sighting, can we afford to wait until tomorrow?"

Peter shook his head. "I think he still doesn't really believe me. But it's better than nothing. He said he wants to do his due diligence."

"So, what are we supposed to do?" I asked.

"Nothing." Peter shrugged. "We are just going to have to trust God and wait." He managed a small smile. "What would Edie do on a night like this?"

"Edie always said worry never did anyone any good. As long as there is nothing you can do, you might as well enjoy yourself. *That's* what Edie would do," I said thoughtfully, then added as inspiration struck, "How about I make popcorn? And some hot chocolate? And we can stay up all night and watch for German spies."

"There won't be any spies tonight," Peter replied. "It's too stormy to attempt a landing."

Grace followed me into the kitchen, and I found the popcorn and began to heat oil in the pot.

"How are you so calm?" Grace exclaimed.

"I'm praying on the inside, trust me. I'm asking for the peace that passes all understanding!"

"Praying?"

As I twirled the popcorn kernels around and around in the hot oil, I looked at her, wondering if she considered that a good thing or bad thing.

She shook her head as she said, half to me and half to herself, "This is not a time to pray. It is a time for *action*." She shot me a dramatic look. "Being here, doing what you are doing, I don't understand how you can take it! There is a sub out there doing who knows what, and we are making popcorn!" She shook her head again and took a handful of popcorn. "It needs salt and butter."

"You need to calm down." I pointed to the table where the butter and salt shaker were. "I have to take it. My husband can't be on the front-lines anymore. And more than that, we are waiting on God to show us what to do and where to go next," I said with more confidence than I felt.

"Come on," I pushed her forward to the living room, "we are waiting, and there is nothing we can do tonight, except read or listen to the radio. To quote my mother, 'God's timing is always perfect. You may think you are too late when you are only too early.'"

I could feel her groan internally.

"I'm not talking about being late! I'm talking about doing nothing at all!" she replied, passion in her voice.

"Let's read," Peter cut in, passing me the manuscript as I handed him the popcorn. "I need to take my mind off of what's going on out there."

I looked at Grace. "Are you up for it? I mean, can you handle more of Edie's book?"

Grace exhaled and grabbed the popcorn. "I guess so. It's better than lying in bed awake doing nothing."

CHAPTER 33

BACK TO SCHOOL, AGAIN

Several days after Yosef's escape, Lorelei looked at her older sister over breakfast and said: "Katrine, you can't just sit around and mope. It's not healthy."

"I know that!" Katrine exclaimed, folding her hands over her lap and trying to look composed. "I have a plan."

"You have a plan?" Lorelei spread butter on her toast and checked the clock. She had five minutes before she had to run to the Spafford Baby Home. It was her day at the clinic, and now that the epidemic was over, everything had returned to normal, for the most part.

"I do," Katrine answered. "I'm going to get a job."

"You are?" Lorelei's toast stopped midair.

"Yes." She looked down at her hands.

"Doing what? More deliveries?"

"Oh, no." Katrine's head shook. "The Agency

will have to deal with one less Mrs. Smith. I want something a little more dependable. And preferably, something that pays."

"Well, what do you have in mind?"

"What any self-respecting single woman has in mind." She bit her lip and then mumbled, "Teaching."

Lorelei tilted her head thoughtfully. "The Spafford Baby Home has a small pre-school, and I heard that they were looking for someone with a college degree. I could put in a good word for you."

"No, no." Katrine laughed tightly. "You know how I am with kids."

"No, I don't."

"Lorelei, I never babysat growing up. You and Grace were the only babies I ever spent any time with at all, and I was a baby myself then. Kids make me nervous. It's one of the reasons I don't want to go back to the kibbutz. Plus the fact I'm not cut out for hard labor."

"So, you want to teach adults?" Lorelei's eyes focused on Katrine. Her sister, to her, had never seemed so sad in her whole life. And yet, despite that, there was also a new sort of determination.

"Exactly." She stood up and began to take her plate to the kitchen. "It's an old dream. But sometimes when a new dream dies, you have to go back to the old dreams."

Following her, Lorelei asked, "You are talking about Harry, aren't you."

"I'm talking about a lot of things." Katrine faced the sink and washed her plate. Then, she took Lorelei's plate and began to wash it too. "Now, it's time for you to go to work. I don't want you to be late."

Later that morning, Katrine found herself in Professor Hildesheimer's office at the University.

He appeared even taller than Katrine remembered him.

"Why, Miss Katrine, it simply is impossible."

Katrine looked down at her brown skirt and back up at the gentle academic's face, eyes filled with compassion. "But, Professor," she paused, "I have to have a job. I have to do something. I can't just sit around the rest of my life."

"A girl like you, a good strong head on her shoulders," he made a tut-tut sound, putting his tongue behind his teeth, "of course not. You must put what God gave you to good use."

"Then give me an adjunct professorship." She locked her blue eyes on his.

"You didn't finish your degree at the University in Berlin."

"They wouldn't let me sit for the final exams because I'm Jewish."

"I know all about such things." He sighed sadly. "But, it still poses a problem in the academic world. The University of Jerusalem only hires those with valid degrees."

Katrine wanted to cry. "Professor Hildesheimer, I have two skills. I can sing harmony with my sisters. We had a rather successful underground trio once, but now... well, the band broke up. And I'd never make it as a soloist."

"And the other skill?"

"I love history. I really do. When I say I would have graduated near the top of my class, it's the truth. I'm not good for much else." She looked away, afraid of what answer she would find when she once more faced the kindly archeologist. "I made a terrible spy."

"How so?"

"I became emotionally involved, I guess you could say."

"I see." He observed her, thoughtfully, "I have the perfect solution. You go back to school."

"I could never afford it. I'm out of money." She sighed. "Don't you understand?"

"Yes, I certainly do. I'm going to give you a fellowship."

Katrine's jaw dropped. "You are?"

"I am." He coughed into his handkerchief. "Now, it won't be medieval history like you studied before. I need a research assistant for my work out at the dig in the City of David. You'll have to switch gears and brush up on your ancient languages. And, of course, you'll have to be okay with being outdoors a lot. It's cold and wet in the winter and hot as blazes in the summer."

"I don't care." Katrine was genuinely smiling now. "I would do anything you asked; I'd even clean the classrooms!"

"No need for that, my dear." He stood up, and Katrine followed suit. "We start tomorrow morning, at seven o'clock sharp." He took two thick books from his bookshelf, *The Basics of Ancient Weaponry* and *The Roman Empire in Palestine.* "I expect these read and analyzed by next Thursday."

Out of her mouth escaped an exclamation that was between a laugh and a sigh.

The professor looked at her questioningly. "What is it?"

"I can't believe it, that's all."

"What?"

She stopped, trying to put into words all she felt. "I gave up ever finishing my Masters. Now, the thought of getting my Doctorate… After so many disappointments, it is a welcome surprise to get something I've always wanted. It's so wonderful, I—" She caught herself before she could accidentally add that it was so wonderful she might even forget Harry.

~

MORRIS, Grace, and Cecilia wandered cautiously into the Citadel Military Hospital outside of Cairo. They found Amos in the last bed of a long line of soldiers in various states of physical pain. A nurse had a record playing in the corner, Bing Crosby by the sounds of it.

Amos was sitting up, chatting away with the soldier next to him, who, apparently, had recently lost his arm.

From down the hall, he saw them coming and shouted cheerfully, "What are you guys doing here?"

"We've come to visit the sick." Cecilia smiled her kind little smile. "Besides, we have the afternoon off for good behavior."

"Sure." Amos glanced sideways at Grace and blushed slightly. "Even that one? I know a troublemaker when I see one."

Morris looked at the thick rolls of bandages wrapped around Amos's shin and then down the line of the wounded. "I feel terrible about this," he said. "I feel like I'm responsible."

"Well, you are. But I would say it was all for the best. Besides, I'll be discharged in two days," Amos proudly pointed to the bandage on his shin. "Forty-five stitches. The rock sliced right through to the bone. Not broken, thankfully. Compared to the rest of the guys in here, I got a cat-scratch."

"I heard that Admiral Wells gave you a medal for bravery." Grace shook her head. "In my opinion, a cat-scratch wouldn't warrant that!"

"You told them what happened?" Morris asked, suddenly concerned. He lowered his voice to a whisper that only they could hear. "What about compromising our mission and all that?"

"I had to tell them something." Amos sat up and swung his bandaged leg over the side of the hospital bed. "I screamed bloody murder at all those guys swimming in the pool, and then they discovered a sopping wet bomb."

"What did you tell them?" Grace asked.

He shrugged his shoulders and answered, "I let them know the Jewish Agency uncovered a conspiracy. We heard someone might try to bomb the club, and together, we made sure it didn't happen."

"That's not exactly true." Morris frowned.

"It's not exactly false either." Amos locked eyes with Grace. "What the British don't know won't hurt them. If anything, we have more trust than ever before."

Cecilia looked from Grace to Amos to Morris. "Well, that's good, isn't it?"

"Very good." He still didn't look away from Grace. "I, uh… It was nice of you to come and visit."

"How's it been? Getting all this rest and relaxation?" Grace asked, grinning.

"Boring. I'm not sure I can take it anymore."

"Yes. Well… I'm glad you are all right and will be allowed to fly. Katrine and Lorelei both say hello by the way." Grace looked at the floor. The hospital atmosphere made her edgy.

"You heard from your sisters?"

"Saw them, actually. I did the last Palestine run. The Adleman sisters," she frowned slightly, "together again and playing in a town near you."

"Grace?" A voice called from behind a curtain several beds down from where they sat. "Is that Grace Adleman?"

Grace's eyes opened wide. "Yes?" she called out. "Who is that?"

"It's Frank! Open the curtain! You remember me, don't you?"

Amos looked at Cecilia and Morris. "Frank? Who's that?"

The two youngsters shook their heads. They had no idea who Frank was either.

By now, Grace had strode over to the curtain and pulled the white sheet away. There, lying on his back, one leg and one arm in traction, was none other than Frank Golden, the first officer of the *Grey Goose*. They stared at one another, stunned.

Amos grabbed a pair of crutches and hobbled over to where Grace stood. "Who's this?"

"This is Frank Golden. He was on the crew of my, well, it's a long story, but the couple who smuggled us out of Germany has a rather lovely yacht, and Frank used to work on it."

"Grace and I go way back," he said, looking up at Amos's face.

"How far back?" For reasons he could not articulate, Amos felt uncomfortable meeting a handsome sailor who was chummy with Grace.

Grace stepped forward and knelt down by Frank's face. "What happened to you? You look ghastly."

Dramatically, he heaved a sigh. "The wounds of war, my dear. You are looking at a hero."

"I got a medal for bravery," Amos stated.

"That's nice." Frank kept his eyes glued on Grace. "I got three."

"Now, tell me what happened, Frank!"

Frank, with an impish grin, looked up at his foot swinging near Grace's head. "I got into a little trouble a couple of days ago. You know how Peter and I volunteered for the Royal Navy and everything?"

She nodded her head. She remembered well. They had all left Scotland around the same time. It felt like a very long time ago indeed.

"We made it through Dunkirk okay."

"I know," she said. "I saw Horatio and Peter's picture in a newspaper. I cut it out and put it in my scrapbook."

"That's real nice."

"So," she prodded, "you obviously got caught in some trouble."

"We attacked the French after they signed the Armistice on the coast of Algeria. It was a mistake. We all knew it was a mistake. The goal was to get the French ships before the Germans did, but now the Vichy government, the French who are not loyal to Hitler, think we betrayed them.[7] My boat got hit. There was some real damage, and it sunk. Almost sunk me too. They sent what was left of me here."

"If that's how the British treat their allies…" Amos trailed off. "I'll bet French-Anglo relations are glowing." His jaw was set and his fists clenched.

Frank nodded a bit too vigorously, and his face contorted as he let out a quiet, "Ow."

"Oh, Frank." Grace could tell he was in terrible pain. "What about Peter? Where is he? Is he all right?"

He shook his head. "I have no idea. We were on different ships. I don't even know if we won or lost the battle. Probably won't know for a while. I never thought I'd see you again, in North Africa of all places." He stopped and looked at her quizzically. "Come to think of it, what are you doing here?"

"I volunteered too, for the RAF."

"You didn't!"

"I'm a pilot."

"You? You're kidding me." He looked prouder than a mother hen. "I knew you'd turn out good." Tentatively, he added, "So, how's that sister of yours, the lonely Lorelei?"

"She's doing fine."

"And the other one? Katrine? Are she and that guy together yet?" He laughed to himself. "I have never seen two people go at it quite like them. Like oil and vinegar. Don't mix easy, but they make good salad dressing."

Grace shook her head. "No, no. Katrine hasn't heard from Harry in quite a while."

"Is Lorelei seeing anyone?"

"No." She looked at him with a slight smirk. "Why do you ask?"

"No reason, no reason. I was just checking. That's all."

"Okay." Grace stood up. "Well, I really ought to go. The bus leaves in a few minutes."

"You'll come back and see me, maybe?"

Her face fell, and her heart went out to the wounded sailor. "I wish I could, but I'm being shipped out."

"Oh, I see." His jaw moved as though he was working up the courage to ask her something, which is exactly what he was doing. "Would you do me a favor?"

"What is it?"

He could tell she would do anything he asked by the look on her face, and Frank exhaled like a great weight was lifted off of his shoulders. "I have a letter I need you to send."

"That's all?"

"It's to Lorelei. I wrote it a while ago. I just haven't known where to send it." With his free hand, he motioned to a small side table with a drawer where he had a few personal belongings. "It's in there."

There it was, just as he said, with the words 'Lorelei Adleman' scrawled on the envelope in his simple square script.

"How'd you write it?" Amos asked, looking at the arm in traction.

"I'm left-handed."

Grace took the letter and put it in her purse. "Take care, Frank," she said softly.

Morris and Cecilia, now behind Amos, looked on.

Frank saw them, two obvious teenagers wearing RAF uniforms, and whistled a low whistle. "What, are we really doing so badly we are drafting kids now?"

Grace stepped back. "It's a long story. One I'll have to tell you when, well, I don't know when, but when we next meet."

Morris adjusted his skull cap and waved. "And I will pray Mi-Shebeirach for you, the prayers of healing."

CHAPTER 34

HARRY'S RETURN

"*E*arly Bronze Age." Katrine pointed to a small shard of pottery. Motioning to an arrowhead, she said, "Late Bronze Age."

"And these?" Professor Hildesheimer motioned towards a handful of gold coins.

"Byzantine, obviously."

"Obviously." He smiled. "You have an eye, you know. I think you are more of an archeologist than a historian."

Shrugging, she continued to carefully brush away the dirt and debris from the pot handle they had uncovered at the dig yesterday in the City of David. In the weeks since she'd returned, she had gone from Mrs. Smith, the girl with no real job, no home, no fiancé and no prospect of one, to Katrine Adleman, the research assistant to Dr. Hildesheimer, working on a very important paper that would one day be published in the Cambridge

Archeological Journal. She had also moved into the living room of Becky and Lorelei's apartment. The couch was comfortable… enough.

The new Katrine Adleman was almost happy. She tried to keep busy, pouring herself into her new life. The busier she was, the less she had to think about the summer and that fateful Fourth of July when Harry had kissed her.

"This is what I've always wanted," she told herself. "Almost, anyway. Research, books, academics." It was all so predictable and safe and comforting. Exciting, too. There was always a new discovery at the dig. She liked wearing khaki pants and pulling her shirt sleeves up. She even liked the dust, dirt, and sun. The moment her fingers would brush up against an old bowl or feel the grooves in the paving stones of streets thousands of years old, a shiver of pleasure would course through her body. She wondered who'd drunk out of this bowl? What had they done all day? Where had they been going? Probably they'd been going home to their husbands.

Then she would stop and swallow and pretend she hadn't thought that thought because it made her feel awful that she didn't have a man to go home to. All she had was a couch. And she should be thankful for that couch because maybe the ancient person hadn't even had a couch. In fact, she knew they probably hadn't because it was a dish for a poor person in the 1st century, and poor people in the 1st century didn't have couches. They slept on the floor.

"So there, Katrine," she'd chide herself. "You should be thankful."

And then she would think of the film she'd seen with Joe Miller, and she was truly thankful.

Sure, there were reminders of what could have been. She had to pass by the Math Department, underneath Einstein's theory of relativity etched into the stone relief, every day on her way to her little office next to Professor Hildesheimer's larger one or on her way to the library. Sometimes it seemed like Harry was everywhere. Other times, it was as though she had nearly forgotten him. But never completely.

She spent little time with Lorelei and Becky. The two nurses were always working, working, working. And they shared a connection she could not grasp regarding faith. Her approach to religion had always been more platonic. More academic. Judaism for her was cultural. It was holidays and sayings and shared history. She believed there was a God, certainly, but thinking he was active in the lives of humanity seemed a far stretch of the imagination. Wisely, Lorelei did not try to push the issue.

Katrine would wake up and quickly eat with Lorelei (Becky, usually, had already left to teach an early morning class before her shift started). Then, the two sisters would take the bus up the hill where Lorelei would get off at the first stop for Hadassah Hospital (except for Spafford Baby Home days), and Katrine would get off at the second stop for the University.

Katrine would take the professor's notes from

the day before and organize them into something that was somewhat coherent. By the time she was finished, it was nearly 10:00 in the morning, and she would take a slight break for tea before catching the bus back down the hill and head straight towards the City of David, the archeological dig site nestled on the side of the Old City.

It was there, with several other students under Hildesheimer's watchful eye, that the Jewish roots to the ancient city were slowly being unearthed. It was an archaeologist's dreamland. Dr. Hildesheimer believed that some of the ruins might even be a part of King David's palace. This was very, very important, the professor explained, because it gave the Jewish people historical precedence to the land. Obviously, if they used to live there, they should get to live there now. It was a convincing argument for a Jewish homeland in Palestine. Why, if Jerusalem had been their capital 3,000 years ago, why shouldn't it be their capital now?

It was a good argument that did little to convince the Arab Jerusalemites, who had been living there for generations after most of the Jews were expelled by the Romans and fully expected Jerusalem to be their *own* capital, sans Jews.

Certainly, Katrine thought, there was room for everyone. Wasn't there? But then, she didn't bother with the politics of the dig or her research. The same way she didn't bother with religion. She was done with politics. Done with all of it. She cared purely for the history, to unearth the lives of the past. There was too much pain in the present. It was much easier looking back, knowing what *had* happened, than looking forward and wondering what *would* happen.

And when Lorelei asked her if she was happy, she answered that she was. She really was happy. She was doing exactly, almost, what she had wanted to do from the time she was 12 years old.

The problem was, she was lonely. Not for people, mind you. She was surrounded by people. Wonderful, caring, intelligent, witty people. Rather, she was lonely for one person in particular.

It was with this foreboding sense of loneliness that Katrine made her way late one evening from the library back to Dr. Hildesheimer's office to let him know she was done for the night and was going to go home.

The light was on, seeping through the door that was cracked open just a hair. He was still there.

"Professor?" she called down the deserted hall.

"Katrine? Is that you? You must come in!"

She pushed the door open and stopped short. She'd know that tousled curly head anywhere.

The head turned. It *was* Harry! Big blue eyes behind round glasses.

Harry jumped out of his seat. "Hey there, pal!" he said, with that playful grin of his. At first, a wave of relief washed over Katrine, instantly replaced by anger. How could he do this to her? Just show up out of nowhere! And in her boss's office, no less! Katrine wanted to punch him.

"When'd you get back?" she asked flatly, trying to control her emotions.

"Yesterday. It's been nonstop meetings and debriefs. You know how it is."

"Yes. I do." She looked at her boss and stepped backward. "Well, obviously you are both busy. I'll excuse myself. I'll see you in the morning, Professor."

Harry followed her out into the hall.

Katrine could feel him behind her. "Why are you following me?"

"Why am I following you? Katrine, stop walking and look at me for a second!"

She spun on her heel and looked at him. "All right. I'm looking!"

He stopped walking and shuffled his feet on the linoleum, "I, um... How are you? What have you been up to?"

That's what you have to say to me? Katrine thought to herself. After all this time? You are asking me what I've been up to?

Katrine struggled to maintain her composure. "What have I been up to? Let's see... After finding myself alone in New York, I took a jaunty trip to Lisbon. Met some friends in Cairo for an impromptu birthday celebration at the movies. Bland, boring, basic espionage work. You know how it is. But after losing my partner to unforeseen causes, I decided, I'm just not cut out for it. So, I decided to go back to what I'm good at. *School*. Except, this time around, they

are paying me to study." She put her hand on
her hip.

"Professor Hildesheimer told me. You look
great, do you know that?"

She raised one eyebrow and pursed her lips.

"I heard at the Agency you are staying with
Lorelei. I was hoping I could drop in later."

"Don't bother," she said with an air that said
she could not care less.

He stepped forward. "Katrine, what's the
matter? What happened? Something obviously is
wrong."

"Nothing is wrong in the slightest."

"You can tell me. We are friends, remember?"

"Friends? Friends! Harry, what kind of 'pal'
just ups and leaves his friend in the middle of
New York?"

"I left you a note." Harry nervously brushed
his hand through his curls, growing more
confused and concerned by the second.

"Some note." She glared at him. "'Yours,
Harry.' And I gave you flowers!"

"Seriously, Katie." He looked very concerned.
"We are in the Haganah. We were on a mission.
There was no way I could let you know where I
was going or when I would be back. I thought you
would understand that! Besides, I didn't know
where I was going or when I would be back
either."

"Please let me pass," she said firmly as he
took her arm. "I have a bus to catch."

"But we have to talk, Katrine! You are not
being rational!" he shouted after her as she
marched down the hall. The door slammed shut

behind her, leaving him alone with the professor peeking out of his office.

"You sure got her riled," he said, eyeing Harry. "What did you say?"

"Nothing. I didn't say anything at all!" Harry stuffed his hands in his pockets. "I asked her how she was. I told her she looked great."

"Then maybe, it is what you did *not* say."

"What I did not say?" Harry paused, thinking deeply.

"So…" the professor baited him. "Do you?"

"Do I what?"

"Love her?"

Harry looked like a deer caught in the head-lights. "Yes, sir. I do."

"And you haven't expressed this to her?" The professor watched as Harry stared after Katrine's wake, nodding. "Case closed. That's what's the matter with her."

KATRINE BLEW into the apartment like a storm. In her head the whole ride home she'd replayed the scene over and over. He had said this. She should have said that. She felt terribly angry at him and herself. Of course, now that she thought about it, it made sense that Harry could not have written more information. One cannot write what one does not know. But he could have called! No, she corrected herself. He couldn't have called. He'd had no idea where she was either.

She hadn't even given him a chance to explain

himself, not really. But then again, why should she? Because they had been friends once, that's why. It made her so… angry!

She slammed the door behind her with the force of the minotaur.

Lorelei was absorbed in a letter from Edie (describing how she and Horatio had taken up Scottish country dancing with the couple from the manor on the neighboring estate, an elderly gentleman and his wife, both in their 80s, and how she really thought Lorelei would excel at it as a hobby) and didn't look up. "Oh good," she said, "you're home."

Not in the mood to answer, Katrine kicked her shoes off and went into the kitchen to heat the kettle for tea.

"Where's Becky?" Katrine asked loudly over the running water.

"I'm here!" the young woman called out from her bedroom. "We thought we could do something fun tonight, just us girls. Maybe go get Paulina and see a film at the Edison Theater. *The Maltese Falcon* is out. Mary Astor's the star."[8]

Katrine blinked a few times. She was in no mood for a movie, Mary Astor or not.

"What's it about?" Katrine heard Lorelei ask as she set the kettle over the flame.

"Let me see." She heard the rustle of a newspaper. "A San Francisco Private Eye becomes involved in an adventure to obtain a jewel-encrusted falcon statuette. Sounds pretty interesting, don't you think?"

Katrine poked her head out of the kitchen. Lorelei was still on the couch with her letter, and Becky was sitting in a chair pulling nylons over her legs.

"You two go ahead." Katrine sighed. "I already lived that movie. I don't need to see it."

"Katrine! You love films. Why—" Lorelei stopped. "What's going on?"

"Nothing at all. I'm perfectly fine."

"Oh no, you're not. I know you better than that. That is definitely not your 'I'm perfectly fine' voice. It's your 'I am most definitely not all right voice.' Now, come here and tell me what happened."

Katrine groaned and took a step out of the kitchen. She'd have to tell Lorelei eventually, wouldn't she? "Harry showed up at the university today."

"He did?" Lorelei's voice rose. "What did he say?"

"I didn't give him much of a chance to say anything, actually."

"Oh, Katrine." Lorelei let the letter slide to the floor. "You didn't."

"Didn't what?"

"Pull one of your tantrums on that poor man."

Becky leaned back, thoroughly interested.

Katrine lifted her shoulders softly. "Maybe. It doesn't matter now. What's done is done. Besides, he's the one who left me in New York to go off and be a hero, remember. Without one kind word at all!"

Lorelei, who had not felt free to ask the details of Katrine and Harry's epic parting in New York, decided that now was the time to crack the jar open, no matter what might come out.

"Katrine, he left you because you both had work to finish, right?"

She nodded. "He didn't have time to give me a proper goodbye…"

It sounded dumb even as she said it.

"You even *know* that he couldn't give you a proper goodbye!" Lorelei answered incredulously.

"He could have written one!"

"Maybe he's not good with words! Maybe he is a face-to-face sort of man!"

Katrine's face froze. She knew that Lorelei spoke the truth.

"He was my best friend, Lorelei!" Katrine cried out. "The best friend I ever had. You should have seen us dance together! We were good. Everyone thought so. He was so kind, so thoughtful, so funny. How he made me laugh. You can't imagine how I've missed him these months."

"*I* can't imagine?"

The words hung painfully in the air, and the sisters stared at each other.

"Oh, Lorelei, I am sorry. I wasn't thinking."

"If you ask me, you are the one who has not been a good friend. You've doubted him, thought badly of him, been angry at him, all for him doing his job."

"You're right."

"So, swallow your pride. Apologize to the man. Give him a chance."

"I don't even know where he is staying."

At that moment, there was a soft knock on the front door. Becky jumped up out of the chair and opened it. It was the eldest Finkelstein boy. "Is everything all right, David?"

The boy nodded, and he passed an envelope to Becky. It had 'Katrine' scrawled on the outside. "A man gave this to me outside and told me it was for the new girl, the one with the black hair and blue eyes."

"I'll give it to her. Did he give you his name?"

The boy nodded his head. "Mr. Smith."

"Thanks, David," Becky said. "Run along now."

Lorelei and Becky stood by Katrine as she opened the envelope. Inside was a scrap of paper that simply read, "The King David, 9:00 on the terrace."

"Curious," Becky said. "Who's Mr. Smith?"

"If it is the Agency, I've retired," Katrine said firmly.

"But it may not be the Agency." Lorelei poked her sister. "What if it's him?"

The girls looked at the clock. It read 8:00 pm. "That gives you 20 minutes to put on a dress and fix your hair and still make it," Becky said, smiling.

CHAPTER 35

CHOICES

"Everyone!" Captain O'Rourke silenced the 32 finalists; all those who had checked and double-checked their chutes that morning, those whose packs were filled with wireless transmitting devices, several changes of clothes, food, and medicine.

They each spoke several languages. They knew morse code. They could climb, run, shoot straight, and look fear in the eye and not tremble. They were the 32 young people that the British Military Intelligence would use to locate and rescue Allied POWs and escapees. They were the 32 that the Jewish Agency trusted to help organize local resistance among the Jewish communities. It was a formidable task, but it was theirs, and they were as ready as they would ever be.

O'Rourke looked at his trainees proudly, and though he'd never say it, he had grown to love each and every one as though they were his own children. The Jewish Unit of RAF paratroopers had become O'Rourke's Unit.

On the ground in Germany, Romania, Hungary, Yugoslavia, Austria, and Italy, members of the resistance prepared for their arrival.

"Hannah Senesh," O'Rourke motioned for the girl to come up beside him under the plane's wing, "has something to share with all of us."

Hanna smiled and opened her small journal, her clear, confident voice piercing the dark Egyptian night sky with the words to her poem *To Die.*[9]

It was a beautiful poem. It carried Grace along, moving her to tears. Hannah spoke of the sun in the Holy Land. She spoke of life. Her words yearned for peace, revealing a kind and gentle heart with no pleasure in bloodshed or war. She was not ready to die. But, if she had to, she wanted to die for The Soil.

All 32 knew that Hannah meant, of course, the land of Palestine. This was why they were flinging themselves back into enemy territory. Because, at heart, they were not soldiers. Because, at heart, they hated war and battle and blood. They were fighting back so they could enjoy their sun in Caesarea, in the Galilee. So they could plow their soil and get married one day and raise their children on it without fear. But they would not die. Certainly. They were, each one, too young to die. They would live. And each prayed silently that God would give them the grace to live. But thoughts beyond that, not one of the 32 had the courage to think.

Grace ran to Hannah and embraced her before she got on the plane that would take her and three others to Hungary. "You are a very good writer, Hannah."

"I just say what is in my heart."

"When we get back…" Grace's voice caught in her throat.

Hannah put her hand on Grace's cheek. "Don't be afraid, Grace. When we meet again, it will be on our own land. Our very own. You'll meet my mother too. I'm going to find her and bring her back to Palestine. You'll love her. She is a wonderful woman." She chuckled as she said, "Admittedly, she is half the reason I left for Palestine years ago. We didn't, what shall I say, understand one another. She loves dinner parties and fancy things. I like the sea and sun and shorts."

Grace grinned. "Me too." She lowered her voice and asked, "But how will you find her?"

Hannah sighed. "Her letters stopped coming a month ago. I'm afraid… I'll find her though."

Grace put her hands on Hannah's shoulders. "You be careful out there."

She laughed off Grace's worry. "I'm not ready to die, Grace. Don't you worry. Meet at the kibbutz in Caesarea, one year from today! We'll drink lemonade with mint, and my mother will make her famous walnut cookies."

"It's a date."

Hannah kissed Grace's cheek and hoisted the heavy pack onto her shoulder. She was ready.

~

It was dark. Very, very dark. And the roar of the plane's engine was very loud. So loud that they could barely hear one another talk.

Cecilia, sitting next to Grace, looked around. "I'm not ready for this, you know. I'm not cut out to be a soldier."

"It's too late to bail out now." Grace looked at her. "Like it or not, you and I are going to be on German soil in less than an hour." By now, she thought, Morris was already in Poland and Hannah in Hungary. The plane to Italy had left the day before. They were the last plane of parachutists.

"I'm afraid."

Grace exhaled, not knowing how to comfort her.

"But you are different. You are not afraid of anything." Cecilia looked admiringly at Grace.

"That's not totally true." Grace smiled.

"Name one thing you are scared of!"

Grace was thoughtful for a moment. "Sleeping alone. I couldn't even handle three days in the bungalow without my sisters at the kibbutz." The two girls broke into nervous laughter. Truth be told, Grace was a little scared of what they were attempting to do. It was only natural, wasn't it?

O'Rourke was pacing up and down the middle of the plane. Grace could tell he was nervous too. They must be nearing the jump zone.

Suddenly, Amos rushed into the back of the plane.

"Grace!" he shouted over the noise of the engine. "I have to ask you a question!"

"What are you doing here? I didn't know you

were flying the plane!" she shouted back. And then added, slightly alarmed, "Who's flying the plane!"

"I got the co-pilot on it," he shouted back.

The red light went on and the door opened. It was time to jump. Grace's heart caught in her chest. She looked at Amos.

"What is it!" she yelled, standing up and getting in the line of paratroopers.

O'Rourke noticed Amos standing there and barked out, "Get back in the cockpit where you belong, young man!"

"I have to ask her a question!"

"Jump!" O'Rourke shouted at the first paratrooper. The young man threw himself out of the plane.

"You better hurry!" Grace answered.

Amos clung to the handrail on the ceiling of the plane. "Grace Adleman, I think you are the best girl I've ever met."

O'Rourke glared at Amos. "Get back in the cockpit!"

"I…" Grace stuttered. Her mind spun a million miles a minute. Mind on the mission. Mind on the mission. The open door of the plane got closer and closer.

The jump light went on.

Cecilia was next. She reached out and kissed Grace's cheek, and on O'Rourke's signal, she shut her eyes and jumped.

Amos waited, not moving.

The jump light went on again. Amos worked up his courage. "Grace Adleman," he began, "will you marry me?"

Would she marry him?

As she hurled herself out of the plane, all thoughts of the mission went out of the window with her. With a vague sense of satisfaction that she had, finally, accomplished her goal of getting Amos to notice her, Grace Adleman realized she needed to pull the chord of her parachute.

～

THE TERRACE of the King David hotel at night was quiet. There were a few tables filled with couples, a politician or two, and a few men there on business. They drank cocktails and ate poached salmon as they overlooked the enormous pool where a late night swimmer was putting in a few laps before going to bed. It was all so civilized. So normal.

Katrine wore her dark green dress made of heavy linen, with wide shoulders and slim hips and a rising hemline just above her knee. It was the American look, and it suited her.

Harry was waiting for her at the far end of the terrace. He stood up immediately when he saw her. She steadied herself and walked towards the table.

It was him, she thought to herself. Not some other Mr. Smith.

He pulled out the chair, and she sat down.

A waiter came to their table but left when Harry told him they would order later.

Awkwardly, they sat in silence.

Well, Katrine thought, now was as good a time

as any. She plunged in. "I'm sorry I was so rude earlier today. It wasn't the way friends should treat one another. Especially friends who were as close as we were… once."

She thought back to their kiss and the fireworks and how being this close to him at this very moment was bringing it all back.

"Don't worry about it," Harry said quickly. "Let's not talk about the past."

Oh dear, she thought. He didn't want to think about what they once were to each other. "I'm a historian. It's what I do… So, what should we talk about then?"

"The future. There's one last mission I was hoping you would join me on."

Katrine was shaking her head. "I've retired, you know. No more missions."

"I thought we made pretty good partners." He looked down and added quietly, "Once."

"I can't ever be Mrs. Smith, not ever again."

"That wasn't quite what I had in mind—"

"Let me finish, Harry, while I have the courage." She put her hands on the table. "I've worked very hard to forget about you. If I put that ring on and then have to take it off again… I don't know if I could ever get over it. I've made a life for myself. A good life. I'm doing what I like. I can't go back and forth from being with you and then not being with you. Never knowing if you are with me just because I am there, or because you really like me." She inhaled and finished, "Harry, don't you see? It would rip me apart. Because I love you."

Harry was looking down at her curiously. "You

know me better than that, don't you, Katie?" He pulled a ring out of his pocket. Was it the old Mrs. Smith ring? No. A glistening diamond! Was it? It was!

"I've loved you, almost from the moment you yelled at me in Yiddish on the *Grey Goose.*"

Slowly, she looked up at him. "You have?"

"I'm not like that other guy back in Germany. All those other guys."

He was standing up now and moving over to where she sat on the opposite side of the table. He got down on one knee as he said, "And I was hoping that you would wear this as Mrs. Stenetsky this round. For the rest of all the rounds."

The choice was hers. She could believe that he loved her. She could believe and never look back.

She felt his hand take hers and slip the ring onto her finger.

'*Mrs. Stenetsky.*' It had a very nice ring to it.

"You'll wear it?" He looked up at her, hoping against hope.

"Till the day I die," she whispered, slowly allowing her heart to believe the truth.

And with that, he kissed her, and Katrine once more heard fireworks.

And so, as Grace and Cecilia began to assemble the transmitting device in a small cave in the woods of Bavaria, and Katrine and Harry were applying for a marriage license, life went on as usual for Lorelei.

It was not a bad life. But it was not, Lorelei knew, as good as it could be. There was something missing, but she couldn't put her finger on what it was, exactly. For some reason, she no longer felt like she truly fit in Jerusalem. The city felt too small. She wanted adventure. She wanted something fresh and new. She wanted to do what God had made her to do, knowing fully well that her final destination was not the Spafford Baby Home or going back to Kibbutz Kinneret, at least for now.

With these feelings swirling inside, Lorelei marched up the steps to her apartment. "And it's not that I'm ungrateful for where I am. I love the people at the Spafford Baby Home. But you know me, I'm just… not that great with babies. And of course, the kibbutz is wonderful, but without Grace or Katrine there. Well, it's not home."

She pushed the door to the apartment open and continued, "It seems like everyone is off on their adventure, or they've been off on an adventure, and now… well." She stopped herself, knowing it was wrong to complain or feel jealous of her sisters. "It's not that I'm unhappy. It's just that I'm—"

"You're what?"

"Becky?" Lorelei noticed Becky on the couch and blushed. "Was I talking out loud?"

"We need to talk, you know," Becky said, standing up and moving into the kitchen. "You've passed all your boards with flying colors and you have completed all the necessary training hours at the hospital. It's time to be posted. The Spafford Baby Home would love to have you full-time."

Lorelei let out a slight groan.

"Lorelei?" She poked her head out of the kitchen. "I thought you liked the Baby Home."

"I do! It's not that. It's just…"

"The kibbutz would take you back in a heartbeat."

"I know," Lorelei answered. "I'll go back. One day. It's the reason I went to nursing school, after all. But I'm not ready. Not quite yet anyway. I feel unsettled, somehow. Like I need to be somewhere else," she finished lamely.

"Well, in that case, there is another posting I want to talk to you about. It's rather dangerous, and I don't think—"

"Where is it?"

"Cairo."

"Cairo? What sort of posting is in Cairo?"

"They want field nurses. They need someone right away."

"Field nurses?" Lorelei let this news sink in. To be a field nurse was the most difficult job of all. It meant facing death every day, her own and the deaths of others.

Lorelei stared at Becky long and hard. She touched her wrist where Rolf's bracelet no longer was. It was clear and free. She was free. Perhaps, she looked up at the ceiling, God was trying to tell her something.

Was going to Cairo to work as a field nurse

what would do her the most good and bring him the most glory?

A warm, familiar peace enveloped her, and she knew it was time to go. She looked back at Becky and said decisively, "I'll take it, Becky. I'll go to Cairo."

"It's a risky job, Lorelei. Are you quite sure?"

Her fingers tingled with nervousness, but the peace was still there. "Tell them I'll do it. I'll do whatever they need."

"But whatever for?"

"Because sometimes you have to risk, isn't that right? You have to risk trust. You have to risk because of love." Lorelei's love of Yeshua was strong. She would go to the ends of the earth for him, wherever he called her. "It's the same reason you came to Palestine, yes?"

Becky exhaled, slowly understanding.

"And I'm going to risk living, for love. I can't live my life in the safety that this city provides. It wouldn't be a real life, not when he is calling me out and beyond." She stood up. "Becky, you tell them Lorelei Adleman will be on the next plane to Cairo."

Lorelei then noticed a letter on the side table with her name on it. The return address was marked *Alexander Military Medical Hospital, Cairo.* Cairo? Lorelei was shocked. Certainly, this was a confirmation that God was opening a new door!

Lorelei tore open the letter, her eyes widening in wonder as she read what Frank Golden had written.

Becky looked at her questioningly. "What's that?" she asked.

"Looks like I have an old friend in Egypt." She smiled. "I think I need to write him and tell him I'll be visiting him rather soon."

THE END OF THE MIDDLE

~

I looked up from the manuscript, shocked. "That's the end?"

Grace was sprawled out by the fire, laying next to Founder. She pushed herself up and ate another handful of popcorn. Yes, that was the end, she said. At least, that was as far as Edie had gotten.

"Somehow, you made it out of Germany," Peter said, leaning forward in his chair.

"Yeah," Grace said. "That is a whole different book. One I do *not* want to read for a while."

"What happened to Cecilia? To Morris?" I asked. "What happened to Hannah? And Lorelei and Frank?"

Now, Peter was with me. "Come to think of it, what happened to Amos?"

Standing, she picked up Founder and began walking upstairs.

"Don't you dare think you are going to get out of telling us the rest of the story!" I exclaimed.

"If I knew the end to the story, do you think I'd be here!" she shouted back at me and then added, for good measure, "I'm tired. Goodnight!"

The door to her bedroom shut soundly, leaving Peter and me in the light of the fire, but other than that, completely in the dark.

"That girl is running away faster than her feet can carry her." He looked at me, a question pooled in his eyes. "What is she so afraid of?"

"Commitment," I answered simply. To Amos. To God. To anything or anyone that might disappoint or hurt her.

I put the manuscript down and slowly followed my husband upstairs. Wordlessly, I went to the bathroom and brushed my teeth and my hair and washed my face, slathering cold cream all over it and down my neck and my forearms. It was never too early to start preventing wrinkles, my aunt always said.

When I returned to our room, Peter was already in bed. I curled up beside him, laying my head on his chest, listening to the beating of his heart. "What will we do, Peter?" I sighed.

"We'll trust God."

I exhaled and felt his hand on my back. "Trust him with Grace, Piper. He can handle her. She's his kid to begin with."

I thought of Lorelei and of Katrine. I thought of Grace. It was true. They were his daughters. His chosen ones. Their faces swirled in my mind in a vast Middle Eastern desert. Oh Lord, I prayed. Help Grace. Help her. Help her know what to do. Bring her to wherever she needs to be to find you. To wherever she needs to be to stop running. And Katrine and Harry. And Frank and... My eyes fluttered shut.

When I opened my eyes again, it was morning. The bright beautiful morning of December 7th, 1941. It was perfectly clear. The storm was over and gone.

Peter was already up and had made coffee by the smell of things. I looked at the clock. It was nearly noon! How had I slept in so late!

I jumped out of bed and slipped on my slippers and my robe. I could hear Grace singing softly to herself as she washed her hair over the tub.

There was a quick knock on the door. The coastguard! Of course! To see Peter's photographs. I groaned. "Peter! Peter, come get the door! I'm not dressed."

But Peter didn't answer. He was busy in the kitchen making his own breakfast. Or lunch. I wasn't sure.

Ugh. I shuffled towards the front door and opened it, frowning.

Two men stood there. An old one and a young one.

The elder one extended his hand and introduced himself as Captain Donahue. He had a white mustache and light eyes. He plunged right in. "Now, I don't know what you saw yesterday, but I'll tell you right now we don't have suspicious activity around here. So, let's get this over with so I can go home."

They were inside now. The younger one had dark auburn hair and held himself very tall.

Captain Donahue continued talking and motioned towards the young man. "Found this one on the road walking to the lighthouse. Can you imagine? Only a dumb foreigner would attempt to do something so stupid in cold weather like this. Snow is a few feet deep on certain parts of the road!"

"Walking here?" I asked, looking at the young man. Perhaps he was an old friend of Peter's.

Grace let out a shocked gasp from the top of the stairs. Her hair was in a towel wrapped up on top of her head. She wore her pajamas. He was handsome and tall and everything she had remembered and more. Any bit of 'boy' that had been there before was gone. There stood a man. And she had a towel on her head. The only rational response, which Grace had, was to plunge back into her bedroom and slam the door and pretend he had never seen her.

509

"Shalom. Grace," Amos said, looking up at the spot where she had stood on the stairs.

Peter appeared in the hall, a spatula in his hand. We looked at each other, mouths slightly open.

No one spoke or moved—except for Captain Donahue, who had no idea what was going on. "So, where are these pictures you called about?"

Wordlessly, I pointed to the desk in the living room where we had laid them out the night before.

Then, I pulled Amos deeper inside and shut the door. His hands were freezing. "Amos," I said. "Your clothes are wet straight through. How long were you out there in the snow?"

He shivered. "A few hours, I guess. It's a long walk from the train station. I thought I could... I've never been in the snow before."

I marched him upstairs and showed him the bathroom and where Peter kept his clothes. "Take a hot bath. Wear Peter's robe until your clothes dry. I'll put some tea on. Can you feel your toes?"

He tested them out. "Yes."

"Thank goodness." I exhaled in relief. At least he didn't have frostbite.

When I returned to the living room, Grace had reappeared, dressed to the nines.

"You look great," I said. And then, upon closer inspection, I asked, "Is that lipstick?"

She didn't answer and flitted over to the radio, buzzing with nervous energy.

Donahue, in the meantime, was trying to convince Peter that the sub in the picture was not a sub but some sort of whale. Peter wasn't buying it. Neither was I, for that matter, as much as I longed to. We'd already seen too much to play dumb.

As soon as she found a clear station playing Brahms' Lullaby, she dragged me into the kitchen, whispering fiercely, "What am I supposed to do? He's come here to force me to make a decision!"

"Calm down!" I whispered back. "You don't have to make a decision you are not ready to make."

She started to breathe more evenly.

"But I have to ask... Grace, do you love him?"

She froze like a possum at gunpoint.

Amos appeared in the kitchen, wearing Peter's bathrobe, and I wondered how he had possibly taken a bath that quickly.

"Hi," he said, looking at Grace.

"Hi," she repeated, clearly gathering her thoughts. "I didn't even ask what you are doing here, in the States, I mean."

"I have to go to Washington DC on behalf of the RAF. I'm going to brief the president on the state of things on the North African Front. I thought I'd make a little detour and see you and talk about..." He faltered and looked down. "You know, the future."

In the living room, I could hear Donahue preparing to leave.

"Excuse me," I said, and they both looked at me, almost surprised I was there. "I need to show the captain out."

Entering the living room, the music suddenly cut short with, *"We interrupt this musical program to bring you the breaking news."*

"What a second." Donahue stopped. "Turn it up."

Peter moved away from the desk and adjusted the dial.

"Hello, NBC. Hello, NBC. This is KTU in Honolulu, Hawaii. I am speaking from the roof of the Advertiser Publishing Company Building. We have witnessed this morning the distant view a brief full battle of Pearl Harbor and the severe bombing of Pearl Harbor by enemy planes, undoubtedly Japanese. The city of Honolulu has also been attacked and considerable damage done... One of the bombs dropped within fifty feet of KTU tower. It is no joke. It is a real war. The public of Honolulu has been advised to keep in their homes and away from the Army and Navy. There has been serious fighting going on in the air and in the sea. The heavy shooting seems to be..." The radio crackled with static for several seconds before the the voice continued, *"We cannot estimate just how much damage has been done, but it has been a very severe attack. The Navy and Army appear now to have the air and the sea under control."*[10]

I could see Amos and Grace in the kitchen, listening intently.

"*Ah, just a minute. . . . This is the telephone company. This is the operator,*" another voice said.

Peter looked at me, his face registering his inner turmoil. "They are broadcasting a telephone call."

"What do we do now?" I exclaimed.

Captain Donahue was hit with reality. He switched gears from Doubting Thomas to Paul Revere, 'ready to sound the alarm through every Middlesex village and farm.'[11] There might be German subs out there! On this coast! "I am commissioning this lighthouse immediately. You are all deputized." He marched towards the desk and grabbed the photographs. "I've got to get these to my superiors. You four are on official patrol until you hear from me."

"I'm not American," Grace stated.

"Neither am I!" Amos repeated.

"Don't care! You youngsters are going to watch out that tower and call this number," he scribbled a number on the pad on the desk, "if you see anything at all. Including a whale! The fate of our fair coast lies in your hands. We are under attack! You heard what they just said!" It would have seemed melodramatic if we had not all felt the gravity of the situation.

And so, Captain Donahue left the lighthouse, with us in his wake.

"It is no joke," Peter repeated the reporter's words. "It is a *real* war." Then he looked at me. "We are not neutral anymore." He spoke as though he couldn't believe the words coming out of his mouth were true. "I knew something big was going to happen. I could feel it. I knew it wasn't time to leave yet. God sent us here for *now.*"

I sunk onto the couch, barely comprehending the morning's events. I felt Grace beside me. "So, that is what it took," she said slowly. "Katrine so wondered what it would take. She said it would take Americans feeling pain. I think she was quoting Joe Miller."

Amos also sat down, and Peter suddenly remembered himself. "I'm sorry. We haven't been properly introduced. I'm your almost cousin-in-law."

"I've heard of you." Amos smiled.

"I see you've found my bathrobe."

Amos turned red. "I sure appreciate it. All my stuff is soaked." He looked at Grace. "I was kind of hoping you and I could talk."

Peter interrupted him. "You two kids can catch up in the tower. You've both got the first watch. I'll relieve you in two hours."

"Peter!" I exclaimed.

He turned to me. "Piper, bring them up a thermos of something hot. And I am going to run into town and buy some binoculars. We are going to need them. Who knows what, or who, could be lurking out there?"

I saluted him and looked out the window. The sea churned, and the wind blew, and the lighthouse clung onto the rocks as it had for decades. A seahawk called and swooped out over the waves, solitary and fierce. It refused to be made into something small and gentle and tameable. It was like my cousins—like Grace and Lorelei and Katrine.

And as Peter's truck tore down the drive to town for binoculars, and Amos followed Grace up to the tower, I wondered how much longer I would call that house home.

ENDNOTES

Part 1

1. Senesh, Hannah. "To My Mother." *Dooble.co.il.* Retrieved May 20, 2019, from http://www.hannahsenesh.org.il/Sc.asp?ID=1958.

2. More Fear of War, and Jewish Immigration, 1937-38. Retrieved May 20, 2019, from http://www.fsmitha.com/h2/ch22.htm.

3. The History Place; Holocaust Timeline. (n.d.). Retrieved May 20, 2019, from http://www.historyplace.com/worldwar2/holocaust/timeline.html.

4. Holy Bible, I Kings 18.

5. Henrietta Szold. (n.d.). Retrieved May 20, 2019, from https://jwa.org/womenofvalor/szold.

Henrietta Szold was an American Jewish woman responsible for creating Hadassah, a Zionist women's groups dedicated to practical aid in Palestine in 1912. By WWII, in her seventies, Henrietta was responsible for direction Youth Aliyah and overseeing thousands of children's removal from Germany and Europe and settlement in Palestine.

6. Holy Bible, New International Version, Isaiah 43:6.

7. British White Papers: White Paper of 1939. Sources: The Avalon Project. Retrieved May 20, 2019, from https://www. jewishvirtuallibrary.org/british-white-paper-of-1939.

8. Anslow, L. (2017, April 06). The Nazis, with the help of an Arab cleric, used Islamic extremists as a tool. Retrieved from https://timeline.com/nazis-muslim-extremists-ss-6824aee281d2.

9. Balfour Declaration: Text of the Declaration. Retrieved May 20, 2019, from https://www.jewishvirtuallibrary.org/text-of-the-balfour-declaration.

10. WWI: Britain Makes Promises. (n.d.). Retrieved May 20, 2019, from http://www.bu.edu/mzank/Jerusalem/p/period7-1-1.htm.

11. Greenblatt, J. (2015, November 19). Closing the Borders to Refugees: Wrong in the 1930s, and Wrong Today. Retrieved May 20, 2019, from https://www.adl.org/blog/closing-the-borders-to-refugees-wrong-in-the-1930s-and-wrong-today.

12. Retrieved May 20, 2019, from https://www. jewishvirtuallibrary.org/charles-orde-wingate.

Deeply religious Christian and military genius, Orde Wingate adamantly believed that Jew's return to Palestine was a fulfillment of biblical prophecy. He became personally involved with the Zionist cause and trained many who became leaders in the Palmach.

Charles Orde Wingate (1903 - 1944). (n.d.).

13. Jewish Defense Organizations: The Palmach. Retrieved May 20, 2019, from https://www.jewishvirtuallibrary.org/the-palmach.

14. Israel National Symbols: National Anthem (Hatikvah). Retrieved May 20, 2019, from https://www.jewishvirtuallibrary. org/israeli-national-anthem-hatikvah.

15. Holy Bible, Genesis 14:18-20.

16. Holy Bible, New International Version, Proverbs 17:28.

17. Shakespeare, W. The Taming of the Shrew. ACT 2, SCENE I. Padua. A Room in Baptista's House. Retrieved May 20, 2019,

from http://shakespeare.mit.edu/taming_shrew/ taming_shrew.2.1.html.

18. Ibid.

19. Ibid.

20. Shakespeare, W. The Taming of the Shrew. Act I, SCENE II. Padua. Before Hortensio's House. Retrieved May 20, 2019, from http://shakespeare.mit.edu/taming_shrew/taming_shrew.1.2.html.

21. Shakespeare, W. The Taming of the Shrew. Act 3, SCENE 2. Padua. Before Baptista's House. Retrieved May 20, 2019, from http://shakespeare.mit.edu/taming_shrew/taming_shrew.3.2.html.

22. Irgun Tz'va'i Le'umi (Etzel): Background & Overview (1931 - 1948). (n.d.). Retrieved May 20, 2019, from https://www. jewishvirtuallibrary.org/background-and-overview-of-the-irgun-etzel.

23. Senesh, Hannah, "Walk to Caesarea."*Dooble.co.il.* Retrieved May 20, 2019, from http://www.hannahsenesh.org.il/Sc.asp? ID=1958.

24. The term 'Arab Jew' was used for decades to describe Jews from the Middle East, North Africa, and parts of the Levant.

Shatz, A. (2008, November 06). LRB · Adam Shatz · Leaving Paradise: Iraqi Jews. Retrieved May 20, 2019, from https://www. lrb.co.uk/v30/n21/adam-shatz/leaving-paradise

25. The King David Hotel was (and still is) a luxury hotel in Jerusalem that catered to the British upper crust throughout the Mandate period.

26. Sheikh Jarrah is a real neighborhood in Jerusalem that is said to be named after Saladin's physician.

27. Einstein's Relationship to Judaism - and Zionism - Were as Fascinating as You'd Expect. (2015, November 23). Retrieved May 20, 2019, from https://www.haaretz.com/jewish/what-was-einstein-s-relationship-to-judaism-and-zionism-1.5425826.

Albert Einstein was chairman of the Academics Committee at the Hebrew University of Jerusalem. He visited the campus in 1923, where he gave the university's first scientific lecture. This was his only visit to Palestine. I have taken dramatic license to imagine what might have happened if Einstein had set out on a secret mission in the 1940s to confer with the Jewish leadership in Palestine regarding the Nazi's production of an atomic weapon.

Part 2

1. Amos, J. (2017, October 05). Athenia: Is This the Wreck of the First British Ship Torpedoed in WW2? Retrieved May 21, 2019, from https://www.bbc.com/news/science-environment-41503664.

2. Einstein's Second Letter to President Roosevelt - 1945. Retrieved May 21, 2019, from http://www.atomicarchive.com/Docs/ManhattanProject/Einstein2.shtml.

3. Art of War Quotes; Sun Tzu Quotes from the Book the Art of War. Retrieved May 21, 2019, from http://www.artofwarquotes.com/.

4. Ibid.

5. Jerome Kern & Dorothy Fields. (1936). A Fine Romance [Universal Music Publishing Group, Shapiro Bernstein & Co. Inc., BMG Rights Management].

6. Holy Bible, New International Version, Psalm 23:1-4.

7. Microfilm Models: Precursors of V-Mail. Retrieved May 21, 2019,
https://postalmuseum.si.edu/VictoryMail/introducing/microfilm.html.

8. The Daughters of the American Revolution is a lineage based organization that is made up of women who can trace their lineage to those directly involved in the American Revolution.

9. Jewish Resistance: Jewish Parachutists in World War II. Retrieved May 21, 2019, from https://www.jewishvirtuallibrary.org/jewish-parachutists-in-world-war-ii.

10. Hannah Senesh (1921-1944). Retrieved May 21, 2019, from https://www.jewishvirtuallibrary.org/hannah-senesh.

Hannah Senesh was one of the Jewish Paratroopers who volunteered with the British Army and trained in Egypt along with 33 others. She was caught almost immediately by Hungarian police and was executed in 1944. Her poetry is beloved to this day.

12. Carnegie's Deli in Midtown Manhattan opened in 1937. Though the original deli closed in 2016, other branches are still in operation.

13. Henry Morgenthau Jr. was the US Secretary of the Treasury under President Franklin D. Roosevelt. Morgenthau was the only Jew in Roosevelt's administration. Throughout the war, he brought various rescue plans to Roosevelt's attention. Roosevelt, though initially reluctant to become involved placed Morgenthau in charge of establishing the War Refugee Board in 1944. It was, sadly, too little too late.

14. Ford's Anti-Semitism. (n.d.). Retrieved May 21, 2019, from http://www.pbs.org/wgbh/americanexperience/features/henryford-antisemitism/.

Charles E. Coughlin. Retrieved May 21, 2019, from https://encyclopedia.ushmm.org/content/en/article/charles-e-coughlin.

15. Breckenridge Long. Retrieved May 21, 2019, from https://encyclopedia.ushmm.org/content/en/article/breckinridge-long.

16. Christ Church History. Retrieved May 21, 2019, from https://www.cmj-israel.org/christchurch/ourhistory.

17. Senesh, Hannah. Song of Hannah. Retrieved May 21, 2019, from http://www.jewishfilm.org/Catalogue/films/songhannah.htm.

Part 3

1. Arms and Armor. Retrieved May 21, 2019, from https://www.metmuseum.org/about-the-met/curatorial-departments/arms-and-armor.

2. 1930 New York World's Fair. Retrieved May 23, 2019, from http://www.1939nyworldsfair.com.

3. Parachute Jump. Retrieved May 21, 2019, from http://www.heartofconeyisland.com/parachute-jump.html.

4. History. Retrieved May 21, 2019, from http://www. spaffordcenter.org/history

The beautiful story of the Spafford Baby home is completely true, and amazingly, the Baby Home started by Bertha Spafford in 1925 is still in operation today.

5. Holy Bible, New American Standard Bible, Proverbs 17:22.

6. Again, the story of the Spaffords is authentic history. History. Retrieved May 21, 2019, from http://www. spaffordcenter.org/history.

7. Horatio Spafford. (1876). It Is Well With My Soul. [Gospel Songs No. 2 by Ira Sankey and Bliss].

8. Shlaim, A. (2003, March 29). Arab Nationalism in the 20th Century by Adeed Dawisha. Retrieved May 21, 2019, from https:// www.theguardian.com/books/2003/mar/29/featuresreviews. guardianreview.

9. Adalian, R. P. (n.d.). Armenian Genocide. Retrieved May 21, 2019, from https://www.armenian-genocide.org/genocide.html.

10. Mallmann, K., & Cüppers, M. Nazi Palestine: The Plans for the Extermination of the Jews of Palestine. Retrieved May 21, 2019, from https://www.ushmm.org/research/publications/academic-publications/full-list-of-academic-publications/nazi-palestine-the-plans-for-the-extermination-of-the-jews-of-palestine.

11. The Gambino's were one of the five 'Crime Families' that dominated organized crime in New York City during the first half of the 20th century.

12. Wein, B. The Gaon of Vilna. Retrieved May 21, 2019, from https://www.jewishhistory.org/the-gaon-of-vilna/.

13. Voyage of the St. Louis. (n.d.). Retrieved May 21, 2019, from https://encyclopedia.ushmm.org/content/en/article/voyage-of-the-st-louis.

14. Keen Detective Funnies #23 (Aug. 1940). Retrieved May 21, 2019, from https://www.comics.org/issue/970/.

15. Ibid.

16. Lohamei Herut Israel (Lehi or Stern Gang/Group). Retrieved

May 21, 2019, from https://www.jewishvirtuallibrary.org/lo-x1e25-amei-x1e24-erut-israel.

17. Santoro, G. (2011, June 2). Lisbon: Harbor of Hope and Intrigue. Retrieved May 21, 2019, from https://www.historynet.com/lisbon-harbor-of-hope-and-intrigue.htm.

Part 4

1. Glenn Osser & Ruth Lowe. (1940). I'll Never Smile Again lyrics [Universal Music Publishing Group].

2. Holy Bible, English Standard Version, John 12:36-40.

3. Holy Bible, English Standard Version, John 12:41-42.

4. Holy Bible, English Standard Version, Philippians 4:7.

5. The Hotel that Saw it All... Retrieved May 23, 2019, from http://www.shepheard-hotel.com/history.html.

Shepheard's Hotel, nearly 200 years old, was the place to be seen and heard in Cairo during the 1930s and 1940s. The original hotel was destroyed by a fire in 1952, but was rebuilt and is in operation to this day.

6. Green, D., & Newport, F. (2018, April 23). American Public Opinion and the Holocaust. Retrieved May 23, 2019, from https://news.gallup.com/opinion/polling-matters/232949/american-public-opinion-holocaust.aspx.

According to Gallup, "Even during World War II, as the American public started to realize that the rumors of mass murder in death camps were true, they struggled to grasp the vast scale and scope of the crime. In November 1944, well over 5 million Jews had been murdered by the Nazi regime and its collaborators. Yet just under one-quarter of Americans who answered the poll could believe that more than 1 million people had been murdered by Germans in concentration camps; 36% believed that 100,000 or fewer had been killed."

7. Operation Catapult: Naval Destruction at Mers-el-Kebir. (2006, August 31). Retrieved May 23, 2019, from https://www.historynet.com/operation-catapult-naval-destruction-at-mers-el-

kebir.htm.

8. *The Maltese Falcon.* Dir. John Huston. Perf. Humphrey Bogart and Mary Astor. Warner Brothers. 1941.

9. "To Die" A Poem by Hannah Senesh With Commentary & Memories. (2012, September 22). Retrieved May 23, 2019, from https://redhaircrow.com/2012/09/22/to-die-a-poem-by-hannah-senesh-with-commentary-memories/.

10. "This Is No Joke: This Is War": A Live Radio Broadcast of the Attack on Pearl Harbor. Retrieved May 23, 2019, from http://historymatters.gmu.edu/d/5167.

11. Longfellow, Henry Wadsworth. "Paul Revere's Ride." Henry Wadsworth Longfellow [online resource], Maine Historical Society, Accessed June 18, 2019. http://www.hwlongfellow.org

BIBLIOGRAPHY

Adalian, R. P. "Armenian Genocide." *Armenian Genocide.org*, https://www.armenian-genocide.org/genocide.html. Accessed May 21, 2019.

Amos, J. "Athenia: Is This the Wreck of the First British Ship Torpedoed in WW2?" *BBC*, October 5, 2017. https://www.bbc.com/news/science-environment-41503664. Accessed May 21, 2019.

Anslow, L. "The Nazis, with the help of an Arab cleric, used Islamic extremists as a tool." *Timeline.com*, April 6, 2017, https://timeline.com/nazis-muslim-extremists-ss-6824aee281d2. Accessed May 20, 2019.

"Arms and Armor." *Met Museum*, https://www.metmuseum.org/about-the-met/curatorial-departments/arms-and-armor. Accessed May 21, 2019.

"Art of War Quotes; Sun Tzu Quotes from the Book the Art of War." *Art of War Quotes,* http://www.artofwarquotes.com/. Accessed May 21, 2019.

"Balfour Declaration: Text of the Declaration." *Jewish Virtual Library,* https://www.jewishvirtuallibrary.org/text-of-the-balfour-declaration. Accessed May 20, 2019.

"Breckenridge Long." *Encyclopedia.ushmm.org,* https://encyclopedia.ushmm.org/content/en/article/breckinridge-long. Accessed May 21, 2019.

"British White Papers: White Paper of 1939. Sources: The Avalon Project." *Jewish Virtual Library,* https://www.jewishvirtuallibrary.org/british-white-paper-of-1939. Accessed May 20, 2019.

"Charles E. Coughlin." *Encyclopedia.ushmm.org,* https://encyclopedia.ushmm.org/content/en/article/charles-e-coughlin. Accessed May 21, 2019.

"Charles Orde Windgate." *Jewish Virtual Library,* https://www.jewishvirtuallibrary.org/charles-orde-wingate. Accessed May 20, 2019.

"Christ Church History." *CMJ Israel,* https://www.cmj-israel.org/christchurch/ourhistory. Accessed May 21, 2019.

"Einstein's Relationship to Judaism - and Zionism - Were as Fascinating as You'd Expect." *Ha Aretz,* November 23, 2015. https://www.haaretz.com/jewish/what-was-einstein-s-relationship-to-judaism-and-zionism-1.5425826. Accessed May 20, 2019.

"Einstein's Second Letter to President Roosevelt - 1945." *Atomic Archive,* http://www.atomicarchive.com/Docs/ManhattanProject/Einstein2.shtml. Accessed May 21, 2019.

"Ford's Anti-Semitism. (n.d.)." *PBS,* http://www.pbs.org/wgbh/americanexperience/features/henryford-antisemitism/. Accessed May 21, 2019.

Glenn Osser & Ruth Lowe. *I'll Never Smile Again.* 1940. Universal Music Publishing Group.

Green, D., & Newport, F. (2018, April 23). "American Public Opinion and the Holocaust." *Gallup,* April 23, 2018. https://news.gallup.com/opinion/polling-matters/232949/american-public-opinion-holocaust.aspx. Accessed May 21, 2019.

Greenblatt, J. "Closing the Borders to Refugees: Wrong in the 1930s, and Wrong Today." *Anti Defamation League,* November 19, 2015, https://www.adl.org/blog/closing-the-borders-to-refugees-wrong-in-the-1930s-and-wrong-today. Accessed May 20, 2019.

"Hannah Senesh (1921-1944)." *Jewish Virtual Library,* https://www.jewishvirtuallibrary.org/hannah-senesh. Accessed May 21, 2019.

"Henrietta Szold." *Jewish Women's Archive,* https://jwa.org/womenofvalor/szold. Accessed May 20, 2019.

"History." *Spafford Center,* http://www.spaffordcenter.org/history. Accessed May 21, 2019.

"Irgun Tz'va'i Le'umi (Etzel): Background & Overview (1931 - 1948)." *Jewish Virtual Library,* https://www.jewishvirtuallibrary.org/background-and-overview-of-the-irgun-etzel. Accessed May 20, 2019.

"Israel National Symbols: National Anthem (Hatikvah)." *Jewish Virtual Library,* https://www.jewishvirtuallibrary.org/israeli-national-anthem-hatikvah. Accessed May 20, 2019.

Jerome Kern & Dorothy Fields. *A Fine Romance.* Universal Music Publishing Group, Shapiro Bernstein & Co. Inc., BMG Rights Management. 1936,

"Jewish Defense Organizations: The Palmach." *Jewish Virtual Library,* https://www.jewishvirtuallibrary.org/the-palmach. Accessed May 20, 2019.

"Jewish Resistance: Jewish Parachutists in World War II." *Jewish Virtual Library,* https://www.jewishvirtuallibrary.org/jewish-parachutists-in-world-war-ii. Accessed May 21, 2019.

"Keen Detective Funnies #23 (Aug. 1940)." *Comics.org,* https://www.comics.org/issue/970/. Accessed May 21, 2019.

"Lohamei Herut Israel (Lehi or Stern Gang/Group)." *Jewish Virtual Library,* https://www.jewishvirtuallibrary.org/lo-x1e25-amei-x1e24-erut-israel. Accessed May 21, 2019.

Longfellow, Henry Wadsworth. "Paul Revere's Ride." Henry Wadsworth Longfellow [online resource], Maine Historical Society, Accessed June 18, 2019. http://www.hwlongfellow.org

Mallmann, K., & Cüppers, M. "Nazi Palestine: The Plans for the Extermination of the Jews of Palestine." *Ushmm,* https://www.ushmm.org/research/publications/academic-publications/full-list-of-academic-publications/nazi-palestine-the-plans-for-the-extermination-of-the-jews-of-palestine. Accessed May 21, 2019.

"Microfilm Models: Precursors of V-Mail." *Postal Museum,* https://postalmuseum.si.edu/VictoryMail/introducing/ microfilm.html. Accessed May 21, 2019.

"More Fear of War, and Jewish Immigration, 1937-38." *Macrohistory and World Timeline.* http://www.fsmitha.com/h2/ch22.htm. Accessed May 20, 2019.

"Operation Catapult: Naval Destruction at Mers-el-Kebir." *History Net.com,* August 31, 2006, https://www.historynet.com/operation-catapult-naval-destruction-at-mers-el-kebir.htm. Accessed May 23, 2019.

"Parachute Jump." *Heart of Coney Island.com,* http://www. heartofconeyisland.com/parachute-jump.html. Accessed May 21, 2019.

Santoro, G. "Lisbon: Harbor of Hope and Intrigue." *History Net.com,* June 2, 2011, https://www.historynet.com/lisbon-harbor-of-hope-and-intrigue.htm. Accessed May 21, 2019.

Senesh, Hannah. "From Hannah's Poem Notebook, 1922-1944." *Dooble.co.il.* http://www.hannahsenesh.org.il/Sc.asp?ID=1958. Accessed May 20, 2019.

Shakespeare, W. "The Taming of the Shrew." http://shakespeare.mit.edu/taming_shrew/taming_shrew.2.1.html. Accessed May 20, 2019.

Shatz, A. "Leaving Paradise: Iraqi Jews." *London Review of Books,* November 06, 2008, https://www.lrb.co.uk/v30/n21/adam-shatz/ leaving-paradise. Accessed May 20, 2019.

Shlaim, A. "Arab Nationalism in the 20th Century by Adeed Dawisha." *The Guardian,* March 29, 2003, https://www.theguardian.com/books/2003/mar/29/featuresreviews.guardianreview. Accessed May 21, 2019.

"Song of Hannah." *Jewish Film.Org,* http://www.jewishfilm.org/Catalogue/films/songhannah.htm. Accessed May 21, 2019.

Spafford, Horatio. "It Is Well With My Soul." *Gospel Songs No. 2* by Ira Sankey and Bliss, 1876.

"The History Place; Holocaust Timeline." *The History Place,* http://www.historyplace.com/worldwar2/holocaust/timeline.html. Accessed May 20, 2019.

"The Hotel that Saw it All…" *Shepheard Hotel.com,* http://www.shepheard-hotel.com/history.html. Accessed May 23, 2019.

"'This Is No Joke: This Is War': A Live Radio Broadcast of the Attack on Pearl Harbor." *History Matters,* http://historymatters.gmu.edu/d/5167. Accessed May 23, 2019.

"To Die: A Poem by Hannah Senesh With Commentary & Memories." *Red Hair Crow,* September 22, 2012, https://redhaircrow.com/2012/09/22/to-die-a-poem-by-hannah-senesh-with-commentary-memories/. Accessed May 23, 2019.

The Maltese Falcon. Dir. John Huston. Perf. Humphrey Bogart and Mary Astor. Warner Brothers. 1941.

"Voyage of the St. Louis." (n.d.). *Encyclopedia.ushmm.org,* https://encyclopedia.ushmm.org/content/en/article/voyage-of-the-st-louis. Accessed May 21, 2019.

Wein, B. "The Gaon of Vilna." *Jewish History.org,* https://www.jewishhistory.org/the-gaon-of-vilna/. Accessed May 21, 2019.

"WWI: Britain Makes Promises." *Boston University,* http://www.bu.edu/mzank/Jerusalem/p/period7-1-1.htm. Accessed May 20, 2019.

"1930 New York World's Fair." *1939 New York World's Fair,* http://www.1939nyworldsfair.com. Accessed May 23, 2019.

cFaith-based historical fiction for the tween, teen, and fun-loving adult!

The Seabirds

TRILOGY

MEET THE GREY GOOSE GANG AND SET OUT ON THE WWII ADVENTURE OF A LIFETIME THAT WILL CHALLENGE, INSPIRE, AND ENCOURAGE READERS!

CURIOUS ABOUT PIPER'S FIRST JOB AS THE GIRL REPORTER? NOW'S YOUR CHANCE TO FIND OUT WITH THESE BELOVED NANCY DREW STYLE MYSTERIES SET BETWEEN VOYAGE OF THE SANDPIPER AND FLIGHT OF THE SEAHAWKS!

GIRL

REPORTER

THE COLUMBA DIARIES

PICKING UP WHERE THE SEABIRDS TRILOGY LEFT OFF, THE COLUMBA DIARIES FOLLOWS THE GREY GOOSE GANG ON NEW ADVENTURES SORTING THROUGH THE AFTERMATH OF THE HOLOCAUST AS THE WORLD SPINS TOWARDS THE COLD WAR.

A WWII HISTORY

The Seabirds Companion Curriculum

To Order
Visit Amazon.com and
Hopehousepress.co

The Seabirds Trilogy World War II Companion Curriculum is a 36 week comprehensive high school level history, social studies, spiritual growth, and college research writing prep curriculum. Your student will learn about the greatest conflict in human history through story, the testimony of those who survived, and award-winning films and documentaries. Along the way, they will sharpen their critical-thinking skills, grow spiritually, and learn how to write a college level historical research paper. Students will dive deep into the years leading up to the war and the war itself by experiencing it through those who lived it. Included are articles by authors like C.S. Lewis and Emile Zola, tutorials and clips of specific events during the war, music by Mendelssohn and the Andrew Sisters, original recordings by Roosevelt and Churchill, and memoirs by Corrie ten Boom and other heroes.

ABOUT THE AUTHOR

Jessica Glasner is an author and screenwriter. Young and old alike agree that her lively characters, colorful settings, and laugh-out-loud vignettes display the goodness of God in the darkest moments of the past. Known for instilling hope, faith, and godly values through page-turning stories, inspiring tears and laughter her books are those that are read over and over.

For more adventures with Piper and the gang, check out Jessica Glasner's other stories on Amazon and Barnes and Noble.com.

facebook.com/jesskateglasner

instagram.com/jesskateglasner

Made in the USA
Columbia, SC
28 November 2021

49863318R10324